SKELETAL HEARTS

SABRE SECURITY BOOK TWO

J ROSE

For those who live with guilt,
you are still worthy of love.

TRIGGER WARNING

Skeletal Hearts is a contemporary reverse harem romance, so the main character will have multiple love interests that she will not have to choose between.

This book is very dark and contains scenes that may be triggering for some readers. This includes physical and psychological abuse, torture, sexual assault and abuse, imprisonment, graphic violence, serial murder, PTSD, Trichotillomania, suicidal ideation and attempted suicide.

If you are triggered by any of this content, please do not read this book.

This is a slow-burn romance, so the relationships will develop over time, and the spice level will build with each book.

"Tell me every terrible thing you ever did
and let me love you anyway."
- Edgar Allen Poe

PROLOGUE

Leticia

Black Water – The People's Thieves

London Bridge is falling down.
Falling down, falling down.
Tugging the hood of my bright-red raincoat up to shield my plaited pigtails, I hum the tune of my favourite song while leaving the school gates.

London Bridge is falling down.
My fair lady.
Rain patters against my coat in a soft drizzle. It's cold, probably a little too cold to be walking home.

Build it up with wood and clay.
Wood and clay, wood and clay.
The hum of cars whizzes past me along the quiet street.

Build it up with wood and clay.
My fair lady.
Staring down at my patent leather school shoes, I count each step. One after another. Cross the road. Check for traffic. Stick to the zebra

crossing.

Wood and clay will wash away.

Wash away, wash away.

There's a loud rumble from above me. Heart pounding, I speed up, heading for the outcrop of trees that marks my path home over the nearby farmer's field.

Wood and clay will wash away.

My fair lady.

My legs are tired as I squelch through wet mud and rain puddles. The village vanishes, swallowed by high bushes clustered with tiny, ripe blackberries.

I stop to collect handfuls of berries and fill my pockets. The droplets of sour tartness burst on my tongue. Grandma Sylvie bakes the best blackberry crumble. I better take some for her.

When my pockets are overflowing and my hands are stained dark purple with juice, I return to the rough path cutting through the shoulder-high crops.

It's scary out here. I wish Daddy were here to walk me home like he usually does. Mummy took me to school in her big, loud car this morning. She wasn't happy. I don't ever see her smile anymore.

Send a man to watch all night.

Watch all night, watch all night.

My quiet humming fills the bleakness of the field's silence.

Send a man to watch all night.

My fair lady.

Grandma taught me that song. She picks me up sometimes, when Mummy is asleep on the sofa with her favourite book and an empty wine glass. Or when Daddy doesn't come home for a few days and makes everyone mad.

We get ice cream and feed the seagulls, even in winter. It makes me laugh when their beaks tickle my hand. If you stand real still, they'll peck the food right from your palm.

Checking the sparkly, pink *Dora the Explorer* watch around my wrist, I bite my lip. It's getting dark fast, and I still have half an hour to walk. I come this way with Daddy sometimes, when he can walk straight.

But never alone.

That isn't allowed.

Tummy rumbling, I dig into my supply of blackberries. The pops of sugary sourness keep me going as I squelch through thick, glue-like mud. The rain has stopped now, but my uniform is soaking wet.

Movement in the distance slows my footsteps. The tall stalks of corn are swaying. A headful of thick, chocolate-coloured hair appears first. Then, a big smile and a scary, hooked nose, almost like a clown.

The man waves. Still frozen, I wave back with a blackberry-stained hand. He doesn't look too scary, apart from his big nose. Kind of old and wrinkled, though, like the man who lives next door to Grandma.

"Hey there," he calls out.

Clutching the straps of my backpack, I tentatively approach him. "Hello."

"Are you lost, sweetie?"

"No. I'm going home."

He looks around the deserted field. "Through here?"

I nod, my lip jutted out in defiance.

"Hmm. It's getting a bit dark, isn't it?"

"I'm a big girl. I can walk home alone."

His laugh is tinkly. I like it.

"Well, a big girl like you should be just fine. I don't like the dark, though. Can you show me the way in case I get scared?"

I blink up at him. "You get scared?"

"Sometimes," he replies with a wink.

"The dark isn't scary! Come on. I'll show you."

I reach out a sticky, purple hand. The stranger squeezes my little fingers tight, laughing when he sees the juices splashed across them.

"Hungry?"

"I was picking blackberries for my grandma," I reveal in a whisper. "Don't tell Mummy, though. She gets mad when my clothes are dirty."

"It's our little secret. Can I have one?"

Fishing a blackberry from my pocket, I offer it up to him. The stranger pops it in his mouth and rubs his tummy. I laugh at him. He's very silly.

"Yummy," he praises. "You keep those berries safe now."

"I will. Grandma can bake a crumble to eat later on."

We slip through the stalks of corn, avoiding deep puddles that will get me even dirtier. I'm already streaked with filth and rainwater. I'll have to hide my dress from Mummy. I don't want her to shout.

"What's your name, anyhow?" he asks me.

"Letty." I stare up at my new friend. "What's your name?"

The stranger offers me a lopsided smile. "Michael."

"Pleased to meet you, Mr Michael."

"Well, aren't you a well-mannered little thing."

I'm not sure I like being called a *little thing*, but I don't complain. I don't have many friends. I'd like a real one, even if he is a funny old man.

"What's that on your chest?" I ask nosily.

Michael looks down at the silvery chain around his neck. He pulls it over his head, offering the shiny necklace to me. Excited by the present, I slip it over my head instead.

It's a funny shape. There's a triangle in the middle that looks a bit like a flower, surrounded by a circle. The metal is cool against my purple fingertips.

"That's a Holy Trinity," he explains. "It represents the Father, Son and Holy Spirit. Do you go to church, Letty?"

"Not really," I answer, distracted by the necklace. "But sometimes Mummy shouts at Daddy and tells him to go to hell. That's to do with church, right?"

His smile is getting big—almost too big.

"A little bit. You see, that's where the bad people go."

"Are you saying my daddy is bad?"

"Maybe. That's part of my job. I help the bad people get better."

"Like a doctor?"

Michael laughs again. "A little bit."

"So… you can help my daddy? I don't want him to go to hell. It sounds like a scary place."

"Maybe. What about your mummy?"

I pop another blackberry in my mouth, still studying the necklace. "Sometimes she gets angry. I don't think she likes me much."

"Now, I'm sure that isn't true."

"Could you fix her as well?"

Michael takes my hand, tighter this time. It hurts a little bit.

"We could make a deal."

"What kind of deal?" I ask excitedly.

"I have a very important job to do that I want you to help me with. Did you learn about Noah's ark at school?"

"The big boat with all the animals?"

"Yes." He beams at me. "Noah built a big boat to save all the good people. Do you know what happened to the bad ones?"

I shake my head.

"When the flood came, they all got washed away," he answers. "There's another flood coming, Letty. A big one. It's my job to clean everything up in time, you understand?"

"Cleaning?" I wrinkle my nose. "I don't like cleaning."

Emerging from the swaying stalks of corn, we stop at another cluster of blackberry bushes. My legs and feet hurt from walking such a long way. We're almost there now. I can see the gravel road through the leaves.

There's a funny-looking van parked there. The dark-blue paint is peeling off, and the tyres look ready to pop, they're so old. This must be Michael's car.

We shimmy through the bush and escape to the other side. There are no lights down this road. It isn't a proper path for cars. The mud is all sticky and smeared about, and there's no painted lines.

"My home's over that way." I point to the trees leading away from the field. "Good luck with your cleaning, Mr Michael."

The van beeps as he clicks the set of keys in his hands. Weak, yellow light spills over the mud, illuminating the thick shadows of early evening.

He pulls open the sliding door on the side of the van and gestures inside.

"Hop in, sweetie. I'll drop you off at your grandma's so she can bake that crumble. You must be hungry."

My belly rumbles again. Lunchtime was a long time ago. But I already broke two rules tonight—walking home alone and talking to a stranger. I don't want to get into more trouble.

"I'm okay to walk," I decline politely. "Goodnight."

With a final wave, I tug up my backpack and set off towards the trees covered in pinecones. The squelch of boots following me registers too late as something trips me up.

"Owww!" I wail.

Landing hard on my knees, I slip in the mud. My ankle burns

from tripping over a big, boot-covered foot, attached to my new friend.

He looms over me, still wearing that smile, but I don't like it now. There's something scary in his shiny, green eyes. Like when Daddy drinks a whole bottle of naughty juice and starts shouting and smashing things.

"Get in the car, Leticia."

Frightened tears well up in my eyes.

"How do you know my name? I said it's Letty."

He jabs a finger into my chest, right above the necklace. I'd forgotten I was still wearing it. Is he mad now? Will he hurt me like other people do? I didn't mean to steal from him.

"I have a job to do," he says in a snarl. "You stole from me. That's a sin. Do you want to go to hell too?"

"No," I cry loudly. "I'm s-sorry! Please."

His hand smacks against my cheek so hard, it rattles my teeth together. I can't see through the tears pouring out of my eyes. My small body is bundled into his arms with a grunt.

"There's a good girl," he whispers in my ear. "Don't worry. The Lord is just and merciful to forgive those who sin. You'll learn soon enough."

Screaming at the top of my lungs doesn't stop him from throwing me into the back of the van. I try to get up and run, but the door slams shut in my face.

Silence.

Darkness.

I'm trapped.

Crying harder as the engine begins to rumble, the van bounces over bumpy ground. Each lurch sends me jolting from side to side. There's nothing to hold on to in here. Flailing around, I realise I dropped my backpack outside.

"Please," I whimper into the dark. "Stop."

He can't hear me.

Nobody can.

The van crashes over a big bump, sending me flying across the cramped space. I hit the wall so hard, my head cracks on the thick, rusted metal. I slump as everything goes blurry.

The last thing I think of is my daddy. He always said never to walk home alone. And I never got a chance to say goodbye this morning.

CHAPTER 1

Harlow

Drown – hometown & young

M y breath fogs up the lined glass of the hospital window. Clouds of condensation drip over the smooth surface, obscuring the view inside the clinical room.

Wrapped in clusters of wires, drips and a feeding tube slicing through the core of his being, my father lies asleep. It's been weeks since he spoke a single word to me.

Now, a machine is keeping him alive—pumping blood and breath through his failing organs, suspending his corpse between this cruel world and the Lord's divine light.

Beep.

Beep.

Beep.

God has forsaken him, like the rest of us left to fight for the right to breathe. His body, awash with the aftereffects of years of heavy drinking and drug use, can no longer function alone. Most days, he struggles to lift an eyelid.

Taking a fortifying breath, I let myself into his hospital room. The scent of bleach and disappointment oozes over me, clinging with the persistence of aching regret.

"Dad," I croak.

Nothing.

He's too out of it to know I'm here.

The word *dad* feels foreign on my tongue. I couldn't call Giana by the name my birth granted her. But this broken shade of a man... somehow, I can relate to him. His pain is my pain.

He never forgot me.

I wish I remembered him.

Taking his papery hand in mine, I sit down in the cracked vinyl armchair. His hair is a dark, muddy blonde colour, ragged and hanging over his bushy eyebrows.

With pronounced cheekbones, thin lips, a narrow nose and ghoul-like skin, he looks more like me than my mother does. The skin hangs from his bones in a humanoid costume.

"What happened to you?" I stroke his knuckles. "Why can't I remember our life together? Before... everything?"

Beep.

Beep.

Beep.

The stillness is broken by the reassurance of his breathing. In and out. Chest rising up and caving down. Life beginning. Life ending. Falling into a brief chasm of death in between each breath.

"Miss Kensington?"

I flinch so forcefully, I almost tug out the needle that's taped against my father's white hand. The door clicks shut as his consultant, Doctor Bannon, pads into the room.

"Sorry," he apologies with a smile. "I wasn't sure if we'd see you today."

"I had physiotherapy for my arm downstairs, and I thought I'd come check on him."

He glances over the machines and writes down some measurements. His furrowed frown doesn't abate.

"How is he?" I make myself ask.

Doctor Bannon spares me a glance. "We're doing our best to keep him stable while we search for a donor match."

"You know I can help."

"No, Miss Kensington. We've had this discussion. You are not well enough to be considered for a partial liver donation."

"You've had this discussion with Hunter. Nobody has bothered to ask me how I feel about it."

His expression softens. "Mr Rodriguez has nothing to do with this decision. I'm prioritising your health. We will find someone else; it just takes time."

I stare down at my booted feet, tears tightening my throat. "My father is going to die unless he gets this transplant."

"He's acutely unwell. We're doing the best we can."

"You've been saying that for the last three weeks."

When he reaches out to place a hand on my shoulder, I screech the chair backwards and shoot upright. Doctor Bannon freezes, his lips pursed.

"I'm sorry, Miss K—"

"That isn't my name," I interrupt him.

He sighs in clear frustration. "Your father is suffering from acute liver failure. He overdosed on heroin and fentanyl. This isn't a quick fix. We're fighting to keep him alive."

"Then let me help!"

"I'm sorry, Harlow. It simply isn't an option while you're still recovering. You should go home and get some rest."

"I don't need to rest," I shout back.

A shadow crosses the window, huge and looming. I recognise the threatening set of Enzo's shoulders without looking up at his stony expression. He's tracked me down.

Huffing, I take one last look at my father's slack face and storm from the room. I'm barely out of the door before a beefy hand encircles my bicep.

"We agreed that I would meet you downstairs," Enzo says gruffly. "You can't just run off like that. It isn't safe."

"I don't need an escort."

He almost yanks me off my feet as I'm forced to halt. Enzo stares down at me, his golden-amber eyes lit with heartache through thick lashes that some would kill for.

Haphazard black hair hangs over his face. Unlike the others, his features are a little too harsh and angular to be classically handsome. He's more rugged and raw, attractive in a different sense. Everything about Enzo is roughened around the edges.

"Is that all I am now? An escort?"

Barbed wire wraps around my throat. I can't even choke out an excuse. Enzo's been there for every single day I've spent despondent and shell-shocked. All I've done is run away from him for the past few weeks.

"I don't know what I want anymore," I admit thickly.

His hand falls from my bicep, curling into a white-knuckled fist. "What are you saying?"

"I don't know."

Nodding, he wipes the look of hurt from his face. "Let's get out of here."

Enzo stuffs his hands in the pockets of his leather jacket and takes off towards the ward's exit. Every step away from me is a sizzling bullet to the heart.

I can't keep myself together right now—how am I supposed to hold his broken pieces as well? Nothing has been the same since we stepped inside that chapel last month.

I'm not the same girl who escaped four months ago, and I've changed again since then. There's a revolving door of Harlows sliding their never-ending supply of masks into place.

All I know is that Pastor Michaels is gone. Mrs Michaels is dead. There is no justice in this lawless purgatory—only more death and destruction. Each breath I take guarantees the suffering of more innocent women.

My real father may die.

Maybe, I should go with him.

Reluctantly following Enzo, we dodge nurses with trolleys and a porter bringing the latest victim to their clinical prison.

Stepping inside the elevator that took me from this same hospital, a whole other Harlow ago, I watch the doors close with a thud.

"Enzo," I begin.

He doesn't even look at me.

"Please say something."

The silence is overwhelming.

"Like what?" he eventually replies.

I watch the flickering light tick down as the parking garage approaches. We can't go on like this. It's killing us both.

"I miss my friend," I force out.

He inhales sharply. "I'm right here."

"None of you have looked at me the same since you saw the basement. I hate it so much."

"Harlow," he interrupts.

"Don't try to deny it. You've barely touched me in weeks. Hunter has withdrawn, and Leighton is miserable. I have no idea where Theo even is right now."

When my lowered head refuses to lift, Enzo suddenly grabs me. My back meets the metal wall of the cage imprisoning us, and two calloused fingers lift my chin. His stare is scorching.

"I look at you the same as I always have," he says softly. "With astonishment and respect. You survived that hellhole. I have no idea how."

My eyes burn with tears. "You don't have to say that, Enz. Just talk to me like a normal human being."

"I am. Nothing has changed."

"You're all treating me like I'm made of broken glass."

At my raised voice, his expression darkens. A thunderstorm settles over him, deadly and dangerous.

Grabbing my shoulders, his fingers dig deep into my skin. The instinct to run screams through my mind. He isn't the gentle giant who last escorted me from this hospital.

"I am trying to protect you," he hisses angrily. "Even from yourself. Can't you see how much I care about you?"

I shrug, unable to answer.

"Fuck, Harlow! You're infuriating."

Giving me no opportunity to argue, I startle when his lips slam against mine. He kisses me like the hospital is collapsing around us, shattering and crushing helpless bodies as it falls victim to God's wrath.

My lips part, granting the wet swipe of his tongue access to my mouth. He tastes like bonfire embers and the tantalising promise of a new dawn breaking the cover of night.

He tastes like home.

Enzo gave me a family again.

When his lips disappear, I gasp for air. His forehead is pressed against mine, our souls straining to reach one another. I can almost hear his heart erratically pounding.

"Still don't know what you want?" he rumbles.

"I'm not... I don't know."

"If you're trying to scare me off, it isn't going to work." He drops a kiss to my temple. "I'm not going anywhere. No matter what you do to push me away."

"I don't deserve you," I whisper back.

His fingers slot between mine. "You don't get to decide that. I'm staying right here. I will never abandon you."

The elevator doors *ding* open, cloaking us in the darkness of the parking garage. Enzo tows me out, refusing to release his grip on my hand. I can't lift my gaze from my feet.

His sweet, generous soul gave me the strength to leave this hospital before. But now, this place serves as a reminder of the lies I've told to them all. The deception I've woven to escape their judgement. I want to be loved.

So did Laura.

I took that from her.

Even if death was waiting for her to succumb, her final moments were godless and excruciating. She choked on blood and the pressure of my hands gripping her throat.

I am a murderer.

Enzo deserves so much more.

Silent tears soaking into my cheeks, I let him drag me through parked cars and covered motorcycles. The hospital hums above us, a nest of activity and sickness. I'm glad to see the back of it.

"We should get some food," Enzo decides. "Leighton has been

filing paperwork all day. He'll be ready to eat his own arm."

"Why is Hunter making him do that?"

"He's gotta start somewhere. I'm going to train him up, but he needs to learn some work ethic first."

His arm curls around my shoulders, and I lean into the furnace-like warmth of his muscled torso.

"If Leighton's working now, I should get a job too." I peer up at him. "It's overdue."

Enzo shakes his head. "We've discussed this."

"You're the second person to say that to me today. I'm getting really sick of decisions being made for me."

He abruptly halts. "Shit."

I almost lose my balance, so I grab his elbow to stop myself from faceplanting. We're metres from the blacked-out company SUV, but Enzo's feet are rooted to the spot.

"Motherfucker," he curses.

"What is it?"

He shoves me behind him. "Stay back. I need to call for backup."

I manage to peek around his massive frame. Gloopy, bright-red paint stains the concrete floor, dripping in great globules.

The car has been trashed, from the smashed windows to the dented, scratched body paint. On the bonnet, a single word has been written in spilled paint.

SINNER.

CHAPTER 2

Hunter

Empty – Letdown

The floor of my spacious office is worn bare from frantic pacing. It's all I've done as of late. Paced. Pondered. Negotiated. Threatened. Every day, more walls are thrown in my path.

I've beaten myself to a pulp trying to knock those obstacles down. We're hunting a ghost who speaks in riddles, facing a crisis of faith in our weary teams and slowly cracking under the pressure of a country desperate for answers.

So much death.

Countless litres of blood spilled.

Pain. Heartbreak. Grief.

It's all been for nothing. Each lead creates a new dead end. More problems. Unanswered questions. Black holes of missing information and money pouring down the drain.

I'm losing control of this mess.

More than that, I'm losing *her*.

Refastening my striped, blue tie, I leave my office and head down the corridor to Theo's lair. I don't bother knocking. His cave is near pitch black, the blinds cocooning him in darkness and stifling warmth.

In the corner of the room, a lump is huddled beneath a blanket on his sofa. I grab a half-finished cup of coffee from his desk and upend it on top of the snoring, balled-up figure.

"Argh!"

"Wakey wakey, sleeping beauty."

Theo shoots upright, his mass of light-blonde ringlets dripping with stale coffee. He's wearing the same flannel shirt and blue jeans as he was three days ago, rumpled and stained.

"What the fuck, Hunter?"

"I'm not paying you to sleep."

With a groan, he collapses back on the sofa. "You're not paying me to work twenty-four seven, either. Doesn't stop me from doing it, though. I want a raise."

"Don't we all?"

I backtrack before he can swing an exhausted right hook. Theo wipes his face on his green-and-red shirt, replacing his black glasses as his clear, blue eyes squint up at me.

"Have you finished compiling the latest Kiera James report from the intelligence department?"

He heads for his cluttered desk. "I have."

"Harlow has been asking me for an update. I'd like to be able to give her a better answer than last time."

"The answer hasn't changed," he grumbles. "Kiera was a plain Jane, through and through. Devoted Christian, no children or notable relationships. Vanished into thin air."

"If I wanted a regurgitation of the last four reports I already read, I could've spared myself a trip down here."

He shoots me a glower. "I've got nothing, Hunt."

"Come on. Give me something to offer her."

"I can't wrap an empty box in a fucking red bow and call it a result. We've got nothing."

"Gee, and here I was thinking you're Santa Claus."

"Ha bloody ha."

Taking a seat at his desk, Theo reboots his monstrous array of computer screens. Stacks of paperwork, strewn post-it notes and empty ramen containers litter his workspace.

We've been working flat out since locating the chapel in Northumberland. It took almost two weeks to process and ship all the forensic evidence to HQ. The place was scrubbed, but we still found traces of two DNA signatures.

Both unidentified.

The infamous Michaels.

Not to mention, the swinging, strangled corpse. That was a head fuck in and of itself. Using dental records, we identified the fictional Mrs Michaels and matched one of the DNA profiles to her. We also have a name.

Rosetta Stone vanished in the late seventies after a stint at a now-demolished children's home. She was sixteen at the time. From there, Rosetta ceased to exist.

No marriage records, mortgage applications, bank accounts. Nothing. She ran away from that orphanage and disappeared. Mrs Michaels was born from that gaping black hole, adopting a brand-new, false identity to hide her crimes.

We have the body of a missing woman, accused of aiding and abetting the crimes of a serial killer and rapist, and the DNA of a ghost. Yet, we're standing here with our dicks in our hands, clueless and out of ideas.

"Who can we speak to from that children's home?" I muse out

loud. "We need someone to verify Rosetta's identity."

Theo takes a sip from a mug and spits the cold coffee straight back out with a wince. He makes a beeline for his coffee machine to make a much-needed fresh cup.

"Files were burned when it shut down. You know the drill. We're still uncovering mass graves from government-funded hellholes running back then. It was clearly corrupt as hell."

"We don't have a single name?"

"It was demolished in the nineties, facing a dozen different lawsuits and accusations of abuse. Management bulldozed it and removed all traces of it ever existing."

Fierce pain pounds behind my eyes with another impending migraine. I'm not coming up with an answer for Harlow anytime soon.

"What about Kiera's sister?" I sigh tiredly.

Theo picks up a folder and waves it in the air. "She's agreed to be interviewed for our investigation to go over everything."

Running a hand over my slicked-back bun, I clap him on the shoulder. The police investigation into Kiera's murder was lacklustre at best. With any luck, they missed something.

"Set it up. I'll interview her myself."

"Already done," he replies absently.

"When?"

"She's flying down to London end of next week."

"Perfect. Good work."

Theo's brows draw together. "Oh, erm… well, thanks."

"You don't have to look like I just suggested you run naked down Oxford Street."

"That would be less surprising than you thanking me."

I turn to walk out, but my feet glue themselves to the carpet before

I can skulk back to my office. Guilt spears me in the chest.

"Am I really that awful?"

Theo's forehead collides with his desk. "You seriously need to ask me that?"

"Clearly, I do."

"You've always been a dick, Hunt. But the last five years have proven you're also a cold-hearted son of a bitch."

My hands clench and unclench at my sides. "It was never about you. Everything I've done has been for this company."

"Including sacrificing your family?"

"I haven't sacrificed anyone," I snap at him. "I've kept you all alive. Even when you didn't want to live."

Storming from the office, I don't give Theo the opportunity to answer. He's always been shortsighted. His existence revolves around solving one puzzle after another, day in and day out, to make him feel alive.

Sabre wouldn't be what it is without his tireless work. I appreciate that fact. But the simple truth is, someone has to get their hands bloody from time to time.

That's my job.

It's a shitty role to play.

I make the hard decisions so nobody else has to. If I wasn't prepared to be unpopular, we'd all be dead by now. The burden of responsibility is heavy on my shoulders. It's a weight I bear alone, or at least, I did.

Harlow is the first person to see past the carefully constructed, professional persona I wear. She took one look at my performance and tore it to shreds without uttering a word.

My phone buzzes in my pocket, and I pick up Enzo's incoming call with a tired sigh.

"What's up?"

"Hunt. We have a problem. I need you to send transport and a team of agents to the hospital."

I brace my hand against the wall. "Is Harlow secure?"

"She's safe. Some asshole trashed the car while we were inside and left a stupid message. We need backup."

Quickly storming back into Theo's office, I snap my fingers to get his attention and fire off rapid instructions. He jerks into action, our sharp barbs forgotten.

Becket and the rest of the Anaconda team are running a reconnaissance op in Central London. We've been paid a hefty sum to investigate a well-loved politician suspected of bankrolling a human trafficking ring.

"Hold tight, the team's coming. What message?"

A photo comes through via text message with a *ding*. I curse under my breath. This is some fucked-up shit. Theo looks over my shoulder and blanches.

"What the hell?" he mutters.

"Pull the surveillance footage from that parking garage," I order him. "I want names."

Down the phone line, I can hear breathless panting in the background. Enzo swears and hangs up the call before I can yell at him. I recognise the sound of Harlow freaking out.

Countless nights spent with her asleep in my arms have given me a shitty ability to sense her distress. Enzo usually joins us, even when I tell him to get lost. Her bed is the only place he manages to get any sleep these days.

"Hunt," Theo calls. "I've got the hospital's CCTV feed. The camera doesn't have Enzo's car in range, but we have three people who enter the garage in the time frame."

I lean over him to take a look. He's right, we don't have a clear shot of the car or who did this. Two middle-aged nurses and a short, stout man come and go, but they look like workers, not crazed lunatics capable of doing this.

"You think one of them did it?" he wonders.

"We have no concrete proof."

"I'll run facial recognition and pull their records anyway. No one else enters or exits through the entrance gate."

"It has to be one of them. Call Hudson and send him to pick them up for criminal damage and harassment."

"Don't you think that's a bit rash?" Theo worries.

"Someone has threatened Harlow's life. I don't give a shit if it's rash or not."

"We've already pissed off the superintendent this month," he reasons. "She's ready to pull the plug without us arresting innocent people and aggravating her further."

"I'm not risking them getting away with this. If these people are innocent, then they'll have nothing to hide."

Theo nods, his lips pursed. "Fine."

We sit in tense silence as we await an update from the team. The alarm clock on his desk ticks down. When half an hour has passed, I redial Enzo with an impatient snarl.

Nothing.

I'll kill him myself.

"Motherfucker isn't answering his phone." I punch in another number. "He knows I hate being ignored."

"Don't we all," Theo comments.

"Watch your tone. I want full profiles on all three of those people. Names, addresses and any connection to Michaels or Harlow."

He gives me a weary salute. "Yes, boss."

The line connects, and Becket barks a greeting. I can hear the hum of his car engine, but it's broken by hysterical crying in the background. Harlow.

"He's found me," she hiccups through sobs. "I'm a sinner. He's found me. I'm a sinner."

"Little busy here," Becket interjects.

"Update?"

"We're twenty minutes out from the house. No sign of a tail or any reporters. Think we're in the clear."

"Put me on loudspeaker."

There's a faint click.

"Go ahead."

"Harlow?" I say urgently. "I know you can hear me, sweetheart. You're safe. Becket is taking you home."

It's excruciating, the sound of her terror. I can't do a damn thing from here. She's out of my reach and unresponsive.

"This wasn't him, Harlow. It's just some punks playing a foolish prank. He hasn't found you."

She still doesn't respond, too busy repeating her frenzied mantra over and over again. I drag my hair tie out and fist the long strands, desperate to crawl through the phone.

"Enz? You there?"

"I've got her," he responds sharply. "What's the latest?"

"CCTV is a bust. We've got three perps in range, but no evidence. Hudson's picking them up for questioning."

"Why would anyone do this?"

"That's exactly what I'm going to find out."

Theo shoots me a thumbs up from his desk chair. He's logged in to our secure server, tracking Hudson's precious Mustang as he peels through Central London, making a beeline for the hospital.

That man is far better than a bloodhound and more likely to tear his victims to shreds with his bare teeth. I hope I'm right and one of those workers did this, or we're sending a paid assassin after three innocent people. Not my best move.

"Send Leighton home to watch Harlow," Enzo demands. "Put the perps in the detention block until I get to HQ."

"Take over here," I suggest instead. "I'm coming home."

"You are?"

"Harlow needs me. She comes first."

Her whimpering quietens, replaced by a relieved inhale.

"Hunter," she manages to say.

I almost fall over from the rush of relief. Hearing her crying in fear makes me want to dismember someone, and not in a fun way. I can't stand knowing someone scared her this bad.

"Hold on, love. I'll be there soon."

Disconnecting the call, I catch Theo looking at me strangely before I exit his office again.

"What?"

He lifts an eyebrow. "You're never one to surrender control, even to Enzo."

"My priorities have changed."

"Since when?"

"Since now. Moving forward, it's family first, and that's exactly what Harlow is to us."

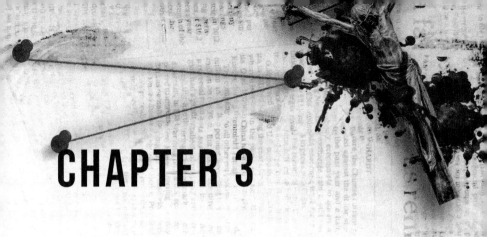

CHAPTER 3

Harlow

All I Have – NF

The first thing I feel is the reassuring warmth of a hard, muscular body wrapped around me. Familiar scents intermingle with the residue of last night's fire.

Lemon and lime.

Toasted marshmallows.

Leftover popcorn.

Someone's trapped beneath me, his chest rising and falling with each deep breath. Opening my eyes, I blink the sleep away and peer down at Leighton's snoring frame.

He's fast asleep.

Sunlight streams through the thick curtains that we forgot to draw in the den last night. The television is still paused on an episode of *The Office*. It's our new thing after finishing *Friends* and bawling our eyes out together at the ending.

I'm secretly rooting for Dwight and Angela to end up together. They're my favourite couple. Leighton's a Jim and Pam fan, so we argue a lot about it over fresh popcorn and over-sweetened cups of tea. Our go-to snacks.

"Leigh?" I gently tap his cheek.

"Go away, Hunt," he complains sleepily. "No work."

I suppress a laugh. "I'm not Hunter, and I really hope you don't wake up with him laying on you like this."

He cracks an eye open before huffing and screwing it shut again. "Too early. Go back to sleep."

Placing a hand on the hardwood floor next to the green, velvet sectional sofa that we're splayed out on, I manoeuvre myself off his body without falling over.

"Harlow," he whines. "Come back."

I stretch to my full height. "Go back to sleep."

He doesn't need more encouragement. His rattled snoring resumes, and I pad through to the kitchen to boil the kettle. Lucky is already waiting at the back door, her tail wagging with anticipation.

"You're never late."

She yips excitedly.

I stroke a hand over her golden fur and unlock the French doors. "Go on then. I'll be out in a sec."

Galloping outside, she stretches her powerful limbs before bounding through the early morning mist. January arrived brisk and cold, bringing frost and the occasional snowfall.

I'm not sure where Christmas went. Our plans were ruined by everything that happened up north. By the time Hunter and Enzo returned home, the festivities were over, and I was in no mood to celebrate anything.

Another year ruined.

I can't say I'm surprised.

It was over a week before I was able to face leaving my room. Facing the real world is still a challenge, even now. After what happened at the hospital the other day, I'm seriously considering becoming a full-time hermit.

The security system buzzes with an alert before the front door clicks open, admitting a sweaty, red-faced Enzo dressed in thermal running gear. He braces his hands on his knees.

"Morning, Enz."

His head snaps up. "You're awake."

"Just about."

I fire up Hunter's fancy machine and set about making him a black coffee. He's barely capable of coherent thought without a constant current of caffeine in his veins.

"Good run?"

Enzo drains his water bottle before chucking it in the steel rubbish bin. "Quiet. Anyone else up?"

"Hunter fell asleep at his desk last night. He hasn't emerged yet. Leighton is doing his best grizzly bear impression in the den. Theo isn't here."

He eyes me suspiciously. "You slept downstairs?"

Sliding him the fresh cup of coffee, I finish my own tea with milk and a generous heap of sugar before shrugging.

"We fell asleep watching TV."

"Must be nice," he complains.

Our eyes connect across the marble breakfast bar, scattered with last night's empty pizza boxes and Hunter's newspaper from yesterday morning.

There are violent purple bags beneath his vivid amber eyes. Shame punches me in the chest. Enzo doesn't sleep unless it's next to me. His skin has to be touching mine for him to finally succumb, usually for a handful of hours at best.

"I'm sorry," I rush to apologise.

"Don't worry about it."

"I should have come up and found you. Did you get any sleep at all?"

"Not important."

I quickly grab his arm before he can disappear to shower. Enzo frowns at where my fingers grip his glistening bicep.

"You're not responsible for my sleep schedule, little one. I've been getting by alone for thirty-two years."

Stepping into his embrace, I wrap my arms around his waist. He smells salty beneath a sheen of sweat, but his earthy, pine tree scent still beckons me in. I rest my head on his hard abdominals and let my eyes slide shut.

"You can call dibs on me tonight."

His chest vibrates with a chuckle. "Dibs? Is that the system we're working on now?"

"I'm not sure there is a system."

"Yeah, me neither."

"We haven't really discussed... well, anything."

Enzo lifts my chin so our eyes meet. A shiver runs down my spine. He still makes butterflies explode in my stomach. The months we've spent living together haven't changed that.

It's like staring up into the threatening grimace of a golden-eyed tiger. Instead of fearing his power, though, I'm comforted by the certainty that he'll tear apart any predator that dares to give me a second glance.

"What do you want to talk about?" he croons.

I squirm as his arms band around me. His grip tightens into a vice-like prison, locking me against his chest. I couldn't run away even if I wanted to.

"Well, the others… erm, us. We haven't really talked about… you know, us."

He cocks an eyebrow. "Smooth. Us?"

A blush creeps up my neck. There's an amused twinkle in Enzo's eyes as the corner of his mouth lifts.

"You've been, um… staying in my bed most nights," I scramble to explain. "And Hunter, you know. He does too. Then Leighton… he… ah, hell. I give up."

"You sure?" He laughs throatily.

"Shut up."

"Oh, no. Feel free to keep going. This is hilarious."

"Stop laughing at me!"

Expression growing serious, his gaze softens with tender affection. Two calloused fingers brush across my cheek before he tucks a strand of long, brown hair behind my ear.

"I know things are confusing right now," he offers. "The case is a mess and we're no better. But I can promise you one thing."

"What's that?"

He leans close, his thick, plush lips ghosting over mine. "None of us are going anywhere. We have a lot of shit to sort out between us, but that fact won't ever change."

I press my mouth against his, my teeth playfully nipping his bottom lip before withdrawing. My confidence is blooming with each touch.

"Do you promise?" I ask huskily.

"Want me to cross my fucking heart?"

"If you're offering."

With a crooked grin, Enzo drags his index finger over his heart. "Then I cross my heart and hope to die. That's what it would take for me to let you go."

Rather than comforted, I feel sick.

"Harlow?" he prompts. "What is it?"

Dread seeps over me in a suffocating cloud. I've already gotten enough people killed. Whether by my hand or not, I enabled all of those women's deaths. I watched from behind the rusted bars of my cage and said nothing.

I can't watch Enzo die too.

Not like Laura.

"Did you find who wrecked your car last week?"

Sighing, he leans against the countertop. "It wasn't one of the people we picked up. I interviewed them myself."

"By interviewed, do you mean that you beat them to within an inch of their lives?"

Enzo's grin widens. "Something like that."

"Jesus, seriously?"

"No, I'm kidding."

I blow out a breath. "Don't scare me like that."

"I sat them down and questioned them. They all had alibis and were working at the time it occurred. It wasn't them."

"Who did this then?"

He shrugs casually. "We've been receiving some weird-as-hell emails, so it could easily be one of those nut jobs."

"Wait, what?"

Enzo hesitates before answering. "There are some people who support what Pastor Michaels is doing to these women. Real Charles Manson shit."

"I don't know who that is."

"Serial killers attract the worst kind of attention," he attempts to explain. "We've been getting people threatening us to let Michaels do his work in peace."

"Why? He's killing people!"

"These psychos think he's some kind of messiah. Reckon he's doing God's work, culling the sinners from the earth in preparation for the rapture or some shit like that."

I wish that freaked me out more. Several months ago, that would have sounded normal. In some ways, it still does. My reality is a confusing combination of past and present.

Indoctrinated and liberated.

Captive and free.

Damned and worthy.

"You think he's been ordering these people to attack us? Was Pastor Michaels behind what happened at the hospital?"

Enzo scrubs a hand over his face. "I doubt it. He's an apex predator. They hunt alone and without a pack."

"He wasn't alone. Mrs Michaels helped him."

"Pastor Michaels slaughtered his only accomplice and hung her like a piece of meat," he highlights. "I doubt he's looking for any more help if she wasn't needed."

Head drooping, I focus on my sock-covered feet. Upstairs, hidden beneath my mattress, Mrs Michaels' golden wedding ring awaits its final resting place.

I'm not sure why I couldn't part with it. On some level, it's a sick fascination for the physical proof of what happened in the confusing blur of those thirteen years.

But deeper, on a more instinctual level, that ring represents the only life I've ever known. Part of me feels safer with it close, a twisted slice of home. I can't bear to let it go yet.

"What about Kiera?" I bite my lip. "She still talks to me. Whispers and snippets of memories are coming back every day."

Enzo's frown deepens. "Talks to you?"

"Like in my dreams and stuff."

"I see. Well, Hunter's going to be interviewing her sister in a couple of days. We'll have more information then."

Grabbing my half-finished cup of tea, I tip out the rest of the liquid. Enzo watches me intently, and I can't stand it for a second longer. They're all just waiting for me to break.

"I want a meeting with all of you." I place the cup down with trembling hands. "I'm involved in this case too."

"Why? I said we'd keep you posted with any updates. That's exactly what we're doing."

"Are you?" I scoff.

When Enzo drops my eyes, I know I've caught him out. My instincts were right. There's something else the team isn't telling me.

"I'm protecting you," he reasons.

"Then stop! I don't need you to."

My control snapping, I grab the discarded cup and throw it so hard, it shatters on the marble countertop. It feels good to watch the broken shards rain down, completely destroyed.

"I gave you Kiera James. I found that chapel. I have done more than my fair share, and you still keep me in the dark."

"You know that isn't the case."

"Isn't it?" I round on him. "What about Mrs Michaels? It's been a whole month. You must have identified her body."

Bingo. Enzo shifts on his feet, blowing out a frustrated breath. After all we've been through and the progress I thought we've made, they still don't trust me.

It hurts.

I'm not one of them.

"Well?" I throw my hands up.

Footsteps approach, breaking our furious stare off. Hunter strolls into the kitchen, wearing his usual soft, green sweats and bare, chiselled abdomen, highlighting his defined Adonis belt.

Intricate tattoos cover his entire chest, wrapping around his torso and dipping into the waistband of his sweats. The inked thunderstorm is depicted in painstaking detail, reflecting the controlled but vicious storm brewing within him.

"I heard shouting," he mumbles.

His burnished, chocolate-brown eyes land on me beneath his long, chestnut hair. The only imperfection on his model-like looks is an old scar that bisects his eyebrow.

"What's going on?"

I fold my arms, lifting my chin with indignation. "Who is Mrs Michaels?"

His shoulders slump. "Sit down, Harlow. This doesn't have to be a fight."

"That seems to be the only way to make you idiots tell the truth. I'm not sitting down. Start talking."

Easing past me to brew his morning fix of tea, Hunter takes a seat at the breakfast bar and gingerly pushes old pizza boxes aside. He looks physically offended by the mess.

"It took some time, but our forensic team has identified Mrs Michaels using old dental records."

Enzo shakes his head as he turns away from us. I'd love to thump him around the face right now. He still doesn't get why I need to know what's happening.

"Her real name is Rosetta Stone." Hunter glances up at me. "She's been missing since the late seventies."

"M-Missing?" I stammer.

He fiddles with his black hearing aid. "We linked her to a dodgy children's home that was shut down in 1994. It wasn't uncommon for these kids to disappear."

"We think she ran away to escape the abuse and neglect." Enzo braces his hands on the counter. "She was sixteen."

"Didn't they look for her?"

"It would've been easy to start again under a new name, pretending to be older to avoid being dragged back there."

My heart pounds faster, exploding into delirious butterflies. It's hard to imagine the monstrous pillar of violence and hatred who haunted my childhood as a little girl.

She was scared and running for her life. Just like me. I hate the way that realisation twists my emotions, leaving me feeling completely lost in the wilderness of my confusion.

"This children's home... have you spoken to the staff? Do they remember her? What if we go there and look around?"

"It's gone," Hunter says gently.

"Gone?" I repeat. "How?"

"Bulldozed and wiped from the records as part of the government's clean-up initiative. They were implicated and wanted to cover their tracks. Any staff members have died or been silenced in the decades since."

My balled-up fist crashes against the counter. "This is such bullshit. You're telling me there's nothing?"

Both men stare at me like I'm an alien.

"She's spending far too much time with your potty mouth of a brother," Enzo complains to his best friend.

"He's teaching her bad habits," Hunter concurs.

"Go and wake the little delinquent up. He can get his lazy backside into the office today to do some damn work."

"I am standing right here," I snap in exasperation. "Any other vital information you've kept from me? Also, you guys say *fuck* literally all the time, but I'm the potty mouth?"

They both burst out laughing, doubled over and wiping away tears. Crossing my arms, I attempt to storm past Enzo to escape into the garden to get away from them.

His arms shoot out to capture me. "Where do you think you're going?"

"Away from you two."

"I don't think so. You wanted to talk, so let's talk."

"You don't get to turn this on me," I defend angrily. "Take me seriously, or this conversation is over."

"Look who's calling the shots," Hunter taunts, an eyebrow raised. "You've changed, sweetheart."

I flush hot, my entire body burning. I'm not sure if it's embarrassment or desire, but the way he's staring at me with a weird look of pride is setting a fire low in my belly.

"Is that a bad thing? People are supposed to change."

Curling his arm around my narrow waist, Enzo tugs me against his chest. We collide with a smack and my face presses up against his heavily beating heart.

"It's not a bad thing," he murmurs. "We're happy to see you figuring out what you want."

"Then why do you keep me in the dark?"

"It's our responsibility to keep you safe while you're healing. You shouldn't be worrying. We have the case under control."

Before I can argue back, Hunter's stool scrapes across the tiled floor and a column of warmth meets my spine. His chin rests on top of my head, imprisoning me between them.

I forget how to blink, breathe or form any logical thought. Enzo's muscles are hard beneath my touch, while Hunter's hot breath stirs my hair. They both smell so good.

"If this is just a job, where does that leave us?"

"Just a job?" Hunter repeats. "Pretty sure I proved otherwise the night you came on my tongue, sweetheart."

Enzo's grip on me tightens. "I didn't consider it my job to make you cry out my name in this very kitchen."

"Careful," Hunter warns him.

My heart seizes with fear. I'm caught between them both. There's no space to run away from the truth. I've been playing a dangerous game without even realising it.

"It's fine by me," Enzo croons.

Hunter's growl vibrates against my back. "I warned you to keep your damn hands to yourself, Enz. Not go behind my back to try to fuck our client."

"Like you didn't do the same thing?" he argues. "We've talked about this. All of us care about Harlow a lot."

"That's exactly why we can't do this."

"Do what?" I ask cluelessly.

I can practically feel their glowers above my head. When I wriggle out from between them, drowning in the testosterone, Hunter's hands grab my hips tight.

His thumbs slip beneath the oversized *Aerosmith* t-shirt that I stole from Leighton's wardrobe to relax in yesterday. He's very precious about his extensive collection, but he never complains about me wearing his clothes.

"Did I say you could move?" Hunter traps me back between them. "Stay right where you are."

His left hand coasts higher, over the scarred expanse of my lower stomach. I bite my lip to hold back a sigh as he teases the waistband of my yoga pants.

"This isn't a game," Enzo hisses at him. "Take your hands off her."

"Why? If I want to touch Harlow, I will. If I want to strip her bare, spread her across the table and fuck her while you watch, I bloody well will."

"Touch her when she doesn't want it and we're going to have a serious problem."

Pushing his taunting hand inside my yoga pants, Hunter's fingers coast even lower. I arch my back, silently pleading for more. He cups my mound over the damp material of my panties, sending spikes of anticipation through my core.

"Seems like she wants it to me," he purrs. "I can feel how wet her pussy is just thinking about me fucking her."

"Stop being a dick." Enzo grabs my shoulders and pulls me closer. "Best friend or not, I'll still put a bullet in your face."

Hunter slips his hand from my yoga pants. "You were the one proposing we share her. How's that plan going, Enz?"

Forehead slick with nervous sweat, I almost teeter when Enzo releases me, on the verge of punching Hunter in the face. He immediately grabs me again, his eyebrows knitted together with concern.

"Share me?" I ask, despite my dizziness.

Neither responds.

"Like you did with Alyssa?"

Her whispered name causes Hunter to step away from us both. The rush of cold air is like a slap to the face. He avoids looking at us both as he storms from the room, a hand fisted in his long, tangled hair.

His office door slams shut down the hall with an audible crack. Enzo shakes his head, running his hands up and down my arms as he tries to comfort me.

"I'm sorry about that."

"Not your fault," I reply in a small voice. "He's got a lot on his plate. I never meant to cause so much trouble."

"You have the right to ask for something... if you want it."

A secret message stares back at me in shades of molten amber through his gaze. I can see the truth. His desires. The future he's so desperately reaching for. It terrifies me.

"What do you want?" I counter softly.

His lips part. "You."

My entire body is humming with anticipation. The embattled, fearful slice of submission left inside me wants to fling open the front door, run until my feet bleed and escape all of these complicated emotions.

"The others want you too," Enzo explains with a sad smile. "That's the problem. We all want the impossible."

I rest a hand over his heart. "What's that?"

His throat bobs tellingly. "Another chance."

Stroking a hand over the razor-sharp line of his carved collar bone, I wrestle with the tears threatening to spill down my cheeks. He still doesn't see it. They deserve every shot at happiness. Far more than I do.

That's why I can't have them.

It's too late for me.

"Maybe I should stay somewhere else."

Enzo's face drains of all colour. "Excuse me?"

"This is all my fault. You're fighting over something that can never happen. If I go now, it'll be easier that way."

He takes a small, protective step away from me. It feels like a knife is twisting in my gut.

"Never happen?" he thunders.

The pain swimming in his eyes makes me feel like the absolute worst human on the planet. He sacrificed everything to make me feel at home; giving me safety, love, their devotion and protection. I've thrown it back in his face.

"I should stand on my own two feet," I reason. "The longer I stay here with you, the harder that will be. I don't want anyone to fight over me."

"You seriously want to leave us?"

I swallow the truth like gulping bullets and nod. Even if it's a bold-faced lie. I'd rather crawl back into my cage than leave them, but I won't hurt Enzo's family any longer.

"You're lying."

"Hey," I snap defensively.

"If you mean it... say it again."

Swallowing down the nausea curdling in my stomach, I try to speak in an even, believable voice.

"I'm an adult, and I have the right to choose where I live. Thank you for everything you've done, but I want to leave now."

Stepping back into my personal space, Enzo slides a finger under my chin. When his mouth slants against mine, stealing a pulse-spiking kiss, I want to collapse in his arms and take it all back.

"That's how I know you're lying," he says huskily. "I expected this bullshit from Hunter, but not you."

Dropping his grip on my chin, he brushes past me. I flinch, trying to grab his t-shirt but failing.

"Enzo—"

"I need to get to the office."

"Please, wait."

Enzo glances back, a wounded bonfire smouldering in his eyes. "Try to leave this house and I'll have the agents guarding the gate drag you back, kicking and screaming."

My haze-filled brain screams out in alarm. I know he'd never hurt me, but the threat is clear. It's the same toxic possession that fuelled Pastor Michaels' abuse. I didn't escape that basement to be controlled by another man.

"You can't do that."

"I'm not bluffing, Harlow. You will stay here until it's safe. When Pastor Michaels is rotting in hell, feel free to leave."

Enzo storms out before I can summon a comeback. I'm left in the empty kitchen, trembling all over and feeling like God has slammed the pearly gates shut in my face with a sneer.

A prison is still a prison.

Even when it's an invisible one.

CHAPTER 4

Theo

The Kid I Used To Know – Arrested Youth

S at behind my cluttered, cup-lined desk, I watch the live feed from
the interview room several floors beneath my office. My head is
pounding with a sleep-deprived headache.

Reagan James, Kiera's younger sister, sits at the plain wooden
table. Her trembling hands are wrapped around a cup of coffee as her
red hair covers her tear-streaked face.

Hunter hasn't begun yet.

She's already a mess.

On the camera feed, the door to the room opens. Our two hard-
faced masters enter with solemn determination. Hunter is dressed
to the nines in his usual three-piece suit, while Enzo is sporting his
standard, all-black clothing and leather jacket.

"Miss James," Hunter greets as he takes a seat.

"Mr Rodriguez," she replies.

"Thanks for coming in. We appreciate your cooperation."

Reagan tucks hair behind her ear, showing off a glinting

engagement ring. "Anything to help get justice for Kiera. Do you have new information?"

Enzo slaps down a thick folder of evidence. "I'm sure you're aware of the recent developments in the case."

"Of course. It's all over the news."

"We have a live witness cooperating with us, and she has shed some light on your sister's death."

"Is she here? I'd like to meet her myself."

Hunter shakes his head. "I'm afraid that isn't possible. We need to ask you some questions about your sister."

She swallows hard. "What do you want to know?"

My office door creaks, and Leighton slips inside, carrying a heavy evidence box from Hunter's office. I gesture for him to put it down next to the fully stocked bookshelf.

He dusts off his hands, appearing bored beyond belief. The past several weeks of him working here have been hilarious to watch. He's suffering Enzo's seemingly endless wrath, and the punishment is going well.

"Enjoying yourself?"

His eyes narrow. "Shut the hell up. I'm only here because Harlow's having her therapy session upstairs. I'm driving her home after."

"I thought you just loved working here, Leigh."

"Not fucking likely," he grumbles.

With a one-fingered salute, Leighton saunters out of the room. He's slacked off in the months since his release from prison, and after the fiasco with Diablo, he has a lot to make up for. Enzo's prepared to train him up once he earns his forgiveness for everything that happened.

Having Leighton around the office so much has been weird. I feel guilty for how I've treated him, but my coldness towards him has never been personal. He simply represents the finality of Alyssa's exit from our lives.

Turning back to the live interview, I watch Enzo rest a hand on Reagan's shoulder. She's silently crying as they run back through the basics of the case to refresh her memory.

The grief is clearly still raw, despite the years that have passed since Kiera's slaughtered body turned up. I know better than most that time doesn't always equal healing.

"From your previous statements, we know you last saw Kiera the day before her disappearance." Hunter scans over the evidence file. "Tell me, how did she seem?"

Reagan blows her nose. "Normal. My sister lived a quiet life. She worked in the local school, attended church, rarely dated or even looked at men. She was happy."

"No boyfriends then?"

"No, never. Her work and religion were her life. The most socialising she ever did was walking her dog."

Reagan's face collapses as she cries harder.

"Miss James?" Enzo prompts.

"Reggie died last year. I know he was just a dog, but he was the last connection I had to her. Now, she's really gone."

"I'm sorry," he offers gently. "I know this must be difficult."

The iron-willed boulder of muscle has a disturbing talent for slipping past the defences of even the most cautious people. Enzo wields his kind-hearted nature as a weapon when it suits him, but he's the first one to snap spinal cords or shatter noses when shit hits the fan.

"I miss her," Reagan admits. "We were close."

Giving her tissues, Enzo sits back down and rifles through the evidence that Hunter hands him. He slides a printed map of woodland across the table. We know that Kiera was snatched somewhere around that location.

"How often did Kiera take this route for her dog walk?"

Reagan picks up the paper and studies it. "Several times a week. She loved to unplug after dealing with kids all day at work. Being in nature was one of her favourite things."

"This was a regular pattern of behaviour for her?" Hunter presses.

Reagan nods. "For sure."

"Who else was aware of your sister's regular walking route? Friends? Neighbours? Colleagues?"

"It's a small town," she answers. "I moved away after university, but Kiera was happy to live in a village where everyone knows everyone."

Looking at the identical file spread out between empty crisp packets and leftover pizza crusts on my desk, I rifle through the next section of evidence. It's a sparse file, even though Kiera's disappearance shocked the local community.

The whole town rallied around Reagan and her family to conduct regular searches and information campaigns. Everything about this victim was different. This was long before the serialised pattern of murder was established.

Only one other woman, a local sex worker, had died before Kiera and in completely different circumstances. She was the odd one out amongst a repertoire of brutality.

Kiera doesn't fit the victim profile at all—she was in full-time employment, living a quiet life as a devout Christian who was loved by her family and church.

Killing her wasn't safe or strategic.

The whole thing screams of rage.

She was ripped from a close-knit community and brutalised despite her faith. Pastor Michaels didn't select her like he did the others, intent on punishing them for what he considered a life of sin. He tore Kiera apart regardless.

"Can you think of anyone who wanted to hurt your sister?" Enzo asks.

Reagan's staring at a photograph of Kiera, smiling with a caramel-coloured puppy cuddled in her arms. She was sweet and attractive, albeit a little older than the other victims, in her early thirties. The crucifix around her neck is prominent.

"She wouldn't hurt a fly," Reagan whispers. "All my sister wanted was to help people. She volunteered at a local homeless shelter and helped teach the younger children in the clergy."

Trailing off, Reagan's eyebrows knit together. Hunter sits up in his chair, dropping his hand from playing with his hearing aid, as he does when deep in thought.

"What is it?"

Reagan frowns at the photograph in her hands. "There was one person she fell out with. Someone in the congregation. I'd forgotten all about it... but she was very angry."

"What did they argue about?" Enzo urges.

"She wouldn't tell me what happened, but she was so upset after attending church. I remember her acting strange during our Sunday night video call that week."

"How long was this before her disappearance?"

"Perhaps a few months?"

Unease brushes down my spine. For a plain, unremarkable woman with little to no social life, fighting with a member of her church had to be for a good reason.

"Did you tell the police about this?" Hunter questions.

"They didn't think it was important."

"Why?"

"You guys don't go to church," Reagan guesses with a thin smile. "Arguments are what keep these places in business. It isn't exactly breaking news for church members to disagree."

"Then why does it feel significant to you?"

She looks surprised by the sharply worded question. Hunter has always had an ability to examine people's darkest thoughts, past the veneer of thinly veiled bullshit.

"My sister was a gentle person," Reagan explains slowly. "She hated conflict. That's why I was so surprised when she was upset. But I just figured it was nothing, you know?"

Flipping through the preliminary report, I search for any mention of a falling out in the written transcript. There's nothing. Police incompetence and lacklustre investigating is half the reason this motherfucker has killed so many people.

The officers presumed that Kiera ran off with a boyfriend. She was old enough to take care of herself and deemed to be sensible, so in their eyes, limited police time and funding were better spent elsewhere.

When her body rocked up six weeks later, they'd already moved on to the next investigation demanding their cash-strapped time. Their failure enabled her death, and all those that followed.

"Who else knew about this?" Hunter asks crisply.

"I think she said something about the argument happening during a church service. Perhaps someone else who was there might have witnessed it. I'm not sure."

Hunter grabs a piece of paper and a pen. "Any names or contact details you have would be greatly appreciated."

Reagan bites her lip. "I might have a name. I wasn't much of a churchgoer, but I know the old pastor fairly well."

"Anything you can give us."

I snap back to reality when someone knocks on my office door. It's light and timid, announcing Harlow's presence before she peeks her head around the corner. Nobody else has the politeness to knock around here.

"Theo?"

My heart leaps into my throat. Fuck. I'd forgotten how gorgeous she is. I've barely seen her since the night when her father turned up, lifeless and half dead. The circles beneath her eyes are even darker now, much like my own.

"Is this a bad time? I have some books to return."

"Oh, erm… sure. Thanks."

She steps into the office, revealing her small, inviting curves and pert breasts accentuated by a long-sleeved white t-shirt and tight blue jeans beneath her parka coat.

In the months since she stumbled into our lives, she's put on some weight, and it's done her so much good. Despite all the shit that's been thrown her way, she's doing her best to stay alive.

Her flowing brown hair brushes her lower back in tumbling waves, highlighting her piercing aquamarine eyes, cute button nose and sharp but dainty cheekbones.

I'm so entranced, my throat tightening with desire, I forget to turn off the live interview feed. She lets me take the box of books from her hands. Balancing them on my shoulder, I use my spare arm to pull her into a tentative hug.

"Oh," she squeaks.

I release her. "Sorry."

"Don't apologise. I missed you."

Goddammit.

"I missed you too," I force out.

"How have you been?"

"I've been snowed under with the investigation. Sorry that I haven't been around much."

"I understand. I miss our late-night book talks."

Her eyes are fixed on the scuffed brown leather of her laced boots, perfectly tied into bows. Dumping the box of books, my fingers spasm with the need to pull her closer.

There are two halves warring within me, both demanding very different things. Despite my growing feelings for Harlow, that voice is still there. *Alyssa.* The memories still talk to me.

Laughing and teasing.

Telling me she loved me.

Promising me forever.

I hate how this feels like I'm betraying her memory. She's dead and gone. I can at least admit that to myself now. Locking Harlow out isn't going to bring Alyssa back.

After months spent trying to do that, it didn't fucking work. I still ended up right here—standing in front of Harlow, desperate to taste her lips, but too scared to make that leap.

"I enjoyed *The Odyssey*," she blurts.

"You did?"

"It was a good story, albeit a little sexist."

I stifle a laugh. "Well, yeah. Most classic books are."

She mock-shivers. "Not quite as bad as *Pride and Prejudice*, though. That was gross."

"Not a fan of classic romance?"

"I prefer reality to stupid pageantry and star-crossed lovers. Frankenstein's monster killing Victor's entire family when he refused to make him a bride was pretty cool."

Barking a laugh, I watch a smirk blossom on her pink lips. Jesus, this girl. It's not every day you find someone who prefers reading about horrifying monsters that are desperate for love over Mr Darcy and his problematic behaviour.

"Got anything else for me?"

I hook a thumb over my shoulder. "Come take a look." Panicking, I glance at my bookshelf. "Um, please don't judge the amount of trashy fantasy novels I have."

She giggles. "Is it that bad?"

"I can't have the world knowing I'm a nerd."

"I think that ship has already sailed."

Harlow walks over to my bookshelf, each footstep bouncing with excitement. I stand back and simply watch her. The way her fingertips trace over the book spines sets my heart pulsing.

She may as well be caressing the fractured pages of my soul, begging the book to open up to her. I want to do exactly that right now. She holds such unspoken power over me.

"You like sad books," she observes.

I wring my hands together. "Why would I want to read about something happy?"

"Most people do."

"Hope is in very limited supply in this world. I don't want to waste it on characters who don't exist. Give me death and tragedy. Like you said… it's more realistic."

Her brilliant blue eyes flick over to me. "What are you saving your hope for then, Theodore?"

My dick hardens at the teasing use of my full name. All I can think about is bending her over that goddamn bookshelf and burying myself deep inside of her. I haven't even thought about sex for a very long time.

"I don't know yet," I admit hoarsely.

Tension crackles in the charged air between us. All of my defences are annihilated with a mere glance. Harlow burns through the layers of numbness I've constructed over the years, and I'm stunned to realise that I'm glad.

"I'm not sure if I have any hope left to save." Her smile is bittersweet. "But if I did, I would keep it close so nobody could ever steal it from me again."

As we stare at each other, both looking for the right words to offer the other, voices filter back into our awareness. My array of monitors is still playing the live interview. Harlow's gaze strays over to the computer screens.

"What is going on?" she asks suspiciously.

"Oh, erm."

"Is that Kiera's sister?"

"Uh, I don't know if I'm supposed to tell you."

She shakes her head, the annoyance clear on her face. "Not you as well."

I feel like a dick as she abandons her small selection of books and heads for my desk. On the screen, Reagan is crying again. Harlow freezes, her fingers clenched over her mouth.

"My sister didn't deserve to die," Reagan sobs. "She should be here to walk down the aisle with me."

I hover a hand over Harlow's shoulder without touching her. "Maybe you shouldn't be watching this."

"Kiera was my friend," she replies. "I have more of a right than anyone to hear this."

Tiny earthquakes are wracking her entire slim frame as she watches Reagan fall apart, overwhelmed by the interview and array of evidence spread out in front of her.

"Miss James," Hunter interrupts, poised in his seat. "We can leave it here. You've been most helpful."

"I want to see her," Reagan demands.

"Excuse me?"

Her tear-logged eyes glance between them. "I want to meet the girl who let my sister die."

Fuck!

I need to turn this shit off.

"Why did she live when all of us have been left to grieve our loved ones? What makes her so special?"

"That's enough." Enzo gathers the evidence into the file. "Interview suspended. Miss James, you may leave now."

"Why won't she speak up?" Reagan's voice raises. "This monster is out there right now, slaughtering innocent women. All for what? She could make him stop."

Enzo grabs Reagan by the wrist, hauling her out of the seat. He wrestles her from the interview room as she shouts and raves, leaving Hunter to glance up at the camera. He looks as weary and bone tired as I feel.

Protecting Harlow is getting harder.

The world is turning against us.

"Is that what everyone's thinking?" Harlow's voice draws my attention. "Does the entire world want me to... to die?"

"Hell no," I hiss back. "She's grieving."

"They're all grieving! I'm the only one who didn't die."

"That doesn't make you culpable. You were a victim of this son of a bitch. Nobody could ever blame you."

She hugs her midsection tight. "Rewind the tape, Theo. Plenty of people are blaming me already."

"I know the truth. They don't."

Her breathing grows shallower as the cloud of panic slowly filters over her. I try to step closer, but she backs away.

"If I surrendered, would all of this stop?"

"Harlow. Don't go there."

"You read those letters he sent. I'm what Pastor Michaels wants. If he gets me back, the killings will stop."

"I don't give a fuck what that psychopath wants! We're going to find him and put an end to all of this."

She slams her hands over her ears, scrunching her eyes shut to block me out. I grip her shoulders and pull her into my arms, burying my nose in her sweet-scented hair.

"You're going to be okay," I whisper against her covered ear. "We will fix this, I promise. It'll be over soon."

"I never should've left that basement."

"Come on. Don't let her get in your head."

Thick, shining tears roll down her cheeks. "Everyone that's died… all the pain and suffering… it's my fault."

"Beautiful, please. Don't think like that."

"What if I killed myself? Would he be sated then?"

Her words slip out in a dark, anguished whisper. So quietly spoken, for a moment I think I've imagined it. Her eyes open, and the limitless lake of blue is cracked with guilt.

"You don't mean that."

"I can't watch anyone else die," she pleads. "My life isn't worth more than whoever he kills next."

The ringing in my head grows louder and louder, until it feels like I'm trapped beneath a frozen lake, battering my fists against the frosted, crème brûlée surface, trying to break free.

She's in my arms. I can feel her. Smell her. Touch her. Yet, our hands are being ripped apart at the same time. Fate is threatening to tear us apart, and I don't know if I can stop it.

If I don't hold on tighter, she's going to drown. I can already see it happening. Defeat has infected her, and it's spreading. Someone has to pull her back to the surface.

"Look at me." I pry her hands from her ears. "You listen carefully."

More tears pour down her red-stained cheeks as I trap her against my chest. She's biting back another pained sob.

"Your death will not stop this bastard from killing again. It won't. He's trying to manipulate you. Don't let him."

Her knees give way all at once. I'm dragged down with her, and we end up collapsing in a tangle.

"Breathe for me, beautiful."

Her chest contracts with each shuddered breath. I'm thrown back into the past—back to a time when there was an ocean of secrets between us, and I offered her Laura's bone to say goodbye to. It worked to bring her back from the edge.

I can fix this.

She needs to feel safe.

Banding my arms around her, I use my feet to shuffle backwards across the rough carpet. The solid wood of my desk looms above us. Dodging computer cables and bundled wires, I slip beneath it, taking Harlow with me.

Curling up in the tight, cramped space, I hold her spooned in my lap like she's a newborn baby. Her back rests on my chest, glueing us together as two halves of the same whole.

I don't say anything.

Words don't matter.

They mean absolutely nothing when you're staring into the abyss and searching for a reason not to take that short walk to oblivion. All I can do is hold her through it.

"Theo," she hiccups after several minutes.

"Yeah, beautiful?"

Her fingers search my flannel shirt, crawling up my throat until her palm rests on my cheek. I place my hand over hers, our fingers fitting together.

"Thank you for being here. You should hate me for all the trouble I've caused."

"I could never hate you," I reply softly.

Her adrenaline finally crashes, leaving her breathing to even out. It's uncomfortable hiding under here, but I don't care. We'll stay until the end of time if that's what she needs.

"Living keeps getting harder," she admits.

I smooth her hair in slow, rhythmic strokes. "Surviving doesn't make you guilty. Even if you feel like it does."

"Then what does it make me?"

Taking a moment to think over my response, I dare to drop a kiss on the top of her head. She feels so good in my arms.

"Lucky."

CHAPTER 5

Harlow

Put It On Me – Matt Maeson

L eighton deposits a bowl of sweetened popcorn in my lap, collapsing next to me on the sectional with a huff. He curls his legs up to his chest and drops his headful of messy, brown hair on my shoulder.

"Ready for this?"

I rest my head against his. "Yep."

"My number one movie. It's been a long time coming."

"The suspense is killing me."

My joke falls flat. I can't hide the exhaustion from my voice. My sleep last night was riddled with dreams of Kiera, her dead, empty eyes watching me as they carved the limbs from her torso.

Her sister's words were the soundtrack.

Why did she live?

What makes her so special?

Why won't she speak up?

"Goldilocks."

Snapping his fingers in front of my face, Leighton's watching me with concerned green eyes. The scent of lemons and tropical fruit clinging to his hair drags me back to the present.

"Yeah?"

"Where did you go?"

I avoid his gaze. "Nowhere. What were you saying?"

Leighton is the youngest of the group at twenty-four. He wears his youth with casual unkemptness. His hair covers his ears, in need of a good cut, while his jeans and revolving door of frayed nineties band t-shirts are always crumpled.

He hesitates, biting his bottom lip. "You can talk to me if you want to. I'm a pretty good listener."

Snatching a handful of popcorn, I shove it in my mouth to avoid answering.

"Is this about your dad?" he guesses.

"It's nothing. Let's watch the movie."

When the hospital called a couple of hours ago to say that my father was a lot more awake this week and beginning to respond to treatment, I didn't know how to feel.

Relieved. Confused.

But mostly, angry with the world.

After finding a donor match, his surgery has been confirmed for next week. It's the first progress we've had in over a month, but I still feel sick thinking about it.

I know it's only a matter of time before he'll want to speak to me. Sitting in a hospital room with a groggy shade of the man I can't remember is one thing. Facing the past head on is entirely different. I'm not sure if I can handle it yet.

Leighton's eyes are still lasered on me, awaiting an answer.

"Look, I appreciate you… but I don't want to talk. Can we pretend everything is normal? Just for one night?"

His face softens into a grin. "Heck yeah, we can."

"Great."

"But I'm warning you, this movie might make your brain hurt a bit. Be prepared to have your mind blown."

Loading the movie, he slides lower on the sofa and positions his head in my lap instead. I automatically tangle my fingers in his hair, sifting the citrus-scented strands as he munches on handfuls of popcorn.

"What delight am I suffering through tonight?"

Leighton chuckles from my lap. "This is *The Matrix*. Ultimate nineties sci-fi classic. Awesome."

"I had to watch a video to explain the last sci-fi movie we watched together."

"*Interstellar*? How could you possibly be confused by that movie? Wormholes, time travel. Very straightforward stuff."

"I know for a fact you were searching for explainer articles afterwards, and it's not even the first time you've watched it."

"I am a big believer in learning something new every time you watch a movie. Besides, you loved it. We both know you cried your eyes out at the end."

I steal some popcorn from his hand. "As did you."

"I'm fully in touch with my emotions."

"And your tear ducts, apparently."

"Don't tell anyone, please?" He makes big, pleading puppy eyes up at me. "I have a reputation as a hardened criminal to maintain, after all."

"Your secret's safe with me."

Relaxing into the velvet cushions, I let the movie take me to a bleak, faraway land, where our problems pale into insignificance. Leighton has well and truly instilled his love of movies in me.

There's nothing quite like the transformative power of stories to put everything you're worried about into context. My life seems almost normal in comparison, and that's the best feeling. More than anything, I crave normality.

"Hang on, I'm confused."

Leighton peers up at me. "What's up, princess?"

"He was living in an alternate reality for this entire time?"

"Erm. Pretty much."

"Well, who the hell would choose to go to the real world? I'd definitely take the blue pill and go back to the fantasy."

His lips twist in a rueful smile. "Not everyone is a pessimist like you. What if the truth sets you free? Isn't it worth the risk? I'd take the red pill."

"I'm not a pessimist," I grumble back. "Sometimes the truth isn't the blessing people think it is."

"What if I had a pill that would give you all of your missing memories back? Would you take it?"

My hand freezes, buried in his hair.

"I… don't know."

Leighton's fingers wrap around my ankle. "I get it. If I could take a pill to forget my time in prison, I don't know if I'd do it."

"Why?" I ask curiously.

"Well, that shit makes or breaks you. I spent three years inside, and I want it to count for something."

His thumb traces the sliver of bare skin exposed by my yoga pants riding up. I shiver at his light, teasing touch.

"Sorry, Goldilocks," he apologises. "I promised you a normal night. Ignore me thinking about this deep shit."

"Deep shit." I laugh as his hand sneaks higher. "You really do have a way with words sometimes, Leigh."

"Just call me a motherfucking poet."

The hand dancing its way up my leg has landed on my thigh. It's a good distraction. Tingles are zipping over my skin with each touch. I have to fight the urge to squeeze my legs together.

Ditching the bowl of popcorn on the floor, Leighton rolls over until he's facing away from the TV and is able to stare straight at me. The movie is abandoned.

Sliding a hand underneath my loose t-shirt, his fingertips stroke a path over my stomach, reaching the underside of my breasts. His eyes widen when he discovers my lack of a bra.

I flush pink. "Leigh."

"Problem?" he teases. "Since when did you stop wearing bras? I'm not complaining, by the way."

"We're having a movie night. I took it off."

His eyes glint with mischief. "Naughty, naughty."

Dragging his thumb over the peak of my nipple, I can't hold back a low moan of pleasure. Leighton gently pinches the bud before palming my breast in his hand.

"I've made a point of keeping my hands off you, but keep making noises like that, and I can't promise I'll behave."

"You… have?"

"Obviously," he quips back. "Things were pretty fucked up after Northumberland. I figured you needed time."

"Time for what?"

"To figure out what you want."

Gently squeezing my breast, he moves to the next nipple, tweaking it until it hardens into a point. I'm turned on and panicking at the same time. I have no idea what I want.

"Well?" he prompts.

"Did you speak to the other two?"

Leighton smiles lazily. "What if I have?"

His thumb doesn't stop teasing me. Warmth is gathering between my thighs as he continues to play with my nipple.

"Did they tell you to speak to me?"

"Nope," he answers easily.

"But what do you think of our... erm, situation?"

"Is that what we're calling it now?"

"Stop playing around."

"Oh! You mean that you've fooled around with my brother and his best friend, kissed the hell out of me and wrapped Theo around your finger without even touching him?"

I agree with a strangled squeak.

Leighton's smile turns dark. "Well, Goldilocks, my opinion of our *situation* is that it's a mess. You're fucking trouble."

"Trouble?" I breathe.

"The best kind."

Tugging my face closer, he plants a kiss against my mouth. "But I don't mind playing dirty to get what I want. Those assholes better bring their A game if they think they're gonna win this fight."

Dancing lower, his fingers reappear and brush over the seam of my yoga pants, right over my pussy. I'm on the verge of begging him to touch me down there.

"Why does it have to be a fight?"

Leighton hesitates. "Because I've been second best for my entire life. Hunter has taken every accomplishment away from me. He doesn't get you too."

He suddenly sits up and pushes me backwards. I flop across the sectional in a breathless tangle. Leighton swaps positions, pouncing on me in one smooth move.

"Gotcha," he declares.

I'm trapped beneath his grinding hips. He holds my hands over my head, leaving me powerless and at the mercy of his body pinning me to the sofa.

"Is that what you want, baby?" he croons. "You want us to fight over who gets to fuck your sweet cunt first?"

I squirm under him. "I d-don't want anyone to fight."

"You've chosen already?"

"No!"

Lips peppering open-mouthed kisses at the base of my throat, his tongue flicks across my pulse point next.

"Choose me then," he commands.

My hips rise automatically, seeking more friction. Every inch of his stocky, muscled frame is pressing into me.

"I'll walk into HQ and break my brother's legs, if that's what it takes."

"Leigh!" I gasp.

"What? I'm being serious."

The tantalising hardness between his legs pushes into me, right where I want it. My body's instincts have taken over. I'm desperate to feel him everywhere. I need his touch.

He feels huge and powerful on top of me. With the lack of air between us, and so much electricity humming beneath my sensitised skin, I feel alive for the first time since we found that damned chapel and my entire life changed.

"I don't know if you're ready to play this game with me."

"What game?" I stutter.

Tugging the t-shirt over my head, Leighton drops it on the floor next to the bowl of popcorn. His smouldering eyes sweep over every inch of twisted, scarred skin on display.

"I want to fuck that pretty mouth of yours, princess, and watch you choke on my cock. That kind of game."

Lips feathering over the swell of my breasts, he takes a nipple back into his mouth. The light graze of his teeth sends sparks through my whole body as he gently bites down.

"Oh God, Leigh."

"I love it when you say my name," he praises, his tongue flicking across my bud. "I don't want to hold back anymore."

All my inhibitions disappear.

"Then don't."

His forehead collides with my chest. "I also don't want you to get hurt. You know I'd never actually make you choose."

Burying my hands back in his hair, I yank his head up. "Maybe I want to get hurt. Maybe I want to feel something."

Darkness crosses his sweet, rounded features as he slips a hand into my hair. Alarm bells sound when his fingertips coast over the ache of my expanding bald patch.

"Isn't this enough pain for you?"

His question leaves me breathless.

"I don't know what you mean," I divert.

"Don't lie to my face. We all know what's going on here. It's gotten worse since Northumberland."

"I'm f-fine."

"Are you? Really? No bullshit."

Every fibre of my being is screaming at me to run far away from him. I'm so confused. My core is throbbing with need while my mind is desperate to hide the truth from him.

That I can't sleep.

Can't eat.

The pulling is worse than ever.

Guilt is eating me alive every single day, and I don't know how to claw myself out of this hole. Not even Richards can help. This is a living hell of my own making.

"I'm not here to lecture you about how you're choosing to cope, even if I don't like it. We all have secrets, Goldilocks. I have no right to judge yours."

A flicker of hope sears my chest.

"What secrets do you have?"

"Wouldn't you like to know," he replies with a smirk. "Everyone has something to hide. Some more than others."

"What if we agreed to a trade?"

"Trading what?"

I tease his lips with mine. "Secrets."

He deepens the kiss, causing my core to tense. His lips are hard against mine, demanding every breath. Each rock of his hips increases the haze of lust contaminating my mind.

Despite my fear, I want to feel him inside me. I want to be needed. Loved. Devoured. Even if we're all doomed to heartbreak and this mess will never amount to anything good. Right now, I couldn't care less.

"Tell me about your secret," Leighton murmurs. "Why are you hurting yourself?"

"It started by accident," I admit between stolen kisses. "The pain is all I can control right now. It feels good."

"Better than this?" he asks, his cock rubbing against the heat burning between my thighs.

Mouth descending over the slope of my belly, Leighton seizes the waistband of my yoga pants. He pulls them down, exposing the pink lace of my panties and more gnarly scarring across my hips.

"Answer the fucking question."

"No," I moan loudly.

Removing each leg, he chucks them over his shoulder. Warm air kisses my skin, setting off fireworks of excitement. I'm left in nothing but lace and gooseflesh.

"Keep talking," he orders sternly.

When his thumbs hook underneath my panties and ease them off to expose the patch of dark hair over my pussy, I see stars. Months of anticipation are sending me into overdrive.

"Harlow. Words."

"God," I curse as his unshaved stubble teases my inner thighs. "I have to punish myself. It's all I've ever known."

"That's what this is? Punishment?"

My spine arches. "Yes."

Leighton clasps my damp panties in his hand, an eyebrow raised. "You're wet, baby. Maybe you chose me after all."

My cheeks flame hotter than I thought possible. The lacy scrap of cotton lands on top of my discarded yoga pants, leaving me completely naked. There's nowhere to hide.

I'm burning under the weight of his green eyes, searching every exposed, vulnerable inch of me. When he glides the tip of his finger over my mound, I shift my hips up to meet him.

"Please," I whimper.

"Please what? I'm not a mind reader."

My teeth pierce my bottom lip. "Please... touch me."

"Where do you want me to touch you?"

His fingertip vanishes, and a wicked grin slashes across his face. He's loving every second of this torment. My secrets aren't enough for him. Leighton wants my complete and utter submission.

"Here?" He pinches my nipple. "Or here?" His other hand cups my aching pussy, his thumb swirling over my clit.

A groan tears from my lips as he pushes his finger between my folds, coating it in slick moisture. Everywhere he touches erupts into unholy flames.

"Beg me, Harlow."

The circling finger pushes against my slit, breaching the tight opening without entering me fully. I try to move and force him inside me, but I still can't.

"Beg me to touch your pussy and I'll give you exactly what your body is screaming out for. I want to hear it first."

My patience fizzles out.

"Jesus, Leigh."

"Not quite. I said beg."

"Please... stop torturing me."

"Why should I?" He crooks an eyebrow. "How do you think it felt to hear that my brother had his hands on you first? You've been torturing me for months."

"I didn't mean to."

His thumb swipes over my clit again, sending bolts of pleasure up my spine. I bite back a moan that would give him too much satisfaction, but he doesn't let me off that easily.

His finger suddenly thrusts inside me, stretching my pussy. He works the wet digit in and out until he steals the moan from my lips.

"Such a good girl," he whispers. "You're going to beg me to let you come."

I cry out when he pushes another finger deep inside me. The sense of fullness is overwhelming. Hunter and Enzo have touched me like this, but Leighton's filthy mouth and need for control add a whole other layer of excitement.

On the verge of exploding into spectacular pieces, Leighton quickly pulls his hand from between my thighs. The building release that was on the cusp of taking over fizzles out.

"I told you to beg," he growls.

Hanging over me, his shaggy hair falling across his forest-green eyes, he looks like Lucifer himself in human flesh. Leighton could be a fallen angel, swooping down to earth to claim the unsuspecting souls of sinners.

I'd like to be sacrificed.

I'll beg at his altar.

Anything to be adored by him.

"Please let me come, Leigh," I plead through the choking hand of embarrassment.

"My name sounds so good on your tongue." His eyes darken. "I'm going to fuck your pretty mouth next."

Sliding back inside me, he thrusts his fingers in a fast-paced rhythm, guiding me back to the edge of an orgasm. I fist his t-shirt as my release finally crests.

"Let go. Show me how well you fall apart."

It hits me hard and fast. One more swipe of my clit, and he's stolen the keys that unlock something buried deep inside. Hips bucking, I let the wave of sensation wash over me.

"Perfect," Leighton praises.

Floating in the aftermath, the clink of his unfastened belt startles me back into the room. Peeking through my lashes, I watch as he reaches into his jeans and pulls out his thick shaft.

It's the first time I've seen a man like this. I haven't even touched Hunter or Enzo. He will be the first. But I want to explore. I'm no longer afraid, not now that they've taken the time to build my trust.

Leighton grips his length, pulling it from his boxers. "It's your turn now, baby. I'm all yours."

I lick my lips. "Tell me what to do."

Settling back on the sofa while the movie still plays in the background, Leighton pushes his jeans down his hips. I study his erection—long, veined and glinting with something round and silver through the velvety tip.

"Ever seen a pierced cock before?"

I can barely form words.

"Um, I didn't know you could do that."

Leighton laughs under his breath. "It was a drunken impulse when I got out of prison."

"Did it hurt?"

"It didn't tickle, princess. Come here."

I take a deep breath for courage and crawl closer on my hands and knees. I'm still naked, but we're alone in the house and he's already seen me. I don't need to hide anything.

Opening his legs, Leighton gives me space to settle between them. My fingers tremble as I reach out to touch his shaft. It feels strange in my hands, like a warm length of steel. Pumping his length, I love the way his eyes flutter shut.

His head hits the overstuffed cushion behind him as air hisses out from between his teeth. Gently squeezing again, I stroke my hand up and down, getting the hang of it.

"What should I do next?"

"Suck my cock. I'm going to ride your perfect mouth."

His demands make me wet all over again. I feel excited just touching him like this, wielding power I never imagined being able to possess. He's at my mercy for once.

"Then tell me your secrets," I order him. "We agreed, fair and square. You need to keep your end of the bargain."

"What do you want to know?"

"Tell me how you ended up in prison."

With a breath for courage, I duck down and take his cock into my mouth. He groans under his breath, fisting a hand in my long mane of hair to hold it out of my face.

"I hurt somebody," he grinds out. "It was one stupid, angry mistake that ruined my whole life. I'll regret it forever."

His shaft slides against my tongue, nudging the back of my throat. It takes some getting used to. The coldness of his metal piercing feels weird at first, but as I circle my tongue around it, Leighton groans in delight.

"Fucking hell," he curses. "I was dating someone for several years. It was going well. We were serious. I even thought about… you know, proposing."

Encouraging him to keep going, I tighten my lips, bobbing up and down while wrapping my hand around the base of his length.

"Something didn't sit right, though I couldn't figure out what. Then, I came home one night and found them together. My best friend was fucking my girl."

Feeling braver as Leighton bares his soul, I slide a hand down his ropey, muscled thigh, reaching around to cup the softness of his balls. He makes a guttural sound when I give them a gentle, curious squeeze.

"Jesus, princess. You're killing me here."

I stop for a breath. "Finish the story."

His grip on my hair tightens as his hand balls into a fist. "I lost it. Got into a fight with the bastard. I'd been drinking, which didn't help, and things got out of control."

Wrapping my lips back around his cock, I move a little faster, teasing the truth from him. Part of me doesn't want to believe that my sweet, lighthearted Leighton could hurt someone. I need to know what he's hiding from me.

"I was punching him, over and over," he says around a moan. "I couldn't think straight. We'd been friends since we were five years old, and he betrayed me."

His hips thrust upwards to feed his dick into my mouth. The tip nudges my throat. It takes a moment for me to adjust, then I suck deeper, loving the intensity of it.

"I smashed him into the wall at the wrong angle," Leighton grunts out. "He broke three vertebrae. Wheelchair-bound for the rest of his damn life, and it's my fault."

There it is. The twisted secret that I've seen festering inside of him. Leighton's original wound. It makes sense now; the broken state he was in after what happened with Diablo. His actions got someone else hurt.

We're not so different.

He knows what guilt tastes like.

"Keep going and I'm going to come in your mouth."

I pause for another breath. "You can do that?"

"Sometimes, I can't take how fucking innocent you are. Keep going if you want to see."

Nodding, I retake his sheath in my mouth and tilt my head to suck him deeper. My eyes burn with the pressure of each upwards thrust from his hips. I kinda like it though.

This is exhilarating, exploring something I've always associated with darkness and sin. Each jerk of his cock in my mouth feels like its own liberation. I'm flying free from my shackles and retaking my sexuality on my own terms. It's a sick thought to have, but a twisted part of me wishes Pastor Michaels could see what's become of his prisoner.

"So perfect," Leighton purrs as he strokes my hair. "Not so innocent now, are you?"

His muscles are tensing beneath my touch. The movement of his hips increases in time to my sucking, causing stray moisture to slip from the corners of my eyes. His pierced hardness is on the verge of making me gag, but I hold it in.

I love how rough he's being with me. I'm just a normal girl, experiencing a first. It's everything I've been looking for since I escaped. I've craved the tantalising glimmer of another life.

"I'm coming. Move if you want."

Gripping the base of his dick, I stay put. I'm too curious for my own good. He bellows loudly, his length spasming against my tongue. I gasp as hot fluid shoots into my mouth.

Leighton pours himself into me, his come bursting with an odd, salty flavour that I can't describe. I hold my position until his hips still, and his seed slides down my throat.

Releasing him to wipe off my mouth, I look up into his eyes and swallow every drop. He watches the show with wild eyes.

"Fuck me, Harlow. That was…"

"Bad?" I worry aloud.

His knuckles stroke against my cheek. "I was going to say hot. You didn't have to swallow, baby."

I shrug with a satisfied smile. "I was curious."

"I can see that. You're full of surprises."

Sitting back on folded legs, I watch him tuck his cock into his boxers and pull his jeans into place. I suddenly feel bare, my body still quaking with aftershocks and nerves.

"Can you pass my t-shirt?"

Leighton grabs it from off the floor. "Here."

"Thanks."

Quickly pulling it on to cover my chest, I fumble around for my panties. A cold voice lashes us both before I can slide them back on to cover my naked bottom half.

"Did I miss the party?"

We both freeze. I can't bear to look over my shoulder. I know who it is. Hunter's presence would startle even a blind man. He's the electric buzz in the air as a thunderstorm sweeps in.

Leighton doesn't bat an eye. "Sorry, bro. Wasn't expecting you until later on."

"No doubt," Hunter thunders. "For the record, this isn't the worst thing I've walked in on you doing. I didn't expect to find you fooling around with my girl, though."

The entire humiliating debacle falls away as my world narrows to those two unfathomable words.

My.

Girl.

I wish it didn't give me an ill-timed thrill to hear the violent note of possession in Hunter's voice, even while I'm semi-naked and straddling his younger sibling. Not to mention the come still staining my throat.

"*Our* girl didn't last long then," Leighton accuses.

"You lost the right to call her that when your stupidity almost cost Harlow her life."

"You never had any intention of letting the rest of us have a chance with her," he argues back. "You're a selfish dick."

"Do you want to join Diablo's dismembered corpse at the bottom of the river? Because that can totally be arranged."

Praying for the ground to swallow me up, I clamber off Leighton while doing my best to pull the t-shirt down to cover my bare behind.

By accident, I briefly meet Hunter's eyes. The hurt I find there leaves me gutted.

Anger is twisting his features into a familiar mask that I thought I'd seen the last of. But beneath that, there's something else—the green-eyed monster rearing its ugly head. He's actually jealous.

I shove my legs through my panties as fast as possible, snatching up my yoga pants in another breath. When I attempt to dart past Hunter to escape the embarrassment, he clamps down on my arm.

"Been busy, sweetheart?" he asks throatily.

"Um, no. Just hanging out."

"I warned you before about lying to me. If you want a war, I'll happily give you one. Don't think I won't burn this house down to walk away with you."

A terrified chill settles over me.

"You don't mean that."

Hunter licks his parted lips. "Don't I?"

Yanking my arm from his bruising grasp, I take a big step backwards. His jaw sets into a hard line as he folds his arms, biceps straining against his white dress shirt. Dark, intricate tattoos bleed through the material, begging to be licked and explored.

I'm losing my mind. They're pushing me over the edge and waiting to see which way I'll fall. I need to get out of here.

Still clutching my remaining clothing, I flee upstairs as fast as my legs will carry me. I can hear their voices bickering with each ashamed step I take.

Bedroom door slammed shut behind me, I collapse on the bed in a boneless, flustered slump. I'm picking up my phone and tapping out a desperate text message in a heartbeat.

Harlow: Hey, Brooke. You around? I could use a place to stay for a few days.

Her response comes fast.

Brooklyn: I've got you. These twats are driving me insane too. Pick you up in ten minutes.

My head hits the soft pillow.

Now, I have to convince Hunter to let me leave.

CHAPTER 6

Harlow

No More Hiding - Gina Brooklyn

"Harlow."

Someone is roughly shaking me awake, their fingertips digging into my arms. I grunt and pull the blanket closer to my chest. I'm comfortable. It isn't time to wake up yet.

"Wake up. He's coming."

"No," I complain sleepily. "Leave... alone."

"You need to get up."

Suddenly, the scents of blood and mould seep into my lungs. My comfort vanishes. I'm freezing cold. Wet. Aching. The basement steals every ounce of warmth from my body as my eyes fling open in a rush of fear.

"You have to kneel. Come on."

Kiera's whispered voice filters through my half-awake brain. I startle upright in the dark, and a smooth object in my hand hits the floor. Light cuts the suffocating darkness of the room as my phone screen illuminates.

I take an unsteady breath.

This isn't the basement.

There's nobody else here.

I'm surrounded by two huge brown-leather sofas framing a massive television. Clutter is scattered around the room, and the walls are filled with framed photographs of someone else's family.

Brooklyn's house.

I'm still here.

Shining my phone around the room, I search for the person who startled me awake. Kiera's gone. Slinked back to her grave, festering at the back of my mind. I'm alone here.

The quilt and pillow that Brooklyn gave me to sleep on the sofa with are damp with sweat. Scrubbing my hands over my face, I make myself take a deep breath.

This is getting ridiculous now. My sleep schedule is so messed up. I need to learn how to sleep alone, without one of the guys there to hold my hand like I'm a child.

The guys.

I miss them so much.

Pain spears me in the chest. I've been staying here for a few days, spending time with Brooklyn and her family while hiding from my problems. The break came at the perfect time as I was on the verge of going insane back there.

The sound of glass shattering from somewhere else in the two-story townhouse causes shards of fear to slice into me. I'm not convinced it isn't in my head like everything else.

"Breathe," I tell myself. "You're in control."

He's a monster, Harlow.

I always knew there was evil in him.

Her voice returns, whispering through my consciousness. I still have one hand in the dream-world. Kiera's playground. She comes to me in fragments—choppy memories, broken flashes, the slow patter of drip-fed information.

You're going to be okay now.

I have a plan to get us out.

One of many failed plans. Kiera was the first to offer me that hopeless promise as a lifeline. However she knew Pastor Michaels, it didn't stop him from terrifying her. In that basement, she unmasked the evil that she'd suspected.

And he killed her for it.

Blow after skull-crushing blow.

Grabbing the woolly pink sweater that I left balled up on the carpet, I throw it over Leighton's t-shirt and my grey sweats. The house is silent around me as I stand up and quietly creep from the room.

Brooklyn shares this generous-sized home with five loud, boisterous men, but it doesn't feel cramped. The house rivals Hunter's in size. It has a smaller garden and kitchen, but an extra bedroom upstairs to accommodate everyone.

Unlike the clean lines, steel accents and polished floorboards of Hunter's modernised, Victorian-style mansion, this is comfortably informal.

The walls are clustered with hilarious photographs from Brooklyn and her family's European adventures, and the personality of each inhabitant is reflected in the little touches dotted throughout every room.

Hudson has a very impressive whiskey collection. Kade leaves discarded silk ties everywhere. Brooklyn has a stack of vinyl records, gifted from an old friend. Those brightly coloured discs I'm particularly jealous of.

Eli has a tiny library tucked under the spiral staircase, brimming with enough books to rival Theo's collection. On another shelf, Phoenix's vast array of video games are safely stored. Even their stuff is close together, like them.

Finally, Jude has a quiet office, tucked away from them all at the back of the house. He disappears in there a lot when his eyes cloud over and his face darkens. Sometimes for hours at a time. The others don't seem to mind though.

Following the sound of cursing and glass being swept up, I find the door to Jude's office cracked open. He's kneeling on the patterned rug, cleaning up the remains of a photo frame.

I hesitate, deciding to turn back and give him some privacy, but his caramel eyes land on me through the open door. He has scarily sharp hearing.

"I… heard a noise," I say lamely.

He pushes the door open further. "You're allowed to walk around, Harlow. I heard you wake up anyway."

"Your hearing is kinda scary."

Jude picks glass from his rug. "So I've heard."

"Are you okay?"

He freezes, his intelligent eyes downturned to avoid mine. With a closely cropped headful of brown hair, a thin but even nose and strong, prominent features, Jude is handsome in a wholesome way that contrasts the person I know lies within.

When you take a closer look, that illusion dissipates. His whole body, while toned from an obsessive exercise regimen, is littered with scars. We have that in common. Some are nastier than others, mottling his skin into a macabre sight.

As he picks up the last shards of broken glass, the stump where his right hand belongs is propping him up. It doesn't seem to hurt him.

The skin is smooth and taut, healed with the passing of time.

"Jude?" I ask again.

His gaze snaps up to me. "Sorry, zoned out. I'm okay, just couldn't sleep. You know how it is."

I slip inside his office, hugging myself tight. "Yeah, I know. Do you want to talk about it?"

"You don't need to be there for me, as much as I appreciate the offer. You've got enough on your plate."

"You were there for me before."

Jude waves it off. "You needed a friend."

In the weeks after our close encounter with Pastor Michaels' brutality, I struggled to anchor myself to the present. Richards says that my episodes of dissociation are a defence mechanism. The frantic paddle of a mind drowning, overwhelmed by a frightening world.

Jude came around to introduce himself soon after. He seemed to know about the war inside my head without me having to explain. His reassurance that the world would come back when it was ready was enough to calm me.

Sure enough, the numb prison I was stuck in for countless blurred days slowly released its grip on my sanity. I came back to myself, bit by bit. It just took some time to remember that I was safe and free. Unlike the remains of Laura's corpse.

"I'd like to be a friend for you too," I offer him. "Or just tell me to go away, if you'd rather talk to someone else."

"I don't like worrying them."

"Brooklyn and the others?"

He nods. "They've spent the best part of a decade worrying about me. Especially Brooke."

"It bothers me that the guys have to worry so much about me too. They tell me off for not talking to them."

"But it's easier not to," he supplies.

"Exactly. Simpler for everyone."

Jude scrubs a hand over his drawn face. "Don't make my mistake. Keeping everything inside isn't healthy."

"You should take your own advice, doc."

Chuckling, he dumps the smashed glass into the small bin under his desk. "I guess I deserve that."

"Richards would be disappointed. He still talks about you as his star patient."

"Great. I love everyone knowing my business."

"He didn't tell me anything else," I rush to explain. "It's just that we've been through similar stuff, I think."

His caramel eyes fix on me, studying the goosebumps across my arms. "You're shaking. What happened?"

"Nothing."

Sighing, Jude climbs to his feet. "Do you like ice cream?"

"Uh, what?"

His mouth hooks up. "I know where Eli keeps his secret stash. He thinks we don't know about it."

Leading the way, Jude pads towards the kitchen with bare feet. I quickly glance around and spot the photo torn from the broken frame he tossed in the bin.

My heart stops.

I know that person.

A pretty, smiling face stares back at me from his desk. It's Alyssa. She's standing next to a younger-looking Jude in a graduation cap and gown. The contrast to the version of him I know is stark. I had no idea he knew her.

"Harlow," he beckons.

"I'm coming."

Closing the door behind me, I follow Jude into the kitchen. He keeps the overhead lights off, and I don't mind. Like me, he's accustomed to darkness. Jude steps into it like he's arriving home, svelte and at ease in the familiarity of shadows.

I take a seat at the huge glass table. This is where they gather each night. Unlike Hunter and the others, Brooklyn's family prides being together above all else.

They love each other with such ferocity, even as they throw food or threaten death for stealing the last slice of garlic bread. I've loved being here for that reason.

Taking a seat, I accept the spoon Jude hands me, a tub of ice cream tucked under his arm. We sit next to each other, and he lets me take the first bite before I pass the tub back. Salted caramel gooeyness melts on my tongue.

"This is good ice cream."

"That's why Eli hides it," he answers as he licks the spoon. "Since he was promoted to head lecturer at King's College, he has to mark all these papers. Hence the need for ice cream."

"Doesn't he enjoy teaching?"

"I'd imagine teaching a roomful of know-it-alls can't be much fun. Eli loves to learn, but dealing with people on a daily basis? Not so much."

"He's a quiet person," I observe.

"But a hell of a lot chattier than he used to be. Trust me."

Passing the ice cream back to me, I take another spoonful. Like Eli, Jude is a confusingly complex person to be around. While he's calm and soothing in a way that only someone who has experienced trauma can be, there's darkness festering in him.

If you look closely, you can see it. Hidden in the tiniest glimpses. His sharp hearing. Fast reflexes. Flashes of bad temper. It's the same darkness that sparkles in Brooklyn's silver-grey eyes.

When I look in the mirror, I see it staring back at me in my reflection too. We're all walking around with madness in our veins—a sickness that, unlike most, is entirely incurable.

Instead, we have to live with the pain that was inflicted by a force beyond our control. Being broken by someone else is fixable with enough time and care. The self-destruction that follows when you miss the familiarity of that pain is far harder to treat.

"What was it this time?" Jude asks quietly.

I swallow my mouthful. "I'm fine."

"You really don't need to bullshit me like you do everyone else. I've been in the game long enough. Nothing you say will go any further. Not even to Hunter or his team."

Placing the ice cream down, I let myself droop. "It's her again. She finds me every single night."

"Kiera?" he guesses.

"Yeah. I'm taking those pills that Richards prescribed me. It hasn't helped. I still wake up screaming."

"Medication doesn't get rid of the shit in our heads." He places his spoon down, now licked clean. "It isn't that easy."

"Clearly not."

"What does Kiera say to you?"

"Mostly, she's warning me. There are bits of memories coming back. We're in the basement, and she's trying to protect me from him."

"Do you remember anything else about her?" he quizzes.

"Not really. Only flashes. I've gone over the memories a thousand times with Richards, but we've hit a brick wall."

"Perhaps you could try a different way."

I send him a puzzled look. "Like what?"

Smoothing the t-shirt he's wearing over loose-fitting sweats, Jude stands back up. "I'll show you what worked for me."

I follow him back to his office, our midnight snack returned to Eli's hiding place in the freezer. Jude flicks the lamp on, lighting the sparse, obsessively organised space.

It almost resembles a prison cell, but with a luxurious rug and a set of blue armchairs. Part of me thinks that's deliberate. Material possessions mean nothing to Jude. Like me, he's lived with nothing for long enough to lose that desire.

Clicking the door shut, he gestures for me to take a seat in an armchair. I sink into the comfortable cushion.

"When I first went into treatment with Richards, I could only remember snippets of who I was before what happened to me. Flashes, here and there."

I know a little of the group's colourful past. Enough to understand why their bond is so unique and indestructible.

"Can I ask you a personal question?"

"Sure," he obliges.

"How long were you held prisoner for?"

Jude leans against the desk. "Seven years, give or take. But it wasn't me who was held captive and tortured. My mind locked the real me away. That's how I survived."

Unlocking a drawer in his dark-wood desk, he begins to pull out a stack of slim, leather-bound journals. Stacking them up one by one, there's seven in total. Jude gestures to them.

"One for each year that I was held. Afterwards, I spent three years at an inpatient facility, piecing myself back together with Richards' help."

"And it worked?"

"Mostly," he answers with a thin smile. "I spent years working through the fragments. Writing everything down helped me to document my life. It's how I regained control."

Reaching back into the desk drawer, he pulls out another journal. This one isn't bent and worn, bound in supple, dark-red leather. I hesitate as he offers it to me.

"For you."

Tentatively accepting the gift, I turn it over in my hands. Jude packs his journals away and locks the drawer again.

"Kiera can't give you the answers you're looking for," he says while cleaning up. "She isn't real."

Stupid tears rise to my eyes. "I know."

"Only you can find your own truth. It's up here." He taps his temple. "Waiting for you to find your way back."

Thumbing through the blank journal, I wrestle with my fear. For months, I've wanted nothing more than to uncover my past and use it to forge a new future.

But Leighton was right when he called me a pessimist. I'm afraid of what I'll find when I start digging, looking for answers. Or more accurately, *who* I'll find.

"Thank you." I hold the journal to my chest. "It helps just knowing that someone else has been through this too."

"Of course. Any friend of Brooklyn's is a friend of mine." His eyes flick back to the broken frame in his bin. "We have to look out for each other."

I bite my lip. "How did you know her?"

"Hmm?" he replies absently.

"Alyssa."

Her name startles Jude, and his head slumps, falling into his single hand. "She was my sister."

"Wait, really?"

"We were separated for years and… well, I forgot about her. By the time we reunited, it was too late. The damage was done. She died before I could fix things."

"I had no idea."

"Nobody talks about her much."

Fiddling with my sweater sleeve, I battle a wave of curiosity. Jude could give me every last detail about the mysterious woman who came before me. I've been desperate to know more since the beginning, but too afraid to ask.

"They were dating her? Hunter, Enzo and Theo?"

His eyes flick over me. "Yeah, the four of them were in a relationship for a long time."

"Like you guys are with Brooklyn? How does it work?"

Jude smothers a smile. "I'm probably not the best person to ask about how this stuff works. I was a latecomer."

Feeling embarrassed, I glance out of the small window to study the dark night. Jude clears his throat.

"If it helps, I found it hard."

"The sharing?"

He shrugs it off. "We made it work eventually."

"Did you ask her to choose?"

"None of us were willing to lose her."

It seems so perfect—a family of choice with no one left out. I know that's what Enzo wants for us, even if Hunter is adamant that it will never happen. I don't know where that leaves me.

I'm not good enough for all of them. They deserve more than me, especially after losing Alyssa. I want them to be happy, and I'll never be able to give them that.

Footsteps pad down the staircase above us, interrupting our conversation. We fall silent until the office door creaks open. A mop of messy raven hair, numerous black facial piercings and arctic-blue eyes peek around the door.

"Thought I heard voices," Hudson greets.

I wave from the armchair. "Sorry. Only us."

"It's two o'clock in the morning."

"Come and join the sleepless club," Jude jokes.

Yawning loudly, Hudson slinks into the room. I watch, slightly fascinated, as he swoops down and smacks his lips against Jude's mouth while gripping the back of his neck.

Quickly looking away, I give them a private moment as they share a kiss. I'm not attracted to them or anything. I just find their dynamic fascinating as a whole group.

Hudson straightens. "Sorry, Harlow."

"No w-worries," I stammer.

He tangles Jude's hand in his. "Come back to bed. It's Eli and Phoenix's night with Brooklyn, so my room is empty."

"I came down because I couldn't sleep," Jude explains hastily. "You go back up. We're fine here."

Hudson glances between us. "Since we're all awake... let's have some fun. I'm off work tomorrow, so no early start."

I'm not entirely sure how we end up spreadeagled across the thick carpet of the den, a pack of cards and a bowl of leftover Christmas sweets laid out between us.

"You got the rules?" Hudson asks me.

Filtering through my hand of cards, I begin to arrange the numbers. "I think so. Can I watch you guys play first?"

"No problem."

Jude lowers his voice. "Watch him, Harlow. He likes to cheat and will lie his ass off to pretend otherwise."

"Hey, dick." Hudson throws a handful of wrapped toffee pennies at his head. "It's not my fault that you lost the last game we played and had to pay the bar tab."

"This is exactly why we need Brooklyn to come as a chaperone on our date nights."

"We do not need a chaperone."

"I disagree. You're too competitive for your own good."

"Am not," Hudson disputes.

Picking up their sets of cards, they play the first round of Rummy. It's hard to wrap my head around the rules at first, but it soon starts to make sense. The winner has to match two groups of four and three cards, either consecutive or across the different suits.

"Too slow," Jude boasts as he lays his cards down. "Give it up."

"Goddammit. How do you do that?"

"By not being a moron."

Hudson tosses his cards. "Motherfucker."

"Alright, Harlow. You're up. Stakes?"

Taking a chocolate finger and a toffee penny, I place them down in the middle. "Here's mine."

Jude reciprocates and awkwardly shuffles the cards with his good hand before dealing them back out. Still grumbling about losing, Hudson accepts them and adds his own sweets to the pile in the middle.

"I'm going to win this time," he announces.

Jude snorts. "Good luck with that."

"Shut up and play."

We take it in turns to pick up a card and swap it out for another, looking for the magical combination. Hudson curses with each new card that he selects. His hand isn't going well.

I can see the combinations surprisingly easily. The numbers click into place in my head as I rearrange the cards I have into a pattern. My trick is to imagine the numbers as I used to when measuring time in the confines of my cage.

One bowl of food.

Two lashes of the whip.

Three punches.

Four broken ribs.

"Got it," I declare, laying down my cards.

Both men blink at me.

"One, Two, Three and Four of Hearts."

Hudson's mouth clicks open. "Huh?"

"Are you just going to stare at me?" I raise an eyebrow.

Jude recovers the quickest. "That was like, thirty seconds into the round. I can't believe it."

"Beginner's luck." Hudson narrows his eyes.

After collecting my sugary winnings, I watch him shuffle the cards and deal them out again. My hand isn't so good this time. We begin taking it in turns to pick up and drop a card, going several rotations with no breakthrough.

"You need an Ace of Spades."

All three of us startle at the new voice. Standing behind the sofa, an ice cream tub in hand, Eli studies Hudson's cards over his shoulder. His brown curls are wild and pointing in all directions, framing vivid green eyes and a contrite smile.

"Thanks for ruining my strategy," Hudson snarls as he tosses the cards down. "You did that on purpose."

Eli snickers. "Maybe. It was fun though."

A heaping of ice cream disappears into his mouth as he collapses onto the nearest sofa. He grins at me before offering the tub.

"Midnight snack?"

I decline with a head shake. "We already stole some."

Eli glowers at Jude. "Do I seriously have to find a new hiding spot? You ate all of my Ben and Jerry's last week."

"It was an emergency," he defends. "What are you doing up anyway?"

He shrugs while eating. "Phoenix is snoring his head off and Brooklyn stole all of the covers again."

"We bought that pillow for him," Hudson complains. "The whole goddamn house vibrates with his snoring."

"It's in his room, not hers."

"That's helpful."

"Not really." Eli snorts. "But that's Phoenix for you. I decided to leave them to it and come downstairs instead."

Going for a fresh round, we quickly reach a stalemate. I abandon my strategy and switch up the suits, aiming for another matching pair. Eli is watching us as he munches.

The next card I pick up is a Seven of Clubs. Perfect. I can see my plan forming. Five beatings, six shattered noses and seven hours of screaming. All I need is an eight.

"Stupid game," Hudson says under his breath.

"You really don't like losing, do you?" I laugh.

"I lived with Kade after I was adopted by his folks. Imagine competing with that asshole."

"I'll pass on that fun," Jude comments.

"Not like there was much competition," Hudson continues with a scoff. "Even now, he's still pissed I found this house first and closed the deal before he could."

"The house he wanted was twice this size," Eli adds.

"Are you complaining about my purchase?"

He licks the last smears of ice cream from his spoon. "You think I give a shit about that? This place is too big as it is."

"Some of us like space and don't sleep on top of Phoenix every night like some kind of sloth." Jude lays down his cards with a grin. "Game's up. I win."

"Fuck!" Hudson bellows.

Jude smacks him around the head, telling him to be quiet. He really hates losing. Agreeing to a truce, they seal the peace agreement with another kiss.

"What should we play now?" I ask around a yawn.

Eli sets his spoon down. "I've got a game."

Surrendering the cards to him, Jude shuffles so Eli can take a seat next to us on the floor. He stops by the adjacent sofa, grabbing the knitted blanket from the back and wrapping it around my shoulders without a word.

My chest burns. "Thanks, Eli."

"No problem," he replies. "It's cold in here. Kade's in charge of the thermostat, and he's a hot bod."

"Someone really needs to steal that remote from him," Jude suggests. "I'd rather be too hot than too cold."

"Leave it with me." Hudson grins evilly. "I'll get it back."

"You promised Brooke that you'd stop winding Kade up," Eli responds. "Especially after you hid his car keys for a month."

"Well, now I'll hide the remote for a month instead." Hudson rubs his hands together. "Problem solved."

Several rounds into the next game, things have gotten serious. Turns out, Eli is a whole league above us and consistently beats all three of us at every game that Hudson suggests. I reckon his brain could rival Theo's any day.

While they shuffle cards and argue about the last result, I excuse myself to grab some water from the kitchen and check my phone in private since I heard it buzzing.

It's nearly four o'clock in the morning, but there's a series of text messages waiting in my group chat with the guys that we recently set up. Nobody is asleep right now.

> **Leigh:** I miss you, Goldilocks.
>
> **Enzo:** Your fault she left, dickhead.
>
> **Leigh:** Aren't you supposed to be getting your beauty sleep?
>
> **Enzo:** I'm not fucking Cinderella.
>
> **Hunter:** Shut up, the pair of you. Harlow, please come home. Let's talk.
>
> **Theo:** Some of us are still in the office working. Give it a bloody rest, will you?

Pain wrings every last drop of annoyance from my heart. It's only been a few days, but I hate the distance between us.

> **Harlow:** Miss you guys too. I just needed a break.

It doesn't take long for the responses to come.

> **Enzo:** Why are you awake? What's wrong?
>
> **Hunter:** Are you okay?
>
> **Harlow:** Same reason you're all up.
>
> **Leigh:** I'm sorry, princess.
>
> **Hunter:** We're here when you're ready to talk.
>
> **Enzo:** Say the word and I'll pick you up.

My phone vibrates with a separate text message from Theo in our own private chat. We usually only talk about books, but lately, things have felt different between us.

> **Theo:** Ignore them. Take the time you need.
> **Harlow:** Still sure you don't hate me?
>
> **Theo:** Not a chance. Sleep tight, beautiful.

I crash my forehead against the fridge. My blossoming feelings for Theo only complicate this mess further. He's become a good friend, and sometimes, I catch myself wanting more. I can't keep up with my own emotions.

We keep going around in circles and it's exhausting. The guys are determined to protect me from the world. I love and appreciate their care, but they don't seem to realise I also need protection from them.

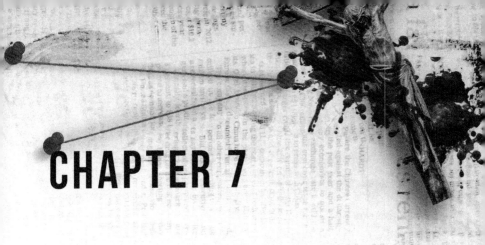

CHAPTER 7

Enzo

Fool & The Thief – THE HARA

My forehead collides with the office wall. I pray that when I open my eyes, I'll be back at home and curled up in bed with Harlow, her sweet body tucked into the crook of my arm.

Instead, I'm stuck in this hellhole. We're running on two hours of sleep, and I am on the verge of losing my shit. Hunter is in another board meeting with the superintendent, getting a thorough spanking for our lack of results.

We're losing steam.

This case is beating us.

"Knock some sense into yourself?" Theo laughs.

"Do you ever wish you could pack up your entire life, jump on a plane and disappear to some foreign island?"

His eyes are glued to a screen full of complex computer code. "Only five thousand times a day. Usually when Hunter is chewing my ear off."

With a sigh, I stomp back over to the black-leather sofa in the corner of his untidy office. Unlike our semi-neurotic overlord, who demands tidiness in every corner of his office, Theo thrives on disorganisation.

How his super-powered brain functions in such a mess, I'll never know. He lives in a perpetual state of chaos, and it doesn't seem to bother him one bit.

Pulling out my phone, I log in to Sabre's secure server and pull up our bespoke tracking program. Harlow doesn't know it, but we added her phone to our list of tracked individuals the day she unwrapped it.

I have no doubt that she'd hate the fact we have constant surveillance of her, twenty-four hours a day. None of us even batted an eye about invading her privacy in such a way.

"She's still with Brooklyn." I toss my phone aside. "We agreed to a few nights. What the hell is she still doing there?"

"Painting Brooke's toenails?" Theo suggests absently. "Having pillow fights in their frilly underwear? Having afternoon tea and discussing eligible bachelors for courting?"

Grabbing the nearest book laying discarded, I curve it through the air, watching with satisfaction as it hits the back of his head. Theo yelps, spinning in his chair to glare at me.

"You've been watching too much *Bridgerton*."

Theo snorts in derision. "Like I have the time. I spend every second of the day on this investigation while you two sit around worrying about Harlow."

I stretch my legs out. "She asked for a break. Hunter gave it to her. That was a week ago. I can't focus knowing she isn't safe at home, protected by an army of agents."

Theo flashes through several programs on his laptop. "Harlow's an adult. She can make her own decisions."

"Her safety isn't a decision. It's non-negotiable."

He rolls his eyes. "She's hanging out with Hudson, the man who salivates over removing people's tongues. He makes you look like a fluffy teddy bear."

"I am not a fluffy fucking teddy bear."

"My point is that she's safe. Focus, we have work to do tonight."

Dragging my sore body upright, I contemplate the huge stacks of paperwork on his mug-clustered coffee table. Since Reagan's interview, we've followed up on the names she was able to provide.

Two members of the church's congregation are refusing to be interviewed. They were cagey and extremely evasive over the phone and reserved their right to remain silent.

No explanation given.

More good news for us.

I think not.

On the plus side, Frederick Houghton, the village busybody, was more than willing to be interviewed. At the ripe old age of eighty-five, he's too frail to travel down to London. Hunter and I will drive to Newcastle next week to take his statement.

During difficult cases, I sometimes get this feeling. My blood boils and I can't focus on anything but chasing down that lead until it reveals its secrets.

Some might call it a gut instinct, honed after years in this messy business. I see it more as a bleak belief that humans will always fulfil your worst expectation of them.

We're circling something big.

I can taste it in the air.

"You get anything on Rosetta Stone from that contact of yours?" I flick through paperwork half-heartedly.

"I'm waiting for him to do a search. All government records are gone, but sometimes hard copies were kept in storage. They could have missed some."

"Sounds like a long shot."

He takes several gulps of coffee. "All we have are long shots. It only takes one to make a difference though. We need to know more about that children's home."

"Mrs Michaels is dead. Why does it matter?"

Theo pauses, and I know he's up to no good. Hunter likes to think that he's the pioneer of this operation, but Sabre runs off a high-powered steam engine that works quietly behind the scenes. Namely, Theo's obnoxiously large brain.

"I have a theory," he says hesitantly.

Dumping the paperwork, I crack my neck. "Go on then. Entertain me, Sherlock."

"What if Rosetta met Pastor Michaels there?"

My head snaps back up so I can stare at him. He's turned in his office chair, a lukewarm coffee clasped in his hands.

"What makes you think that?"

"Why not?" he counters.

"Well, there's no evidence."

"So what?" Theo cocks an eyebrow. "They had to meet somewhere. Rosetta disappeared for a reason."

"Because she lived in an abusive shitshow?"

"And vanished into thin air," he finishes. "Pastor Michaels is a ghost. We've got nothing on either of them. What if his files were erased along with Rosetta's during the cleanup?"

My mind whirrs with possibilities. We've been banging our heads against the wall for too long. Perhaps this is why. The trail we need to follow has been conveniently wiped.

"What motivates a killer to kill?"

Theo stares at me. "You want me to sit and list the reasons? We'll be here all day."

"Humour me. We've been working on the assumption that Pastor Michaels is a religious fanatic, punishing sex workers for what he categorises as a sin."

"He's an unhinged religious extremist," he points out.

"Yes, who butchers innocent women for pleasure."

"We already know this, Enz."

"But why? Where did this impulse come from?"

Theo rubs a spot between his brows. "I'm too fucking sleep deprived for this conversation."

"This was your theory, dumbass. All this time, we've been looking at the victims, searching for a connection. We never stopped to consider whether Pastor Michaels had family."

"Or... whether he started killing because of them."

"If Rosetta came from this place, maybe her future phoney husband did too. He learnt his violence from somewhere."

He nods in agreement. "We need proof."

"You reckon your contact will find anything?"

"I think we need a back-up plan. The government has gotten good at covering its tracks over the years."

"Don't we know it," I mutter.

Falling silent, we wrack our brains. All we need is a smoking gun. These children's homes were a dirty secret for a very long time.

They took public funding and used it to exploit the charges under their care. When the truth was exposed, the government took every precaution to bury it.

"Hunter and Leighton's dad," Theo exclaims.

"You want to call Ben in?"

"He ran the local police department for twenty-five years. If anyone knows where to start with this, it's him."

My heart sinks. "You know that breaks Hunter's rules. We agreed never to involve our families. It's too risky."

"Fuck the rules."

"He'll crucify us both."

Theo shoots me an impatient look. "This business *is* our family, Enz. We have to do whatever it takes to end this."

Pacing his littered floorspace, I wrestle with our options. Locating Rosetta's lost identity was a strike of luck that fell into our laps when we needed it most.

It's given us a much-needed step up to bring this tower of lies tumbling down. We owe it to Harlow to see this through and squeeze every bit of information out of the lead.

"All we're asking for is some information," Theo justifies. "We aren't involving Ben with anything else."

"That's still involving him."

"Maybe he has an old buddy who knows something, or he can point us in the right direction. Just think about it."

I massage my temples. "Fine, I'll make the call."

"Good." Theo nods. "This is the right decision."

"We're keeping this between us, alright? Hunter's enough of a dickhead these days as it is. He doesn't need to know."

"You got it, boss."

Retrieving my phone again, I unlock the screen and prepare to fire off a text message to Ben Rodriguez. He's a decent bloke, despite being headstrong and strict as hell after years spent serving in the police force.

My phone unlocks on the tracking program, and I frown down at the screen. Harlow's on the move, along with the little purple dot that signifies Brooklyn's tracker.

What the fuck?

Constant monitoring is a condition of employment when you join Sabre. That's why the entire Cobra team is also being monitored. Hudson's marker hasn't moved from their home a few miles away from ours. He isn't with them.

Harlow and Brooklyn are heading into Central London, coasting along the main road and heading for the bright lights of Soho. Unbelievable.

"You've got to be kidding me."

Theo perks up. "What is it?"

"Brooklyn is taking Harlow into the city. Are they seriously going drinking right now? Is she out of her mind?"

"That can't be right. Brooklyn isn't that stupid."

I meet his puzzled gaze. "Wanna bet?"

"Well," he admits after a beat. "If Hunter forbade her from taking Harlow out, you can bet your ass that Brooke's doing exactly that just to spite him."

He's fucking right.

Son of a bitch!

"I'm going to kill that woman, once and for all." I sling my leather jacket over my t-shirt and gun holster. "Send their location to my car. I'm going to drag them home."

Theo offers me a salute. "Want me to send backup?"

"Call Hudson and find out why the fuck he let them go out alone. I'll deal with him myself. He doesn't need his arms attached to work for this company."

Swooping from the office before Theo can point out what a terrible idea dismembering our best agent is, I bypass the elevator and skip each step down to the parking garage.

With my car ruined and stuck in the shop for the past few weeks, I've been driving one of our spare company SUVs around. Peeling out of the building, Theo programs the tracker's location into the built-in computer within seconds.

They have arrived in a popular drinking district, right outside a well-known bar I've scouted out on a previous case. I watch Harlow's and Brooklyn's trackers move inside.

They're going clubbing.

Oh, heads are going to roll.

It takes me over an hour to cut through the bustling traffic of London on a Friday night. Despite the frigid February temperature, the streets are lined with tottering heels, alcohol-tinged smiles and hopeful expectations.

I'm ready to flatten the three cars in front of me for holding the queue. The row of taxis releases their inebriated passengers into the throng of clubbers outside several popular venues. There are people everywhere.

Pulling up on the curb, I park—very much illegally—and slam the door shut so hard, it rocks the stupid car. Fuck the inevitable parking ticket. We won't be staying long.

There's a shivering queue of punters outside the bar I'm heading for. I cut past them and pull a stack of notes from my wallet, palming them to the bouncer without a word.

"Mr Montpellier," he greets.

I've done enough undercover work in Soho for every staff member working this street to know who I represent. Funnily enough, the dangerous and disturbed criminals who pay Sabre's salaries often frequent Soho's array of seedy bars.

"Evening, Zayne."

"You looking for anyone in particular tonight?"

"Two female suspects. First one is five foot four, brunette, probably being strong-armed by a tall, blonde-haired chick with a big mouth."

The corner of his mouth lifts. "She's got a mighty gob on her, that one."

"Sounds like my target."

"Even threatened to castrate me if I didn't let them inside to get out of the cold. She paid good as well."

Brooklyn motherfucking West!

"Yeah, she would," I grumble.

Slipping inside the dark, smoky space, the thump of loud bass music pounds into my head. I'm too goddamn tired for this shit. Writhing bodies pack the nightclub to the rafters. The queue for the bar alone is several people deep.

When a hand lands on my shoulder, I react on instinct and yank the perpetrator forwards. A tattooed mass slams into my shoulder, breaking my hold with a level of precision that only I could have taught.

"Jesus, Enz."

"Hudson?! Fuck."

He plants his feet. "Theo called while you were driving."

I grab him by the scruff of his black t-shirt. "Why did you let them leave? Are you seriously that thick?"

He shoves me backwards, unkempt hair hanging over his hardened blue eyes. Hudson Knight is the kind of man that inspires fear in the hearts of his enemies without uttering a single word.

"I was asleep, dammit."

"Asleep?" I repeat incredulously.

"Yes, asshole! Your sadistic best friend has had me working overtime for a month. I had no idea they snuck out."

"Hunter told you to keep Harlow safe! That was the sole reason he allowed her out to spend time with Brooklyn."

"Allowed her out?" Hudson's pierced eyebrow lifts. "Do you hear yourself? Harlow isn't your fucking pet. She's allowed to have a life as well."

I am going to pulverise his face.

He's really fucked me off now.

"If a serial killer was stalking Brooklyn, plotting to imprison and torture her, would you let her out of the house?"

His mouth snaps shut.

"Yeah, I didn't think so."

"Brooklyn has a gun," he offers.

"Oh, awesome. Brooklyn West and a deadly weapon in a nightclub full of grabby hands. What could possibly go wrong with that?"

Dismissing him before I commit a very public murder, I begin to filter through the melee of people. Hudson follows hot on my heels as we part the sea of people with nothing but sheer intimidation and scowls.

Clearing the dance floor, we scan through the crowd and eliminate several writhing couples trying to subtly snort cocaine off each other's hands. Definitely not our girls.

Hudson lifts his chin towards the back of the club, where the emergency exit signs point towards the smoking area. Stepping outside together, we gulp down fresh air.

If you want to enter an introvert's version of hell, go nightclubbing in London after pay day. This place is a cesspit of revelry and cheap hook-ups. Not my kind of scene.

"There."

I follow Hudson's stare. Bingo.

"You wanna deal with Brooklyn?" he asks.

"She's your problem, Hud."

"Since when?"

"You're marrying the lunatic, not me."

Hudson groans loudly. "Fuck, don't remind me."

Smoking a cigarette with her feet propped up on a bench, Brooklyn watches us approach with palpable exasperation. She wears her shoulder-length, blonde hair loose, but her usual jeans and band t-shirt have been replaced by a tight, black-leather dress and Doc Martens.

"Here come the party poopers!"

"Fancy seeing you two here," I snarl at them.

"Seriously, guys. That was barely an hour."

Marching up to his fiancée with a thunderous expression, Hudson takes the cigarette from her fingertips and crushes it.

"I'd expect this from you, blackbird. But bringing Harlow out unprotected? What were you thinking?"

Brooklyn wears a smarmy grin. "Harlow has been cooped up for months. She needs to live a little."

"It isn't safe, and you know it."

"I can keep her safe!" she argues.

Ignoring the smart-mouthed hellion, I step in front of Harlow to gain her attention. She's staring at the ground, her shoulders slumped and aquamarine eyes averted.

At least she's wearing more than Brooklyn. Her tight blue jeans and a loose, floaty blouse show off her naturally pale complexion and defined collarbones.

"Little one?"

Her eyes don't lift to mine.

Things have been strained between us lately. I'll admit that I have been an overprotective douchebag. I've felt shitty about how we left things after our argument, too shitty to crawl between her sheets and take her into my arms.

But I wasn't wrong.

Her safety will always be a priority.

"I'm sorry," she murmurs quietly.

"I know, angel."

"I just wanted to do something normal."

Sending Brooklyn an accusing look, she winks at me and lifts her chin in defiance. Fucking smartass.

"Told you," she mouths.

"Take her home," I order Hudson.

Brooklyn shakes her head. "I'm fine here."

I jab a finger at her. "We'll be discussing this tomorrow, wildfire. Get out of my face."

"Or what?" Brooklyn fires back.

"You don't want to find out."

"Wake up, Enz! You need to stop wrapping her up in cotton wool, or you'll lose her for good."

"Brooke," Harlow whispers. "Please don't."

"He needs to know how you're feeling."

"Got it," I shout before lowering my voice. "Seriously, Brooke. Go home and be thankful you're a woman, otherwise I would've beaten the shit out of you by now."

"Take a shot, big guy. My fucking gender has nothing to do with it. I'll still win in a fight against you."

"Go!" I roar, my patience fizzling out.

Still scowling, Brooklyn shoves Hudson aside when he tries to grab hold of her. She leans closer to whisper in Harlow's ear before giving her a tight squeeze and sashaying away.

"Sorry," Hudson offers.

"Just take her home and fucking keep her there."

With a nod, he disappears. Once they've gone, I take a seat next to Harlow on the bench. It groans beneath my weight, threatening to collapse into dust. The frozen statue next to me releases a tiny laugh.

"Shut up," I tease, trying to cut the tension.

"Please don't break it."

Nudging her shoulder, I rest a hand on her thigh. "If you want to go drinking, I could take you somewhere way better than this shithole."

"Really?" Harlow says hopefully.

"You should see Hunter dance. It's a sight to behold."

"I can't imagine that."

"After enough tequila and lime, nothing can stop him. I'm not sure it qualifies as dancing, though. More like a crime against humanity."

"That bad, huh?"

Harlow finally looks up and meets my eyes. I'm stabbed in the chest by the bleak, bottomless pit of loneliness looking back at me. It's the same empty stare I used to see in the mirror. That was before she came into my life.

"I'm sorry," we say at the same time.

Her cheeks flame. "That was my line."

"Mine too."

I reach for her hand and take it in mine. Her bones are so delicate and bird-like, I feel like with one wrong move I could snap her entire body without batting an eye.

She's all wrong for me.

Fragile. Broken.

Vulnerable.

But I'm falling for her even more with each day that passes. Curiosity has melted into mindless infatuation. I need her. She's the air in my lungs and the choking hand at my throat all at once. That's the power she holds.

"You didn't swap one prison for another."

"Didn't I?" She scoffs.

I stroke her knuckles. "All I want is to keep you safe, little one. But I know that sometimes I get carried away."

"You're right, though. Coming here was stupid."

"I get it."

She gives me a side look. "You do?"

"Yeah." I slide our fingers together. "We're not the easiest people to live with, and you've been cooped up for too long."

"It isn't you. I needed to do this for myself."

"Well, there are better ways to cool off than by running away with Brooklyn as your sidekick."

"Seemed like a good idea at the time," she offers with a sigh. "I needed to get away from Hunter and Leighton."

Hunter was tight-lipped about why Harlow decided to go on an impromptu overnight visit that turned into hiding from us at Brooklyn's for the rest of the week.

"What happened last week?"

She anxiously fiddles with her hair. "The inevitable. I know you think we can make this work, but it isn't going to happen."

I slide a finger along her jawline, tilting her brilliant blue eyes back up to mine. Staring at her is like escaping a burning building by jumping into the sea, no matter the very real risk of drowning.

I know the risk.

I'll still take it.

Whatever she's willing to give me is enough. We're under fire, and a storm of acid rain is threatening to hammer down on us. I'll fill my lungs and let my own skin slough off to keep her dry, if that's what it takes.

"Why not?" I breathe.

"Because I'm going to hurt you. All of you."

"You don't know that."

She bites her lip, her eyes sparkling with emotion. "I'm not like Pastor Michaels. I can't hurt the people I'm supposed to... to..."

Drawn to one another by an invisible string lacing our two hearts together, I let my lips brush hers in a tender caress.

"Finish that sentence."

She shudders. "I can't."

My self-control snaps. I won't let her slip away again. We've already been down this road before. I seal my mouth on hers, needing to taste her sweet essence.

Harlow doesn't see herself like I do. She's everything that's good and pure in this world. Everything that I'm not but hope to be. Around her, I can feel the darkness inside me melting.

I want to shackle her inside the protective depths of my soul, safe and secure, where no motherfucker can bruise her skin again. The world is full of people trying to break us. It's my job not to let them.

Her lips part on a blissful sigh as she melts into the kiss. A natural, silent symphony guides our colliding mouths. My hand slides up to bury in her thick, flowing tresses.

She breaks the kiss. "Enzo, don't."

But it's too late.

My fingertips are already sifting through her hair, following the grooves of her skull. When velvety softness is replaced by scabbed, raw skin that feels hot to the touch, I pull away.

"Is that—"

Her face crumples. "Please don't look."

Leighton told me her hair pulling has gotten worse since Northumberland. Amidst the chaos, we've let our surveillance slip. She's careful not to do it when we're eating together or watching TV in the den.

I grip the back of her neck. "It's okay. You don't need to be afraid. I need to see, or I can't help you."

"But I don't need help."

"Harlow," I say gruffly. "I swore an oath to keep you safe, no matter what. You can trust me with this."

Her eyes shut as she nods. "Okay."

Lifting her mousy-brown hair to expose what used to be a small-sized bald patch, violent armies of rage filter my vision into shades of red.

Beneath a thin layer of untouched hair to hide the truth from the world, almost the whole left half of her head is bleeding and scabbed over with bright patches of soreness.

She must be in agony.

This is months' worth of pulling.

I can't begin to fathom the determination it must have taken to tear all of this hair out by hand. Strand by strand. Pluck by pluck. I want to roar in fury just thinking about it.

"That." She cracks an eye open to study me. "That look right there is exactly why I didn't want you to see it."

I let her hair drop and carefully smooth it over. Tears are racing down her cheeks in thick rivulets. Pressing my lips to the side of her head, I kiss above the secret she's kept from us all.

"We need to get you some more support."

"Richards already knows," she whispers.

"And? What does he think?"

Harlow shrugs. "He gave me a bunch of coping techniques. It's just hard to use them when everything's so... loud."

Fuck. This is bad. Even worse than I thought.

"You need to try," I attempt to encourage.

"Yeah, I know."

I trace a finger over her lips. "You're not in this alone, even when you feel like it. It will get easier with time."

"And if it doesn't?"

My lips meet hers in a breath-stealing kiss. Salty tears are burning my skin. I can feel her pain taking on a life of its own and crawling inside me. It's sending my protective instincts into overdrive.

"I will not let you give up," I murmur into her mouth. "Not in a million years."

"You can't fight all my battles for me."

"But I can hold your hand while you fight for yourself. I'll do everything in my power to make this easier for you."

Harlow lets me tuck her into my side, her face burying in the crook of my neck. We sit there, curled around each other, in the smoky darkness of the biting London air.

"I didn't mean what I said the other week," she says in a timid voice. "About wanting to leave. I was feeling overwhelmed, and I needed some space to breathe."

"You don't need to apologise."

"But I shouldn't have said that to you."

"We both said things we didn't mean in the heat of the moment." I sigh against her head. "I could communicate better instead of threatening you with house arrest."

"Probably, yeah."

We both laugh, the last drops of tension dissipating. I take her hand and tug her onto her feet. Right now, I want to hold her close and never let go. That's step one to begin fixing this.

"Let's go home. The other idiots are on strict orders to behave or find somewhere else to live."

Harlow winces. "You didn't have to do that."

"Nobody upsets you on my watch and gets away with it. Hunter's lucky I love him, or he'd be dead and buried by now. Don't get me started on his asshole brother."

"Thought you were going to stop threatening?"

"Threatening *you*," I correct her. "I can't commit to not beating the living daylights out of my teammates on a semi-regular basis. Especially when they behave like jealous teenagers."

Harlow summons a weak smile.

"Guess I can't complain about that."

CHAPTER 8

Harlow

Me and My Brain – Airways

With a red-plaid blanket wrapped around my shoulders, I take my steaming cup of tea and click my tongue for Lucky to follow. She zips to my side, preening as I rub her ears.

Having her with me calms the itching static of anxiety humming through my body as I wait for my phone to ring. My stomach cramps aren't helping me feel any better.

"Good girl." I stroke a finger over her crown. "Why hasn't the doctor called yet? It's been hours.""

Her pleading eyes stare up at me.

"What if his operation went wrong?"

The steady, reassuring love in her animal eyes answers me without the need for words. I have to be patient. My father's operation commenced at eleven o'clock this morning.

I'm afraid.

Even if I don't know why.

I didn't think it was possible to care about someone that you don't know, but the past few hours of waiting have proven that I do care. Perhaps more than I should. He's still my father, even though we don't know each other.

Lucky trots by my side as I approach Hunter's office, tucked behind the wide staircase leading upstairs. He left early this morning with Enzo to begin the long drive up to Newcastle.

They're both trying to be more open. It's a new development after my stint with Brooklyn and my later heart-to-heart with Enzo. True to his word, he spoke to Hunter and the others about the new status quo.

We're starting fresh.

Hunter revealed last night that they're interviewing an elderly pastor for the case. This man worked at the church Kiera attended. We're hoping to understand more about her life, and why Pastor Michaels decided that it had to end.

Like Jude said, the answers are there.

I just have to find them.

Despite spending hours spilling the inky darkness of my soul onto lined paper, my memories are still disjointed. I can only remember flashes. Whispered promises and pleas.

It's going to be okay, Harlow.

I won't let him hurt you again.

She should have been afraid. Pastor Michaels slaughtered her with a lascivious smile on his face. Her empty carcass was torn apart, limb for limb. Now, she's trapped.

Kiera has joined the faces that I wish I could go back to not remembering, all pointing their accusing fingers at me. Every breath I take is an insult to them.

You lived.

You lived.

You lived.

My hand spasms with the urge to grab a tantalising handful of hair and rip it clean out. I need a distraction. Enzo wrote down a few things, along with the password to Hunter's desktop computer in his office before he left.

I've got a few hours before I'm due to meet Richards for a session. He moved up the appointment—another one of Enzo's ideas, along with the additional security that's been posted at the front gate while they're gone.

With the thump of Leighton's terrible music pounding through the floor, I slide into Hunter's office. The residue of his spicy aftershave seeps over me. I take a breath, running my fingers over a discarded checked scarf on the sofa.

He has an impressive selection of books, but unlike Theo's insatiable thirst for classics and science fiction, Hunter seems to enjoy memoirs and tear-inducingly boring business books.

Yikes.

Glossy black shelving fills an entire wall, casting shadows over a brown sofa, overhanging lamp and sheepskin rug that covers the floorboards. Taking a seat at his desk, I wiggle the mouse and input his password.

The screen opens on a background that makes my heart twinge. Hunter and Leighton both look younger, their faces softened and pulled taut in bright, almost identical smiles that advertise their shared genes.

On either side of them, two older people are smiling at the camera. The resemblance is stark. Della, their mum, is short and grey-haired, with an understanding smile and hazel eyes softened by wrinkles.

Their father, Ben, wears a sharp haircut, and he's in good shape despite his older age. With an unwavering brown stare, I can see where Hunter gets his intense air of authority.

Sometimes, I forget that Hunter and Leighton are family. They weren't always imprisoned in this fractured phase. Hunter is ready to murder his younger brother most days, and Leighton is determined to put him in a premature grave.

Lucky harrumphs as she settles beneath the huge desk, her fur brushing against my feet. Reaching underneath to rub her ears, I bring up the browser and head for the online education website that Enzo suggested.

They're adamant that getting a job is out of the question, but the idea of going back to school gave me food for thought. I don't remember ever attending school.

I love reading and learning new things about the world. This could be a way for me to escape the constant feeling of oppression that comes with my current situation.

"Goldilocks?" Leighton calls out.

"In the office."

He thumps up the staircase from the basement gym. "You hungry? I'm just going to take a quick shower."

"I'm fine, thanks."

Engrossed in a course catalogue, the choices available are endless. Half of the subjects are unrecognisable to me. I'm going to be learning with children laughing and pointing at the idiot adult. I feel sick at the thought.

There's so much I don't understand about this world. I'll never recapture the normalcy that was stolen from me. It will forever be a far-off dream. Crap, this was a mistake.

The door creaks as Leighton pokes his sweaty head around it. "Harlow? You want tea?"

I gesture to my cup. "Beat you to it."

"Just trying to look after you." He hesitates before leaving. "You should eat something. I make a mean grilled cheese."

"You're fussing again."

He slips inside the room, revealing his loose workout shorts and bare chest, glistening with droplets of sweat that define the slopes of his tightly packed muscles. My throat tightens.

Raising his hands, he mimes clawing the air. "Grrr, grrr. Little Harlow. Must. Eat."

"What on earth is that?" I frown at him.

"Are you not impressed by my best Enzo impression? Should I growl more? Did I not threaten enough?"

"Erm, he usually follows up his fussing with action."

I yelp when the office chair spins. Leighton grins down at me with amusement dancing in his eyes. He boxes me in with a hand on each side of the leather chair.

"You want action? I'm more than happy to give it."

"Knock it off, Leigh. I'm trying to look through this stupid catalogue. Stop distracting me."

He flashes two gorgeous dimples. "What is this, anyway? Are you seriously going back to school?"

"Maybe. Why not?"

"Most people can't wait to leave it."

"I'm not most people." I glance back at the computer. "All I want is to experience what other people take for granted. I had none of that."

Leighton leaves me to flop across the leather sofa, propping his bare feet up on the armrest. Lucky launches herself across the office and barks until he starts rubbing her belly.

"So, what is this then? Online classes?"

I glance over another course description. "Richards recommended it to me. You can attend online in your own time, no pressure."

"Sounds good, Goldilocks."

"I guess so."

"Why the long face?"

Struggling to understand another paragraph of information, I exit the website and turn in the chair to face Leighton.

"Do you think I'm stupid?"

"What?" He chuckles.

I try to shrug off my embarrassment. "None of it is making any sense to me. How am I supposed to catch up?"

"Hell, it doesn't make sense to me either."

"Not funny. You went to school and can understand basic things like maths and science. I feel like an idiot."

"I flunked both of those subjects," he reveals.

"Seriously?"

"School was not my strong suit. I liked sports and drinking beer at the back of the football pitch. That's about it."

"No wonder you flunked out if you spent all day drinking beer and kicking a ball around."

"Ouch, princess."

Leighton flashes across the room, banding his corded arms around me. I squeal as I'm lifted out of the office chair.

"Hey! Put me down!"

"Not a chance," Leighton replies.

My legs automatically wrap around his waist. He holds me against his bare chest and pins me. When his nose buries in my hair, he takes a deep, indulgent inhale.

"Are you sniffing me?"

"You smell incredible," he whispers back. "For the record, I don't think that you're stupid. If you want to go back to school, then we can all help you catch up."

"Thank you," I hush. "That means a lot."

"Always, Goldilocks. Lunch?"

"I'm not really hungry."

Leighton looks me in the eye. "What's really going on?"

Busted. He knows me far too well.

"The hospital still hasn't called." I bite down on my sore bottom lip. "He's been in surgery for hours now."

"Give it time. Doctor Bannon will call."

That doesn't ease my anxiety. He reads it on my face, stroking his thumb along my cheek.

"I can practically hear your brain churning." Leighton kisses the tip of my nose. "What else is bothering you?"

"I don't know what happens if the surgery is a success."

"Well, Jude and Phoenix have found a bed in the rehab centre they work at. They will take care of your dad there."

I don't realise I'm twirling a long strand of hair between my fingers, tugging roughly with each rotation. Leighton's eyes narrow on the movement, and he catches my hand.

"Stop," he murmurs.

"I'm sorry."

"You don't need to do that. I'm here."

I blow out an unsteady breath. "What if he doesn't pull through? I haven't even spoken to him."

"Do you want to now that he's responsive?"

"Maybe. I think I have questions."

His eyebrows pull together. "What about talking to Giana instead?"

Nose wrinkled, I suppress a full-body shudder.

"She calls every week," he adds. "Hunter stopped passing the messages along to you after Northumberland."

At the mention of my estranged mother, my already aching stomach twists painfully. It's been in knots all morning.

"Maybe I'll feel better if I talk to her again," I concede with a sigh. "We left things in a pretty bad way."

"You don't have to if you don't want to."

"I think some closure might help. If she can tell me what she knows about my childhood, the memories might return."

Leighton pecks my cheek. "She's due to come into HQ for a second interview in a couple of weeks. You could see her then, rather than travelling back to Devon."

"Yeah, I don't want to go back there."

"Then it's settled. Come on, let's go make some lunch. I'm withering away here. I'll shower after."

"Withering away? Hardly."

He narrows his eyes. "What are you saying?"

"You're making Enzo look small with all the working out you're doing at the moment."

Grin darkening with deliciously malevolent intentions, he flexes for my benefit, his growing biceps rippling.

"I warned you. This is a fight I intend to win. Trust me, I look even better naked."

"Christ, Leigh."

"Wanna see the rest of me?" he proposes.

"Keep your pants on and make me a sandwich instead."

Leighton links our fingers together and drags me away from the office. In the kitchen, he grabs my hips and lifts me onto the marble breakfast bar.

I cross my legs at the ankle and watch him pull a teetering tower of sandwich ingredients from the fridge. He sets up a chopping board, bread and two plates before constructing our sandwiches. I steal bites of cheese while waiting.

"Patience, young Jedi."

"Don't Yoda me." I grab a slice of tomato before he can smack my hand away. "You're the last one to be patient when food is involved."

Leighton squeezes mayo into my sandwich. "Point taken. I'm not a good example to follow, as we've established."

"I learned that a while ago."

He slices off the crusts on my sandwich without being told and cuts it into neat, bite-sized mouthfuls. My heart skitters with appreciation. Large portions of food are intimidating.

"Get that in you." He hands me the plate. "Then, we're going to go back to that course catalogue together."

Chest burning, I touch my lips to his stubbly cheek. "Thank you for being amazing."

"I know, I'm fucking awesome. Eat up. I'm gonna go take that shower."

"You're not eating with me?"

"Harlow, I stink."

With a mouthful of sandwich, I sniff the air. "You really do smell bad."

"Don't be mean now. I fed you, didn't I?"

Depositing a kiss on my head, he crams his sandwich into his mouth and disappears. Left alone, I munch through another bite-sized chunk before my stomach twists again.

With Leighton gone, I push my plate away. The stomach cramps are making me feel nauseous. A dull, throbbing pain pulses through my abdomen and lower back.

When I stand up to make another cup of tea, hoping to ease my nausea, a strange warmth soaks into the fabric of my jeans. Oh my God. It's coming from between my legs.

Biting my lip, I run out of the kitchen, making a beeline upstairs for the privacy of my bedroom. The door is barely shut before more warmth rushes out with a spike of pain.

This can't be what I think it is.

Not after all this time.

I didn't think it was even possible. The doctors said it might never happen after years of malnourishment. Hands shaking, I unfasten my jeans and slowly push them over my hips. My heartbeat is roaring in my ears.

With denim swamping my knees, I blanch at the bright-red stain on the fabric. Blood. I'm bleeding. Kicking the jeans aside with a cry working up my throat, I look down at the soaked material of my panties.

Blood is smeared on both of my thighs, painting my skin with swirls of dark crimson. It's definitely coming out of me. Panic sets in as the past takes over, and I'm too freaked out to stop myself from spiralling.

The bedroom melts away.

Darkness slinks back in.

The sound of crying shreds my grasp on sanity. It was grief, tinged with the paradox of twisted relief, that fuelled her screams as the blood poured out of her.

"Adelaide," I sob.

I can feel her, invisible and wrapping her arms around me when my knees buckle. Crumpled on the bedroom floor, I hug my midsection as the memories overwhelm me.

The swell of her belly.

Every syllable of her anguished lament.

The thump of fists on flesh.

Bruises blossoming like oil paint.

Covering my ears, I try to block it out. Her petrified cursing. Pastor Michaels' hissed promise of retribution as she stole the unborn life from him that he intended to puppeteer.

A mother, protecting her kin.

Even by means of death.

No matter how hard I clamp down on my ears, it gets louder. She lives inside me, surrounded by ranks of tortured souls, all waiting for their own turn to tear a slice off me.

"Harlow?"

Leighton's voice slips through my closed bedroom door. I should scrub my tears and attempt to hide the mess I've found myself in, but I can't move a muscle. I'm tucked in the corner of my cage, cowering out of sight.

If I move, Pastor Michaels will remember me. He'll abandon the other cage and return to mine. Unlock the door. Prowl inside. Beat, whip and break his way to domination.

You'll always be a sinner.

It's my job to teach you.

One day, you'll thank me.

Two strong hands grip my shoulders and peel me off the plush, grey carpet. I'm too scared to open my eyes. He's here. Pastor Michaels blamed me for that baby's death.

When Adelaide died, his rage exploded out of him. He stomped my bones into broken dust while the scent of her blood poisoned the basement around us.

"Harlow," the voice snaps.

I recognise it. That isn't Pastor Michaels. He wouldn't be stroking my back or whispering reassurances.

"Talk to me. Where are you hurt?"

"Leigh," I gasp.

"It's me. I've got you."

"I c-c-can't breathe…"

Cradled in his arms, my cheek is pressed against the hot skin of his pectorals. I suck in a stuttered breath and focus on the rise and fall of his chest, using it to anchor myself.

"That's it, princess."

Dragging my eyelids open, I find Leighton staring down at me, searching for answers. Shame colours my cheeks.

"What happened? Where are your clothes?"

"I f-freaked out when I saw the blood."

"What blood?"

"I'm so sorry, Leigh."

He cups my cheek. "Why are you bleeding? Did you fall or something?"

"Oh my God." I attempt to scramble off his lap as his arms tighten. "Let me go. I'm going to get it all over you."

Six feet of toned muscle and tanned skin holds me prisoner. He's only wearing a pair of tight blue boxers, leaving nothing to the imagination. I fight harder to escape.

"I'm going to lose my shit in a sec. What is it?"

I bury my face in his chest to hide. "I d-didn't think I was ever going to get it. The doctors warned me."

There's a beat of hesitation.

"Oh," Leighton breathes. "*Oh.*"

"Yeah," I deadpan.

"That. Okay."

"Let me up. This is gross as hell."

His hand moves to my back to hold me in place. "Don't be ridiculous. It's just a bit of blood. I'm not bothered."

"Well, I am bothered."

Leighton ignores my squirming and lifts me up. I'm carried into my en-suite, where he finally drops me back on my feet before turning on the walk-in shower.

"Get cleaned up. I'll sort out some supplies."

"Supplies?" I repeat.

"You know, girly shit. Tampons and things." He mock-shudders with a wink. "We don't keep that stuff around the house."

"Ground, please swallow me up," I mutter.

He ruffles my hair. "No can do. Are you... erm, gonna get in? I'll find you some clean clothes to wear."

My sweater is loose enough to cover my body and upper thighs, but I'm standing in nothing but stained panties from the waist down. My legs are crossed tight to hide the mess from him.

"If you breathe a word of this to anyone, you're dead meat," I threaten him. "Promise?"

Leighton laughs as he leaves the bathroom. No answer. Humiliated, I slam the door and pull my sweater over my head, dropping it in a heap on the tiled floor with my bra.

My sodden panties go next. Stepping into the thick steam pouring from the shower, the hot water beats down on me, soothing the last spasms of anxiety. Water makes me happy.

She's still here.

Adelaide.

Lingering in the outermost frontier of my mind, like the others, she's biding her time. I watch the pink swirls escaping down the drain and fight to silence her screaming.

"I'm coming in," Leighton warns.

The bathroom door creaks open as I'm sloughing jasmine-scented shower gel off my legs.

"Leigh!"

"My eyes are covered. Got you some comfy clothes. I'll be downstairs."

"Wait," I rush out.

He freezes before escaping, a hand clamped over his eyes. Breath held, I crack open the shower door. Leighton lifts his hand to peer at me.

"Climb in."

"You sure?" he double-checks.

"I don't want to be alone. I might freak out again."

Closing the door, he shrugs. "I should warn you that you'll find me irresistible when you see me naked."

"Just get in here before I change my mind."

Reaching for the shampoo, I hear Leighton approaching as he finishes stripping down. The shower door closes, and hard planes of muscle meet my back.

Leighton reaches around my waist to take the shampoo from my hands. He lathers the fragranced liquid and begins to work it into my hair, taking care to avoid the stretch of sores running across my scalp.

"Harlow?"

"Mmm," I moan back.

"What scared you so badly about getting your first period?"

Hands braced on the tiled wall, I let my head slump. "I had a flashback to Adelaide's death. The blood triggered me."

"You weren't expecting it?"

"I didn't think I'd ever get my period."

"You've been eating better and putting on some weight." He gently massages the safe side of my head. "I guess your body is starting to catch up with where it's supposed to be."

"I guess so."

"That's a good thing. Trust me."

146

Leighton guides my head back under the spray of water to wash the shampoo out. He's moved closer, and I can feel his erection pushing against my behind.

My breath catches. "Leigh—"

"Sorry," he says quickly. "Can't help it."

Reaching for the conditioner, he begins to lather it into my hair. His hard length brushes against my ass again, causing my pulse to spike.

I can't help shifting against his crotch, my breath held. The friction is a delicious tease, distracting me from the remnants of ghosts still haunting my mind.

"Princess," he warns. "I didn't get in here to take advantage while you're still upset."

"You're not taking advantage."

"Potato, patata. It's taking advantage in my books, no matter how you slice it."

He begins to rinse the conditioner out, and I glance down at the shower basin. The bleeding has stopped for now. I swivel around to face him.

"All clean," he announces.

My eyes flick down. "Want me to—"

"No," he says firmly. "I'm not the kind of guy that asks his girl to get him off just because she's on the blob."

"On the blob?" I laugh.

"You've never heard that before?"

"Nope, never."

"Ah, man. I'm going to have so much fun with this."

Smacking his water-laden chest, I slip out of the shower and wrap myself in the towel he put on the rack to get warm for me. He turns off the shower and disappears to get dressed.

On the bed, my favourite pair of sweats have been laid out with clean panties and fluffy bed socks. I pack my panties with some tissues as a temporary measure.

My phone is vibrating where I left it next to the bed this morning. The group chat has been going crazy for the last half an hour I've spent in the shower.

> **Leigh:** Theo, can you swing by the pharmacy on your way over? Harlow needs something.
>
> **Theo:** Erm, sure. Everything okay?
>
> **Enzo:** What the hell happened?
>
> **Hunter:** Answer my fucking phone call, Leigh. Why does she need something from the pharmacy?
>
> **Enzo:** If she's hurt, I'll personally skin you alive and sell your hide for profit on the dark web. Answer the phone.

"Bloody hell." I flush hot with even more humiliation as I read the next instalment.

> **Leigh:** Calm down, assholes. She needs some of those tampon thingies and whatever else girls use.
>
> **Enzo:** It came?
>
> **Leigh:** Good inference, genius.
>
> **Theo:** I have no idea what girls use.
>
> **Hunter:** Ask the pharmacist.

The next message comes fifteen minutes later. It's a picture of a brightly coloured aisle, overflowing with different brands and types of neon packaging.

> **Theo:** A little help here? Why are there a million different kinds of tampons? And what the fuck are extra-large wings?

Enzo: Google that shit.

Theo: Tried that, not helpful. Now I'm even more confused.

Collapsing on the bed, I tap out a response.

Harlow: Oh my God. I'm never speaking to any of you ever again. This is humiliating.

Leigh: Sorry, Goldilocks. I needed to enlist help.

That asshole is in serious trouble. I can actually hear him laughing all the way from his own bedroom right now.

Harlow: Stay out of my room, Leigh. I do not want to speak to you.

Enzo: You upset her, shithead. Prepare to be skinned.

Leigh: Princess! Help me.

I shake my head with a snort.

Harlow: Not a chance.

Hunter: Can we save the first-degree murder for later? I'm trying to concentrate here. Some of us have a case to solve.

Theo: On my way over with ice cream.

Harlow: Theodore, you're allowed in my room.

Theo: Uh, thanks?

Leigh: Dammit.

Storming back into my bedroom, Leighton's weight bounces on the bed next to me. I've ditched my phone and buried my face in my pillow to hide from the world.

"What's up, buttercup?" he singsongs.

"I officially hate you."

"Hey, I'm the one getting skinned alive."

"You deserve it. I'm never speaking to you ever again. You promised not to tell anyone."

He yanks the pillow off my head and begins tickling my ribcage, forcing me to roll over and gasp for air.

"I'm sorry." His eyes are twinkling. "I didn't want to leave you here alone. Theo is coming over later anyway."

"They were debating different tampon brands!"

"I mean, you want the best, right?"

Stealing my pillow back, I smash him around the head with it. Leighton slumps on the mattress with a cackle, dodging the swinging feathers clasped in my hands.

"Okay, okay," he says between laughter. "I'm sorry. Can I bribe your forgiveness with pizza and a movie?"

"Fine, but I'm choosing both."

"You drive a hard bargain."

Offering me a hand, Leighton pushes me towards the door. He stops to grab my pillows and duvet, hefting them over his shoulder to carry downstairs.

We end up snuggled together under the duvet, sprawled out on the sectional sofa. Leighton is passing me handfuls of my favourite chocolate-covered pretzels as I scroll through the pizza menu on his phone.

"Hey," Theo shouts as the front door opens. "Your delivery man has arrived."

I let my head hit the sofa cushions. "We are so not doing this. I've been humiliated enough for one day."

Strolling into the room with a huge brown paper bag in his hands, Theo offers me a sweet smile in greeting.

"You okay?"

"Peachy," I drone. "Good day at work?"

"It was alright. Did you guys eat already?"

"We're ordering pizza." Leighton takes the phone back from my hands. "Want your usual?"

"With extra olives, please." Theo drops the paper bag in my lap. "For you. Hope it's okay."

"Thank you for getting the stuff."

He peels off his denim jacket and tosses it on the other sofa. "No worries. I was about to come over anyway."

"Here. Sit down."

Vacating my spot for him to take, I clutch the paper bag to my chest and run from the room before their chuckling can catch up to me.

In the bathroom, I open the bag and my mouth drops. Theo has brought enough stuff for an army of hormonal women. At least five different brands of tampons and pads, all varying in sizes and thickness.

Panic creeps back in. I have no idea what to use or where to even begin. Tears burn my eyes as my emotions swell back up to the surface. This is so stupid.

Sliding my phone from my back pocket, I ignore the still-pinging group chat and pull up Brooklyn's contact. It takes a few seconds for her to answer the video call.

"Hey," she greets with a lit cigarette dangling from her mouth. "Is everything okay?"

"Brooke, thank God," I whisper under my breath. "Wait, are you smoking?"

"Wedding planning is fucking stressful, alright?"

"Noted. I need your help. Are you alone?"

Flicking the cigarette aside, she walks away from the hum of another two voices behind her. I can make out the tinted-glass structure of HQ in the background.

"Am now. Who do I need to kill this time?"

"I got my period, and I have no idea what to do."

Her playful smile softens. "Take a breath. Need me to go to the shop?"

"Theo already went."

"Bloody hell, Theo buying sanitary pads. I would've paid to see that. Okay, let's see what we're working with."

I tip out the entire contents of the bag and flip the camera to show her. She whistles under her breath.

"Damn, Theo went to town."

"There's so much!" I hiccup.

"I don't know if this is cute or crazy."

"What should I do?"

Snickering, she pulls a pair of headphones from her pocket and plugs them in so nobody can overhear our conversation.

"Start with the pink pack. I'll talk you through it."

CHAPTER 9

Hunter

2008 — cleopatrick

Knocking back a handful of headache pills, I wash them down with a swig of tea from my thermos. Enzo is draining his own coffee as he drives us through the village streets.

We set off for Newcastle early this morning, leaving Harlow still curled up in bed with her thumb buried in her mouth. It was my turn to sleep in her bed last night, but Enzo soon found his way in to sandwich her between us.

He's stubbornly clinging to the idea that we can somehow share her, even after he had to rescue her from some dingy London nightclub. We drove her away with our fighting and he still won't let it go.

I have zero interest in dividing Harlow's attention between us. I want her eyes on me, and me only. We fooled ourselves into thinking we could all have what we wanted before, and it resulted in death.

I won't watch Harlow die.

Not for us fools.

"Ten more minutes."

I drain the last of my tea. "Good. What do we know about this guy?"

"Theo printed his records off." He jerks a finger over his shoulder. "He ran a full background check too. Seems trustworthy enough."

Straining to reach the briefcase in the backseat, I manage to unclip the lock and pull out a sheath of paperwork in a manilla folder. Theo has compiled a full and detailed profile.

Frederick Houghton is a wizened, shrunken slip of a man at eighty-five years old. He's lived at the same address since 1975 and was married for almost sixty years before his wife passed away from bowel cancer.

He has paid his taxes, mortgage and bills, all while serving the local parish and running St Peter's church for his whole career. On the surface, he seems to be a normal, law-abiding Christian. And potentially, our golden fucking ticket.

This could be our big break.

It's come at last.

"Kiera knew Pastor Michaels," Enzo reiterates. "If we can identify him from the congregation, we're in business."

"You think Michaels would risk everything by killing a fellow church member and potentially blowing his cover?"

He shrugs. "Harlow made it clear that Kiera's death was some kind of punishment. I'm betting that Michaels is the one she fell out with."

It feels a little too good to be true. We know that serial killers tend to live in plain sight, often leading normal lives under the alias of their alter-egos. We could be on to him.

"We need to wrap this up fast. I'm not comfortable being this far from Harlow while her father is under the knife."

"Agreed," Enzo mutters.

"She's far too worried about that son of a bitch."

"Theo's there now with the stuff from the pharmacy." He watches the traffic lights change. "He's going to look at that schooling programme with her later."

Pulling my compact black handgun from the glove box, I check it over before slotting it into my holster. Old age pensioner or not, I'm not taking any risks.

The case is too widely known for people not to recognise us. Every single day, the newspapers and airwaves are dripping with criticism. The country is reaching a boiling point. Disgusting hate speech against Harlow and the company is whipping everyone into a frenzied mob.

"You think she'll apply?"

"I have no idea," he replies. "Richards thinks it will be good for her to have some routine. I think it's a great idea."

"And safer, doing it online."

"Exactly."

My phone rings in the pocket of my navy quilted jacket. I clock Giana Kensington's name before answering with a sigh. She'll only keep calling until I do.

"Giana," I answer stiffly.

"Mr Rodriguez. Thanks for taking my call."

"This isn't a good time."

"I've been informed that my ex-husband's surgery was successful," she states. "I'm still registered as his next of kin along with Let—uh, Harlow."

"I'm glad to hear it."

Her voice chills. "Under no circumstances must that man be allowed anywhere near my daughter. Do you understand? No circumstances."

"Giana, with all due respect, Harlow is an adult. She's entitled to make her own decisions about whether or not she wants to see him."

"She won't even return my phone calls," Giana accuses. "She's my daughter, not his. I won't sit here and allow that monster to poison her against me. I want to see her."

"I'm afraid that's up to Harlow."

"Then you will have to convince her."

"No, I won't do that. I cannot force her to speak to you. She's still coming to terms with all that she's been through."

"It's been months. I cannot go on like this!"

Holding the phone away from my ear, I wince as her voice reaches a hysterical whine. My hearing aid buzzes in protest. Enzo is silently laughing, able to hear her ranting.

Returning to the phone call, Giana is breathing heavily, but silent. I clear my throat as Enzo parks up on the curb outside a small cottage, draped in glossy green ivy and winter moss.

"I'll speak to Harlow," I offer her.

"You will? When?"

"No promises. Goodbye."

Ending the call, I tuck my phone away with an annoyed growl. I still don't trust her story. I'll tolerate her for as long as I need to, but that doesn't mean I have to be polite.

The moment Harlow says the damn word, I'll cut Giana from her life like the cancerous tumour she is and ensure that she never bothers her again.

"Having fun?" Enzo snickers.

"She's off her rocker, that woman."

"Oh, she's clinical for sure."

"I don't care what crap is going on between Harlow's parents. They need to keep it away from her."

"Seconded. She doesn't need that stress."

"Apparently, Oliver's operation went well." I straighten my knotted tie and check my reflection. "I'll call Jude on the way back and see when he can be moved to the centre."

"How do you think Harlow will react?"

"Well, he isn't dead. That has to offer her some relief."

Enzo shakes his head. "I don't understand why she wants to hear the scumbag out in the first place. He was an abusive piece of crap who landed himself in prison."

Grabbing my briefcase and voice recorder for the interview, I climb out of Enzo's new Audi and crack my neck. He follows, stretching his trunk-like arms above his head.

"There are two sides to every story, and Harlow's figuring out who to believe." I slam the door shut. "I, for one, want to know what Oliver has to say about Harlow's disappearance."

We crunch up the gravel path that leads to the cottage. Enzo thumps on the door before stepping behind me. If I saw his two hundred pounds of pure muscle hammering on my front door, I'd sure as hell run away.

We don't want to scare the elderly pastor before the interview has even begun. When the door creaks open, it reveals a short, young woman dressed in pressed medical scrubs.

"We're here for the interview," Enzo snaps.

I stifle an eye roll at his bad manners. "Good afternoon. I believe Mr Houghton is expecting us?"

She ushers us inside with a tight smile. "Sure. I'm just taking Mr Houghton's blood pressure. Come through."

The low-ceilinged living room is lit by crackling flames from the open fireplace. The nearby high-backed armchair is occupied. Frederick Houghton waves us in, an open copy of the Bible on his leg.

"Mr Houghton," I greet.

"Gentlemen. Please, sit down."

I stick a hand out for him to shake. "My name is Hunter Rodriguez. You spoke to my colleague, Theodore, on the phone. This is Mr Montpellier."

"Please, call me Frederick," he gushes, pumping my hand. "Helen, bring us some tea and biscuits, will you?"

"We're fine," Enzo interrupts with a forced smile. "If you'll excuse our bluntness, we're on a tight schedule."

He snaps the Bible shut with wrinkled, pale hands. "Well, that's quite alright. How may I help you? I understand you're investigating these dreadful murders."

Opening my briefcase, I pull out a full-page photograph of Kiera. It was taken on her last birthday before her future was ripped away from her. I hand it to the retired pastor.

"Kiera is one of almost twenty victims we're investigating at this time. Do you remember her? We've been informed she attended your church services regularly."

He squints at the photograph. "Such a pity. Kiera was a wonderful woman, so devoted to her faith."

"Did you know her well?"

"Oh, I did. She attended my services for a number of years. The church mourned her loss deeply."

"What do you remember about her disappearance?" Enzo starts the slim recorder to capture our conversation.

"I was interviewed by a couple of detectives at the time."

"We're conducting our own investigation." I sit down in the nearby armchair. "If you wouldn't mind going back over it for our benefit."

He nods, fingering his gold-paged Bible. "Kiera was very active in the church. She helped with a lot of our charitable work. When she disappeared, it was out of character."

"Did you raise your concerns with the police department?" Enzo asks.

"I'm afraid to say the police weren't particularly interested. It was suggested that Kiera was romantically involved with someone, and that she took off without informing anyone."

"And that didn't strike you as suspicious?" I shake my head, disbelieving. "What did the church do to find her?"

"Hunt," Enzo mutters.

Taking a deep breath, I scrape a hand over my slicked-back ponytail. "My apologies, Mr Houghton."

"That's alright." He touches the golden crucifix resting on his clavicle. "A concerned member of the church organised a search party that turned up no results."

Enzo nods, a small notepad in hand. "Do you have a name for this individual? We'd like to interview them."

"Oh, Lee moved away several years ago with his wife."

"Do you have a contact number?"

He shakes his head. "I'm afraid not."

"Going back to Kiera," Enzo redirects the old man. "We've been informed that she had a disagreement with a member of the church. Do you recall this?"

Clearing his throat, Frederick looks uncomfortable. "I wouldn't want to speak out of turn."

"Mr Houghton." I plaster on a fake smile. "All we want is to give Kiera's family some closure. Help us to do that."

"Well, I wouldn't want this *sensitive* information getting into the wrong hands. We're a traditional bunch around here."

It's taking all my self-control not to ram his stupid Bible up his ass. We don't have time for this.

"Sensitive?" Enzo prompts.

He sighs, his brows knitted. "There was a rumour going around that Kiera had been involved with a married man."

That doesn't sound right.

"A member of the church?" I ask him.

"Indeed. This led to a bit of a heated moment between Kiera and the gentleman's wife. If I remember correctly, Kiera was most upset by the accusation."

He's looking back down at his Bible again, his eyes clouded over with the confusion of time. Enzo coughs deliberately, attempting to startle him back.

"Who knows what took place back then," he concludes. "Like I said, I wouldn't want to sully Kiera's name."

I sit on the edge of my seat. "Who did this accusation involve?"

"Lee was distraught when she vanished. He organised the search to find her. I'm sure he felt guilty for the rumour, which Kiera always maintained was false."

Stricken silence ensues.

He… organised the search?

Exchanging loaded glances with Enzo, we both grip our notepads a little tighter. "You're telling me the man accused of infidelity with Kiera, a claim she denied, also organised the search party to find her?"

Frederick nods emphatically. "They moved away from the village not long after Kiera's body was found."

"I need full names and addresses." Enzo flips to a clean page in his notebook. "Everything you can tell me."

Frederick looks taken aback but calls for Helen to return and fetch his address book. I pause for a moment to take a breather and gather my thoughts.

We've worked in this industry for long enough to understand the sickest of minds. Serial killers are depraved, calculating creatures, driven by the most heinous of desires.

Most people don't realise they are also entirely fallible and, ultimately, human. They have to revel in their crimes. It's like oxygen to them. The attention feeds their addiction.

Sometimes, they will insert themselves into criminal investigations, even flaunt their facades in front of law enforcement to seek a twisted thrill.

It's clear that Kiera was devastated by the accusation levelled against her. We know she had no romantic relationships, and I doubt she became embroiled in an affair.

So, what happened?

Was this man involved?

What if it wasn't consensual?

If Pastor Michaels was hiding behind a false identity, he could have hurt Kiera, even imprisoned and tortured her, all while directing a neighbourhood-wide search to locate her. His old base of operations isn't far from here.

Stepping into the corridor, I dial Theo's number. He takes a moment to answer, and I can hear the rumble of the TV in the background.

"Hold on," he whispers.

My heart pounds when I hear Harlow's voice, sweet and sleepy, asking where he's going. Theo mutters something about grabbing a drink before returning to the line.

"Hunt. What is it?"

"How is she?" I ask urgently.

His sigh rattles through the receiver. "The hospital called. She's still worried, but we're trying to keep her mind off it."

"Good. Listen, I need you to send the intelligence department some information. We need an urgent confirmation."

"You've found something?"

"Maybe. I want a full background check on Mr Lee Heston and his wife, Natasha. I'm texting you their old addresses now. They moved away around five years ago."

The tapping of his fingers on his phone echoes down the line as he begins texting the team.

"Do you have a photo?" Theo asks.

"Of what?"

"This man," he clarifies. "You think he's Michaels, right? If we have a photo, we can show Harlow. She'll confirm it."

"We can't do that to her."

"She wants to help, Hunt."

"This won't help her though."

"Actually, I think it will. I'm not sure how much longer she can go on like this, powerless and afraid. It's killing her."

"How is involving her in this bloodbath going to help?"

Theo hesitates. "She needs to be back in control of her own life. I can't watch her sit there, tearing her own goddamn hair out, for a second longer. Let her help."

Eyes screwed shut, I battle the impending migraine that's causing my stomach to revolt. Uncertainty isn't something I've dealt with in recent years. I've always known the right path to take.

Every step is planned, timed and organised to the finest fucking degree of detail. The guys laugh at Kade and his obsessive, control-freak ways, but he's a disorganised toddler compared to the life I lead.

That is, until Harlow.

She invaded my world, set the entire ocean alight and left me on a sinking life raft with no land in sight. I wasn't prepared to lose every ounce of control I've spent years perfecting. It all fell to ruin in the path of her blue eyes and staggeringly sad smiles.

"I'll see what I can do. If it is this asshole, she's going to be triggered. Stay with her until we get home. Understood?"

"Understood," he complies.

"Keep your phone on."

Hanging up the call, I slip back into the musty living room. Enzo's head snaps up as I approach them both, my phone clutched in a white-knuckled grip.

"Mr Houghton, I don't suppose you have a photograph of Lee Heston and his wife?"

Frederick taps his lips with a papery finger. "If I do, it will be in one of the old Parish booklets we distributed at Christmas time. Helen! Come here, dearie."

The weary care worker slinks back into the room. I spare her an apologetic look. She deserves to be paid a hell of a lot more than I'm sure this old bastard is giving her.

Bringing his Zimmer frame in front of the armchair, she helps Frederick stand up on spindly legs. They walk over to the tall, mahogany dresser at the back of the room beneath a pair of ugly net curtains.

Frederick grumbles under his breath as he searches through the drawers, pulling out odd trinkets and scraps of clipped newspapers along the way.

"Maybe I didn't save one, after all." He frowns at a stack of news articles. "My wife used to collect obituaries before she passed on."

"Charming," Enzo comments.

"You'll be old one day too, young man. Appreciate your youth and family while you have it. My wife left me for the Lord's grace far too early for my liking."

Enzo shoots me a desperate look. On a good day, his patience is a shoestring verging on disaster. Perhaps he was the wrong person to enrol for this particular assignment.

"Oh look, my winning scratch card." Frederick hands it to him with a smile. "I won three pounds in 1987. It was quite the excitement at the time."

I watch Enzo faceplant and mouth a pained *fuck my life*. I have to swallow my laughter.

"Ah! There's the ticket."

Flourishing a crinkled, palm-sized booklet, Frederick flicks through the pages with his lips parted. When his expression lights up as he taps a page, I know we've struck gold.

"Here he is," he declares. "This was taken seven or so years ago. Oh, Kiera is in this photo too. How precious."

Enzo snatches the booklet from his hands and scans over it. Lips pursed, he passes it to me and watches as I snap a picture for Theo. I hate doing this when I'm not there to hold Harlow's hand at what could be a pivotal moment.

Lee Heston looked to be in his early fifties, wearing an unassuming, cheap suit and sparkling gold crucifix over his white shirt. His wife, Natasha, wore a demure, flowery dress and a thin smile that didn't reach her eyes.

"Why are you sending it to him?" Enzo asks quietly.

I pull him aside for some privacy. "Harlow's going to check if she recognises him."

"What the fuck? Why?" he exclaims.

"Because she needs to. If not for the investigation, then her own sanity."

"You should have waited. What if she needs us, huh? We're five damn hours away."

"And if Michaels has another girl in a cage right now? Raping, beating and brutalising the poor sod? Can she wait?"

His mouth clicks shut as my phone vibrates with a text message. We both stare down at the two words.

Six letters. Nineteen murders. One living victim… and one chance to finally nail this motherfucker.

Theodore: It's him.

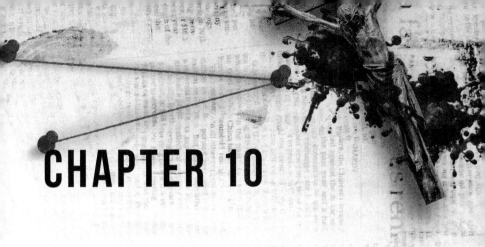

CHAPTER 10

Harlow

Do It For Me - Rosenfeld

Excruciating pain flares through my entire body, twisting and writhing in an inferno of agony. I try to pull my arm from Pastor Michaels' grip, but his knee is pinning my elbow to the stained, blood-slick concrete as he attaches the pliers to my next fingernail.

"I told you to pray, filthy demon spawn," he hisses, hot spittle hitting me in the face. "Why do you defy me? Don't you love your daddy?"

"No! You killed my friend!" I scream hoarsely.

In the adjacent cage, Tia's dirty, bloodstained face is gone. There's nothing left. Just a pummelled, oozing meat salad where her pretty features once resided. Beaten to a crimson paste by Pastor Michaels' ring-laden fist.

On his sneering face, a small cut is spilling blood down his stubble-peppered cheek. Tia's feistier than the other girls… or rather, she was. When he pinned her naked body against the bars and shoved a hand between her legs, she fought back, managing to get in a blow of her own.

It only enraged him more.

I no longer recognise her demolished corpse.

"Please," I beg, my face slick with sweat.

"I have to hurt you." He traces his lips against my dirty cheek. "It's the only way for you to learn, daughter of mine. The Lord spared you, unlike this sinful whore. You're Daddy's special girl."

Tugging the pliers away from my finger in one brutal move, he rips the other fingernail out with a snarl. My voice cracks and the endless screams erupting from my throat fall silent. My face is slick with a waterfall of tears.

"When I bring the next girl down here, what are you going to do?"

The stench of his breath stops me from succumbing to unconsciousness.

"P-P-Pray harder," I wheeze out.

"Good. Now, let's hear those prayers. From the top."

He moves the pliers to my final fingernail, primed and ready for the taking. Blood is seeping across my palm from the other tender, torn-out wounds. The pain is almost numbing, it's so overwhelming.

"Harlow," he warns, tugging on the nail.

"Our F-Father." I choke down a bubble of vomit. "Who art in H-Heaven…"

My head falls to the side, dizzy from pain, and I stare at the place where Tia's eyes used to be. Squelchy, red-slick sockets stare back at me. In my semi-conscious daze, I swear her visible jawbone moves, shifting to mouth an accusation.

"Your fault."

†

Sliding out of the sweaty bedsheets and almost falling to my knees, I battle to remain upright. Hunter groans in his sleep, snuggling closer to my vacated pillow.

He takes a deep inhale of the fabric where my head rested and relaxes with the comfort of my familiar scent sending him back to sleep.

Clamping a hand over my mouth, I stumble as fast as possible for the en-suite bathroom. The door has barely clicked shut behind me before I'm crouched over the toilet, throwing up over and over again.

It's only stomach acid coming out. I haven't eaten anything since yesterday's breakfast. My stomach revolts again, forcing more acid up my aching throat.

When the onslaught finally stops, I curl up on the cold, tiled floor, my entire body slick with sweat and limbs trembling. Nineteen women are screaming inside my head in a deafening chorus.

Your fault.

Your fault.

Your fault.

"Please stop," I whisper to the invisible ghosts. "He k-killed you, not me. I t-tried to stop him... I really did."

Your fault.

Your fault.

Your fault.

"Stop it! Stop!"

Scrambling to my feet, I hoist myself up and make it over to the sink basin. Running the tap as quietly as possible, I splash my face and scrub hard enough for my skin to ache.

I need to get Pastor Michaels' poison out of my pores. It's infecting me from the inside out. Hands braced on the sink, I try to catch the breath that's determined to escape my lungs.

I can't suck it in before it disappears through my fingertips like sand. My head is spinning so fast, I'm on the verge of passing out.

A strange, deep gurgle emanates from the plug hole. The water that just washed down begins to rise back up the pipe, bubbling and spitting, but it's no longer clear.

Crimson-soaked droplets fill the sink basin in a bloodied tidal wave, growing higher and higher. Taking a step back, I cover my mouth in horror as blood begins to spill over the edges, pooling on the tiles.

It's everywhere.

Covering everything.

Red trails leak down the walls, adding to the macabre scene of death. Every corner of the bathroom is stained with the dark tinge of blood.

"Hunter!" I scream.

My back hits the wall as I scratch at my own throat, physically trying to grapple the air and shove it into my lungs. The blood has started to gather into a huge, dramatic crest.

"Sweetheart? Where are you?"

The bathroom door cracks against the wall with such force, the glass pane shatters and collapses into jagged pieces. Bare-chested and frantic, Hunter hops over the mess, his hair sticking up in every direction.

"Harlow?"

I'm scratching so deep into my neck, blood and skin are gathering beneath my nails. The same fingers that Pastor Michaels attached his pliers to, threatening with each sharp rip.

"H-Help me," I stutter.

"What is it? Did you have a bad dream?"

Gesturing towards the sticky trails of blood pouring from every corner of the room, I launch myself towards him before I'm swallowed whole by the devil.

Hunter grunts when I smack into him so hard, we both stumble and hit the towel rack. He narrowly avoids landing in a pile of smashed glass.

"Woah." He runs his hands over my back. "Harlow, I need you to breathe. You're going to pass out if you don't."

"The b-blood!"

He grips my chin tight and drags my eyes up to meet his. "What blood? Where?"

"Everywhere! Can't y-you see it?!"

Heartbreak sizzles across his expression.

"Baby… there's nothing here. No blood."

Tilting my head to the side, he encourages me to look. With tears still stinging my cheeks, I take a tiny, terrified glance around the bathroom. The entire scene has changed.

It's spotless.

Completely, irrefutably spotless.

My chest rises and falls in a bruising rhythm, causing my heart to slam against my ribcage. It's all gone. Not a single speck of blood. Where did it go? Am I losing my mind here? Everything has changed before my very eyes.

"Harlow," he murmurs. "Breathe for me. Come on, like Enzo showed you. There's a good girl."

Easily lifting me up, Hunter exits the bathroom. I'm met by softness as he deposits me on the edge of the bed and kneels in front of me.

His face is laced with uncertainty. It hurts me to see him so afraid, far from the lion-hearted dictator who swept into my hospital room months ago to lay the law down.

I did this to him.

I'm breaking them all.

"Tell me what you need," he pleads, his thumbs circling my bare legs. "Want me to call Enzo? He's at the office with Theo. I can get them both here."

I shake my head. "The b-blood and Pastor Michaels… he killed her. It was my fault… all my fault."

"What are you talking about? Come on, sweetheart. We've talked about this."

"It's m-my fault!" I sob harder.

"Harlow, you did nothing wrong. Watching isn't the same as perpetrating. You couldn't have saved them from him."

I raise a trembling hand and grab a handful of loose hair hanging over my shoulder. Hunter curses as I yank hard, pulling several strands out at once.

The faint *pop* of snapped hair follicles causes pain to race over my sore scalp in a blissful release. More. More. More.

I have to hurt.

Just like they did.

Taking more strands of hair, I dodge his hand clamping around my wrist and pull again—harder, faster, ripping a handful out. When Hunter captures my hand and slips a finger beneath my mane of hair, his skin comes away wet with fresh blood.

"Jesus Christ," he swears in a panic. "Please, tell me what you need. I'll do anything. Just stop hurting yourself."

"No, I need to hurt. He hurt them… I have to hurt as well. Let go of me!"

"I won't," he yells back. "Don't expect me to sit here and watch you tear yourself apart."

More frantic sobs gnaw at my chest, demanding an outlet. His drawn face hardens into a mask of determination.

"You need to hurt?"

"Yes," I choke out. "It's the only thing that works."

"Fine. I'll fucking hurt you."

Standing up, Hunter roughly yanks me to my feet. I almost fall over from dizziness, but he refuses to let me fall. I'm still wearing

Leighton's t-shirt, stolen from his wardrobe as he fell asleep on the sofa downstairs.

Beneath it, I'm only wearing plain panties. My period left several days ago, as abruptly as it arrived.

"Arms up," he orders in a harsh voice.

"What?"

Hunter grabs the hem of my shirt and yanks it over my head. He tosses it over his shoulder without a second glance. I stand beneath his towering, muscled height, my breasts bare and torso scarred with the carving of the Holy Trinity.

"Hunter," I whimper.

He drags a hand down my arm, moving to the curve of my hip. "Do you trust me?"

Hesitating, I muster a timid nod.

"Then let me take care of you. We can deal with this together, without you hurting yourself. I have another idea."

Still gripping my hip, he ducks down and places a gentle kiss against the slope of my stomach. I let my eyes flutter shut as his lips lower, tracing the line of my plain white panties.

Hunter hooks a finger underneath the elastic and pulls them down inch by torturous inch. His warm hand wraps around my ankle, and he guides them off.

"You won't be needing these," he says with heavy-lidded eyes peering up at me.

When he rises back to his full height, I'm completely naked and feeling more than a little vulnerable. Everything is on display. There's nowhere to hide from his fearsome gaze.

"What are you g-going to do to me?"

His mouth hooks up. "Turn around, sweetheart. Hands on the bed."

When I don't move, he wraps his fingers around one of my stiffened nipples and tugs. I gasp at the sudden burst of pain.

"Turn around. Now."

With chills sweeping over my skin, I follow orders and face the bed. His fingertip touches the top of my spine and dances downwards over gooseflesh and vertebrae, leaving a burning trail of heat that pools between my thighs.

"Bend over, little Harlow," he breathes in my ear. "I'm going to give you the pain you're looking for."

My entire body is screaming out for a release, awash with building tension. I want to tear every last hair from my head and bathe in my own blood as penance. Hunter can't save me, no matter what he thinks.

It's too late.

I'm already broken.

Placing my hands on the rumpled sheets, I arch my back, pushing my behind outwards. It feels wrong to expose myself like this, without a single scrap of fabric covering my body.

But instead of fear, anticipation is thrumming through my veins. I can't help my curiosity. Hunter promised pain. Relief. A punishment of sorts. He's toyed with me for months, offering only the barest flickers of affection.

Even if I don't deserve it, I want more. I'm dying to be consumed by him. Controlled. Silenced by a hand other than my own. It's the only light at the end of a very dark tunnel.

I bite back a moan as Hunter's palm strokes my left butt cheek in a slow, tender caress. "Such a beautiful girl."

I'm just relaxing into the soothing contact when his hand slams against my ass in a punishing spank. Pain lances up my spine, setting off exploding fireworks.

Stroking my sensitised skin, I can't hold back a gasp when Hunter hits me again. Harder, against the same cheek, causing thunder to crackle across my entire frame this time.

"Does that hurt, sweetheart?"

"Yes," I pant.

"Do you want more?"

Arching my back more, I push my ass against the hardness tenting his sweatpants. "Yes. Please, more."

He soothes the sting across my skin with another reverent stroke. "Please what, Harlow?"

"Please hit me," I say in a strangled whisper.

"Why, baby?"

"Because… I need it. I need the pain to survive."

He smooths a calloused palm over my other butt cheek. Tingles from his last spank race through my system. When he hits me this time, it toes the line between pain and pleasure. Each aching blow makes my core clench tight.

"I could get used to the sound of you begging," he teases, still stroking me. "Do you want it harder this time?"

"Yes."

"Ask me properly then."

It should be humiliating to be bossed around by him. I don't think I'd let any other man control me with such blatant lust for my submission. But with him? It comes down to trust.

I want to please him and satisfy the demanding creature beneath his human skin. His whispered praise is the tonic to Pastor Michaels' cruel poison. I can't get enough of it.

"Hit me harder, Hunter." I smack a frustrated hand on the mattress. "Stop being gentle with me."

"You're not triggered?" he checks in.

"No. Keep going."

My pulse spikes as his hand snakes around the curve of my hip to dip between my legs. His bare foot nudges between mine, pushing my thighs open. When he cups my mound, I realise how wet I am for him.

"Such a good girl, aren't you?" he purrs in my ear. "You're so wet for me, sweetheart, and I've barely touched you."

Another moan escapes as he slips a skilled finger through my folds. Circling my entrance, sparks of pain race over my earlobe with the light bite of Hunter's teeth.

I gasp loudly when he pushes a thick finger deep inside my slit. His delicious hardness is pressing up against my tingling ass cheeks, separated by the friction of his sweatpants.

"Goddammit, love," Hunter grumbles. "I want to bury my cock in you so badly. Tell me to stop."

I'm panting with need as he slips another finger inside me. The pressure intensifies. Both digits move in a steady, teasing rhythm. His thumb circles my nub with each rotation, adding to the flames of desire.

"I want... I..."

"What do you want?" he coos.

"Everything. I want it all."

His tongue flicks against my ear. "I want to fuck you so bad, Harlow. But I won't do it. Not until you choose me."

"Choose?" I moan.

With his fingers teasing the tender spot that sends sparks across my skin, a traitorous part of me wants to submit. I'm so tired of the fighting. But I can't. I won't do it. Not like this.

Before I burst, Hunter's hand disappears from between my thighs. I cry out, my eyes burning with unshed tears. I'm so overwhelmed. All of these twisted feelings need to escape my body before my sanity finally snaps.

He raises his glistening fingers to my mouth and pushes them inside. "Suck. Taste yourself."

My throat clenches as his fingers glide against my tongue, spreading the salty tang of my own come. I lick over his digits before Hunter pulls them back out.

His hand disappears, ghosting back down the length of my spine. I'm still bent over the bed, trapped and powerless to his divine will. He could do anything to me right now, and I wouldn't give a damn.

"You want me to prove myself? I can make you feel even better than that, sweetheart. Just wait."

My legs tremble as his moistened fingers stroke over my pussy from behind, daring to skate higher. He isn't going to… is he? I try to lift myself, and his hand pushes against my lower back to shove me down again.

"Trust me," he says simply.

Letting the tension drain out of me, I hold my breath as he pushes between my cheeks. The intrusion is nerve-wracking. My instincts are still yelling at me to run as his wet fingertip circles the tight ring of muscle at my back entrance.

"Pleasure can take many forms," Hunter whispers. "I want to know what makes my baby feel good."

"Oh God, Hunt!"

His finger pushes deep inside me, using the coating of saliva to ease the ride. It's a burning intrusion at first. Unwelcome. But when the first flash of anxiety dissipates, the pleasure comes barrelling through me.

"Can you take both?" he wonders.

Rotating his hand, Hunter pushes another finger back into my pussy. With both holes filled, I grip the sheets tighter. It's too much. My entire body is spasming with waves of pleasure.

"Ready to let go?"

"Yes," I mewl.

"Then come for me, baby. Scream my name."

It keeps coming—stronger than the time he teased my orgasm with his lips, or when Enzo tasted me in the kitchen. Even more intense than Leighton toying with me on the sofa.

The tip of his covered cock is pushing against me, feeling like it's going to burst free from its fabric prison. I can imagine how it will feel, sliding deep inside me for the first time.

He drives right to the edge and leaves me to freefall as my orgasm takes over. I writhe and moan, my whole world shattering with the spasms wracking over me. Hunter buries his face in my hair, savouring the power he holds.

"Perfect," he praises.

Carefully turning me over, I'm spread across the bed on my back. His smile is crooked as he adjusts the tight material banded across his erection.

When I try to reach for him, intent on putting the lesson Leighton taught me to use, he brushes my hand aside.

"I don't want anything from you," he says with a smouldering look. "This was about proving a point."

I summon the remaining wisps of my voice.

"You want me to choose you."

His eyes refuse to leave mine. "Yes."

"Just you."

"Yes," he repeats.

An invisible hand chokes my windpipe. "You know I can't do that, Hunt."

His smile drops. "I won't share you. I'm a selfish fucking bastard, and I want you to myself or not at all."

"Not at all?"

"You heard me," he confirms.

Covering my bare breasts with my arms, I pull myself up, needing some space to think. Hunter's expression shuts down into familiar coldness as I inch backwards on the mattress.

"I... need them too," I whisper. "You can't ask me to stop caring about the others. I can't just turn my feelings off."

His feet drag backwards, widening the distance between us. "And what about my feelings, Harlow?"

My hand flashes to my hair and back down again, wracked by indecision. He looks ready to lock me in a brand-new cage. This time, it's one of his construction, shiny and deceptive, where the other pieces of my heart can't reach me.

"I can't let them go," I answer around my rising tears. "I just can't."

"Even if I've fallen in love with you?"

I feel like I've been slapped across the face with a brick. Hunter's eyebrows are drawn together in an accusing frown, and the space keeping us apart feels like an endless ocean.

I suddenly wish Leighton would wake up and come rescue me. Violence clings to Hunter like a second skin, and though I know he'd never hurt me, his words cut just as deeply.

"You're... in love with me?" I repeat.

"I've spent the last five years living the life of a ghost. I didn't know I was capable of feeling such things again."

I have no idea what to say.

He knows it too.

Hunter turns his back and tries to escape. Leaping up from the bed, I snake my arms around his naked, tattooed torso from behind and hold him in place. He'll have to drag me.

"Please don't leave," I whimper against his skin. "I'm so confused, but I know I can't do this without you."

"You don't mean that."

"Hunter." I dive in front of him. "It's true. You have saved my life, over and over again. Nobody has ever cared about me the way you do."

Insecurity flashes through the molten depths of his irises. I draw his lips down to mine and kiss him, unable to find the words to express what I need to say. My wordless desperation is all I have to offer him.

"I'm falling in love with you too," I whisper against his lips. "Don't close yourself off from me again. Please."

His forehead leans against mine. "Fuck, Harlow. All we're going to do is hurt each other in the end."

"I don't care. I'll get hurt if that's what it takes. I need you to stay, but please, don't ask me to choose. You know I can't."

It feels like the entire house is burning to ashes around me as I wait for his answer. I'm silently pleading with an uncaring God to give me this one tiny thing—their patience.

I'll find a way out of this mess because I have to. It's a matter of life and death. Light and dark. Salvation and destruction. Living with them... or dying without them. I can't see any other alternative.

"I know." He sighs, his two hands landing on my shoulders. "Get back into bed. You need to rest."

My eyes dart over to the tangled sheets. "I'm s-scared to sleep. The dreams... they feel so real."

"I can get Leighton instead."

"No!" I raise my voice and cling on tighter. "I don't want him to hold me. I want you."

I don't need to look up to see his smile. I can feel it. He lifts me into his arms and walks over to the bed. We crawl between the sheets together, and I'm settled in the crook of his arm, so he's spooned behind me.

His face buries in my neck. "Sleep, Harlow."

"You'll protect me?" I murmur.

"No one is going to hurt you while I'm here. Not even the nightmares. I'll always keep you safe."

My eyes fall shut, commanded by the authority in his voice. The blood-slick nightmares don't return. Not with Hunter's promise still ringing in my ears.

CHAPTER 11

Leighton

My Hand/Lawless Dream - Matt Maeson

The large conference room in Sabre HQ is bustling with bleak conversation, cracked-open energy drinks and the splash of fresh coffee being poured. It's a bleak morning.

Everyone is here at Hunter's urgent command. Last night, we received word from Derby's police department that a young sex worker has vanished without a trace.

Candace Bernard was reported missing by two friends when she didn't return from a job. They saw her leave with a customer around midnight and called the police the next morning after searching for her.

What they found terrified them.

That's when we were called in.

Her skimpy, sequinned dress was found in a nearby alleyway, covered in fresh blood. A note was tucked into the pocket with a written message and a hand-drawn calling card—the Holy Trinity, etched in fresh ink.

Surrender, Harlow Michaels.

Or the next death is on you.

Harlow has barely spoken since we broke the news. There wasn't even a glimmer of satisfaction when Enzo agreed she could attend this emergency meeting. He's determined to do right by her and fix his mistakes by keeping her in the loop.

The Anaconda and Cobra teams have gathered, plus the whole intelligence department. Everyone involved in the case so far has been put on high alert by this violent development.

"I don't think I can do this."

Harlow's voice is cracked with fear.

"We can go in together," I offer.

She lingers behind me, bouncing on the balls of her feet, which are cloaked in thick-soled leather boots to protect against the February chill. Her usual skinny jeans and sweater seem rumpled, like she got dressed without paying attention.

I tug her closer until she collides with my chest. Harlow buries her face in my grey t-shirt, her breathing unsteady.

"Hunter, Enzo and Theo are all in there with the teams. It's safe. We're going to deal with this together."

Her head shakes. "Every single one of them is thinking the same thing; the longer I hide, the more death there will be."

"You know that isn't true."

"Isn't it?" she scoffs.

"Nobody here is going to let you fall for this sicko's trap. This is part of his game. We can't play into it."

Catching her wrist as her fingers attempt to tangle in her long mane of hair, I push them aside before she can begin pulling. Harlow glances up at me, her shining blue eyes filled with embarrassment.

"I have just the thing." I press a soft kiss to the corner of her mouth. "Let me try something."

Pushing back my coat sleeve, I reveal the collection of elastic hair ties I've been wearing around my wrist on a daily basis. Her eyes widen as I take one and gesture for her to turn around.

"How long have you been carrying those around for?"

Taking three big bunches of her hair, I begin braiding. "A few weeks."

I work fast as the plait begins to grow in length, stretching down her back in a corded rope of hair. Tying it off with the elastic, I drop a kiss on top of her lowered head.

"I figured that if it's out of your way, you won't be tempted to pull without realising."

Harlow turns around to stare up at me, her eyes brimming with sparkling tears. One dares to leak down her cheek, and I use my thumb to gently brush it aside.

"What did I do to deserve you?"

"Plenty," I reply easily. "If you need to take a breather or it gets too much, poke me and we can step outside. Deal?"

She summons a smile. "Deal."

Taking Harlow's hand, I tuck her into my side. We enter the room together and approach the table where Enzo and Theo are talking in low, urgent whispers. They both fall silent and look up at us.

"Good morning," I say cheerfully.

"What are you so chipper about?" Enzo stares at me.

"Just trying to lighten the mood. I had a great sleep last night, snuggled up with Harlow. You should work late more often, Enz."

His glower deepens. "Hilarious."

He looks like he wants to obliterate me with his stare alone. Since their little excursion to Newcastle earlier this month, Enzo's been working most nights alongside Kade and Theo to gather information on Michaels' false identity.

Pulling out the chair next to Theo, I guide Harlow into it before she can have second thoughts and bolt from the room.

She shoots Enzo a strained smile and wraps Theo in a quick, tight hug. To my surprise, he hugs her back, his eyes closing briefly. Enzo watches on with his own smile.

"You okay?" she asks Theo.

"Been better. We worked through the night."

"You need to sleep." Harlow glances at Enzo too. "And you. The pair of you look ready to keel over."

"We're fine, little one," Enzo offers as he knocks back more coffee. "Sleep can wait for when we find this girl."

"I'm sorry I wasn't there when Hunter told you last night," Theo apologises. "I couldn't get away."

Harlow shrugs it off. "I understand."

"Things have been crazy for the last few weeks, and now all this shit too. We must have a stack of books to discuss."

She helps herself to a mug of tea. "More like a whole bookcase. I've been reading lots."

Avoiding the empty seat next to Enzo, I take the other end of the table, where he can't beat my ass for rubbing last night's cuddle session in his face.

He really does look like shit. The dark circles beneath his eyes are full-blown thunder clouds, while his untidy mop of jet-black hair is getting unruly as it awaits a needed haircut.

"Did you complete the registration for online school?" Enzo asks her.

Harlow takes another sip and nods. "Theo helped me do it while you were away last week. Basic Maths and English for now. I want to catch up on what I missed."

"You'll do fine," I reassure her.

"We'll see about that."

Silenced by a flash of bright-blonde hair and two scarred arms circling her neck from behind, Brooklyn draws her into a bear hug, squeezing before quickly releasing.

"I didn't know you were coming," she greets. "Are you doing okay with the news?"

"Peachy," Harlow replies. "How are you? Aside from the case. I feel like that's all I've thought about."

Helping herself to our cafetière of coffee, Brooklyn rolls her eyes. "Oh, you know. Planning a wedding to five dickheads is a challenge. Hudson wants to hold it in a graveyard."

"You're kidding?" Enzo chuckles.

"He thinks it'll be ironic." Brooklyn gestures towards the table where Hudson and Kade are conspiring. "I'm seriously outgunned as the only female."

"Do you want some help?" Harlow asks uncertainly.

Brooklyn's face lights up. "You'd do that?"

"I know absolutely nothing about weddings, let alone planning one. I'm happy to give it a go though."

The squeal she makes is so unlike Brooklyn, I clamp my hands over my ears. This woman has slaughtered whole rooms full of people without blinking an eye, yet here she is getting excited about choosing wedding flowers.

"Blackbird!" Hudson bellows.

The Anaconda team and intelligence department fall silent as they watch her turn, a hand propped on her hip. Becket pauses halfway through showing Rayna and Fox something.

"Yes, Hud?" Brooklyn beams.

"Mind keeping the screaming down? You, Phoenix and Eli

fucking like rabbits kept me awake last night."

Rather than blushing like a sane human being, Brooklyn's grin widens. "Hey, we invited you and Jude to join in."

"That is not the mental image I need this early in the morning," Enzo grumbles under his breath. "Brooke, go deal with your fiancé before I throw up."

Winking at us both, Brooklyn thumps away in her tightly laced, patent leather Doc Martens. Ethan, Becket's second-in-command, wolf whistles as she passes.

"That's my future wife you're checking out." Hudson shoots him a death glare. "I'd shut up if I were you."

His smile drops. "Oh, uh. Sure."

"That's what I thought."

Breaking their standoff, the door to the conference room slams shut. Hunter storms in, flanked by our PR agent, Lucas. Both are dressed in pristine suits and wearing identical grim expressions.

"Sorry we're late."

"Everything okay?" Enzo frowns at him.

Hunter pulls off his jacket and gun holster. "We're moving the building to level three security with immediate effect."

He stiffens, reaching for his own weapon. "What happened? Are we secure?"

Lucas pours himself a coffee. "There was a leak from Derby's police department."

Enzo's head thumps on the table. "Fuck."

"Every newspaper in the country has a copy of Pastor Michaels' note printed across its front page this morning."

"With Harlow's name included?" Theo asks.

Hunter nods, his jaw clenched.

"There's also a protest being staged outside." Lucas drains his coffee with a wince. "The media has turned up to film it and a crowd's gathering already."

"P-Protest?" Harlow stammers.

Hunter clears his throat. "We're facing increasing pressure to capture the killer… or give him what he wants. Pastor Michaels has a number of supporters."

Her face turns white. "Me."

"That's not fucking happening," Enzo barks. "They'll have to tear the building down to get their hands on Harlow."

"Nobody is suggesting we do that," Hunter placates him. "These lunatics are exactly that. Lunatics. We ignore them."

Mumblings of agreement sweep over the room. Humans disgust me sometimes. Giving Michaels what he wants won't stop the killings, no matter what the media prints.

He will continue to slaughter and terrorise the country, even with Harlow back in his possession. Rule number one in prison? You never give a bully what he wants because they will keep taking until you've got nothing left.

Harlow sacrificing herself won't keep people safe. She would lose her freedom, and her life, for nothing. Our biggest job is convincing her of that fact, not the public.

"We've tripled security. The protest is contained," Hunter explains. "Let's move on to the case. Where are we at?"

Enzo shuffles through the paperwork. "We know Michaels cleaned house in his previous kill site and left Rosetta's corpse behind. He must be holding this victim in a new bolt hole."

"Why speak up now?" Kade questions.

"It was only a matter of time," Hudson finishes for him. "He killed Rosetta Stone to cover his tracks, and an accomplice is an unnecessary risk. Her death didn't sate him."

"No, that's not right," Harlow disagrees.

She catches herself and flushes red, her lips pursed. Rather than scold her as she seems to be expecting, Hunter smiles and gestures for her to continue.

"Well, he relied on her for everything." Harlow fiddles with her nails. "Mrs Michaels did all the dirty work. Killing her didn't make his life easier. She was his biggest asset."

"Then why do it?" I ask the room.

Raising a hand, Rayna waits for Hunter's nod of approval before speaking. Her purple hair is loose today, spilling over her oversized sweatshirt and tight leggings.

"He didn't just kill Rosetta," she explains nervously. "It was a message. He didn't even take her wedding ring with him. It's like… he wanted Harlow to find her."

"For what purpose?" Hudson growls.

Twirling the end of her braid in a trembling hand, Harlow looks at me. I raise a single brow, asking if she wants to leave. Taking a deep breath, she shakes her head.

"Did he want us to identify Rosetta?" Brooklyn suggests. "We're missing something. He wants us to know whatever that is."

"Or whoever she is," Theo finishes. "Rosetta is the key to his past. He's taunting us."

"To what end?" Hunter sighs.

"Well, we have a theory. My contact in government was useless, so I… uh, went in search of answers elsewhere."

He stares at Theo. "What did you do?"

"I might have hacked the High Court's criminal database and looked through some sealed case files."

"Might have?" Hunter exclaims.

"It was… an accident?" Theo offers.

"Jesus Christ. You are costing me a fortune in legal bills. The High bloody Court, Theo. This is serious!"

"I know this is serious," he answers evenly. "That is exactly why I did it. We need answers that no one can give us."

"There are only so many times I can stop your stupid ass from being thrown in prison on computer misuse charges."

"I was careful," Theo defends. "Nobody even knows that I infiltrated their system. Easy peasy, lemon squeezy."

"No, it's not. You're a loose cannon!"

"Hunt," Enzo says calmly. "Hear us out."

"You were in on this too?" Hunter accuses.

"We needed to test if our theory was right," he replies before glancing at his accomplice. "Fill them in."

Smoothing his blue flannel shirt and tight, faded-grey jeans, Theo connects one of his laptops to the projector. A series of images are painted across the empty back wall.

Four old, peeling cardboard boxes of paperwork have been emptied out to be manually scanned. The array of evidence is vast, all sealed by the court's authority.

"An estimated eight hundred children's homes were operational between the fifties and nineties," Theo explains. "This was before the government cracked down, facing lawsuits and allegations of severe neglect."

He moves to the first image. It's a black-and-white shot of a four-story manor house. Dark vines of ivy creep over the antiquated bricks, and the sinister structure is surrounded by a thicket of towering trees.

"Genesis Home for Wayward Children."

"This was the place?" Hunter clarifies.

"Rosetta spent four years here. It was a Catholic-run orphanage that has been implicated in countless cases of child abuse and sexual violence."

"Why haven't we heard of this scandal?" Ethan speaks up as he studies the images. "If government funding was involved, we should've heard of the fallout."

"None of this is public knowledge," Theo responds. "The victims reached a settlement and the clean-up initiative buried everything, including this court case."

"Any prosecutions?" Kade asks next.

"The home was managed by a string of well-paid Catholic churches." Theo checks his notes. "Several priests were liable for prosecution, but they bought off the defendants."

I study the images. "Do we have a list of the victims?"

"Negative. It's safe to assume that Rosetta Stone was not among them. She left custody and shed her identity to avoid being dragged back there."

One hand stroking his beard, Hunter listens while sparing Harlow glances every few seconds. He seems desperate to keep his eyes on her at all times.

She's also studying the projected photograph of the children's home with creased eyebrows, as if the grainy pixels will reveal the secrets of the universe if she stares for long enough.

I shuffle closer to her. "What is it?"

"The answers are all in that place." She shakes her head. "What is he trying to tell me? Why leave Rosetta behind?"

"I don't know, princess."

"It's just another dead end, isn't it?'"

"That's not exactly true," Theo intervenes. "We may have found someone who worked on the original investigation in the eighties."

"What? How?" Hunter urges.

"We did some digging around with a police contact," Enzo

answers for him. "A retired constable got back to us, but he's unwilling to go on record."

"Even the superintendent refused to touch this place." Hunter eyes them both. "Who on earth did you speak to?"

Neither answers him.

"Does this have anything to do with the missed calls from my father?" he continues in a lower voice.

"We did what we had to." Enzo clears his throat. "Whether this guy goes on record or not, he has information about that place. I'll get it out of him."

Hunter's eyes narrow. "You involved my father."

"All we asked for was a contact."

"That's fucking involving him!"

"It was a calculated risk," Enzo defends.

Turning his back to take a breath, Hunter mutters a colourful curse. I sure as hell am not getting involved in anything to do with our parents. Fuck that.

When Hunter turns around, I can see he's buried his annoyance for a private bollocking later. Theo gulps hard. He's going to get shafted for breaking the rules.

"We have a lead on Michaels' false identity," he redirects. "What information have we uncovered about Lee Heston?"

"Not a lot," Theo admits. "No birth certificate. There's a record of his marriage to Natasha in 1983. Their address was half a mile from the church that Mr Houghton ran."

"Nothing else?" he pushes.

"No registered employment. The house was rented from a private landlord who was part of the parish. They were quiet, unassuming. No reason for anyone to suspect their lives were a sham."

"Do you think he would go back there to hide out?" Becket asks from his table. "Given the chapel has been uncovered."

"Unlikely," Hunter dismisses. "Let's send a team to Newcastle to search the property regardless." He looks at Hudson and Kade. "Take forensics with you."

Kade quickly nods. "We'll leave today."

"I'm sorry, but how is murdering nineteen women quiet and unassuming?" Brooklyn interrupts angrily. "Someone should've caught this guy years ago."

"Brooke." Kade rests a hand on her shoulder. "We have no control over what the police did back then."

"So what? We can't be angry? He was living a happy fucking life while Harlow was locked in a basement."

"That's enough," Hunter scolds.

"No, it's not. How was he allowed to get away with this for so long? Now another woman is about to lose her life."

"I said enough!" he shouts at her. "Harlow is here, and she doesn't need to hear this right now."

"Don't tell me what to fucking do!"

Brooklyn storms out of the room. Kade hesitates for a second before chasing after her, leaving Hudson to shrug.

"She's pissed about the news report."

"What news report?" Harlow speaks up.

Everyone looks uneasy. I know that the Cobra team is protective about their past. Sabre is a pretty accepting place, but even here, people talk. They prefer to keep it private.

"A few newspapers are running some old stories about us." Hudson stares at his clenched hands. "I tried to stop her from reading them, but you know what she's like."

"Motherfuckers," Enzo curses. "The minute they see our name in the press, the vultures come circling."

"They'll move on soon enough."

Brooklyn's outburst makes more sense. She can't protect her family from the cruel bullshit that the newspapers print. Just like she couldn't protect Harlow from this sick bastard.

Where people she cares about are concerned, her temper runs incredibly hot. Brooklyn loves deeply, and it comes out as rage. That's how she shows her devotion, through violent, territorial friendship that would scare most people.

Theo touches Harlow's hand and recoils when she shudders at the contact. She's closing in on herself, hugging her stomach tight and staring down at the table.

"Someone should have stopped him," she agrees hoarsely. "If not the police, then me. All I did was watch."

Hunter turns away again, looking on the verge of a furious meltdown. He's really struggling to be professional today.

"I don't know how we can convince you that none of this is your fault." Enzo sighs. "You weren't responsible."

It's the same crap that my mum shoved down my throat before she knew what I did to Thomas Green. I didn't believe her. This is different, but the same thing applies.

"It doesn't matter what we think, does it?" I try instead.

Harlow looks up at me, her eyes wide.

"What matters is how you feel about it, not us."

She nods in acknowledgement. Enzo slumps in his chair, defeated. For a smart guy, he can be a hard-headed idiot when it comes to Harlow and her emotions.

"I know I could have done more," she admits. "Regardless of what you think. Every single person protesting out there is thinking the same thing."

"What do you need to let this go?" I propose.

The whole room is watching our exchange with bated breath, including Hunter from the corner of his eye. Even Enzo is waiting for her answer.

"Justice," Harlow decides.

Hunter's phone rings at the worst possible moment. He answers the call, listens, and swiftly hangs up.

"Giana is here for her second interview. I forgot to cancel it last night." He looks at Harlow apprehensively. "You don't have to speak to her with all this going on. We can postpone."

"No, I need to see her. The rehab unit keeps calling. I can't speak to my father until I hear Giana out first."

"Harlow," Enzo warns. "I don't think—"

"I'll be fine," she cuts him off.

He bites back whatever macho bullshit he was about to suffocate her with. I think the gruff idiot is finally learning.

"I can come with you," Theo offers.

She doesn't flinch this time when he takes her hand. I first noticed their blossoming friendship when he ate pizza with us. It's the first time I've seen Theo initiate contact with anyone.

"Let's get it over and done with." She tightens her grip on Theo's hand. "Will you interview her after?"

Hunter nods. "Yeah. Go first."

Smoothing her sweater, Harlow bends down to press a kiss to my lips in front of the entire damn room. My chest burns with pride as both Hunter and Enzo glare daggers at me.

"Wait for me?" she whispers.

"Like I'd go anywhere without you. Good luck with Giana. Be strong."

"I'll try my best."

Before she can follow Theo out, Enzo thuds around the table to reach Harlow. She squeaks as he bundles her into a back-breaking hug, her head barely reaching his ribcage.

"Remember, you don't owe her anything." He smooths her braided hair. "Just shout if you need us."

"I will, Enz."

"I mean it."

She crosses her finger over her chest in a silent promise. Enzo gives her a secret smile before kissing her forehead.

"I won't hesitate to toss her outside by her hair if she upsets you. With fucking pleasure."

"I know," she murmurs back.

When Enzo releases her, Hunter completes the ridiculous show we're giving the whole room by sweeping her into a bear hug. God knows what everyone will think now.

"Enzo's right." Hunter kisses her temple. "Get what you need, but don't let her make you uncomfortable."

"Guys." Harlow struggles to break his suffocating embrace. "I'll be fine. I just want to ask her a few questions."

"Hug her any tighter and I'll need to call an ambulance," Hudson heckles them. "Run while you can, Harlow."

Grinning, she pecks Hunter's fuzz-covered cheek and slips out from between his muscled arms. Theo offers her his hand again and the pair exit the room together.

Enzo rounds on me. "What the fuck were you doing in her bed last night? While she was upset, no less."

"What were you doing in it last week?" I counter, checking no one is listening. "Or Hunter over the weekend?"

Hunter scrubs his face. "This is ridiculous."

"She isn't going to choose," Enzo hisses at his partner. "Get on board, or let us move ahead without you."

"I am not having this conversation here," he fires back. "We have work to do. Candace's friends are waiting to be interviewed."

Hunter walks over to the Cobra team as Brooklyn and Kade return from the corridor. Her expression is hard and pissed as hell, but she looks a little calmer.

"You think he'll come around?" Enzo sighs.

I glance up at him. "Hunter? Doubt it."

"If we don't compromise, this is only going to end one way. I won't let Hunter fuck up our chance with Harlow."

"Enz, I can't pretend to understand a single thing that goes on inside my brother's head. We can only hope."

"I don't believe in hope."

"Real optimistic of you."

"I'm going to win him over," he vows.

Slapping his shoulder, I help myself to another coffee. "You better start plotting. Good luck. You're going to need it."

Enzo harrumphs. "Fucking watch me."

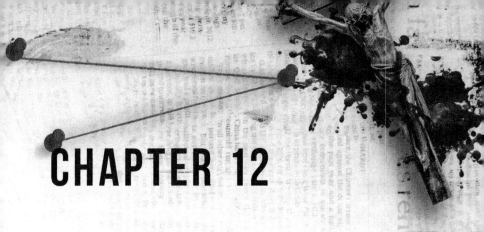

CHAPTER 12

Harlow

Pray – Ready the Prince

Sitting on the overstuffed brown sofa, I attempt to focus on the task at hand rather than the fact that another innocent woman is being stripped, beaten and tortured right now.

Candace Bernard.

Another name across my heart.

The clock hanging on the wall in the interview room is ticking loudly, worsening the anxiety gripping my throat. Every second is another slice against her skin, another bruise, another rape.

Pastor Michaels is laughing at us.

We're losing this endless fight.

Hearing voices down the corridor, I scrub my face and take a deep breath. I haven't seen or spoken to my estranged mother, Giana, since the incident in Devon last year.

Being reunited with her and confronted by the picture-perfect family she's created was traumatising. I've had zero desire to repeat the experience, but with my father back in the picture, I can't hide from the past for much longer.

I need to know her side of the story before I can consider giving my father a second of my time. He's done nothing to earn it. My relationship with Giana may be rocky, but I owe it to her to hear her out. That's only fair.

The door beeps with a security pass being scanned. I force myself to take a deep breath as it swings open and Theo's headful of blonde ringlets enters the room.

He shoots me a look and mouths, *"Breathe."* All I can do is nod, unable to speak. Following behind him, Giana's green eyes immediately land on me.

Bouncy brown hair hanging loose over her shoulders, she's wearing a smart cream blouse and pressed trousers, paired with shining court heels. She's even wearing lipstick.

"Harlow," she gushes, dropping her handbag. "I saw the news last night. I've been calling and calling—"

"I know," I interrupt her. "I wasn't ready to talk."

She tries to mask the hurt on her powdered face. "I understand. Last time we spoke, things didn't end well."

"That's one way to put it," Theo mutters as he takes a seat in the corner. "I'll be right over here if you need me, Harlow."

I cast him a grateful smile. "Okay."

Giana narrows her eyes on him with a look of displeasure that bothers me. So much of the bad feeling she sparks within me is silent. It defies explanation, but something about her doesn't sit right. I wish I could remember why.

Yet, I was the first one at my father's bedside. I've forgotten him too, but my instincts guided me there. I know I'm missing something important in this tale. The truth is right there, and it's up to me to solve the riddle.

"Sit." I gesture towards the chair opposite.

She takes a seat, crossing her legs at the ankle as she sweeps her perceptive eyes over me again. I'm sure I look different. I've put on a few more pounds, and my arm is healed now. The way she studies every single detail makes my skin crawl.

"How have you been?" she asks nervously. "That poor girl, and those people out there… you must be feeling so…"

"I'm fine," I deadpan.

"Well, we should talk about what happened."

"I don't want to talk about Devon. That's not why I asked to speak to you."

"I wanted to apologise," she continues in a rush. "I'm sorry you were overwhelmed. That's the last thing I wanted. I know you've been through a lot."

"A lot?" I repeat.

"Well… yes."

"I want to know about the man who turned up half-dead at our front gate. You said my father was gone forever."

Giana twists her fingers together. "He's been missing since he was released from prison. Frankly, I was happy for him to stay that way."

"How could you say that?"

She looks startled by my tone. I'm not the same person she met, trembling and afraid in her kitchen. I've donned a new mask today, one I've spent months perfecting.

"He's still my father," I reason.

"That man is nothing," she spits. "He has no right to hold that title. I raised you myself, not him."

"Why?"

"He was abusive, physically and emotionally. You were too young to remember most of it."

Looking away from her, I stare at the potted plant in the corner of the room. It's drooping, shrivelled, gasping for a single drop of sustenance.

Theo's pretending to be immersed in his laptop, but I can tell he's listening to every word. His eyes briefly connect with mine, but he doesn't smile. It's a silent show of support.

"Abusive how?" I ask carefully.

"I'd rather not go into specifics."

"Then why did you come here?"

Her bottom lip begins to wobble. "What has gotten into you? I thought you'd be happy to see me."

Swallowing the nausea crawling up my throat, I try to lift my mouth in a smile to appease her, but it doesn't come. Imprinted over her face is another. The only mother I can remember. She's stolen that title and won't give it back.

Mrs Michaels.

Only, my memories have warped and changed. Gone is the caustic lash of her voice, the hammer of her fists, my bones crunching beneath her boot.

Now, I see a scared girl, abandoned in a children's home and left to flee from a violent man with a Bible. I've been that girl too. I hate how this bloodied cord now binds us.

Rosetta.

That's her name. In death, she's earned herself something. The confusing paradox of my pity. But that can't be right. Monsters don't deserve our pity.

Do they?

Her wedding ring still rests beneath my mattress, protected from harm. I get it out daily and spin it around my pinkie, remembering the glimmers of goodness coming back to me now.

Hunks of bread.

A cup of milk.

Once, a meagre bar of soap.

"Harlow!"

I nearly leap from my chair. Giana has leaned forward, a hand resting on my jittery leg.

"You zoned out," she says with a frown.

"I'm sorry, got distracted."

"It's like you couldn't hear me. What happened?"

I can't help but reach for the flyaway strand of hair that's escaped my braid. When she looks away to adjust her blouse, I quickly tear it out and brush it aside.

"It happens sometimes."

Her frown deepens. "Are you still seeing that therapist?"

"How do you know about him?"

"I'm your mother. It's my job to know these things."

That tastes like a lie. I don't know why, but I don't trust her intentions. This so-called concern doesn't ring true.

"Going back to Dad," I deflect.

Head lowering, she rubs her temples. "The truth is, I was planning to leave him before you were taken from us. He was a heavy drug user. Heroin mostly."

My throat closes up.

That's what he overdosed on.

"Why didn't you?" I ask more gently.

Giana flicks invisible lint off her leg. "You were so young, and we didn't have any money. I was trapped."

In the corner of the room, Theo's phone buzzes with an incoming phone call. He mutters an apology and slips outside to answer it, leaving us alone.

"What happened after I was taken?"

"Your father spiralled out of control in his grief." She sniffles. "He began forging identities to buy more drugs. The abuse got a lot worse until he was arrested."

I'm not sure what drives me to reach across the coffee table and take Giana's hand in mine. She looks up, surprised, but flourishes a smile of appreciation.

"When the authorities caught up to him, it was a relief. He was convicted, and I tried to rebuild what was left of my life."

Her fingers are gripping mine, and I note the sparkling diamond band wrapped around her ring finger. The reminder is a sharp slap around the face.

She rebuilt.

Her life continued.

My anger comes racing back, justified or not. I can't see past it. I suddenly regret initiating contact with her.

"You made yourself a new family."

"I never stopped searching for you," she insists. "We didn't just forget about you."

"I've seen my gravestone, Giana."

Her face falls at the formal name.

"You buried me after the police closed my case. Life continued, and you let everyone forget I ever existed."

Her hand tightens around mine. Sharp nails bite into my wrist. At first, I think it's an accident.

"How old is your son? Does he know that he has a half-sister?" I blink away tears. "Does he care?"

"Ulrich is just a child."

"So was I."

Giana's emerald eyes narrow on me. "It's my job to protect him.

He's too young to understand all this."

"Protect him?" I laugh weakly. "Like you protected me?"

"I am not the bad guy here, Letty."

My wrist is searing with pain. Her nails are cutting into me so deeply, I can feel blood welling up. Still, she doesn't move to release me. It's on purpose.

"Stay away from your father," Giana orders me. "Do not visit him. Do not speak to him. No contact. Understood?"

Teeth gritted, I wrench my arm backwards. Her nails slice across my skin with the move, but I manage to separate us, rubbing my sore wrist. Crescent-shaped marks are left behind.

"It's a little late to start protecting me from monsters, isn't it?" I say in an empty voice. "Thirteen years too late."

"You need to listen to me."

"I don't need to do anything for anyone, including you. I'm sorry, this was a mistake. I'll leave you to your interview."

"Please! Don't go."

Tears are sliding down her cheeks, matching the sparkle of her diamond wedding ring.

"I'm begging you for a second chance," she pleads. "I want to fix our relationship."

"You can't."

She tries to grab me again. Standing up, I dance backwards, running from the flames of her deceit before I'm burned again.

A better person might forgive her. Maybe they'd even admit that she was put in a shitty situation. Giana simply made the best of the rest of her life.

I'm not a better person.

I don't believe those things.

While I can't control the decisions she has made, I can control one thing—who I choose to forgive, and how. Right now, I'm not ready to reconcile with her. That's my choice.

"That's it?" She stands up and tries to follow me. "Months of silence, and that's all you have to say to me?"

When I look over my shoulder, she's watching me with soaked cheeks, her hands clenched into fists.

"I'm sorry that I'm not the person you hoped for. I know that must be hard for you. But more than that, I'm sorry Leticia didn't come home."

Escaping before she can answer, I quickly close the door behind me and slump against the frosted glass. The tears spill over as my facade finally crumbles.

I'll never be her daughter.

She'll never be my mother.

There's too much water under that bridge for us to cross it now. I'm not willing to risk drowning in the current as I attempt to swim back into her perfectly ordered life.

Glancing up and down the thickly carpeted corridor, I spot Theo in front of the tinted, floor-length window adjacent to the elevators. He's staring outside, his phone forgotten.

Approaching him, I rest a hand on his flannel-covered shoulder. He startles, his blue eyes colliding with mine. The palpable fear and anxiety there makes my stomach churn.

"What's wrong?"

He glances outside. "This is bad."

The roar of shouting and rhythmic chanting penetrates through the tinted, bulletproof glass protecting us from sight. We're on the tenth floor, closer to the ground than where I've spent most of my time here.

Outside, what Hunter described as a small protest is in fact a furious mob. Countless people are being held back by temporary metal railings and the brute force of Sabre's security team.

Placards are waving in the air, accompanied by frenzied chanting, even some scattered prayers as they call up to the heavens in desperation. Fanatics and protestors blur together.

"End the slaughter!"

"Who is funding this investigation? The taxpayer!"

"Hand her over! Save our streets!"

"Oh my God," I breathe out.

Theo's hand takes mine. "We're safe up here. They can't breach the perimeter."

"I don't understand why they're doing this."

"People are afraid. They're grasping at straws." He pushes his glasses back up his nose. "The media is a powerful force."

One man is screaming at an agent who attempts to push him back. In his hands, the placard shows a wide-angled shot of a pretty, young woman with curling red hair.

My heart somersaults behind my rib cage. I recognise the woman from the police report that Hunter showed me on his phone last night. Candace Bernard. Our missing girl.

"I did this," I whisper to myself.

"This wasn't you," Theo combats. "It was the devil."

"Are we so sure the devil isn't in me too?"

He gently turns my shoulders, tearing my gaze from the army demanding my head on a stake. Behind his glasses, crystalline blue eyes are cracked with unease.

"We will never let them take you."

"Wouldn't me disappearing solve all of your problems?"

Hesitating, his hand slides higher. "No."

He holds the back of my neck, drawing me even closer until I'm pressed against the flannel of his shirt. I can taste the thick tension sizzling between us.

"It wouldn't," he finishes.

Closer still, the scent of antique books and peppermint rolls off him in an enchanting wave. I'm drawn into the warmth of his embrace as my arms wrap around his narrow waist.

Theo stops breathing, his eyes darting from side to side. I wait for his anxiety to pass. I know he can't control his reaction.

He gradually relaxes against me. His lips are close enough to taste, but I can't cross the chasm between us. Not yet.

"Do you want to get out of here?"

"What?" I laugh awkwardly.

"Let's just leave. Me and you."

"But… it isn't safe."

My mouth falls open when he lifts the flap of his shirt, wearing a smirk that looks foreign on his face. He's wearing a loaded gun holster attached to his belt.

"I may be a techie, but I can still keep you safe." Theo lets his shirt fall back down. "Let's get out of here."

Anticipation travels down my spine.

"And go where?"

His thumb slides along my jaw, featherlight and exploring. He lifts my chin so that my lips are exposed to him and leans closer. Our mouths are almost touching.

"I'll go anywhere with you. Anywhere but here. We can leave the death and destruction behind for one night."

My eyes fall shut as his lips brush against mine in the most excruciatingly light touch. It's almost imperceptible.

"What about the case?"

"I'm not the only person working for Hunter," he replies in a whisper. "They can find someone else to boss around and treat like shit. I'd rather be with you."

His thumb is still stroking my cheek, even as his lips retreat. Pain rips through me at the loss of contact. I want more. So much more.

"What have you got to lose?" he challenges.

My eyes stay shut with implicit trust.

"Nothing. Let's go."

CHAPTER 13

Theo

Fantastic – Blame My Youth

"**A**re we safe?" Harlow asks again.

"Nobody saw us sneak out of the back entrance. They were too busy protesting in front of the media's cameras."

She worries her bottom lip with her teeth. "I don't know about this. The entire world knows my face."

Reaching out, I tug the beanie lower on her head. Between hiding her face and the darkness of night, her identity is well concealed.

Unlike Hunter and Enzo, nobody knows what I look like. My seclusion from the world is strategic, beyond my social anxiety. I don't want to be known or seen. I'm much happier working in the background.

"Not much further," I console.

Harlow's beginning to drag her feet after walking for a couple of hours in the phosphorescent glow of London at night. We pass red phone boxes, double-decker buses and the roar of drunken students exiting packed pubs.

I'm sure Hunter has the entire intelligence department looking for us by now. He won't get anywhere. I built that team myself, and I know their pitfalls by heart.

When I joined Sabre, I took great care to make sure I could leave undetected if needed. For many years, I didn't trust Hunter or his motives in recruiting me.

He swooped in and saved my life when I was staring down the barrel of a fifteen-year prison sentence. To me, that was far too good to be true. That's why my phone and laptop run off invisible redundancy systems that I coded myself.

They're impenetrable.

Not even Rayna, whose coding skills rival mine, could hope to infiltrate the systems I've installed to protect my privacy.

"Where are we going?" she questions.

"I want to show you something."

Harlow's arm links with mine. "We're going to get thrown in the back of a dark van at any moment."

"Hunter won't find us." I let her snuggle closer. "I might have sent the team a false location ping on the other side of the city. That should keep them busy for a while."

She looks up at me beneath her cute purple beanie. "You sent them on a wild goose chase, didn't you?"

I shrug it off with a smile. "Hunter should know that you're safe with me. We're both adults, and I think we've earned ourselves a break."

"Yeah, he's going to kill you."

"He's certainly welcome to try." I direct her across a quiet street, slick with rain. "I could hack into his car's control system and blow it up from across the world."

"You could?" she squeaks.

"Probably with my eyes shut."

Checking up and down the road, I spot the deserted, age-spotted building I'm looking for. It screams of abandonment, but I'm not afraid to approach the derelict structure.

"People with real power don't talk about it," I explain. "We leave that to the Hunters of the world. Everyone knows his face. Nobody knows mine."

"That's exactly how you like it, right?"

My chest burns with a strangely warm feeling. It feels weird to be seen by someone, and not fading into the background, unnoticed and forgotten. I'm stunned that I like it so much.

"Right. I like to be invisible."

"Doesn't it get lonely?" Harlow queries.

We pause on the pavement, trapped in a bubble amidst the hustle and bustle of England's capital. Nobody can find us here, lost in the darkness and steady patter of falling rain.

Her sparkling blue eyes stare up at me, wide with curiosity. She isn't repulsed by my awkward social skills or inability to function like a regular human being.

Harlow sees… me.

Unfiltered and unafraid.

That's what has drawn me in from the beginning and strengthened my determination to serve her justice. What began as a professional endeavour has grown into a full-blown, unhealthy obsession to know every inch of her mind.

"Yes," I reply honestly. "It gets lonely, and for a long time, I was perfectly fine with that. I wanted to be alone."

"And now?"

I startle from staring at her lips and meet her eyes again. She's looking at me like she can peel my skin away from my bones, unveil the darkest depths of my soul and drag out the entrails for her own examination.

"Now what?" I respond.

Her mouth quirks in a smile. "Do you want to be alone now, Theodore?"

Fucking Christ, the way my body tingles when she uses my full name. I want to kiss her right here in the middle of the damn street.

"I don't know anymore. Not right now, I don't."

Harlow nods. "Me neither."

Taking a leap of faith, I take her hand from my arm and let our cold fingers tangle together. Her smile bulldozes any misgivings I have about being vulnerable.

"Then it's a good thing we have each other."

"I guess so," she agrees.

I don't need to be scared of her. Harlow understands me in a way that few people do. She sees beneath the veneer I've painted on, and she isn't running away screaming.

"Where are we?" She looks up at the building. "This looks like a quiet spot for a murder. Did we have to walk all this way for you just to kill me?"

I reach for the heavy padlock bolting the metal door shut. "You're not getting out of this that easily."

"Well, there goes my plan for an easy exit."

Inputting the code into the rusted dials, the padlock unlocks and falls into my hands. I tuck it in my pocket and check the street before wrenching the iron door open.

"Need a hand?"

"I've got it." I gesture for her to step into the darkness. "After you."

Harlow tentatively peeks inside at the cloying shadows and heady scent of damp. "Um, are you sure?"

"Just trust me. You're safe."

Taking a deep breath, she nods and sinks into the impenetrable darkness. I heave the door shut behind us and lock it from the inside, checking the three locks I installed to the interior. Nobody's getting in.

"Theo?"

Harlow's voice is high with fear.

"Hold on, beautiful."

Activating my phone light, I illuminate the narrow, brick-lined alleyway. Harlow zips to my side and burrows close to me, her breathing a little unsteady.

For someone who grew up in darkness, she's developed an incredible fear for her natural habitat, despite a part of her seeing it as home. I guess that's the same for all humans.

We like to shed our skins and pretend like we've moved on from the past, even as it burrows beneath our bones, ready to emerge again when we least expect it.

There's no avoiding the inevitable realisation that we're all just a little too broken to forget. No matter how hard we try.

"What is this place?" she whispers.

Leading her down the corridor, the whistling wind grows louder. Bare lit bulbs hang from wires attached to the ceiling, left behind when construction work ceased two decades ago.

"When I joined Sabre, I was on the verge of being convicted for computer hacking," I reveal with a wince. "This was eight or so years ago. I was nineteen at the time."

"Wait, who did you hack?"

My cheeks flush in the dim light.

"I worked for the cybersecurity department in the Ministry of Defence. During a routine check, I came across a hidden partition in

JROSE

the server, full of classified information."

"What happened?"

"Turns out the department head was selling privileged information on the black market to the highest bidder."

Her hand tightens in mine.

"He was getting paid to protect a cartel moving illegal weaponry through London. Probably earned a small fortune while others were killed with those same guns."

At the end of the gloomy alleyway, we reach a metal grate protected by a keypad. I lean close to punch in the ten-digit code and heft it aside, revealing a steep set of concrete stairs.

"After you," I invite with a wave. "Anyway, I needed to prove what I suspected before taking it any further. If he was dirty, who knew if anyone else was involved, right?"

Harlow takes the first few steps, gripping the rusted handrail. I drag my eyes from her tight ass waving in my face with each step, sculpted through her skinny blue jeans.

"Let me guess, it went further than that?"

"And some." I follow her up, my chest tightening. "I hacked into his hard drive and compiled years' worth of evidence. Fraud, corruption, taking bribes. He'd done it all."

We emerge into a cavernous space, our voices echoing off the cold bricks. Harlow is rooted to the spot as I locate the nearest industrial switch and reboot the generator.

"When I took it to his superior, I was arrested and thrown into a prison cell. Senior management was in on the whole thing. I'd stumbled into a criminal conspiracy by accident."

The abandoned, half-constructed London Underground platform is lit by dim, yellow light as the power comes on. It stretches out all around us. The tunnel was sealed long before I came across this place on a dark web auction.

Down the platform, clusters of glimmering lights reveal the remains of a rusted carriage, forever frozen in time. Inside, the destruction gives way to a miniature home.

"Do you live here?" Harlow gasps as she looks around. "This is insane."

"I don't live anywhere. Sometimes, I need to get away from the world. I bought this place years ago. According to public records, it doesn't exist."

Her unease forgotten, Harlow steps inside the furnished carriage. I installed strip lights along the ceiling, framing the small kitchenette and a sagging, mustard-yellow sofa.

"You sleep here?" she asks, aghast.

"There's a bedroom on the other end, behind the partition door. Bathroom too. Mr Talahan in the gym above us knows me. I'm hooked up to his electric and water."

"You're stealing from him?"

Dropping my backpack and plugging the portable space heater into a socket, I laugh off her snap judgement.

"More like I hacked his competitor and fucked with their payment system. They closed down and went into retail instead. Mr Talahan kept all of their customers."

"Theo!"

She sounds horrified, but when I glance up, Harlow is grinning from ear to ear. Hell, she looks fucking impressed.

"You really don't care, do you?"

"About what?" I ask with a shrug.

"The law. I didn't believe Enzo when he told me that. You seem so... uh, normal. Law-abiding."

Setting the heat to high, I wrench the carriage doors shut to block out the wind's current. It'll warm up in here soon.

"It took years of court battles and looking over my shoulder for my name to be cleared and the conspiracy dismantled," I answer her. "Hunter and Enzo saved my life. Not the law."

Tugging off her purple beanie, Harlow pulls her braid over her shoulder. She begins to poke around the space, and I feel like I'm lying on a shrink's sofa, under examination.

She's inspecting the most private corners of my life in here. Nobody knows I own this place. It's the last bit of respite I have in a loud, overwhelming world full of people that trigger my social anxiety.

Dragging her fingers over the spines of books I have stored on a shelf fitted to the low ceiling, she studies the different titles. Fuck, I should've hidden the comic books.

"You wanna eat?" I ask, hoping to distract her.

She's engrossed as I pull the two ham and cheese subs from my backpack that we picked up en route. Setting them down on the cluttered table, I shift on the balls of my feet.

She still isn't speaking.

Have I blown this shit?

What am I even doing?

This wasn't some elaborate plan to lure her down here, away from the others. She was in pain, and I wanted to fix it. This is the only way I know how. Hiding until it stops hurting.

"What are the odds of the others finding us?" She breaks the silence with an old, dusty book in hand.

"Zero."

"That's the point, right?"

"Pretty much." I chuckle.

Harlow turns around to face me across the carriage. "Why are you showing me this, Theo?"

Spasming with nerves, I inch closer. She stands stock still as I ease the book from her hands and place it down. There's only a scant breath between us.

Her sweater is brushing against my flannel shirt. She's biting her lip again. I can't maintain a safe friendzone when she looks at me like that.

"Because I want you to know me," I answer in a low rasp. "The real me. Not many people do these days."

She brushes her fingers over my chest, still staring up at me with wide eyes. "Then tell me who the real Theo is."

I awkwardly gesture around the space—comic books, old cereal boxes, second-hand coding manuals and a thick coating of dust, wrapped in a coffin of loneliness.

"I am, this is him."

"A closeted comic book nerd, who eats stale cereal, hacks people for a living and hangs out in an abandoned train station on his own?"

I can't help but grin at her.

"Pretty much, yeah."

Her fingers are tangled in the material of my shirt. Unable to help myself, I pick up her braid and stroke my thumb over the plait. Her hair is so soft, and it smells amazing, like jasmine shampoo and fresh blossoms in springtime.

"How do I know you're not wearing a mask?" Her eyes search over me. "Just like the rest of us?"

I let my hand travel to the back of her neck, tilting her head upwards. "We can't always live in our masks. Every now and then, we have to take them off to breathe."

"And this is where you do that," she answers for me.

"Precisely. If you want… it's where you can do the same."

Her eyes narrow. "You think I'm wearing a mask?"

Closer still, I let our noses brush. "I think you've been wearing one since the day we found you. I think you're wearing one right now. I think... you don't know how to live without it."

"You're wrong. I'm not hiding."

But she is. I'm the only one that knows it.

"I know about what you did to Enzo's car," I blurt out.

Ah, fuck. That was a secret I had no intention of bringing up. I really need to stop interacting with other humans.

"The c-car?" she stammers. "What are you talking about?"

"It was you. Or at least, a version of you."

Her blue eyes are blown wide with a heavy dose of fear. "I have no idea what you're talking about."

"You're the one who trashed it."

Whether she believes me or not, a part of her knows. I can see the truth dancing in her eyes. Her dissociated mind just locked those memories away, along with everything else.

"But it was those people."

"What people, Harlow?"

"The people!" Her voice rises, bordering on hysterical. "The ones that worship Pastor Michaels... his fan club. Enzo told me about them sending emails and stuff."

"A couple of anonymous troublemakers sending shitty emails because they have nothing better to do?"

"Yes, them!" she insists.

"It wasn't them. Believe me."

Harlow sinks down on the small sofa and buries her face in her hands. Every inch of her is trembling like a leaf. This is where the mask meets reality, and it's never a pleasant sight.

I crouch in front of her and rest my hands on her knees to gain her attention. Her cheeks are wet with tears, and she touches them in confusion. Even her body knows what's happening.

"I've torn the hospital's CCTV systems apart," I spell out. "After leaving physiotherapy on the ninth floor, you snuck away and headed downstairs alone."

She shakes her head again. "Stop."

"There was maintenance work taking place in the reception." I ignore her. "Nobody noticed you swiping a small can of red paint that they were using to freshen up the place."

"I didn't do this… I would know."

"From there, you took the elevator downstairs and ducked beneath the single CCTV camera. You don't reappear for almost ten minutes, sweating and without the paint can."

"Theo, stop it! I don't believe you."

"From there, you take the elevator back up to see your father, stopping at a bathroom to wash up on the way. When Enzo caught up to you, he was none the wiser."

She's having a full-blown panic attack now. *Shit. Great job, Theo. Awesome work.* I reach up to cup her cheeks, my thumbs stroking beneath her screwed-shut eyes.

"Breathe, Harlow. You're not in trouble. I just wanted to know if you remembered or not. The others don't know what I found when I checked the surveillance."

"W-Wasn't me," she falters.

"I'm not wrong, beautiful. It was all there. But I know that it wasn't you who did those things."

"Then who w-was it?"

"Your mask," I say simply.

Tears stream thick and fast down her pink cheeks as she shakes her head from side to side. I should've known this wouldn't be an easy pill to swallow. That's why I kept her secret. She didn't need the guys obsessing over this.

There's nothing worse than realising that no matter your best efforts, you are not in control of your life. Mental health is too fucking cruel for that to be true.

We're all victims of its violent tide, rising and falling to an unchanging rhythm, no matter how loud we scream for it to stop. That Godless infliction doesn't listen.

"You can't remember when you escaped from the chapel, right?" I point out.

"N-No."

"Or chunks of time inside the cage?"

She peeks a bloodshot eye open. "No."

Her tears soak into my skin, stinging with the harsh lash of grief. I can feel her pain slipping beneath my skin, poisoning what's left of my nonchalance. I hold her even tighter, hard enough to creak bones.

"Why can't I remember these things?" she keens.

"Because it's too much. Your mask is keeping you safe. Like it did for all those years in the cage that you can't remember."

"You mean... d-dissociating?"

I nod. "Yeah. Richards talked to you about this?"

"A little. I can't control it."

"I know, it's okay. We can figure this out. But first, I need to ask you something else."

She looks afraid, peering up at me. "What is it?"

"Do you remember telling me that you killed Laura?"

Face draining, Harlow shoves my hands away. If I wasn't blocking the carriage, she'd be running at full speed to escape above ground.

"It's okay," I quickly placate. "We can talk about this."

"No," she weeps. "H-How? I didn't... I..."

"You told us on the way home from Northumberland. None of us have wanted to bring it up since."

Chest rising and falling with each panicked breath, she shakes her head. "No… no… I didn't say anything!"

"Just breathe. You were pretty out of it at the time."

I feel awful for ripping the rug out from under her feet, but we're already down the rabbit hole. Her periods of dissociation are dangerous. Ignoring it won't help us.

"You told me that you killed her. Why do you think that?"

Her oceanic eyes meet mine. "I did."

"It was Pastor Michaels. We all know that."

"After he performed the ritual… she was bleeding out," Harlow says in a choked whisper. "She was in so much pain. I didn't want to, but she begged me to make it fast."

The realisation connects all the dots that have been bothering me for some time. Suddenly, so much of her destructive, guilt-ridden behaviour makes sense.

Hunter was wrong.

She did it. I believe her.

"You're telling the truth?" I double-check.

Harlow manages a nod. "It's true."

My mouth clicks open and shut. I thought she was rambling on the plane. None of us thought she ended Laura's life. I feel sick at the thought that she's been struggling with this alone for months.

Laura's life was already earmarked for death. That's not the same thing as killing. Harlow isn't the guilty one. She's spent all this time blaming herself for someone else's brutality. Her actions were merciful.

"Why didn't you tell us this before?"

"I… I didn't want you to know that I k-killed her," Harlow sobs. "I wrapped my h-hands around her throat and squeezed until she s-stopped breathing. It w-was me."

"She was already dying. You gave her peace."

"So? I still ended her life!"

Leaning in, I rest our foreheads together. I want her closer, beneath the protective sarcophagus of my skeleton, where she can't hurt herself any longer. This is exactly why I kept my distance. Already, it's too late to turn back.

After losing Alyssa, I vowed to never again allow myself to care about someone. I stayed away from Harlow to stop that from happening, but I can't watch her go through this alone. Regardless of the fear screaming at me not to get involved.

"You did not kill her," I say emphatically. "Pastor Michaels did. You saved her from something far worse."

"I n-never wanted you guys to know."

"I promise you that I'm not judging you. Don't worry about that. Worry about forgiving yourself first."

"Forgiving myself?" She laughs weakly. "I deserved to be the one left rotting in a cell, not Laura. She should've gotten out instead of me."

"That's complete crap."

"You can't tell the others," she urges. "Please."

"They need to know. We can help you get through this. And frankly, they've probably already figured it out."

Harlow cusses, her eyes scrunched shut.

"Let me help," I plead again.

"The only way you can help is if you tell me that you hate me," she demands. "Tell me this is all my fault. I need to hear it."

"That's never going to happen because it isn't true."

"Then why am I here? What do you want from me?"

I carefully pull her up, banding an arm around her back so she doesn't topple over. She's pinned against me, and I can feel every stuttered intake of her struggling lungs.

"Because I care about you, and I won't watch this world break you any more than it already has."

Her lips part on a cry. "I'm not yours to protect, Theo. You need someone who can make you whole."

"Who are you to say that you're not that person?" I reason with her. "That's my decision to make. Not yours."

Before she can run, I finally take the risk I've spent months wrestling over and let all of my fears melt away. I've spent the best part of six years running from the possibility of grief and allowing that same loss to dictate my future.

I'm tired.

I'm alone.

I'm fucking done.

"Can I kiss you?" I ask awkwardly.

Harlow's bottomless eyes widen, flecked with surprise.

"You d-don't have to ask," she stutters back.

My lips seek hers out, securing our mouths together in a frenzied panic. I feel like she's slipping through my fingers, even as I grip her arms tight and let our mouths collide.

Harlow tastes exactly as I imagined she would—the sweet, terrifying taste of hope, dawning on a shadowed sky. That light reveals all of the damage inflicted in the dark, but with it comes the chance to begin again.

She's kissing me back.

Over and over again.

Running my hands over her body, I touch the curves I've longed to explore for the last six months. The times I've imagined doing exactly this don't bear thinking about. I never thought it would actually happen.

JROSE

With more confidence than I expected, Harlow pushes me backwards. My legs collide with the nearby sofa. I slump on it, and she follows, placing a leg on either side of my waist.

Her arms wind around my neck, drawing us back together. When her lips land on mine again, the heat has grown unbearable. Our tongues touch, hesitant at first, before tangling together in a pleasured waltz.

She must be able to feel how fucking hard I am for her right now. I can't remember the last time I even slept with a woman. There were only a handful of hook-ups after Alyssa.

I stopped pretending to be even remotely human a long time ago and quit one-night stands in favour of complete isolation from the human race.

Breaking the kiss to gasp for air, Harlow's mouth is bee-stung and swollen. I run a thumb over her bottom lip, feeling my cheeks and neck burn with a fierce blush.

"I wasn't expecting that."

"I'm sorry," she rushes to apologise.

I stroke her jawline. "Don't be. I've been thinking about doing that for a long time. It's a good thing you did it before I could chicken out again."

Smiling sweetly, she rests her head against my collarbone. I tuck her closer to my chest and cuddle her tight, drinking in the reassurance of her weight on top of me. She isn't leaving. The world didn't end because we finally kissed.

I can't lose her.

Not now, not ever.

I was wrong, for all this time. Pretending like keeping my distance could protect me from heartache, even as I stock-piled evidence to fight her case and obsessed about her from afar. It was all a delusion.

She was under my skin long before I started playing this futile game. All I've done is hurt us both by avoiding the chance of something good, something pure, in favour of letting fear rule my life.

No more.

"Harlow," I murmur against her hair. "I know you've got shit going on with the others too, but I need you to know that I really care about you."

"You do?" she whispers.

"I don't just want to be your friend. I'm not sure where that leaves us, but I thought you should know."

Her head doesn't lift. "I'm tearing your family apart, Theo. You can't care about me. I'm going to ruin your lives."

I force her to look up at me. The tears are back, helpless and afraid. I brush them aside, the salty proof of her anguish soaking into my thumb pads.

"I want you to ruin my life," I tell her.

"What?"

"Please ruin this miserable, lonely life that's slowly choking me to death. Please. I'm begging you to hurt me."

Her lips twitch in the tiniest of smiles.

"This is going to end in disaster," she predicts.

I kiss her again with so much certainty, it unnerves me.

"I really fucking hope so."

CHAPTER 14

Harlow

Hard To Be Alone - Barns Courtney

"Harlow? Can you give me a hand?"

Enzo's voice carries through the open front door, where cold, rain-laced air is leaking into the warmth of the house. He's already brought in three bags of food, alcohol and ice.

Apparently, there's more.

"Coming," I shout back.

Putting the last bottles of flavoured vodka on the packed countertop, I tighten Leighton's lemon-scented hoodie around me and head back outside into the falling rain.

Enzo is smiling today, his mood improved by the newly repaired SUV parked in the driveway. It came out of the shop last week, much to his delight.

"How many people are coming to this party?" I cringe at the mere thought.

He grabs another two bags from the car. "All of us, Brooklyn and her lot and Hunter's folks. We're a big bunch."

"Hunter's parents are coming?" I squeak.

His amber eyes pin me to the spot. "Well, it is their son's thirty-fifth birthday. I couldn't not invite them."

"Does Leighton know about this?"

That's when his smile drops.

"Well, the surprise is for both of them."

I pinch the bridge of my nose. "Hunter's going to kill you for throwing him a surprise birthday party. Now, you're saying Leighton has no clue they're coming either?"

"He has to see his parents sometime," Enzo rationalises as he closes the boot. "It would've happened at Christmas if shit didn't go down. He can't put this off forever."

"I don't think you've thought this through."

Balancing several more armfuls of alcohol, Enzo nudges me to head inside. "Like you didn't think through running off with Theo two weeks ago and giving me a heart attack?"

"I thought I already apologised for that."

Slipping off my Chucks, I pad back into the messy kitchen. Hunter would have a heart attack of his own if he saw the chaos in here in preparation for tonight's family reunion.

Leighton is on his way home from meeting his parole officer, and Theo's in charge of delaying Hunter at work until everyone arrives. This whole thing was Enzo's idea. It's been hard to carve out family time amidst the recent chaos.

I had no clue it was even Hunter's birthday. I feel crappy about that. Things have been rough since the latest girl was snatched, and Pastor Michaels is being suspiciously quiet about it, beyond his initial note.

We're all on edge. The guys are working overtime to hunt down any potential clues before it's too late, not to mention working on the false identity lead. Hunter's birthday didn't even scratch the top ten of things I'm worried about.

Unpacking the whole bag dedicated to crisps and dips, I accidentally drop a tub of hummus. It explodes across the tiled floor, and Enzo immediately bursts into laughter.

"Shit," I curse. "I'm so sorry."

"Language, little one. We're going to start a swear jar for you soon."

"Bite me, Enzo. I'm nervous, alright?"

Dodging the mess, his intimidating height towers over me. He backs me against the marble breakfast bar, his wide hips pinning my back to it as his huge, calloused hands circle my wrists.

"Is that an invitation?" he purrs. "I don't mind biting."

My breath catches. "Maybe."

"We're home alone." Enzo trails a fingertip down the uneven slope of my nose. "The party doesn't start until later. What trouble can we get up to in that time?"

"Brooklyn's coming around to help me get ready." I writhe to escape as he pins my wrists to the marble surface. "We need to clean up before then."

"Fuck the mess. I know what I'd rather be doing." His fire-lit eyes search my face. "Tell me, how was it?"

"H-How was what?" I stutter.

"Your kiss with Theo the other week."

I feel myself turn beetroot red. Enzo reads the truth on my face without me having to say a traitorous word.

"So, it did happen," he concludes smugly. "Thanks for the confirmation. I was wondering what his intentions were when he smuggled you away from us."

"I d-don't know what you're talking about."

"No need to get all shy and squirmy. You know I'm in favour of us pursuing a shared relationship. Kiss him all you want."

I buck and pull, attempting to break his hold, but I'm completely stuck. Enzo chuckles as he stares down at me.

"You want to share me," I point out. "Hunter wants to murder you all, and Leighton wants to steal me away. Theo is the only one acting like a sane adult about this."

"Sane?" Enzo lifts a thick eyebrow.

"Yes! Unlike you testosterone-fuelled idiots, bickering over whose turn it is to do what. That's why I left with Theo."

Nose nudging mine, Enzo takes a sharp inhale. "So, you've chosen him? Is that what you're saying?"

"I haven't chosen anyone, and I'm not going to do that to your family. Besides, I didn't think you wanted me to."

"I don't," he fires back. "Hunter thinks he's the one keeping this family together right now, but he's wrong."

I gasp quietly as his leg slides between mine, nudging them open until the denim of his jeans is pressed up against me. I'm tingling from the slightest of touches at the moment.

"In fact, he couldn't be more wrong," Enzo murmurs, his lips meeting my ear. "You're the one keeping us all together."

"That isn't true."

"But it is. I'm scared that if you choose…"

"It will all fall apart," I rasp.

"That's what Hunter doesn't get. He has never been more wrong about anything in his life. The sooner we make him see that we all belong together, the better."

"And what about what I want?"

Eyes darkening with desire, Enzo's lips crash against mine in a heart-pounding kiss that scrambles my thoughts. When he releases me, I feel a tingling warmth gather down low.

"I know exactly what you want," he utters. "Say the word, little one, and I'll bend you over this breakfast bar and fuck you so hard, all of London will hear."

My legs turn to jelly, until his solid weight is the only thing holding me up. Every inch of honed muscle that builds his powerful frame is pressed against me in a cruel taunt.

"I want to bury my cock so deep inside of you, not even Hunter could argue that we don't belong together."

"And then?" I practically pant.

Enzo's teeth sink into my earlobe as he kisses his way around to the slope of my exposed throat.

"Then I'll own every inch of you. Those three knuckleheads can watch as you're dripping in my come, head to fucking toe."

The hard press of his erection is rocking against me, driving my pleasure higher and higher. The anticipation is torturous. I want everything he's said and more.

On the verge of agreeing to an impromptu fuck amongst the dips and melting ice, the security system buzzes with an alert as the front door clicks open. Enzo doesn't move an inch, even when Brooklyn steps inside.

She's shaking rain from her choppy blonde hair and leather jacket. Bellowing our names, she peeks into the kitchen and freezes.

"Am I interrupting?"

"No," I retort.

"Yes," Enzo cuts me off.

Grinning, Brooklyn kicks off her usual Doc Martens and hitches the backpack she's wearing higher on her shoulders.

"I'll be upstairs setting up," she says with a wink. "Don't keep her for too long, Enz. We have hair and makeup to do. Phoenix and Eli are coming soon with the speaker system."

"Bloody party," he grumbles.

"Your idea," I remind him.

With an eye roll, Enzo releases me and takes a step back. "Brooke, didn't we discuss you being a cockblock before? I don't need Hunter's permission to fire you."

She's already halfway upstairs. "You know the company would crumble without me!"

"But it would be a damn sight quieter," he adds. "Go on then. I'll sort this shit out and wait for the others to arrive."

Standing on my tiptoes, I peck his stubble-strewn cheek. "Don't forget to clean up the hummus."

His annoyed cursing follows me upstairs. Closing my bedroom door, I find Brooklyn rifling through my wardrobe, her belongings haphazardly deposited everywhere.

"I know that you hate doing hair and makeup." I sit down on the end of the bed. "So, why the ruse?"

She scrutinises my clothing with a frown. "You were about to be mauled by Enzo. I was doing you a favour, trust me."

"How so?"

Turning around, her smile is devious.

"Would you take your driver's test in a monster truck?"

"Excuse me?" I splutter.

"Your first time is always a bit awkward. I'd advise choosing a smaller, *ahem*, model. Hell, Hunter is probably gentler in bed than Enzo's caveman ass."

"Brooke! Oh my God."

"What?" She cackles. "This is what friends are for, right? I figured we'd have this talk soon, though I'm surprised they've behaved for this long."

Grabbing one of my pillows, I flop backwards and cover my head with it. Every inch of me is on fire. The bed bounces with Brooklyn's weight falling next to me.

"Hey." She pulls the pillow from my head. "Trust me, now's the time to ask questions. Once they know you're fair game, things are going to move very fast."

"We are so not talking about this."

Her playful expression grows serious. "If anyone has pressured you, I will personally hospitalise them with a baseball bat. Just say the word."

"It's not like that. No baseball bats."

Brooklyn turns onto her back. "Fuck, there go my plans for this evening's entertainment. What's stressing you then?"

Twirling a strand of hair between my fingers, I fight the urge to pull it out. "Whoever I choose to sleep with first, it's going to send a message to the others that I've chosen."

"And you don't want to do that?"

"Of course not."

"Just checking," she snickers.

"No matter what, I'll end up hurting someone. I'd rather be alone than put any of them through that kind of pain."

"Pain happens, whether you think you're in control or not," she says seriously.

"That isn't comforting."

Her smile is bittersweet. "You want my advice?"

"Always."

Grabbing my hand, Brooklyn squeezes tight. "Take exactly what you want and never let go, because this world will tear you apart. It's your job not to let it."

"What if I want... all of them?"

She smiles again, and the devil rears its threatening head within her. Confidence gleams in the silver flecks of her eyes, unapologetic and ready to dance in the dark.

"Trust me, they're yours," she whispers conspiratorially. "I think they were from the moment you met."

The strength of sheer determination in her voice steels my spine. I nod back, feeling my own demonic smile rise. Brooklyn squeezes my hand again before releasing.

"Come on, we need to sort that mess out on your head." She gestures to my rain-mussed hair. "Now, I have no fucking clue what I'm doing, so bear with me."

"You can't be any worse than me."

"Wanna bet?"

She bounces off the bed and begins setting up various appliances, glaring at each one as she attempts to figure out a game plan. The nerves set in fast.

I don't like people touching my hair, but more than that... I don't want her to see the damage. I'm sure she knows. They all do by now. But knowing and seeing are different things.

"I think I'll be fine," I blurt out. "Let's just leave it, yeah? Everyone's attention will be on Hunter anyway."

With a curling tong in hand, Brooklyn shoots me an unreadable look. "Harlow, I am the absolute last person you have to worry about judging you."

"It's not that."

"Then what?" she quizzes.

Trapped, I rub the pain in my chest. "I... um, I... fuck."

She arches an eyebrow. "Yes?"

"Fine, you're right. I'm worried about you judging me."

Pulling out the armchair tucked into the corner of my room, that

Hunter once insisted on sleeping in, Brooklyn pats the cushion with a weirdly patient smile.

"You're safe with me," she reassures. "I'm better qualified than most to understand this shit. I'll be gentle and avoid the bad areas. We don't even have to talk about it."

"Promise?"

"Always," she throws back at me.

With a breath for courage, I take a seat and stare straight ahead at the wall, avoiding my reflection. She picks up a hairbrush and begins to comb through the snarled knots.

"Yell at me if I pull too hard."

"Got it," I grit out.

Working her way around my head, she's surprisingly gentle, holding the long length at the root to avoid tugging. I force myself to breathe, focusing on each painful inhale.

"You got an invite too, huh?"

"What?" I reply in a daze.

Her finger appears over my shoulder to point towards my desk in the corner of the room. The memorial invitation rests on top of my journal, tucked back inside its envelope, hand addressed to me.

"Kade told me about it on the phone last night. He's on his way back from up north with Hudson. Forensics are tearing the Michaels' old house apart now."

"They haven't found anything?" I check.

"Not yet. Some other family's been living there for the past five years. They're going to do a thorough search though."

"It will be another dead end."

"You don't know that yet," Brooklyn disputes. "So, are you going to go? The memorial's next month."

"Laura's brother asked for me specifically. He wants me to give a eulogy or something. It was on the invite."

"Well, it's going to be a pretty private event, now he's got the whole… you know, body back."

"Why would he even invite me to come?"

The curling tong beeps as it heats to full temperature, and she begins sifting through the layers of hair on my head.

"You were the last person to see her alive," she guesses. "He probably wants to meet you for that reason."

The pain in my chest intensifies.

"You were on the plane with me on the way home at Christmas, weren't you?"

"I was," she answers neutrally.

"So, you heard… what I did."

"That you killed her? You said something about it."

I recoil like I've been whipped. Since hearing how much my broken mind has been hiding from me, I've been feeling sick to my core. I can't trust myself at all.

"You believed me?"

Brooklyn sighs as she fiddles with a curl. "I've hurt enough people I care about to know what it feels like. I looked in your eyes. I knew you were telling the truth."

"Is it sick I'm glad you believed I was capable of doing that?" I ask honestly. "Sorry. I'm just struggling to know what to believe at the moment."

"We're all sick," Brooklyn says with a laugh. "If that makes you feel better, then sure. I believed it."

Somehow, it does.

She's never underestimated me.

"But I'm not here to judge anyone for how they think or feel," she remarks. "Especially not my friends."

Looking straight into the mirror I've been avoiding, I find her eyes boring into me, the curler forgotten. I didn't want them to know, but on some level, I'm glad.

The mask has slipped.

My control has frayed.

The secrets that've been eating me up inside are out there now, and I can finally confront them. I know Brooklyn won't let me do it alone. She's a good friend like that.

"Then how do I face Laura's brother?" I croak. "I'm the reason he no longer has a sister. How do I stand up and read a eulogy like it wasn't my fault?"

Placing the curler down, she moves around the armchair and kneels in front of me. Her hands grip my knees, and I'm held prisoner in the ferocious emotion of her gaze.

"You stand up there knowing that you granted Laura the last shred of control she had left," Brooklyn says fiercely. "You gave her what she wanted when everything else had been ripped away from her. That's how."

"But… what if you're wrong?"

"About what?"

"What if I killed her because I'm a monster, just like him?"

She reaches up to brush a tear off my cheek. "You're human, Harlow. All humans are monstrous. Some of us just hide it better than others."

"Including you?"

"Especially me," she replies flatly. "I've done some fucked-up shit. Trust me when I tell you, there isn't a bad bone in your body. I'd know if there was."

"You seem confident." I laugh nervously.

"I sure am. Shall we finish this hair then?"

With a shuddered breath, I nod. "Let's do it and crack open the vodka downstairs before everyone arrives."

"You got it."

Before she can stand up, I grab her hand. "Brooke?"

"Yeah?"

"Thanks for not running away screaming from the crap inside my head. I'm glad you're in my life."

Her smile is lopsided. "Not much scares me, so you're in luck. I'll always have your back."

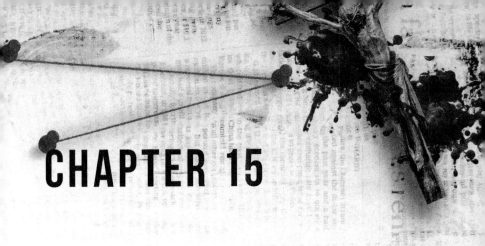

CHAPTER 15

Harlow

Villain – MISSIO

"There is no way I'm drinking that."

Kade eyes the pint glass surrounded by playing cards with a look of distaste. It's swirling with a mixture of different drinks, blended together to form a disgusting, grainy cocktail.

Brooklyn said this card game was a bad idea. Every time someone selected one of the kings, they had to add some of their drink into the glass. It's full now as the game nears its conclusion.

"You know the rules for Ring of Fire." Hudson nudges the drink towards him with a wink. "You picked up the last king. Now, you have to drink."

"This game is fucking stupid," Kade complains.

Leaning over Hudson, Phoenix claps him on his shirt-clad shoulder. "Don't puke either. No one wants to see that."

"Wouldn't be the first time," Jude comments, glued to something on his phone. "Clearly, you've forgotten Mardi Gras in Paris. Red wine everywhere."

"That was Eli's fault." Kade narrows his eyes at the silent, green-eyed suspect in question. "We drank to make him feel more comfortable around all those people."

Eli shifts on the carpet, avoiding eye contact. "Didn't help. That festival was hell."

With a headshake, Kade picks up the pint glass and swears as he begins to down it. The entire room starts clapping and cheering, causing Lucky to yip with excitement from the rug.

I nudge Leighton's shoulder with mine. "This is your fault for suggesting this game. Where did you learn it?"

He takes a pull from his beer. "I used to hang out with the university crowd a lot. England's full of drunk students playing this game and throwing up their guts."

"For what possible reason?"

His eyes meet mine. "Fun. You want a sip too?"

"Not a chance. I'm not falling for that."

Snickering, Leighton wraps an arm around my shoulders and pulls me close for a side hug. "We'll make a party animal out of you yet, Goldilocks."

"You'll be waiting for a long time."

His lips tease the shell of my ear. "What can I say, I'm a patient guy. I'll wait forever if that's what it takes. Remember that."

Flushing red, I wriggle out of his embrace. Enzo is watching us with such piercing interest from his perch behind the sofa, his amber eyes seem all animal tonight, leaving no glimpse of humanity behind.

I half expect him to tear Leighton limb from limb, no matter what he preaches about sharing me. Clearly, the poised Bengal tiger biding its time beneath his tanned skin didn't get that memo.

The alarm on the front gate's security system cuts through the cheering as Kade finishes downing the pint of death. He looks almost green. Brooklyn leans in to give him a congratulatory kiss.

"Motherfucker," Phoenix swears.

He's forced to surrender a ten-pound note to Hudson, having lost his cruel bet that Kade wouldn't finish the pint.

"Who's at the gate?" Leighton asks.

Straightening from his perch, Enzo runs a hand over his hair. "I'll go and see."

I want to bury my face in my hands and hide from the incoming car crash. Enzo shoots me a loaded look before he disappears from the room.

Ignoring my instincts, I stay put. Leighton's going to need me. He was in prison for three years, and in the seven months we've both been home, he's refused to see his parents.

That's about to change.

A couple of tense minutes pass before the front door buzzes open and shut again. Lucky barks loudly, and she races out of the room to greet our guests, her golden tail wagging.

From their seats in front of us on the woven rug, Brooklyn and Hudson have a perfect view behind us. Her eyes bulge when she spots whoever has walked in.

The tinkle of a female voice sneaks into the room over the ruckus of drunken laughter and conversation. I feel Leighton tense beside me as his back goes ramrod straight.

"Did we make it in enough time? You know how slow Ben drives in the city."

"You'd rather get here safely, wouldn't you?" a man responds in a grumpy bark. "Damn traffic."

"You've got to be fucking kidding me," Leighton whispers to himself. "Is that my parents?"

I grab his hand before he can run. "Leigh, breathe."

He looks up at me. "Did you know about this?"

"Well, I…"

"You did," he concludes. "Fucking hell, Harlow. You know why I don't want to see them!"

I grab his stubble-covered chin, gripping tight. "I didn't want any of you to see that chapel, or my scars or my bloody hair."

"That's not—"

"Don't think about telling me it's not the same thing. I didn't get a choice either. Grow up and go see your mum."

Mouth hanging open like he's witnessed a brutal murder, Leighton gapes at me. I refuse to back down, channelling the dominance that Hunter wears like a protective shield. I can be that person too. I'm learning.

"Go," I repeat firmly.

Fear crackles across his expression.

"Come with me?" he pleads.

Standing up, I keep our fingers entwined. "Of course."

Following Enzo's path out of the crowded room, Leighton's grip on my hand tightens to a bone-crunching vice. Enzo leads our two newcomers into the kitchen, giving us a second to prepare before entering behind them.

"Fuck." Leighton suddenly stops. "I can't do this."

I rest my hand over the erratic beat of his heart. "You're not alone, Leigh. All of your family is here with you."

"That's exactly the problem. My family."

"Could they be any worse than mine?" I joke.

He chuckles under his breath. "Point taken. I just haven't seen them since I was sentenced. Fuck, I'm nervous."

"All the more reason to go in there. You've got nothing to be ashamed of."

"Haven't I?" he mutters.

I brush a kiss against his cheek. "No. You haven't."

He shudders a breath. "I'm scared of what they'll think, princess. I let them down. I let everyone down."

"You're their son," I remind him quietly. "That's all that will matter to them. Come on."

With a nervous breath, Leighton smooths his plain black jeans and button-down shirt, the collar casually gaping open.

"Alright. Let's get it over with."

In the kitchen, Enzo is fixing two glasses of red wine. His eyes meet mine and he smiles reassuringly as we approach. Our two guests are facing away from us, depositing bags of presents on the breakfast bar.

Leighton stops inside the kitchen, still crunching the bones in my hand with his grip. He clears his throat, and his father is the first one to turn around.

"Dad," Leighton forces out.

"Well, I'll be damned."

With short, buzzed silver hair, formidable features and tension lines afforded by a lifetime of service to his country, Benjamin Rodriguez is an intimidating presence.

He steps closer, his dark-blue jeans neat, matching an unbuttoned white shirt that shows off his still-toned physique. His eyes perfectly match his son's, but seem colder.

"Let's get a look at you." His fuzz-covered jaw clenches tight. "You look well."

Leighton coughs awkwardly. "I am."

With her pink trench coat removed, his mum turns around next. Her deep hazel eyes are already shining with tears, highlighting smile lines and a sweet, hopeful smile.

"Oh, Leigh." Her delicate, wrinkled hands move to cover her mouth. "I can't believe it's really you."

"Hi, Mum."

Rushing across the kitchen, she bundles him into a back-breaking hug so fast, Leighton almost falls over. His mum is a full head shorter than him, but clearly, very strong.

"Get over here and hug your son," she orders her husband.

Ben unveils a small, strained smile and joins their hug. Leighton is caught between them, his shock of chaotic brown hair peeking out between their sealed chests.

Inching around them, I dart to Enzo's side and let him tuck an arm around my waist. He's watching the reunion with a pleased smile on his face.

"Nice job," I whisper to him.

"Someone had to push Leighton." He shrugs while grinning down at me. "He needed to get over himself."

"You did good, Enz."

"Thanks, little one."

With the hug disbanded, Leighton subtly wipes under his red eyes when he thinks we're not looking. His mum is trying hard not to sob as she blows into a tissue pulled from her designer purse.

"Let me introduce you." Enzo puts a hand on my lower back to guide me forwards. "Della, this is Harlow. She moved in with us last year."

Tissue pocketed, Della steps closer with a bright smile. "Of course! Harlow, we've heard so much about you."

I briefly panic, thinking she's going to try to hug me as well, but she keeps a respectful distance.

"Hello," I say nervously.

"This is my husband, Ben. We're so happy to finally meet you.

Hunter has kept us updated on your case."

Hunter's eagle-eyed father is studying me in an authoritative way, like he can see all of my darkest secrets.

"Nice to meet you," he offers.

"You too, sir."

"Drinks," Leighton declares, breaking the awkward introduction. "Harlow, want a beer?"

I nod, thankful. "Please."

He disappears inside the fridge and returns with two beers. Della and Ben both take seats at the formal dining table in front of the French doors.

"Come and sit down, son." Ben pulls out the chair next to him. "We've got a lot to catch up on."

Yanking the cap off his drink, Leighton takes several gulps for courage and heads over to sit opposite his parents. They're both staring at him like he's an exotic animal.

"How's retirement?" he begins.

Ben takes a sip of red wine. "Quiet. Your mother had me join a walking club last year."

She swats his arm with a laugh. "Don't sound so affronted. You needed to get out after your fall."

"You had a fall?" Leighton replies.

"He toppled over in June and broke his collarbone!"

"Jesus, Dad. Why didn't you tell me?"

"How? By telepathy?" Ben frowns at his son.

I watch Leighton's face crumple. He rubs the back of his neck, polishing off his beer in one long gulp. I want nothing more than to wrap my arms around him, but he needs to do this alone.

"I needed some time," he offers them both. "It took a lot of adjusting when I came out of prison."

"We wanted to help you." Della brushes a tear from her powdered skin. "Three years, Leigh. No visits, no calls. Not even a letter."

"We tried to visit," Ben adds. "You refused every request."

"Yeah... I know," he hushes.

"Eventually, we stopped trying." Della's tears intensify. "It was like you had died. We mourned you every single day."

"Mum," Leighton mumbles. "Don't say that."

"It's the truth. I felt so powerless."

Glancing away, Leighton swipes under his eyes again. I'm desperate to protect him from their disappointment, but they're not wrong. He chose to block out his family and old life to survive behind bars.

Unlike them, I can't blame him. Captivity, whether legally sanctioned or not, forces the new, embattled version of yourself to tear free from the carcass of who you used to be.

Loneliness kept Leighton alive.

His family would've made it worse.

"I don't have a good enough reason for what I've done," he explains thickly. "But I needed to do this alone. All I can hope is that you'll forgive me."

Reaching across the table, Della takes Leighton's clenched hand in hers. She brushes her thumb over the scarring across his knuckles, evidencing years of violence to survive a world behind bars that most will never understand.

"There's nothing to forgive, Leigh."

His head snaps up. "But, you said..."

"You may have hurt us with your choices, but I know for a fact that it hurt you far more than it did us. You were all alone."

Leighton shrugs. "I lived."

"And you did your time," she confirms with a tearful smile. "All we ever wanted was for you to come home again."

"Even after what I did?" He shakes his head.

Della looks to her silent husband for help. Ben is staring at his folded hands, still frowning. He looks so much like Hunter when he does that. They're clearly cut from the same cloth.

"You're still my son," he finally cuts in. "Regardless of the mistakes you've made. Nothing will ever change that fact."

Della nods. "We love you so much."

Releasing a breath that's poisoned him for three long years, Leighton looks between his parents with tears in his eyes. Everything about him seems lighter, relieved, unburdened by the constant fear of rejection.

"I'm sorry I shut you out."

She seizes his hand and kisses it. "You're here, and that's all I care about. We can be a family again."

"You're getting back on your feet," Ben agrees with a chuckle. "I hear you've been driving your brother up the wall too."

Deeming it safe to approach, Enzo claps Leighton on the shoulder. "He's keeping us all on our toes."

"Someone has to," he comments.

"We'll make an adult out of you yet, Leigh."

The front door buzzes as it clicks open again, followed by loud cursing as the beat of heavy rain travels through the air.

"Here we go," Enzo announces.

I slip out of the kitchen to meet them first. Shaking his long, wet ponytail out, Hunter peels off his navy peacoat and holds the door open for Theo to sneak in behind him.

"Hey, guys."

"Sweetheart." Hunter's eyes eat me up as he drags a tie over his head next. "Wow. You're looking different."

Smoothing my purple skater-style dress, paired with thick tights and a black cable knit cardigan, I try not to blush. Hunter stalks towards me, his warm gaze lit with interest, but he's halted by a roar of voices.

"Surprise!"

"Happy Birthday!"

Brooklyn and her guys have swarmed out of the den and surrounded us, clapping and smacking Hunter on the back. He spares me an eye roll before Hudson wrestles him into a man hug.

Leighton and Enzo appear in the doorway next, with Ben and Della behind them. Hunter does a comical double take when he sees his parents still cuddled up to Leighton.

"Mum, Dad," he wheezes. "You're here."

"We couldn't miss your birthday," Della explains, her arm around Leighton's waist. "The family is all together again."

I feel someone approaching me before warmth circles my waist. The scent of books and peppermint drapes over my skin in a comforting mist. It's fast becoming my favourite scent. Theo cuddles me from behind, kissing my temple.

"Hi, beautiful."

"Hello, Theodore," I answer breathily.

"You look stunning. Purple is your colour."

"I can't take the credit. Brooklyn helped."

"I'll have to thank her."

Enzo takes charge, directing everyone into the kitchen to start attacking the mountain of food we've laid out on the table. Hanging back to let everyone pass us both, Hunter blocks the doorway with a muscled arm.

Stopping in front of him, I strain onto my tiptoes to land a featherlight kiss against his bearded cheek.

"Happy Birthday, Hunt."

His hand grips my hip as he catches my lips in a fast, passionate kiss. Even with the boom of voices, cutlery scraping and beers being popped inside the kitchen, it feels like we're alone in the world.

Hunter's bottomless brown eyes trained on me always have that effect. Since the moment we met, I've felt the pressure of the pedestal he puts me on, even though he fought against it at first. He was so ready to give everything to me.

That's exactly why Brooklyn is right about our current situation. It's up to me to fix what I've broken. I want them, and I finally realise that doing nothing will only make this worse. I have to be the one to win Hunter around.

"Let's go on a date," I blurt against his lips.

His eyebrows knit. "A date?"

"It will be fun. We can celebrate your birthday."

His chocolatey eyes blow wide with surprise, and it takes a moment for the corner of his mouth to hook up in a pleased smirk. He looks like the cat that got the cream.

"Just us?" he clarifies.

I push my mouth against his again. "Just us."

With a low growl, his hand cups the back of my head, and he deepens the kiss. His lips work like the magnetic pull of steel train tracks, luring me closer into the depths of his tempting embrace.

I can taste his excitement, feel it running through every sinewy muscle pressed against me beneath his dress shirt. Regardless of our surroundings, he quickly flips us around and pushes me up against the wall.

"I would love to go on a date with you," he says between kisses. "But why now?"

"Because I want to do something fun with you. We can act like a normal couple for once."

The tiniest flash of insecurity sneaks across his expression. For a nanosecond, I can see Leighton in him, putting on a front to avoid rejection. It's soon smoothed over into Hunter's mask of self-assuredness.

"What about the others?" he asks pointedly.

I stroke a fingertip over his brows. "One date, Hunt. No fighting, no jealousy. Give me one single night of normalcy with you alone."

Hunter deliberates before answering. "We can talk after," he eventually submits. "I want to do something normal too, without worrying about what it means for us all."

"Then it's settled."

"I'll plan something nice." He strokes a hand over my curled hair. "Leave it with me, sweetheart."

"Nothing fancy," I warn him.

"We'll see about that."

Someone shouts our names from inside the kitchen, bursting the bubble of privacy that's protecting our intimate moment. Hunter strokes his hands down my shoulders.

"We should go back in. I can't believe my parents are here. How did Leighton take it?"

"He'll be okay, I think. It went well."

"Enzo must be a miracle worker."

"For his family?" I shrug. "I think he might be."

Tangling our fingers together, Hunter pecks my lips a final time and lingers for a teasing second before dragging me back into the kitchen. The buffet of food looks like it's been ravaged by a pack of hungry wolves.

Phoenix is neck deep in three plates full of food, rivalling even Leighton's impressive tower of snacks. In the corner, Eli and Jude are both drinking beers and talking, neither eating.

They both dislike big crowds, even when it's family. Their trust is hard won, and it took me a while to break down their defences. They offer me smiles from across the room.

Hudson, Kade and Brooklyn are gathered in the corner of the kitchen with Della. The wedding talk must be boring Hudson—his darting eyes and silent plea for a distraction are obvious even from here.

I wink at him as I pass. He mouths the word *"traitor"* when I don't offer to intervene as Brooklyn's official co-wedding planner. He's clearly having such a good time. I wouldn't want to ruin it for him.

We join Enzo and Theo at the table, and Hunter pulls the chair out for me to slip in next to our awkward techie wearing his usual flannel shirt, faded-blue jeans and slightly crooked glasses.

"Did you get your class schedule?" he asks quietly.

I eat a curly fry from his plate. "It came through yesterday to start next week. Two hours a day for three months."

"That's good, right?"

"I guess so."

"I've set up one of our work laptops for you to use. It's in my backpack. You can attend the classes online that way."

"You did that for me?" I ask in surprise. "I was just going to use Hunter's computer in his office."

"I know that you hate using it. Now, you don't have to."

My chest burns with gratitude. The tips of Theo's ears turn pink when I quickly kiss his clean-shaven cheek before retreating. I can feel Ben's attention on us both.

"Thank you," I whisper to him.

"Don't mention it. Oh, and those books you asked for are in there too. Help yourself."

"*The War of the Worlds*? I've been dying to read that after finishing *The Time Machine* last week. Early-era science fiction is my new obsession."

"It's the best," Theo agrees happily. "I'm wondering if my reading tastes are rubbing off on you."

"I think they might be."

"Feel free to ignore me and read more Jane Austen shit, no judgement."

"Hard pass. I'll stick with alien invasions and time travel."

His smile widens. "That I can help you with."

Sitting down next to Ben with his several servings of food demolished, Enzo ducks his head low and begins a rapid-fire conversation in conspiratorial whispers.

With Theo engaged in conversation, I'm free to eavesdrop. I subtly move my chair under the pretence of grabbing a cocktail sausage and catch a few words.

"NDA agreement… off the record."

My heart rate triples.

"Time for cake!" Della shouts above the noise.

Startled back to the room, Enzo offers Ben a solemn nod, and the pair disband. I sit back in my seat, attempting to slow the racing organ in my chest. Doubt and fear have slipped back in while my defences are lowered.

We're all sitting here, drinking and eating, while Candace could be taking her dying breath. She feels so out of reach. I can't save her, no matter what I do. I'm just as powerless now as I was then.

The team has been working tirelessly, attempting to gather any information on Genesis Home in the hope it will lead us to Pastor Michaels.

It's like searching for a needle in a haystack. These government-endorsed children's homes used to be littered all over England. Rosetta was one horrifying case among many tragedies.

It doesn't change the fact that Pastor Michaels wanted us to find her. She wasn't left as a boast of divinely ordained power, not like the others. He was whispering into my ear with a hidden message.

I don't know what it is yet. Our one lead is Lee Heston and his past, left behind like rotting breadcrumbs. Until the house search is complete, we won't know if it's just another dead end.

This normal, happy family life will always be hollow until then. I'm surrounded by loved ones. We're safe and secure. My guys are okay. But it doesn't stop the pain creeping back in and ruining every good moment.

"Harlow. You okay?"

Theo's voice cuts through the fog that's descended over me. Everyone is gathered around the table, and the gleam of flickering candles lights the space doused in darkness.

"Fine," I choke out.

Everyone starts to sing. The chorus of "Happy Birthday" rings hollow around me. I brush Theo's concerned hands off and mouth along, plastering my perfected mask back into place.

Smile. Sing.

Breathe. Blink.

I'm a living mannequin, hiding the festering cancer inside me that no one can see. I never celebrated my birthday. Candace may never do that again.

As Hunter blows out the number thirty-five with another eye roll, everyone starts clapping. I follow suit, stuffing my emotions back down before someone catches on. I promised myself that I'd try to enjoy every last moment of freedom.

If they can't find Pastor Michaels before it's too late, then this will be the last birthday I spend with the family that found me in that hospital. I'm planning for a future part of me believes I'll never see.

Hunter's eyes meet mine from across the table. His lips move with a silent message. Words only meant for me. No one's allowed to know what he whispers in the dark, exposing the bare violin strings of his heart. Three words that make my heart hammer and body hum with butterflies.

I love you.

I wish I could say it back. All I can do is smile and hope that God forgives me enough to grant me the luxury of living to see his next birthday. Maybe I can say it then.

In perfect sync, all four of the guys' phones begin to blare with loud alarms. Adding to the chaos, the security system in the hallway screams for attention, cutting off our festivities.

"What the hell is that?" Ben exclaims.

"Front gate emergency alert." Theo stares at his phone as it falls quiet. "Looks like the system is malfunctioning."

Hunter curses at his phone. "The gate is opening. I think we've got company."

Opening the glass door to the wine fridge behind him, Enzo pulls out a hidden silver handgun from between the bottles and checks the barrel. Della's frightened squeak does little to deter him.

"You all armed?" he barks.

Kade lifts the flap of his usual suit jacket to reveal a gun holster. Hudson and Brooklyn nod with their own assent, both pushing an unarmed Eli and Phoenix behind them.

"Alright, on me." Enzo sends the rest of us a sharp look. "Stay here. We'll check it out."

"Enz," Hunter begins.

"I've got it. Stay with Harlow."

Rising from his perch in the corner, Jude zips past everyone and grabs Brooklyn's arm. He's snatched the hunting knife from her grasp before she can block his theft.

"Don't fucking move," he snarls at her.

"Give me the knife back. I'm going out there."

"Sit your ass down, Eight! I mean it!"

The entire room stills at the strange word that's escaped his mouth. Kade and Hudson both gape at him with matching looks of concern.

"Brooklyn," Jude corrects. "I meant Brooklyn. Fuck, wait here. Don't move."

Face paling, she slumps backwards into Eli's open arms. Jude storms from the kitchen ahead of Enzo, Hudson and Kade, his shoulders pulled back.

Everyone stills as the sound of raised voices filters inside when they open the front door. I can hear someone shouting, over and over. A repeated, choreographed taunt. It sounds desperate. Frantic, even.

"Who is it?" I ask through my panic.

"We lost visual, but it looked like a male intruder." Theo's fingers dance across his phone screen as he attempts to reboot the security program. "He appeared to be armed."

Stepping in front of his wife, Ben touches Hunter's arm. "You got more guns stashed in this kitchen of yours, son?"

"There are seventeen hidden across the house," he replies.

"Good. You remembered your training."

"You drilled it into me enough, Pops."

Straining to reach underneath the dining table still full of plates and drinks, Hunter reappears with a gun and checks the safety is on before tossing it through the air to his father.

Ben catches it with ease, clicking off the safety and holding it steady in his expert grip. He prowls across the room to step in front of me, pushing me backwards into the safe zone.

"They're not taking you anywhere," he snarls protectively. "Alright, out the back. Both of you."

"Outside?" Della repeats.

Ben jerks his head. "We'll keep whoever it is occupied."

She snakes an arm around my waist, murmuring reassurances, but a fierce shriek halts us both.

"Letty! I'm here!"

That's when the penny drops.

The name I've heard being called, over and over again, isn't mine. It's *hers*. The broken, damaged girl curled up in the depths of my fragmented mind, never to be seen again.

"Letty! Let—hey, get off me!"

"Wait!" I escape Della's clutches. "That's my father. What is he doing here?"

"We'll deal with him," Hunter interjects while stepping in front of me. "He's supposed to be in rehab."

"Move! He might be in trouble."

"For breaking my front gate?" he accuses. "He sure as fuck is in trouble."

The sound of a scuffle echoes from outside. I throw myself at Hunter, desperate to get past him. I won't allow Enzo to hurt my father in the name of protecting me.

He's sick and needs our help. Whatever drove him here on a freezing cold, dark night, leaving the safety of his spot in a rehab unit behind—it must be important.

Staring up at Hunter, I meet his steely eyes. "Please. I need to see if he's okay."

"It isn't safe. I won't say it again."

"I'm not a fucking child!"

"Then don't act like one!" he yells at me.

With a huff, I pull my arm from his grip and reluctantly slump back into my empty chair. Brooklyn gently touches my leg underneath the table in a show of solidarity.

"Breathe," she murmurs.

"This is ridiculous."

"I know. Just hang on for an opening and make a run for it." She checks Hunter isn't listening. "I'll cover you."

"You'd do that?"

"Obviously. On my mark, alright?"

It's another five minutes before footsteps enter the house. I shoot back onto my feet. Hudson and Kade return first, both muttering under their breaths.

Enzo's unmistakable footsteps announce his presence next. I gasp when I see who's trapped in his huge arms, two hands restrained behind him.

My father looks different from the time that I haven't seen him. There's colour back in the sickly pallor of his skin, and his dark-blonde hair is washed, clean even.

The biggest difference is his crystal-clear blue eyes. They're open and alert, pinned on me as he struggles against his captor. Jude follows behind them, an unfamiliar gun being inspected in his hands.

Enzo shoves my father against the wall. "Alright, we agreed on ten seconds. Better start talking before I lose my patience and shoot you in the skull."

"Letty," he gasps in pain.

"Enzo, let him go!" I yell. "He isn't here to hurt me."

"I just want to talk to my daughter," Dad groans.

"Then do things the right way," Enzo growls back. "Don't break into our home, armed with an illegal gun, and act surprised when we don't trust your intentions."

"I didn't have time! It isn't safe!"

"What isn't safe?" I stare at my father.

"She isn't on your side, Letty! I came to warn you." His eyes are bugged out with fear. "You have to believe me."

"More family crap?" Enzo tugs his arm higher, causing my father to yelp loudly. "You and Giana need to keep away from Harlow."

"Giana is lying to you," he shouts louder.

"Alright, that's enough," Hunter announces as his short patience expires. "Enz, get him out of here."

"No, stop!" I implore them. "I want to hear him out."

"Not like this." Hunter gestures towards my gasping father. "He can set a meeting and follow protocol. He's lucky I'm not having him arrested for breaking and entering."

"I had no choice." My father moans in pain, losing steam. "She isn't safe here. I came to warn you all."

Enzo pulls him back and smashes him into the wall again, even harder this time. My father screams in pain, and the sound lances through my skull like a bayonet.

"Time's up, asshole," Enzo snarls in his face. "Be thankful Harlow's here, or else your brains would be splattered across the driveway right now."

"You h-have to b-believe me… Giana's behind it all."

"Take him away," Hunter orders before meeting my father's eyes. "If you leave rehab again, I'll have you thrown back in prison instead."

Enzo begins to strong arm him away, and I catch Brooklyn's eyes. She steps in front of Ben and his gun, allowing me to dart around the table.

Before I can get far, Hunter catches me and pins me against his firm chest. "Not so fast, sweetheart."

I batter his back with my fists, screaming at the top of my lungs for him to let me go.

"You have to run, Letty! Get away from her!"

"Let him go," I shout helplessly.

Following Brooklyn's lead, Leighton steps in front of his brother and shoves his shoulder, helping to break me free. I land back on my own feet with a grunt.

"This isn't right, Hunt," he argues. "Harlow can make her own choices. You can't do this."

"That lunatic broke in here with a gun," Hunter hisses back. "He's unhinged and dangerous!"

Ignoring their arguing, I take Leighton's distraction and make it outside as Enzo's wrenching his car boot open. He easily plucks my thin father off his feet and tosses him in the back, despite his continued yelling.

Something drops.

"Letty," he screams. "Take it!"

A sizable, tightly bound package has landed on the paved driveway, fallen from my father's grip. Enzo is too busy to notice. Darting outside, I snatch it from behind him before he can steal it away too.

"Take her back inside," Enzo orders as he climbs into the driver's seat. "I'll deal with this one."

Suddenly, two steely iron bands ending with a single hand wrap around my waist from behind. Jude captures me this time. I'm dragged like a sack of potatoes back into the house, staring down at the package clutched in my hands.

It's a bound collection of sealed letters. I quickly shove it inside my cable knit cardigan to conceal it. I have no doubt they'll confiscate this too, in the name of bloody safety.

"I'm sorry, Harlow." Jude finally releases me inside. "It's for your own protection. He could be violent."

With my feet back on the floor, I see red. Violence spikes through my veins as my fist draws back and slams straight into Jude's face. He falls and hits the wall, seeming more surprised than hurt.

"You, of all people, should know better than to do that to me." I clutch my aching fist. "Screw you."

His face falls. "I'm sorry."

Ignoring his useless apology, I turn to include the others in the sentiment. "Screw you all."

Theo abandons his perch against the wall, fiddling with the security system. He attempts to approach me, his hands raised. I take several large steps back.

"Don't touch me! Any of you."

He freezes, his face paling. "I'm sorry, Harlow."

"Sweetheart," Hunter begins from inside the doorway. "We had to ensure your safety. He could be dangerous."

"How many times will you use that excuse?"

Stumped for an answer, he's silent.

"That's what I thought," I finish.

Turning on my heel, leaving them all gaping after me, I flee upstairs with the package held against my chest. None of them dare to follow.

This time, they've gone one step too far. I'm not their prisoner, and I won't be treated like one. Never again.

CHAPTER 16

Harlow

Into It – Chase Atlantic

"**P**lease sit down."

Pacing in the spacious therapy room, I turn the handwritten letter over in my hands. It's one of almost three hundred, spanning several years. I only managed to read the beginning before the tears and grief took over.

I know you're still out there, Letty.

I'll never stop looking for you.

No matter what the world thinks.

I put it back in its envelope and counted them all instead, over and over again, attempting to calm down last night. Not even the knocks on the locked bathroom door or Hunter's pleading convinced me to open up. I cried myself to sleep on the tiled floor, surrounded by letters and torn out hair.

"Harlow," Richards urges.

"He wrote to me, year after year, while the rest of the world presumed me dead. He kept writing. It's all here."

"Sit down and talk to me."

"I don't want to talk!"

"Well, I want to help you," he pleads.

"Then tell me what my father meant about Giana. Is he trying to manipulate me?"

Richards watches me, his spectacles balanced on his nose. "We can work through this, but you need to calm down first."

"How can you possibly fix this?"

"I understand that you're angry," he tries again. "You experienced a scare last night."

"A scare? I'm not scared of my father. I'm scared of the people I'm living with."

"Sabre is contractually obligated to maintain your security," he points out. "I understand that your father was armed when he broke in."

"He's sick and afraid. He needs our help!"

Richards clears his throat. "Harlow... I'm sorry, but look at yourself. In their eyes, you are exactly the same. This is their way of helping you."

I freeze on the carpet. His words punch into me like needlepoints, slashing deep with the bitter pill of truth.

"You think I'm sick?" I repeat. "I should've known that you'd be on their side. You don't want to help me."

"That isn't true at all," Richards argues softly. "You're self-harming again." He nods towards the hair I've torn out during our session. "This isn't a healthy way to cope."

"Who are you to tell me how to cope?"

"I'm your therapist, but I also care about you. We've come so far since our first session last year. Don't throw all that progress away now."

Tossing the letter back on his desk with the rest of the pile, I scrub my hands over my face, smearing hot tears. I haven't felt this out of control for a while. I'd forgotten how terrifying it is.

Nothing is working to stop the barrage of untamed emotions and anger from flooding through me and distorting everything. Not even the pain that's led me here.

"Your coping techniques don't help." I shake my head. "You expect me to sit here and meditate while Candace is being held captive, my father is sick and my entire life is falling apart?"

Richards tidies the bundle of scattered letters on his desk. He neatly ties the package and places it back inside my discarded handbag.

"I understand you're at a breaking point. It's up to you whether you continue down this path or accept my help."

"What is your help, exactly?" I ask him. "Another seven months in this room, doing nothing to fix my problems?"

Richards hesitates, his smile tight. "I'd like for you to agree to an inpatient stay at the local hospital."

His words almost knock me over. I have to grip the back of my empty chair for balance.

"Wait, what?"

"Here me out," he says quickly. "It's nothing to be afraid of. You can take some time out, away from all of this."

My feet begin to backtrack. "You want to lock me up. Just like you did to Brooklyn and Jude."

"They weren't locked up," Richards placates. "You need time and space to heal. You're in a dark place right now. Let me help."

"What if I say no?" I challenge.

"Then I can't force you. But if you continue down this path and I think your life is at risk, we may be having a different conversation."

The walls are closing in. Another prison. Another cell. He wants to lock me up, steal my freedom, my life, my future. I'm staring down the barrel of an inevitable gunshot to the head.

"I won't be put in another cage." I walk towards the door. "Not now, not ever. I can't go back to living like that."

"Nobody is putting you in a cage. I want to give you the space to heal and get help in a safe environment."

"No! I don't want to go. I'm done talking."

Picking up my handbag, I leave Richards staring after me with sadness in his clear eyes. The door slams shut behind me as I escape into the silent corridor in Sabre's HQ. Down the stretch of dark carpet, Leighton's sprawled out in an armchair, scrolling on his phone.

He's the only one of the guys I allowed near me after last night's debacle. At least he attempted to reason with Hunter and allowed me the chance to chase after my father.

He drove me here today for my regular session, respecting my need for silence and distance. The others have all been notably absent and unable to face me.

"Leigh," I gasp through tears.

He sits up, abandoning his phone. "Harlow? You've still got half an hour to go."

"I'm done talking to him."

"Why? What happened in there?"

I hug my handbag. "I want to get out of here."

Tucking his phone into his jeans pocket, he twirls a set of car keys on his finger. "You sure?"

Nodding, I bounce on my feet. "Let's go."

"Well, I have good news. Hunter has his tail between his legs, so we're off the hook for the day."

"What do you mean?"

Leighton flourishes a shiny black card from his pocket. "I have his credit card and free rein to turn your frown upside down. Let's get into some trouble."

"Hunter's trying to make this better by throwing money around? Seriously?"

"Well." He plasters on his best holier-than-thou expression, complete with an invisible halo. "He told me to take you to buy school supplies. Technically, that's free rein."

I manage a tiny grin. "What's the plan then?"

"We should check into a crazy expensive hotel, eat everything on the menu and leave those dickheads to come to their senses. Maybe even some online shopping."

That sounds too good to be true.

"I want his bank account to hurt," he adds.

"Can we do all that? Is it safe with the protests going on outside and Candace still missing?"

"Fuck everyone and the protests. We can take security." He sticks his hand out for me to take. "Come on. I'll text the others and tell them to give us some space."

I squash my fear and tentatively take his hand. The pressure of his long fingers gripping mine grounds me back in the present. I'm not locked in the back of a faceless van, being driven to Richards' fancy prison disguised as a hospital.

"Hey," Leighton murmurs. "What is it?"

"I f-feel like everything is spiralling out of control."

His green eyes soften beneath shaggy chestnut hair, and Leighton tugs me closer. I wrap my arms around his waist and bury my nose in his citrus-scented t-shirt.

"I'm here, princess," he whispers against my lowered head. "I know things feel bleak right now, but I swear to you, we're doing our best to make this right."

"You saw what they did to my father last night. How can I ever trust them?"

"Because the one thing that Hunter and Enzo agree on right now is their love for you," he replies easily.

Love.

There's that word again.

"Sometimes it makes them behave like wankers." He laughs under his breath. "But they care about you."

"Enough to hurt someone I care about?"

"In the name of keeping you safe? Yes. They didn't blink an eye last night, and I'm sure they'd do it all over again."

I release his waist. "Maybe that's the problem."

Leighton strokes a hand over my messy, uneven hair. There's no point even attempting to hide it. The right side is thinning so severely, it's enough to be noticeable now. I can tell it's bothering him.

"Harlow," he begins. "You have to know how much we all fucking adore you. I can't imagine my life without you in it. It's killing me to watch you go through this."

"I'm sorry."

"Don't be." He tucks a strand of hair behind my ear. "Tell me what you want me to do, and I'll do it. Shall we stain all of Hunter's clothes pink? Set Enzo's car keys in jelly?"

"I was thinking something bigger than your usual pranks."

Leighton waves the credit card. "In that case, I think we'll head for the best hotel in the city. Come on, milady. Hunter's inevitable bankruptcy is calling."

Linking my arm in his, Leighton escorts me down to the car parked in the garage and we head out into the busy city traffic. The blacked-out windows of security tailing us in their expensive SUV threaten to derail my mood, but I block them out, pretending we're alone.

Half an hour of terrible singing along to the radio later, Leighton pulls up on the curb beneath the towering shadow of a glitzy, multistory hotel rising above us. I feel my mouth drop open.

Turning off the engine, he hops out of the car and surrenders his keys to the beaming man in a fine suit that appears. I take an unsteady breath before Leighton opens my door and offers me a hand.

"Shall we?" He waggles his eyebrows.

"Sure about this?"

"Hell yeah. Come on."

We're steered inside the bustling reception of the five-star hotel, tailed by two plain-faced agents pretending to be invisible. With thick, red carpets, high ceilings and gilded chandeliers casting sparkling light across the polished mahogany furniture, I feel a little out of place in here.

"Damn," Leighton mutters. "This is fancy as fuck."

"What are we doing here?"

"Being fancy," he teases.

At the front desk, Leighton charms the concierge with the promise of his brother's limitless credit card. She accepts it with a bright smile, racking up a two-thousand-pound bill in less than ten seconds.

"You're lucky the master suite is available," she chatters animatedly. "It comes with its own butler service and valet parking. The three on-site restaurants are at your disposal."

"Perfect." Leighton grins as he curls his arm around my waist. "My wife has very expensive tastes."

I choke on air. "Um."

"Isn't that right, honey?" He winks at me. "She insisted on visiting London on the way to our honeymoon. I'll be needing a new credit card before much longer."

"You are such a beautiful couple!"

"She's my little honey bear. Aren't you, pumpkin?"

"Mmm," I respond, internally dying. "That's me."

Leighton plants a big, sloppy kiss on my cheek. "Do you want anything else, my sugar pea? Perhaps a massage?"

"No... *darling*."

"Oh, that's right. I'll be doing all the massaging later."

I smack his chest, on the verge of a giggling fit.

"Tell you what, I'll throw in a complimentary bottle of champagne," the concierge offers. "Congratulations on your wedding. I hope you have a lovely stay!"

Leighton is doing his best to hold in a laugh. "That's kind of you. I'm sure we will. Come on, darling wife."

He tows me away before I fall into a fit of laughter. Following a well-dressed busboy in his perfectly tailored suit, we ride the gleaming elevator up to the sixteenth floor.

"Don't laugh," he whispers to himself.

I'm biting my tongue to hold my own in. Plush carpets swallow our footsteps down to the hotel room. Leighton lets me in before closing the door in the faces of our security and finally bursting into hysterics.

"You are insane," I break down.

"The look on your face was priceless."

"I can't believe you pulled that off."

Leighton chucks his coat aside. "I am a master."

Inside the suite, I take a moment to look around. It's huge, spanning across two giant rooms. Rich brocade wallpaper meets polished accents in the sitting area, showcasing velvet sofas, a huge flat-screen television and a fully stocked bar.

In the bedroom, through gleaming sliding doors, the world's

biggest bed is covered in decorative pillows and sheets. There's an attached bathroom, glistening with flashes of crystal, marble and shining glass.

Leaving Leighton to inspect the mini bar, I peek out of the floor-to-ceiling curtains held back by silk ties and gasp at the panoramic view of Canary Wharf.

It's pulsating with light and lunchtime activity. Business drinks, first dates and the reunion of friends meeting in the city all add to the menagerie of life unfolding beneath us.

"The city is beautiful."

Leighton sidles up to me. "You think?"

"I'm not sure I could ever live here, but I love watching the people. There's so much energy everywhere."

Leaving me to approach the massive bed, Leighton flops on the crisp, gold-accented linens. His t-shirt rides up to flash a sliver of abdominals and soft, black hair trailing into his fitted blue jeans.

He picks up the leather-bound menu from the bedside table and the nearby telephone to begin reciting his order—dish after dish, until there's nothing left that he hasn't charged to Hunter's credit card.

"Food's coming. Hope you're hungry."

"Your brother is going to flip out."

"He makes this kind of money every thirty seconds. Consider it a lesson for next time he decides to be a colossal controlling asshat."

Pulling off my parka and boots, I take two steps and collapse on the bed, narrowly avoiding crushing Leighton with my body. He rolls onto his side, propping his chin on his hand to study me with a crooked grin.

"You likey?"

I relax into the butter-soft mattress with a sigh. "It's away from home and HQ. That's good enough for me."

"Wanna get naked and watch a movie?"

"What?" I laugh.

His eyes are twinkling with mirth. "Watching TV while naked is one of the best perks of being an adult."

"Is that a fact?"

"Well, along with taking a pizza into the bathtub or eating your whole advent calendar on December first."

Staring up at the chandelier, I clutch my belly, which hurts from laughing so hard. He's certifiably insane.

"I'm not sure you've quite grasped the concept of adulthood," I wheeze out. "But for the record, I prefer your definition. It sounds a lot more fun."

Leighton fist pumps the air. "I knew it. I'm totally winning at adulting here. So, how about it? Shall I run us a hot bubble bath?"

"Did you order pizza as well?"

"Obviously," he quips back. "You know it's one of my five a day."

"Then I guess it would be rude not to."

Depositing a kiss on the corner of my mouth, Leighton bounds into the attached en-suite with the excitement of Lucky when I take her for a sunset walk.

By the time the food arrives, the cloth-covered trolley checked by our overzealous security, Leighton's half naked and the bath is full of steaming water.

He pushes the trolley into the room and dismisses the waiter, already cramming several delicate, miniature cakes into his mouth and spilling crumbs on his bare chest.

I stare at his hamster cheeks. "You're an animal."

"What?" he replies around his mouthful. "I'm hungry. These cakes are so small, you have to eat three at a time."

"Have to?"

"Obviously."

Pulling the complimentary bottle of champagne from its ice bucket, he sets to work removing the cork. With the bottle popped, I watch as he disappears into the bathroom with it.

"Bring the pizzas," he yells over his shoulder.

"Plural?"

"I ordered six, plus sides. Everyone knows these fancy restaurants serve tiny portions and charge twice as much."

Lifting the lids on various serving platters, I gape at the ridiculous amount of food he's ordered. I have no idea how eating in the bath will work. I grab two pizzas to start with.

In the en-suite bathroom, a headful of shaggy hair pokes out from an avalanche of honey-scented bubbles. Leighton is naked in record time, drinking champagne from the bottle.

"I have no words to describe how crazy you look right now." I bark a laugh. "You don't want a glass?"

He sits up, letting slick bubbles cascade over his defined pectorals. "Do I look that sophisticated?"

"Not right now, no."

Leighton looks at the platter in my hands. "You gonna get your clothes off and climb in with that?"

Flushed, I bounce on my feet. "Shut your eyes."

"Princess, I've seen you naked before. Stop being a pussy and come feed me before I get hangry."

"I'm being a pussy? Really?"

His defiant gaze doesn't waver. "Yup."

"Well then."

Balancing the platter on the edge of the clawfoot bathtub, it's big enough to fit at least four people. Leighton's searing eyes are locked on me, and I feel a burst of confidence. He's seen every inch of me, good and bad. There's nothing to be afraid of.

I kick off my jeans and toss my long-sleeved t-shirt next. He doesn't look away once, even as he begins stuffing pizza in his mouth using a soapy hand.

Moving fast, I whip off my bra and drop my panties, leaping into the bath. The water sloshes loudly as I slide into the welcoming heat.

"Not even a twirl for me?" he pouts.

"That wasn't a striptease, Leigh."

"Rude. No pizza for you."

Parting the cloud of fragranced bubbles, I move closer and ease the slick bottle from his hands. Leighton watches with amusement as I take a gulp of the gross, fizzy alcohol.

"This is so disgusting."

"Champagne always is."

"Then why drink it?" I chuckle.

"I reckon the rich-as-fuck assholes who drink it are pretending to be fancy and secretly necking rum and Cokes when no one's looking."

Ditching the bottle on the tiled bathroom floor, I snag a slice of cheese-covered goodness, narrowly avoiding covering it in a carpet of bubbles.

"Eating pizza in the bathtub is impractical."

"But fun." Leighton inhales a slice. "You'd rather eat downstairs in one of those stuffy, pompous restaurants?"

"I'll pass."

He grins widely. "Knew it."

When I go in for another slice, Leighton shifts his huge leg to knock me off balance. I fall forwards in the warm water, sloshing and landing straight in his lap.

His arms wrap around my torso, pulling me up against his chest. My legs move without being told to slip around his waist, until we're pressed together in the steam and bubbles.

"Whoops," he singsongs.

"You did that on purpose!"

Leighton drops a kiss on my shoulder, his lips leaving a path of static electricity up to the curve of my neck. Teeth playfully nipping against my throat, he plants a gentle kiss.

"I could get used to you naked and wet in my bathtub."

I moan as his hips shift to grind into me. The solid press of his dick brushes right against the heat gathering between my thighs. There's nothing between us.

Leighton's mouth caresses mine. His lips move in a perfect, merciless attack formation, nipping and teasing until his tongue touches mine.

I hold his shoulders, my entire body quaking with the sudden rush of desire that obliterates my previous shyness. Every wet, glistening inch of his muscles is on display.

When his hand cups my bare breast and squeezes gently, I gasp against his swollen lips. The darkness metastasising in my mind is overtaken by one single thought.

I want him inside me.

Right now.

I'm done playing it safe.

"Leigh," I gasp as his lips wrap around my stiffened nipple. "Please…"

"Hmm?" he replies, teeth tugging on my hardened peak before he sucks my breast into my mouth.

Grabbing a handful of his dripping brown hair, I yank his head back up. Leighton gasps in pain, but his eyes are lit with excitement.

"I need you," I plead breathlessly.

Reaching into the depths of the water, his hand begins to skate down my stomach to slip between my legs. I'm still holding his hair tight, and I tug again to regain his attention.

"No. Not like that."

His brows furrow. "I don't understand."

I channel my best inner Brooklyn and lean close to capture his mouth in a searing, confident kiss. She's been coaching me for this ever since I admitted that I'm ready.

I stop for a breath to speak. "I need you inside me, and I'm not talking about your fingers."

He searches my face. "You want to…"

"Yes."

Leighton hesitates. "Harlow, I know I've been joking around about this, but seriously, there's no pressure."

"You've given me time and respected my boundaries. I love you for doing that, but I'm ready now. I trust you."

"But… last night. You're still upset and—"

Frustrated, I sink a hand beneath the bubbles and find the promising steel of his pierced cock in the water. Leighton cuts off mid-sentence. I stroke his shaft, showing him my intentions.

"Stop talking and take me to the bed."

"Fuck, princess. Are you sure?"

"Ask me one more time and I'll walk out of this hotel and find one of the others to do this with."

His lust-filled eyes harden. "You wouldn't dare. I'll never hear the end of it if Hunter or Enzo fuck you first."

"This isn't a competition."

"It sure as fuck is, and I'm gonna win."

Water cascades off his toned body as Leighton steps out of the bath and grabs a towel. I lift my arms up and let him pluck me out. Wrapping me in laundered cotton, I'm cradled in his arms.

Leighton walks back into the bedroom, scattering water across the expensive carpet. He kisses along the exposed skin of my neck, his teeth nipping and lips sucking.

I'm deposited on the end of the bed with a thump. Unwrapping the towel, he exposes my naked body. Standing in front of me, every inch of his long, thick length is on display, a glint of silver piercing the velvet tip. I swallow hard.

"We need to get a few things straight."

I shiver under his watchful stare. "Like what?"

Resting a hand on my shoulder, he pushes me backwards. I land on the mattress, my bare legs hanging over the edge.

"Are you going to be a good girl?" he asks.

"M-Me?"

"Do you see anyone else here? Answer the question."

"Yes," I recite softly.

"And you'll do as you're told?"

A quiver of desire sparks deep inside me. I press my thighs together, gasping at the ache between my legs.

"Yes."

"You'll say if I make you uncomfortable or if you want me to stop?"

Leighton didn't bother with a towel. He's hanging over me, stark naked. Fisting his erection, he begins to pump it with lazy strokes. It's so big. How will it fit in me? I'm suddenly nervous while watching him.

"Harlow," he snaps. "Words."

"Yes, I'm sorry. I'll tell you."

Scanning the hotel room, he heads for his discarded jeans on the floor and searches in the pocket for his wallet. I wait, shivering with need and splayed out for his perusal.

"What are you looking for?"

"As much as I'd love to watch my come drip down your thighs, we're in too much shit to have a kid right now. Unless you want to, that is."

"Huh?" I squeak in shock.

Leighton snorts as he walks back over, a foil packet in his hand. "It's a condom, Goldilocks. I was only joking."

"That was a terrible joke. I'd be a crap mother."

He returns to his position of power looming over me. I watch with fascination as he rolls a length of plastic over his erection, checking that it's securely in place.

"I'd be a shitty father, hence the rubber. Hunter would hospitalise me if I knocked you up."

Despite my nerves, I burst out in inappropriate laughter. Leighton snorts as his cheeks flush pink in the most adorable way. He always knows how to set me at ease.

"Last chance. You sure about this?"

Rather than answer again, I hook my foot around his powerful thigh and tug him forwards. Leighton lands above me with a huff, his arms holding him upright.

I squirm on the bed, my thighs rubbing against each other. I'm so flustered and desperate for a release. We've been dancing around this moment for months and I'm done.

"Poor little princess," he teases with a sly look. "If it hurts so bad, why don't you touch yourself?"

"Touch… myself?"

Leighton bites down on my earlobe. "Make yourself ready for me. I want to see your fingers covered in juices."

His mouth should be illegal. It adds fuel to the fire burning me up inside, and I don't feel my usual shyness or embarrassment. Leighton builds me up. He makes me feel powerful and confident in a way no one else does.

Biting down on my lower lip, I move my hand over my body to dip it between my legs. I'm quivering all over.

"Legs open wider," he instructs.

I follow orders, spreading them apart.

"Perfect. Let me see you touch your pussy."

It feels like there's no air to breathe in the room. It takes all of my bravery to hold my legs open so he can scrape his eyes over every inch of my exposed body.

My fingers travel over the now-neat patch of hair above my mound. I spent some time taming it after a thoroughly embarrassing conversation with Brooklyn about girl stuff.

"Lower," Leighton orders. "Don't be shy."

Finding the furnace between my folds, I slip a finger downstairs and stroke over my clit. It feels good, but nowhere near as pleasurable as when the others do it.

Biting back a moan, I gather the slick promise of moisture across my fingers before circling my tight entrance. I've touched myself a couple of times, mostly in exploration.

This is something different.

Leighton's simmering emerald eyes are locked on me with a look of pure fascination. He's enraptured by my every move. There's no hiding from him.

With a sharp inhale, I push my index finger inside myself and groan out loud. It feels so good to swirl it in a slow rotation, my thumb swiping over my bundle of nerves.

"That's it, princess," Leighton encourages in a raspy voice. "Let me see you fuck yourself."

I slide another finger inside, and my lower stomach clenches with pleasure. The pressure of his gaze locked on me is what makes this so hot. I'm performing for him.

"Faster," he orders. "You need to be nice and wet for what comes next, Goldilocks."

Copying the moves I've watched the guys use several times, I begin to move my fingers in and out. They stroke deep inside me, reaching for an invisible chord that sets off fireworks.

It's not quite the same, but when Leighton hovers over my spreadeagled body and sucks my nipple into his mouth, the pleasure intensifies. His mouth is so hot and teasing.

"Look at these perfect tits."

"Leigh," I gasp.

"That's it, baby. Keep going."

Thumbing my clit as the pressure begins to build, I let him guide my legs even further open with his spare hand. I've got a foot propped up on either side of him.

He releases my nipple to lean back and study me, inch by inch, leaving no part of my naked skin untouched by his eyes. When his hand slides between my legs, I writhe on the bed.

Placing his hand over mine, he takes over and pushes my own fingers deeper. The pressure is reaching a breaking point as I hit that strange spot of ecstasy.

"Does it feel good?" he teases me. "I want to see you come before I even think about touching you."

"I can't... do it myself."

"Sure you can. Let me help."

With his guidance, my fingers thrust faster inside me. The feeling begins to peak into an approaching wave. I'm working my own nervous system into a frenzy.

"Your cunt is so wet." Leighton leans closer to bite down on my bottom lip. "Make yourself come, baby girl."

He disappears from above me as I crawl closer to my breaking point. Leighton takes a step back, giving him a perfect view between my thighs.

I thrust my fingers deep into myself, pausing to swipe a thumb over my nub every second or so. It feels so good to be on display, trapped in this sexy, vulnerable state of objectification.

"That's a fine fucking sight," he comments.

Grabbing my left breast with my other hand, I tweak my nipple, needing some inexplicable push to cross that final line. I'm so close, pinching my nipple again, but harder.

The sharp burst of pain shatters the expanding bubble of anticipation. I cry out in pleasure. My back arches off the bed as warmth sweeps over my fingers, still buried deep in my slit.

Leighton's fisting his hard cock, watching every last detail. Heat sweeps over me, and I let my legs go limp, easing my fingers back out of myself as I come down from my high.

"Did I say you were finished?" he scolds.

The fire in his eyes is mesmerising.

He captures my glistening hand mid-air. "Give me your fingers so I can clean up your mess."

I'm tensed up with desire and excitement from the filth that escapes his mouth alone. Bringing my fingers to his lips, I hold his eye contact as he licks my wet, salty digits.

"See how wet you are for me? You're such a good girl, coming all over yourself like that."

Crawling back on top of me, he rests his weight on an elbow and grips my wrist tight. I watch my fingers disappear into his mouth again and his tongue glides over my skin.

"You taste heavenly," he groans. "Dammit, Harlow. The things I want to do to you."

My legs begin to quiver with nervousness. I'm trembling all over and wetter than I've ever been before. That little show was just a warmup. Leighton's tongue runs along my jawbone before he kisses my throat, his breath a teasing whisper.

"I'm going to fuck you now, and you're going to scream my name for the whole hotel to hear. Understood?"

I see stars as he grabs my nipple and twists.

"I understand. Please…"

"Please what? I can't hear you."

His hips brush against mine as he settles between my splayed legs, two hands resting on the bed to hold himself up.

"Please… fuck me," I mewl.

"That's what I wanted to hear—the sound of you begging. Fuck, how I've dreamt about this moment."

My legs are pinned open as he positions himself, and his eyes refuse to grant me a sliver of privacy. Leighton's staring deep into the unreachable wilderness within my psyche.

Lungs seizing with anticipation, I forget how to draw in a breath. The hard press of his sheath is pushed up against my entrance, on the verge of entering me fully. I'm ready to scream in frustration when he stops at the last moment.

"Are you okay?" he checks again. "Tell me to stop if you want. It's not too late to change your mind."

I draw his lips in for a kiss of confirmation. His mouth slants against mine in a perfect, God-given fit. We were always meant to be. This moment feels more right than anything.

He starts to push inside me, and I'm overcome by sharp, shooting pains. Leighton moves slowly, watching me closely for any glimpses of hesitation.

"Still okay?" he worries.

"It h-hurts, but it's fine."

He kisses me again. "Want me to stop?"

"No. Keep going."

"It'll start to feel good soon."

The bonfire crisping my skeleton from the inside out intensifies with each inch of steel sliding into me. I've never felt such intensity before.

The moment it's all in, Leighton's eyes roll back with a satisfied sigh. I can just feel the cool kiss of his piercing through the protective rubber.

"You feel so good around me," he whispers, gripping my hip. "I'm going to start slow, okay?"

I gasp as he retracts before pushing back into me. It burns at first, the pain threatening to unlatch a box full of dark memories, but Leighton won't let me drown in the past.

With each tender thrust, the sense of pressure eases. A new feeling takes over. Pain melts into the first wisps of sweet, welcome relief, before blossoming into euphoria.

"Does that feel good, baby?"

"Fuck... uh-huh."

He pushes even deeper into my pussy. I grab his hard biceps and dig my nails in, a moan tearing out of my parted lips. My nerves are on fire. It's all too much.

"You like my cock buried deep inside your cunt?"

"God, yes."

Leighton moves a little faster, broadening his strokes to slide into my slit. He nudges that mysterious place hidden away that feels so good. I cry out, louder this time.

My mind and body are both overwhelmed. Not even Pastor Michaels or the bottomless pit of traumatic memories can steal my attention from this single, perfect moment.

Leighton is the only thing that exists in my world right now. His tongue darting out to lick his lips. The verdant depths of his eyes, pinned on me with awe. His tanned skin, with lean muscles carved like hewed beams of steel.

"Shit, Harlow. I can't hold on for long."

I have no idea what he means, but I think I know what's coming. I'm tensing up without realising, the edges of my mind beginning to fray with sensory overload.

He's moving at a steady pace, pushing into me with each pump. The pain is completely gone. It feels incredible, so far from the depraved torture I've associated sex with for so long.

Leighton pulls out with a grunt, and I growl at the sudden loss. His cock is standing proud, glistening with moisture and a smear of blood as he waits at the end of the bed. Wrapping his hands around my ankles, I'm yanked down to stand up too.

"Turn over," he grunts.

Too boneless to move, I let Leighton lift my sweat-slick body with a chuckle. My hands land on the sheets and he places me on my tiptoes, raising my backside into the air.

The fierce heat of his body presses against my legs from behind. Unable to see him, I wiggle and moan, silently praying for his length to slide back inside me.

"Look at this gorgeous ass."

His hand smacks against my right cheek, sending warm tingles across my skin. He spanks me again, harder, the sizzling pain blurring into waves of agonising bliss.

"I love seeing my palm print on your skin."

"Leigh," I whine. "Please."

"Sorry, princess. Did I leave you hanging?"

Arching my back, I push against him, loving the tantalising promise of his cock nudging against my ass. He clasps my hips and drives back into me, eliciting a high squeak. From this angle, every sensation is intensified.

Deeper.

Faster.

Harder.

His caution disappears from sight as our bodies collide, his cock slamming back into me in a feverish tempo. Leighton isn't holding back anymore, and it's mind-blowing.

"Goddammit, baby."

My hands are twisted in the sheets as another release begins to reach its apex. This rush of ecstasy feels bigger. More threatening. I'm on the verge of being swept up by the tide, adrift and lost in the sea of intoxication.

"Let go," Leighton growls out. "Let's come together, princess. Fall apart for me."

His barked command is all it takes to knock me over the edge. I fall into a destructive meltdown as sensation explodes through me.

Screaming out his name in a voice that doesn't sound like my own, I hold on for dear life as Leighton chases his own release. His hips are crashing into me with each punishing thrust until he roars in my ear.

"Fuck!"

I've never had an orgasm like it. My entire body feels like it's burnt to a crisp, and I can't move a muscle. Leighton's breathing is ragged as he slumps on the bed, pulling me into the welcoming cradle of his arms.

Burying a hand in my hair, he pulls our lips together. I let him consume me. Over and over. Kiss after kiss. I'm his and he is mine in a way that not even God could dispute.

Our kiss is slower, more tender, silently reassuring the other after taking that inexorable step together. I can hardly keep my eyes open. Exhaustion has slipped over me as the aftershocks of my release fade.

"Jesus Christ," Leighton says after a minute. "Are you okay? Did I hurt you? I didn't mean to get carried away."

"I'm good. Better than good."

Cursing, he pulls the condom from himself and ties it off to be tossed out. I protest when he peels himself from me to disappear into the bathroom. He returns with a damp washcloth and gestures for me to open my legs again.

I hesitate. "Um, I'm fine."

"You seriously can't still be shy? After that?"

"Well, a little bit."

"You are too fucking adorable for me to handle."

Stifling a nervous giggle, I spread my legs, still shuddering with the final whispers of pleasure. Leighton holds my eyes as he dips the warm washcloth between my thighs, gently cleaning me up before tossing it on the floor with my towel.

"Thank you for trusting me, Goldilocks."

When he lies back down, I tangle our legs together and rest my head above his heartbeat. "How couldn't I?"

"I dunno. I'm far from perfect."

"You've been the most incredible friend to me, Leigh."

"Friend, huh?"

"At first." I squash my fear down. "But I think I've loved you since the first day we met, when you made popcorn and forced me to watch *Friends*. You cared so much."

The word slips out before I can stop myself. I'm not sure when I stopped seeing him as my best friend and started referring to him in my head in a different way. I don't like him. I don't even care about him. I love him—fully and irrevocably.

His hand brushes my cheek, allowing his thumb to stroke beneath my eye. I savour each circle of his skin on mine. His malachite irises are muddled with emotion.

Shock. Hope. Relief. Fear. A kaleidoscope of humanity at its best and worst. His broken pieces are calling out to mine. He's pieced me back together, one shattered shard at a time.

"You love me?" he hushes.

I bring our faces closer so our noses brush. It's an intimate embrace, with every single part of our bodies touching somewhere, until we're breathing the same air.

"Yes," I admit. "I love you."

His mouth warps into a painfully wide grin. It's so big and comical, I worry his lips will actually split with happiness.

"I love you," he echoes without hesitating. "I have for so long. All I want in this world is you."

I curl up against him, letting his arms swallow me in safety and protection. His heart is still working overtime. The steady thump is the best sound I've ever heard.

"You have me, Leigh. Forever."

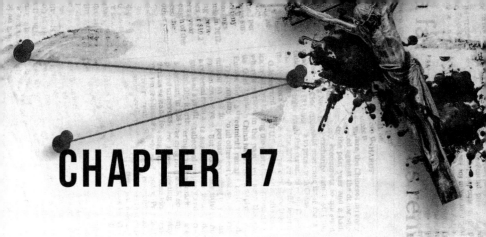

CHAPTER 17

Enzo

Via – Voices From The Fuselage

Sitting next to Theo in his office, we're both leaning forward in our chairs. On his array of monitors, Giana's perfectly choreographed sadness plays out in real time.

She dabs at her reddened eyes with a tissue, looking anywhere but at Hunter. Every time she sniffles, unease twists in my gut. I don't buy it. Not for a second.

"You see, we have a slight problem."

"What kind of problem?" she snips back.

Hunter watches her from across the table. "Your ex-husband disputes your version of events relating to Harlow's disappearance."

"He's a liar! I warned you."

It's hard to decide who is telling the truth in this cesspit of complicated family dynamics and falsehoods. Our conversations with Oliver Kensington have been very interesting, to say the least.

We paid him a visit in the rehab centre to warn him against invading our property again, and he sang like a fucking songbird when given the opportunity to comment.

He shredded Giana's version of events, throwing everything we thought we knew into dispute. Everything Giana has offered us now has to be re-evaluated and torn apart.

"Oliver insists that Harlow must be protected from you," Hunter continues. "He claims that you orchestrated her disappearance before arranging his own incarceration."

With the bomb dropped, Giana turns a bright shade of purple beneath her perfectly curled hair. She looks up at the camera recording the interview, scolding us both with her eyes alone.

"Do you see what kind of monster he is now? You never should have listened to him. He's full of shit."

"Oliver is still Harlow's father," Hunter defends.

"Who would make up such a twisted lie? This is exactly why I wanted Letty to stay away from him."

"Because she didn't want him to tell Harlow what she doesn't remember," Theo supplies next to me.

"You reckon Oliver's telling the truth?" I wonder.

"That Giana was an abusive witch who hated her own family? It's plausible. Maybe she wanted them both gone."

"We don't know that for sure."

"Not yet," he agrees. "But something's off here."

"What happened the day that Harlow was taken?" Hunter redirects, drawing our attention back to the interview.

"We've been over this!" Giana protests.

"I want to hear it again."

She shakes her head in disgruntlement. "I was dealing with an emergency at work. Letty was told to stay inside the school until I arrived to pick her up. Instead, she decided to walk home alone."

"Oliver claims that she would never leave school grounds of her own accord. You've said that she decided to disobey your instructions, leading to her abduction."

"I do not wish to blame her; she was a child." Giana's eyes flit around the interview room. "But Letty was known to be rebellious and… difficult. She's a lot like her father."

"We've interviewed Oliver extensively this week," Hunter combats. "He also rejects your accusations of domestic abuse and claims that it was you who was abusive towards him and your daughter. Violence, both mental and physical."

"That son of a bitch. I can't believe it. You know this is the drugs talking, don't you? He's an unstable addict."

"We know that he's had a drug problem for many years. Oliver says that it was worsened by the severe domestic violence he endured."

"That's nonsense!"

"It was rather convenient when he was arrested, wasn't it?"

Giana splutters. "Excuse me?"

"The authorities were spoon-fed all the evidence they needed to convict him. You were left with full access to the court settlement. That's a lot of money. All yours."

Chair scraping back, she launches to her feet. "I don't have to sit here and listen to this."

"Sit back down, Giana."

"No, I don't think I will. If you have any further questions, please direct them to my legal counsel."

"Lawyering up already?" Hunter chuckles.

"I don't appreciate this spiteful character assassination," she hisses at him. "I had nothing to do with Letty's disappearance. I lost my daughter. My whole life."

"But you still tried to silence your ex-husband." Hunter stacks his paperwork and stands. "If you're innocent, the question is why. What does he have on you?"

She jabs an accusing finger in his face. "Tell my daughter that I want to speak to her immediately. I will not allow that animal to turn her against me with these lies."

"Harlow doesn't want to speak to anyone right now." Hunter squares his shoulders. "I suggest you think carefully about what you say next. All I want is the truth."

Fucking hell. The tension is practically leaking through the screen. I almost miss the soft vibrating of my phone, enraptured by the drama. Fishing it from my pocket, I punch the icon below Hudson's name.

"Yeah?"

"We just got to HQ," he rushes out. "We heard back from Forensics in Newcastle. Where the hell are you?"

"Theo's office. Come down."

"Be there in five."

Hudson hangs up with the sound of raised voices blurring in the background. I leap up, my spine crackling with impatience. We've been anticipating this report. Forensics accessed the family-owned property where Pastor Michaels once lived and performed a thorough search.

"What is it?" Theo asks from his desk.

"Update from Newcastle."

"About time."

Pulling up Hunter's contact, I drop him a quick text message. He'll want to hear this. On Theo's computer screen, Hunter checks his phone and stiffens. Giana continues to rant and rave as he quickly wraps up the interview.

"You'll be hearing from my solicitor," she threatens. "Whatever you're trying to pin on me, it won't stick. I'll see you in court."

Hunter shoves her out the door at lightning speed, paying zero attention to her idle threats. We both wait impatiently until the door to Theo's office slams open and he strides in, short of breath, and tosses his suit jacket on the nearby sofa.

"Having fun?" I tease him.

Hunter narrows his eyes. "Oh, I'm living the life. That woman is a fucking loose cannon. I have a headache."

"You and me both."

"What's the update?" he barks.

"Hudson called. They're coming now."

He scrapes a hand over his loose ponytail. "Giana's being escorted off the premises. Apparently, she's going to sue me for defamation of character."

"She loves a court case," Theo comments.

"Franky, I'd enjoy the chance to drag her over the coals in court. She needs taking down a peg or two."

I approach Hunter. "Why did you push her so much? She's going to shut down completely now. We've shown our hand."

"She was never going to deviate from the narrative she's been pushing for months," he returns with a shrug. "I wanted to catch her off guard. Her defensiveness is telling."

Despite his risky tactics, I reluctantly agree with him. Innocent people don't threaten investigators with legal action for no reason. We're supposed to be on the same side.

If she had nothing to hide, she wouldn't be fighting us at every turn and attempting to control Harlow's life from afar. I didn't trust her from day one. She knows more than she's letting on.

We wait in fraught silence until the office door reopens, admitting Hudson and Kade inside. Both look pale and worn out after several days spent on the ground in Derby, interviewing locals and tracing Candace's steps.

"Where's Brooklyn?" I ask first.

"She's at home with Harlow," Kade answers, out of breath. "They're writing the eulogy for Friday's memorial."

"Good. Tell us what you've got."

Hudson braces his hands on his knees, gulping down air. He really needs to stop smoking before he hacks up a whole lung.

"They found something big."

Hunter leans forward. "What is it?"

"You know the property is owned by a new family," Kade explains. "This delayed the search. Forensics were packing up to leave when they noticed a notch in the floorboard behind a bookcase."

My stomach bottoms out. I don't like where this is going.

"It leads to an old crawl space from the original property, before it was renovated in recent years," Hudson interjects. "It was sealed years ago, but they managed to get inside."

"And?" I urge them.

"They did a cursory search and called me immediately. We need to send major reinforcements right now."

Motherfuck.

For once, it's silent.

None of us want to know what's coming, even if we've been scrambling for any tiny clues for months now. People don't have hidden crawl spaces for no reason.

"What did they find?" Theo asks uneasily.

It takes a lot to make Hudson Knight look queasy. I wasn't sure that it was even possible, but right now, he looks ready to throw up his guts in front of us.

"The skeletal remains of multiple corpses."

"Multiple?" Hunter repeats in disbelief.

"They were all hidden under the family's home. Undisturbed for years now. It's a mass grave."

I have to sit back down before I fall on my stupid, clueless ass. Hunter's mouth is open, but no words are coming out. Theo hasn't moved an inch as he processes the news.

"Are we sure it's him?" he muses.

"Forensics found the bodies buried with a copy of the Bible and a hard-carved crucifix. A specific page was marked."

Pulling out his phone, Kade passes it around for us to see. There's a Bible passage marked with a gold filigree bookmark, inscribed with the symbol of the Holy Trinity.

God himself will kill tens of thousands if it pleases him. Samuel 6:19.

The silence resumes.

Sick, suffocating silence.

It takes a lot to stun us into submission. We've dealt with the outermost fringes of humanity's sickest souls. This has accelerated far beyond our worst nightmares.

Michaels has already killed nineteen women. Nineteen innocent lives brutalised and stolen. That number is about to be pushed a hell of a lot higher with this discovery.

"Fuck," Theo swears, his head in his hands. "*Fuck*. If this gets out, we can kiss the remaining public support we have goodbye."

"We'll be crucified for missing this." Hunter's mouth is pinched tight. "We're in serious shit now."

"But we didn't miss anything!" Hudson argues. "It's the police and their shitty investigations. Why are we taking the heat for them?"

"Because the case is ours now," Hunter replies grimly. "And this family has been living on top of a crime scene for years. The public won't care whose fault that is."

"Their anger will hit us all regardless," I agree.

"Some good news. This evidence ties Lee Heston to multiple

counts of murder." Kade crosses his arms, contemplating. "We can use this."

Hudson perks up. "Let's put out a nationwide call for information leading to his arrest."

"Any number of people have lived at that address over the years." Theo hits his forehead with the heel of his palm. "We can't assume Lee is responsible yet."

"You're kidding me?" he seethes.

"We'll be dragged in front of an ethics board within the hour if we do. There's no connection without proof."

"For fuck's sake!" I snap at them. "This is ridiculous. We know that motherfucker is really Pastor Michaels. We have his picture. Let's release it and end this bullshit right now."

Hunter's hand lands on my shoulder. "Theo is right, Enz. We can't do that. The superintendent will shut us down."

"I don't care. We need to find him! Screw her money. We don't need it. Let her punish us."

"Think this through," he urges. "If the case is taken away from us, Harlow's security will be reassigned."

"We'll lose her," Theo deadpans.

That stops me.

Fuck, he's right.

Seeing red across my vision, I stomp over to Theo's overflowing bookshelf and roar in frustration. It topples easily beneath my rage. Books, trinkets and folders of paperwork fly across the room. I'm left standing amidst the carnage, Theo's office semi-destroyed as he watches on without a word.

"You're telling me that our best shot at finding this asshole will take Harlow away from us."

Hunter's jaw clenches. "If the SCU resumes control of the case, she'll be moved into their witness protection program instead of ours. We'll never see her again."

Nope. Not a chance.

They won't protect her.

"Then how the fuck do we fix this?" I ask frantically.

"We need to tie the bodies to Lee Heston," Theo answers. "When we have probable cause, we can issue a warrant for his arrest and use that to smoke Michaels out."

Kade grabs his phone and turns to leave. "We have Michaels' DNA from the basement in Northumberland. All we need is a match to any DNA found in that mass grave."

"You think he'd be that sloppy?" I clench my fists tight. "He's never left evidence before. All the other victims were spotless."

"It only takes one slip-up. We could be lucky."

"Wouldn't that make a change," Theo mutters.

"Call Forensics," Hunter snaps at Kade. "If there's any DNA to be found in that grave, I want it. We'll send another team and pull every bit of evidence we can."

Kade nods in agreement and leaves to make the call. Scrubbing his tired face, Hunter pulls the scar bisecting his eyebrow taut.

I still remember the day he got it, way back in Sabre's long and colourful history. It was an early security job gone wrong. That seems like so long ago now. We were so naïve, clueless as to the dark and twisty path this business would take us on.

"We have to hold a press conference," he says with a sigh. "Appeal for any information from locals in the area. We need to identify when these murders took place."

"And Lee Heston?" I supply.

"If we get the evidence that we need to name him, we'll release his photograph to the press later on. If anyone's seen Michaels recently, they'll make the connection."

It's another stupid, bureaucratic delay, but we have to play by these ridiculous rules. I won't allow Harlow's safety to be jeopardised by letting the SCU take her from us now.

If it means playing ball until we have the evidence we need, I'll have to suck it the hell up. No fucker on this planet will take my girl from me. Not without a fight.

"We'll announce the update today and start appealing for information," Hunter decides. "That buys us some time while we sort Heston and make the connection."

We all nod in agreement.

Hunter steps aside to make the call to Lucas. He'll have a shit fit when he hears this fiasco. I drag my phone back out and bring up Leighton's name. He's with Harlow and Brooklyn, keeping an eye on them.

> **Enzo:** Make sure Harlow doesn't watch the news and stays away from the internet.

His response comes quickly.

> **Leigh:** What happened?
>
> **Enzo:** We've got more bodies. Under wraps for now, but it will hit the media soon. We should be the ones to tell her.
>
> **Leigh:** Fuck my mouth. Alright, I'll handle it.
>
> **Enzo:** We'll be home when we can. Sit tight.

"Leighton's gonna keep Harlow occupied until we can get home and update her ourselves."

Theo nods as he begins picking up stray books and stacking them haphazardly. I should offer to help given I just fucked his entire library, but I'm too mad to see straight.

Finishing his phone call, Hunter returns to our group. Hudson is texting rapidly from the corner, updating his own family that we're going to be working very late tonight.

"Lucas is organising a press conference," Hunter fills us in. "We won't disclose Frederick Houghton as our source on Heston or what led us to the property."

"When they ask how we found this place?"

"We tell them jack shit," he says tiredly. "The less they know, the better. We need to protect an active investigation."

"Are we sure this is the right approach at all?" Hudson questions, his phone discarded. "We've never played ball with the media before."

Hunter strokes a hand over his beard. "Our best shot is facing this head on. If we leave them to find out for themselves, we'll be buried alive. We're on our last life as it is."

"I don't like it either," I offer him. "But we're short on time and this is the quickest way to get information."

Hudson nods in defeat. "I hate this."

"Ditto." I clap his shoulder. "But let's get it done."

But if we leave this, we'll be facing a full-blown shitstorm when the story leaks. Which it inevitably will. This way, we're cutting out the middleman and getting out in front of this.

"Fucking hell," I curse, my eyes gritty from exhaustion. "This is going to hit Harlow hard. We need to go home."

I leave out the fact that she isn't even speaking to us right now. Not after the way we dealt with her nut-job father at Hunter's birthday. My apologies have fallen flat ever since.

This chaos is spiralling.

The situation is already a hair's breadth from imploding in a spectacular manner, and I have a very bad feeling this update might just be the final straw for all of us.

CHAPTER 18

Harlow

Too Far Gone – The Plot In You

H unter's hand lands on my rapidly bouncing leg, wrapped in a thick pair of black tights beneath my simple, black shift dress. I snatch his hand up, too nervous to fight him off.

Our falling out feels insignificant in light of the recent discovery. I can't think about it, let alone say it out loud. We're still waiting on a final body count from Forensics.

More victims.

More death.

More despair.

There has to come a point when everything stops. The world falls off its axis. Gravity ceases to function. Pain reaches a level of saturation that reality can no longer contain.

I'm close.

Too fucking close.

"Just breathe," Hunter advises. "Say the word and we'll turn this car around and go home. You don't have to do this."

Looking out of the car window at the first glimmers of spring emerging from the chrysalis of cold and rain, I shake my head.

"I have to, Hunt."

"Why? You owe Laura nothing, sweetheart."

"This is my chance to say goodbye."

He nods in understanding. "What about the eulogy? If it's too much—"

"I'll be fine," I interrupt.

His hand releases mine and skates higher, brushing over my inner thigh. The warmth of his body heat curls around my cold sarcophagus. I've been chilled since the news came in.

Staring straight ahead at the back of Enzo's head in the driver's seat, he's silent and wearing a hardened grimace. I let him back into my bed last night. We were both too tired and emotionally raw to sleep apart.

Hunter's lips touch my ear. "You don't have to lie to me. None of us are fine. We won't survive this if we don't talk to each other."

"Talking won't help the families of those people."

"We're doing everything we can to identify the victims. I know it's hard, but I need your patience right now."

"I'm sorry, Hunt. I have no patience left. It's only a matter of time before we find Candace's body next."

"You don't know that," he returns.

"Don't I? Just leave it. I told you that I don't want to talk."

"How about we discuss your impromptu hotel visit with my little brother instead? Either way, you're going to talk to me. I won't let you shut me out."

Jaw clenched, I turn in the backseat to look up at Hunter's handsome features. His hair is slicked back in a severe bun, highlighting his tired, cocoa-coloured eyes and the slim black hearing aid fitted to his left ear.

He looks good enough to eat in an expensive Armani suit, complete with a black shirt, silky tie and the bulge of a concealed weapon strapped to his body. I swallow the bubble of fear in my throat.

"You hurt me," I whisper to him.

"Harlow…"

"No matter your intentions, you took my choice away from me. I had every right to speak to my own father."

"I was trying to protect you from him," he grits out.

"And who's protecting me from you?"

He recoils like I've slapped him. "You don't need protecting from me. Hate me if you want, but I'll always stand between you and danger. That's my job."

"Why?" I raise my voice. "I don't need you to."

"Because I love you too goddamn much to watch you die like everyone else." His eyes burn bright with determined fire. "That's why."

I catch Enzo watching our exchange in the rearview mirror. The same fear and anxiety stares back at me in his amber eyes. I'm caught between both of them.

Their terror of losing me has infiltrated the air in my lungs. I'm choking on it. We all are. The fear is contagious.

"That's what you're supposed to do for someone you love." Hunter's hand grips mine. "And I know it's real love, because I don't give a fuck that you slept with my brother last week."

Busted. I try to summon a response and fail.

"I've spent months trying to keep you all to myself," he adds in a rasp. "But it doesn't matter anymore, does it?"

"Why not?" I force out.

"All I care about is keeping you safe from the world. I need you to be okay. We're in too much danger to bicker amongst ourselves right now. No more fighting."

Enzo stares at him instead of the winding country lane that we're driving down. I never thought I'd hear Hunter change his tune. We've been battling this problem for months.

It's over.

We won.

All it took was for Pastor Michaels to exceed our worst expectations. His inhuman depravity has finally tipped the scales in Enzo's favour. I gave Leighton my virginity, but they're all still here, demanding a slice of my heart.

The intimate confines of the blacked-out car are interrupted by the roar of distant voices. We turn a corner, approaching the quaint village chapel buried amongst pine trees in the distance.

My heart explodes with fear. We're not alone out here in the peaceful countryside, far from London's smog and traffic.

"Oh shit," Hunter curses.

Outside the chapel where Laura's final goodbye is being held, a swarm of news vans, reporters and screaming protestors are shattering the morning's fragile peace.

Camera crews record the cluster of people waving placards and yelling at the top of their lungs. I have no idea how they found out about today's service, but the usual suspects from outside HQ are all here. An unruly, furious mob.

"How the fuck did they find out?" Enzo barks as he hits the brakes. "We told them to back off and let us do our jobs in that damned press conference."

"The media must've leaked the memorial's location. They're desperate for a glimpse of us."

"Dammit! This is a disaster." Enzo scowls ahead.

I scan the crowd and my stomach somersaults. Something has changed. Amongst the calls for justice, several new faces have infiltrated the angry horde. It takes me a moment to realise what they're doing.

"Praying," I surmise flatly.

Hunter leans between the seats to look. "What the hell?"

Where others are here to torment Sabre and release their own anxieties about the crawl space full of corpses, a new faction has decided to pile on to the madness.

Pastor Michaels' fans.

I can see the gleam of crucifixes around their necks as they fervently pray. One middle-aged woman is leading the group, dressed in a demure frock that screams of Mrs Michaels and her cold-hearted ways.

Rolling down my window a crack, I listen in on their calls to the heavens. The frenetic whisper of prayers is an awful, familiar taunt that tosses me back into the throes of the past.

"Oh, Lord Almighty," she calls out. "Protect our saviour on his quest to save the souls of those cursed with damnation."

"The emails," I whisper to myself. "This is them."

Enzo punches the steering wheel. "They're seriously picketing the funeral of one of his victims. Who does that?"

"You'd be surprised." Hunter wrinkles his nose. "That's it, turn the car around. It isn't safe here. We're going home."

"No!" I shout in a rush. "I have to do this."

"Harlow, this is a volatile situation. I won't put your safety at risk while these fanatics are on the loose."

"Laura's brother invited me himself. I can't let him down now, not after… what I did to her." My voice catches. "Please, Hunt. I need this closure."

His eyes soften. "You owe him nothing."

"Maybe not, but I have to do this. Not just for him, but for myself."

That breaks his resolve.

"Fuck. Don't make me regret this." He points towards the back of the stone chapel. "Enz, take the rear entrance. I'll call the others and redirect them."

"Tell Theo to call the police," Enzo instructs as he reverses away from the mob. "They need to be here to contain this shit. It isn't right."

Barking off rapid orders down the phone, Hunter instructs the rest of our convoy to park around the back of the chapel. Theo, Leighton, Hudson and Brooklyn are following behind us with a back-up security car.

Killing the engine after parking, Enzo hops out with a thud and opens the door for me. He's dressed in his usual armour, an all-black ensemble, adding to his threatening presence as he checks his gun is in place.

I grab my handbag, a hand-written eulogy inside, and let him lift me out of the backseat. I'm crushed into his side. He feels like a furnace, his black t-shirt saturated with the woodsy scent of forests and bonfires.

"Stick with me." He buries his face in my hair and inhales. "I don't like this one bit."

Allowing myself to relax a fraction, I fist his leather jacket and hug him tight. Things have been difficult recently, but right now, I need him. Enzo is my stable foundation.

When I raise my head, his lips are on mine before I can react. Enzo's kiss is an agitated plea for the world to cut us some slack. I can taste his trepidation. He's petrified of losing me again.

When the kiss breaks, his forehead meets mine. "Sorry."

"Hey, it's okay," I whisper back. "I'm sorry for being a pain in the ass recently."

"Don't even think about apologising. I should be saying sorry. We're gonna get through this. I know we will."

The squeal of tyres approaching interrupts our moment, and we separate. Theo's still on the phone with the police as he climbs out of the matching SUV, closely flanked by Leighton and Hudson in their own all-black clothing.

Brooklyn hops down from the driver's seat, a lit cigarette caught between her red-painted lips. When her eyes meet mine, she offers a tight, reassuring smile. All I can do is shake my head in dismay.

"Goldilocks!"

Zipping to my side, Leighton drags me into a lung-squeezing cuddle before kissing my temple.

"You okay? This shit is crazy."

"I'm fine, Leigh."

"Stick close to us, yeah?"

He sandwiches me between himself and Enzo as the last of our security detail arrives. Several burly agents offer me emotionless nods. Sabre's finest are here to defend us.

"Police are aware of the protest," Theo informs us all. "Until it's a case of public disorder, they aren't getting involved. They don't want any more bad press."

"Public disorder?" Brooklyn laughs. "People are praying for the victim's fucking murderer at her bloody memorial!"

Hudson drops a hand on her shoulder. "Keep your voice down. We don't want them to spot us."

"I ought to go around there and beat the shit out of every single twisted fuck chanting their stupid heads off!"

"Brooke," Enzo interrupts her rant. "We're trying to keep a low profile here. Shut up."

She flicks her cigarette butt at him. "Eat shit, dickhead."

"Love you too, wildfire. Come on, let's move."

Trapped in a protective nest of muscled shoulders, loaded holsters and fierce scowls, I'm escorted into the rear of the chapel.

It's an older building, carved from slick stones and brightly coloured stained glass. The smell of old Bibles and damp meets my nostrils with sickening familiarity.

I clutch my handbag tighter and remind myself to breathe. This isn't the basement. I can walk out of here. I'm safe. Memories are bubbling up, attempting to overwhelm me.

Low conversation emanates from the chapel as we cut through the outdated kitchen, and that's when my anxiety decides to punch me in the face. I grab a handful of Theo's dark-wash flannel shirt in front of me and tug.

He looks over his shoulder. "You good?"

"I can't d-do this... I c-can't..."

Turning on the spot, he parts the sea of security and people surrounding us to take me into his wiry arms.

"Shhh, beautiful. You can do this."

"I can't!"

"We're all here with you."

"What if... what if he hates me? I killed his sister. It's all my fault that she's gone."

Theo grabs my face and traps me between his warm, dry hands. I latch on to the scent of old books and minty freshness clinging to his denim jacket. It's just him. My Theodore. Nobody else.

"He invited you to speak about his sister and honour her memory," he reminds me. "That kid doesn't hate you."

"He's alone because of me."

"Because of Pastor Michaels," Theo adds meaningfully. "Hold my hand, Harlow. I've got you."

Forcing myself to take a stuttered breath, I let our fingers entwine. Theo doesn't even flinch anymore. He's allowed his sky-high barriers to melt around me.

"Promise you won't let go?" I whisper.

Even with the press of people around us invading our bubble of privacy, he comes close to feather a kiss against my lips.

"I won't let go. I promise."

He squeezes my hand to reiterate his vow. We separate and I let him guide me forwards, following the mammoth set of Enzo's shoulders ducking through arched doorways.

The chapel falls silent as we enter, extinguishing the low murmur of conversation from the small group of guests. Rising from his front-row seat, a slim, auburn-haired teenager watches us approach with slightly widened eyes.

I don't need an introduction to recognise Laura's brother, Carlos Whitcomb. He's barely eighteen years old and far too young to be dealing with all of this alone. Laura was the only family he had left.

With agony constricting my heart, I clutch Theo's hand even tighter and approach the inevitable confrontation. Hunter directs everyone to take seats in the second row, leaving me to stop in front of Laura's brother.

"Harlow?"

"Hi, Carlos."

"You look different from the photos I've seen on the news." A dusting of pink colours his freckled cheeks. "Thanks for coming. I wasn't sure if you'd turn up."

"I wanted to be here. Laura was my friend." I watch the sheen of tears rise in his eyes. "More than that. She was my ray of hope in a very dark time."

Carlos nods with a heartbroken smile. "I'm sure she'd say the same thing for you."

The guilt is choking me alive. Every inch of my mind is flooded with shame and resentment. I wasn't Laura's ray of hope. In the end, all I was to her was an escape route.

The perfect executioner.

He lowers his voice as the tears spill over. "Thank you for bringing her back to me."

The backs of my eyes burn as the devil's claws wrap around my throat. I try to release Theo's hand, but he holds on.

"It was nothing," I answer stiffly.

"It meant a lot to me, so thanks."

Shivering from head to toe, I manage a final nod and escape to my seat. Hunter, Enzo and Leighton are already sandwiched in down the aisle, leaving me to take the outer seat, with Brooklyn and Hudson behind me.

The tinkle of the organ suffuses the air, calling the service to order. I'm surprised that Carlos chose to hold the memorial here of all places, although the grey-haired chaplain notably doesn't hold a Bible. That's a relief.

"We're gathered here today to honour the life of Laura Whitcomb. Beloved sister, co-worker, and friend, she is greatly missed by all who knew and loved her."

Fire ants are itching at my skin, whispering their mindless taunts. I can feel every single hair on my head—heavy, suffocating, begging to be torn free. The pain is so tempting.

As I stare ahead, ignoring the hum of gossip behind us from the small gathering of people, the chaplain's voice is accompanied by shouting from outside.

Theo's thumb draws circles against the skin of my inner wrist.

Each rotation tugs my escaping lucidity back down to earth, forcing me to remain strong.

He's got me. I'm okay. This will all be over soon. The words should be calming, but instead, my own inside voice begins to morph into a familiar, cold taunt.

You fucking whore!

Thwack. Thwack. Thwack.

Watch your friend, Harlow.

Thwack. Thwack. Thwack.

Watch her bleed out for her insolence.

I tried my best to cower and make myself small as Laura was raped and carved into blood-slick ribbons. I tried to block my ears. I tried to pray for her. None of it worked.

She screamed so loud.

All while I was fatally silent.

Carlos takes his place at the front of the chapel, a scrap of paper caught in his shaking hands. He looks over us all, his eyes briefly landing on me. Nausea engulfs me.

He can see the guilt written across my face. I know it. Everyone can. The words of his short, grief-stricken speech don't penetrate my cotton-wool brain. All I can hear is her endless, excruciated screaming.

When he steps down from the pulpit, turning to glance at the printed photograph of a smiling Laura displayed for the whole chapel to see, Carlos blows his sister a final kiss.

I watch his lips move.

Goodbye. I love you.

Theo gently nudges me when I don't move. He's pulled the speech from my handbag and slips it into my hands. I can feel the others all staring at me, searching for any warning signs of a breakdown.

Falling back on years of practiced silence, I plaster a blank mask into place. I don't need them inside my head. It's loud enough in here as it is.

The long walk to the front of the room is the loneliest I've felt in months. I smooth out the folded piece of paper, avoiding looking up at the eyes locked on me.

I stare down. Blink. Gulp air. Plead for courage. The entire chapel is waiting for me to speak, but nothing's coming out. In the silence, the outside sneaks back in.

Shouting.

Chanting.

Praying.

"Laura was a bright, beautiful soul," I begin with downturned eyes. "The day we met, she made me a promise. One that she fought until her last breath to keep."

My words are drowned out by the protest and steady sobbing of a woman a few seats behind Carlos. I recognise her face from Sabre's case files. She worked with Laura.

"Laura protected me. She kept me alive with her stories, her laughter, the promises she made to get us both out alive."

My voice breaks on the final syllable as horror takes over. When I dare to glance up, the chapel has melted away. Shadows, cobwebs and soulless darkness infect the aisle, framing the steady footsteps of a skeletal ghost.

Laura doesn't resemble her beautiful, hopeful photograph displayed to my right. In my imagination, she's skin and bone, blood and flesh, all hashed together in a crimson-soaked patchwork quilt.

I watch her approach. Closer, closer, the entire chapel ambivalent to her movements. They can't see her. She's dead and gone, but her ghost lives on in the fibrous connections between my nerve cells.

"I w-wanted to save you," I rasp through painful breaths. "Please,

Laura. You gave me no choice."

The low murmurings of the audience don't halt her steps. Paper scrunching in my hands, I feel my chest catch on fire. Searing hot tears flood down my cheeks.

Before Laura's ghost can lay her bloodstained hands on me, I turn and flee the room at full speed, leaving my speech scattered across the floor.

Shouts of my name chase after me. I can hear Enzo and Hunter, both trapped in the aisle and bellowing at mourners to move out of the way.

Without looking over my shoulder, I know that she's following, invisible to all but me. The girl who died at my hands. Now, we're tethered together, body and soul.

Caught in the grasp of a panic attack, I shove the rear exit door open and spill outside into the spring air. That's when terror spikes through me. Our ruse has been uncovered.

"Harlow Michaels!"

"Over here. Give us a statement!"

"Harlow! Smile for us!"

Blood-thirsty reporters have clustered around the back of the chapel, battling with the three burly security officers who we brought with us. They're overwhelmed by people.

The protestors have followed them in earnest, bringing their anger and hatred with them as they crowd the back entrance. It's a confusing mixture of political anger and frantic shouts of Bible verses, prayers and insults.

They're here.

The devil's brood.

Clutching my aching chest, I attempt to dodge the nearest microphone being shoved in my face. Hyland, our biggest agent, grabs the reporter by the scruff of his neck and tosses him down to the cracked concrete.

It's an explosion of chaos and opposing sides, all battling for one thing—me. For their exclusive, for the killings to stop, for a sacrificial lamb to offer their careless overlord.

It doesn't matter.

They all want me.

Common sense abandons my sputtering mind. All I want to do is run. Full speed, without direction, as far away from these snakes as possible. When I stumble down the set of stone steps, I'm bombarded by the protestors first.

"He's killing because of you," someone screams in my face. "End the slaughter! Surrender yourself."

The chants grow more extreme. Placards are waved with malice, all depicting familiar faces. Girls who I outlived and failed to protect. Now, these people want justice for them.

"I'm sorry," I try to shout above the riot of noise. "I never w-wanted any of this to happen."

"The Lord is just and merciful! We must protect his servant and pray for our salvation!"

These chants overwhelm the tangle of angry people. Pastor Michaels' deranged fan club, clutching their own crucifixes and Bibles, intermingle with the protestors.

The two sides collide in a riot of anger. I scream and duck as one woman attacks another, wrapping her hands around her throat to cease the mindless barrage of Bible talk.

"How can you support that monster?"

"God bless his divine work. Those sluts deserved to die!"

"They were people!"

When the first punches fly, I know I'm in trouble. I can hear the guys screaming and shouting my name after catching up, but I'm stuck amidst the fighting.

"Take that back! You're as bad as that piece of shit!"

"He will rejoice in our salvation and save our souls from damnation."

Thuds of fists meeting flesh accompany the wail of punched faces. Bibles are thrown as nails scrape down cheeks, drawing blood and screams.

I can see Enzo wrestling with a fearless reporter, attempting to shove her aside and get closer to me. Theo is back on his phone, yelling at the police for backup.

Ducking and weaving in a blur of determination, Hunter abandons Leighton and Hudson, trying to restrain various protestors. He's the closest, leaving Brooklyn to fight behind him to move a single inch.

His fearful brown eyes bug out, and my heart freezes dead in my chest. I can't hear the shouts pouring from his open mouth, frantic and afraid. We're both watching the same horror show in slow motion.

Death.

Its claws are unfurling.

Behind a fight blurring with fists and battered knuckles, one of the protestors has inched closer. His cheeks are tear stained. Resolution fills his gaunt face. I know who he is immediately.

Candace's older brother.

He was interviewed a few weeks ago by Hudson and Kade. I heard about his heartbreak second-hand in one of Hunter's very sparse updates about the case.

That heartbreak has changed now. Morphed. Grown into a new branch of rage. Pastor Michaels demanded my surrender in exchange for Candace's life, and I'm still here.

His sister is going to die.

That's on me.

And he knows it.

The gun clutched in his wavering hands registers too late. It glints in the sunlight, a deadly weapon that holds no fear for me. If I die right here, right now, the slaughter will end.

I want him to pull the trigger. My feet refuse to move. I won't run. I won't fight. If my path is set to end here, I will go with the knowledge that my death ensures the safety of countless more women.

"Harlow!" Hunter screams my name.

I ignore him.

Candace's brother draws closer, fingering the trigger. He's at almost point-blank range. Still, the panic doesn't set in. Numbness is all I can summon in the face of my end.

Seconds pass in fragments. Disjointed. Individual cuts of a wider movie scene that are haphazardly stuck together. The crowd parts. Hunter's fingers touch my arm. The gun nears.

BANG.

I'm not sure what happens first. The piercing gunshot, the spray of blood across my face or Hunter throwing his entire body in front of me at the last moment. It's all a blur.

Candace's brother is barrelled over by Hyland, bellowing for his two fellow agents to follow suit. The gun hits the ground, but it doesn't make a sound. Nothing does.

Silence.

It's all around me.

Floating above my body, I watch my eyes tilt downwards, expecting a flow of blood to pour from the bullet wound in my chest. Instead, my dress is untouched. Pristine.

A river of blood coats the cobblestones of the car park instead. But it isn't mine. Is it? I can't feel any pain. Only the petrified hammering of my heart. The organ knows what's happened here before I do.

A body is tangled at my feet. Collapsed and limp. No signs of life. Blood pours from his head, growing into a rapidly expanding puddle. His ear is a ragged hole.

That's when reality kicks me in the teeth, and I scream at the very top of my lungs.

"HUNTER!"

CHAPTER 19

Leighton

The Way That You Were – Sleep Token

For my entire life, I've withered in my brother's impressive shadow. As kids, we'd bicker and fight. He wanted to help me. Push me. Inspire my success. All I cared about was seeing him fail.

I wanted our parents' love, and for him to know how it felt to be the odd one out. The family screw-up. Not smart enough. Hard working enough. Handsome enough.

Hunter's all of that.

I wanted to take it from him.

Standing at the bottom of an occupied hospital bed, accompanied by the hum of a heart monitor and ventilator, I'd do anything to take it all back. I've been so selfish.

He can have our parents' love.

Success. Money.

The dream house.

A glittering career.

Fuck, he can even have the girl he wants. I'll surrender Harlow to him and kill the last shreds of hope left inside me. I'll cut my own heart out and squash it beneath my shoe if it will bring him back.

I need my brother to live.

Hunter cannot fucking die.

Someone touches my shoulder, but I don't move. If I tear my eyes from the rise and fall of his chest, I know it'll stop. He'll slip away. I have to stand here and keep guard so the devil doesn't end his life when no one's looking.

"Leigh," Enzo says quietly. "You should go home and get some rest."

I shrug him off. "I'm fine here."

"You've been camped out in this room for days. Go eat and shower, at least."

I'm not sure how it's only been two sleepless days since the gut-wrenching moment that I almost lost my sibling. He still isn't out of the woods after being placed in a medically induced coma while the swelling on his brain eases.

The gunshot was so close, it tore through his left ear and fractured his skull in the process. He's got to be the luckiest son of a bitch alive that the shot was shitty at best and his brains weren't painted across that car park.

"Where's Harlow?" I summon the energy to ask. "She was gone when I woke up."

"Asleep in the waiting area. Theo took her home yesterday, but she didn't stay long. Maybe you can convince her to go home with you tonight."

"I'm going nowhere."

Sighing with a level of exhaustion most can't even imagine, Enzo collapses in the creaky chair next to Hunter's bedside. The circles under his eyes are a vivid purple, much like mine. We've been camped out here since our lives changed in a split second with that single bullet.

"Your mum's making a few phone calls in the corridor," he reveals in a flat voice. "And Ben's lecturing the security outside for bad posture."

I brace my hands on the bed's railing. "They don't know what else to do but fuss while Hunter's sedated."

"You heard what the doctors said. The swelling on his brain is severe. It needs time to go down before he'll be safe to regain consciousness."

Glancing up at Enzo, his huge frame is blurred by a sheen of tears. I can't remember the last time I properly cried, not counting the few stray tears that escaped when I reunited with my parents. Hell, I didn't even cry as they read my sentencing and I was shipped off to prison for three years.

"I never thanked him."

Enzo's eyebrows knit together. "For what?"

"For saving my life when I left prison. He gave me a home, money, a job. Everything. All I've ever given him is grief."

With a heartbroken nod, Enzo's head falls into his hands. I know he doesn't want me to see him cry, but the rhythmic shake of his shoulders betrays his despair.

"Hunter never wanted your gratitude," Enzo says into his hands. "All he ever wanted was to see you happy again. That was enough for him."

I grab the clipboard hanging on the end of the hospital bed and throw it so hard, it hits the wall and breaks in half. Enzo's head shoots up as he glares at me.

"Leigh, what the fuck?!"

"Stop using past tense!" I bark at him. "Hunter is lying right there in front of you. He's still alive."

His face falls back into misery. "Hunter's in a coma with a fractured skull. We came too fucking close this time."

I'm so tempted to lay him out across the linoleum with a broken nose. Hunter doesn't quit. Not once. His whole life has been an exercise in conviction. This is no different.

"Go home," Enzo says again.

"I can't leave him here."

"I'll stay and watch him."

I want to protest, but I haven't showered in days. I smell like absolute death incarnate. My head is dizzy from lack of sleep, and my muscles are steadily burning. I need to lie down before I end up in here myself.

"Swear to keep your eyes on him at all times?"

Enzo crosses his heart with a half-hearted smile. "I won't leave him alone in here, Leigh. He's my brother too."

"Alright. I'll take Harlow with me."

"Richards had some more sleeping tablets delivered. Stick some in her tea if she refuses to lie down again."

"Jesus, Enz. I'm not drugging her."

"She hasn't spoken! Not a single goddamn word in days. All she does is cry and stare. Drug her if you have to and make sure she gets some bloody sleep. That's final."

Shaking my fuzzy head in disbelief, I leave him to his guard post. His shoulders are still trembling with silent tears that he won't let anyone else see. Enzo's hope has gone already.

He's expecting the worst. I can see it on his face. Losing his parents, then his baby sister, really fucked him up. Add Alyssa passing away on top of that, and he's far too used to the people he loves being ripped away.

Hunter's death would break him.

Irreparably so.

I offer my father a terse nod as I pass him in the corridor. He's taken the phone from my mum and leans against the wall, pinching the bridge of his nose as he quietly speaks.

"Leigh," Mum exclaims.

Flinching, I dodge her rumpled embrace. "You okay?"

She looks as rough as the rest of us, her clothes worn and sweat stained. "Yes, darling. Are you leaving?"

"I'm going home," I say robotically. "Enzo's going to take this shift. I'll be back in the morning."

She strokes a hand over my hair. "Need a hand with Harlow? She's just making another cup of coffee."

"I'll convince her to come with me. Stay with Enzo." My throat seizes with emotion. "He needs looking after too."

"I left a message for Hayley and asked her to call me back," Mum reveals. "We'll fill her in when she does."

"Good idea." I watch my father begin to pace the corridor. "Who is he speaking to?"

Mum's eyes glance over to her frustrated husband. "The Chief Constable. Hunter's attacker has been charged with attempted murder."

Murder.

He came so close to death.

"What about the protestors?"

"We're slapping them all with criminal charges," she says defiantly. "Public disorder and abusive behaviour offences for every single one of them who incited the violence."

"That's something."

Burying my face in her wrinkled neck, I allow myself a sliver of weakness. I can crumble with my mother's arms around me. She won't tell the world that I'm not the strong one. That has always been Hunter's job.

He's the glue who holds this dysfunctional family together. We've taken him for granted all this time, ignoring the fact that he's the one keeping us all alive and well. We owe him our lives. Now, he's fighting to keep his.

"Your brother needs you to step up, Leigh. If he pulls through… he's going to be in for a long recovery."

I swipe my damp cheeks. "Yeah, I know. I'll speak to Enzo. We'll figure something out about the company."

Mum smiles weakly. "Be the man I know you're meant to be. If not for yourself, then for your brother."

Her words add weight to the growing pressure of responsibility piling on my shoulders. With each day that Hunter has remained unconscious, my resolve has grown.

Now, I have to step up.

It's time to be a fucking adult.

We still have a violent serial killer to catch, decomposed bodies to identify and teams to run. We can't afford to let the darkness win. Hunter deserves more from us than that.

Pressing a soft kiss to my mother's cheek, I leave her to wrangle my father. He spares me a blank nod as I pass, heading for the waiting area where we've been camped out.

I emerge into the quiet, yellow-painted room and wince at the sound of loud banging. It hasn't woken Theo up yet. He's still passed out and snoring, his head covered by a magazine.

In the corner of the room, a disgruntled Harlow is beating the shit out of a vending machine. Her mousy-brown hair is matted, emphasising the visible bald patch beneath the thin layer of protection.

She's been ripping it out nonstop.

"Kicking the machine won't make the coffee any better," I try to joke, but it falls flat. "What's up?"

She braces her hands on the cheap hunk of metal. "It swallowed my coins."

Those are the first words I've heard her speak. All we've exchanged is a constant stream of anguished tears and exhausted half-hugs.

"Well, that's a good reason to go home. I need to shower and eat some real food."

Harlow waves absently. "Go."

"No. You're coming with me."

Her head is lowered with defeat as she ignores me. I crouch down next to her and peer underneath her braced arms, attempting to catch her line of sight.

"Harlow," I repeat. "Home. Now."

She shakes her head, sending stray tears flying.

"That wasn't a request. We both need to get some decent rest and a hot meal. We're no good to Hunter like this."

"I'm not leaving here until he does," she says, barely above a whisper.

I tuck her curtain of dark, curling hair over her shoulder. It reveals the swollen slits where her eyes should be. She's cried herself to the point of being sick in past days. I've heard her throwing up between sobbing gasps and lamentations.

"When Hunter wakes up, he's going to need us," I remind her. "Come home and clean up, at least."

"I can't sleep, Leigh. Every time I shut my eyes, I see him lying at my feet, bleeding across the ground."

Moving slowly, I ease my arms around her and hold her against my heaving chest. Harlow struggles at first, but she's too exhausted to

JROSE

put up much of a fight. Her head collapses on my slumped shoulder.

"You don't have to sleep," I murmur into her ragged hair. "Just come home and eat something. Please? For me?"

"I don't want to eat."

"Bloody hell, Harlow. Enough!"

She recoils at my raised voice.

I grab her chin tight to implore her. "My brother is in a fucking coma. I can't worry about you keeling over as well. You're coming home. Now."

Her usually clear blue eyes are fogged over and uncertain, staring into mine with such intense guilt, it physically burns me. Fucking hell. How on earth did we get here?

"Okay," she says in a tiny voice.

"Okay," I repeat.

"What about Theo?"

"Let's go wake him up and drag him home too. He'll appreciate sleeping in a proper bed."

I tow her back over to the cluster of empty seats to grab her parka and handbag. Theo yelps loudly and shoots upright when I tug on his left leg.

"How's that bed working out for you?" I pull again, causing him to fall on the floor. "Get up, sleeping beauty."

His jaw cracks with a yawn. "What time is it?"

"Just after midnight."

"Fuck, I need to go to the office."

"Now? It's the middle of the night."

"Forensics are moving the unidentified bodies to HQ's morgue in a few hours. I need to be there to sign off."

"You're coming home to sleep and eat first. None of us are travelling alone right now."

334

"Leigh—"

"No fucking arguments," I cut him off. "Get downstairs and in the car before I have Enzo escort you out instead."

His mouth pops open before snapping shut again. Without another word, he grabs his heavy backpack and laptop before taking Harlow's trembling hand.

The pair trail towards the exit, exchanging low murmurs. Harlow's leaning heavily on him, almost limping with exhaustion. My mother offers them both a tearful smile of farewell as they head for the elevator.

"Mr Rodriguez?"

I turn to find Hunter's main doctor approaching with a steaming coffee balanced along with her thick notepad.

"Yeah?"

"Can I have a moment?" Doctor Lane takes a sip of coffee. "I was just on my way to speak to your parents."

"They're dealing with the police investigation right now. What is it? Is there an update?"

Glancing around the empty waiting room, she gestures for me to take a seat. I wave off my mother before she can approach, gesturing for her to stay with Dad for now.

"We've got the results back from your brother's CT scan." Her grey eyes soften with sympathy. "We've ruled out any permanent brain damage at this time."

The air whooshes from my lungs.

"Thank God."

"The skull fracture is significant, but the surgery was successful, and it will heal with time. There are no signs of internal bleeding. He's lucky to survive a direct hit like that."

"And the ear?" I ask next.

That's when her smile droops.

"Our cosmetic surgeon has done her best to salvage Hunter's left ear. She performed a partial reconstruction, but the scarring will be extensive."

"He's alive. Scars are a small price to pay."

Doctor Lane nods. "We'll keep him in intensive care until the swelling reduces before easing him off sedation. Only time will tell how he responds from there."

Slapping my knees, I stand up and straighten my creased t-shirt. "I'm taking my family home. We'll be back tomorrow."

"Mr Rodriguez, before you go, I want to discuss something else with you. It's a little sensitive."

My burst of hopeful optimism fades.

"What is it?"

She looks down, her mouth twisted unhappily. "Your brother is already partially deaf. The ear that was affected in the attack is the one that retained some functioning."

"Yes, there was an accident several years ago. His left ear still works with a permanent hearing aid."

"I'm aware of his medical history," she inserts with that damned pitiful smile again. "This gives me some concern, given the localised nature of the bullet wound."

My tired brain doesn't compute what she's saying. I blink with gritty eyes, the pounding of a headache causing the low-lit room to tilt on its axis.

"What are you saying?" I sigh tiredly.

"His head injury and the damage to his ear are extensive," she clarifies. "We have reason to believe this may impact his current level of hearing, given the pre-existing damage."

Jesus Christ.

Is she saying what I think she is?

Authoritative footsteps slap against the cheap hospital linoleum to join us. I know it's my father from the beat of his feet. He halts beside me, resting a hand on my shoulder.

"Dad," I begin.

His hand squeezes hard. "I overheard. Be straight with us, doc. How much damage can we expect there to be?"

"Difficult to say," Doctor Lane offers. "But his hearing was minimal to begin with. I'm expecting there to be a reduction in line with the severity of his injuries."

A lead brick settles in the pit of my stomach. I reach up to grab Dad's hand, resting mine on top as our fingers entangle. I need someone to comfort me right now.

"How bad could it be?"

The doctor's grimace seals my dread.

"We're looking at total hearing loss."

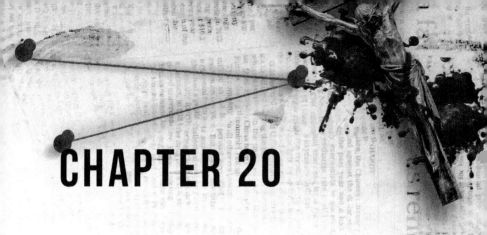

CHAPTER 20

Harlow

Two Weeks – FKA Twigs

Standing in the freezing cold bowels of HQ, the usual hum of chatter and activity is absent. I'm deep underground, far from the staff and their sympathetic glances.

On the other side of the two-way mirror, post-mortem examinations are taking place. Three skeletal, decomposed bodies are being picked over by Sabre's on-site pathologists.

They found five bodies in total.

Five more lives turned to dust.

Sitting next to me, Theo's fingers are hammering against his keyboard as he takes notes. With his black-framed glasses holding his blonde ringlets back from his face, I can see every tired line and eye bag on display.

It's been a long week.

None of us have stopped.

We've been attempting to identify the bodies with a series of post-mortems. Sabre's morgue is overflowing. Using dental records, two families have been brought in for interviews with the Cobra team. The other relatives have yet to be located.

With Hunter still in intensive care and the outside world deemed unsafe for us to enter without protection, we've all holed up at HQ, mucking in to push the case forward.

"This is the last round of post-mortems," Theo comments. "Then we're done. You don't have to be here for this."

"What else do I have to do?"

"Studying?" he suggests.

My tongue is heavy with the bitter taste of disappointment. I've had to make some hard calls this week.

"Richards spoke to my school tutor. They've deferred me to the next cohort. So, I have nothing else to do."

Theo halts. "You did that?"

"I can't focus on school right now. Not with the case going on and Hunter in the hospital. It was the right decision."

He nods thoughtfully. "Then I'm proud of you for making that call. You're prioritising your mental health."

"And failing again."

"Beautiful, it's not a failure."

"After attending two classes? Not a failure?" I laugh without humour. "It doesn't matter anyway."

"You can still change your mind."

"Hunter is more important than school right now."

Turning my back on the endless stainless-steel tables of blackened bones and decomposed bodily matter, I rest my aching head against the white wall.

"Where's Enzo?"

"Upstairs speaking to one of the families," Theo answers from his laptop. "I've got the intelligence department building case files on the new victims for the next press briefing."

"Any leads?" I hold my breath.

"Nothing yet."

Pastor Michaels is out there somewhere, enjoying the chaos that he's created from miles away. He has the entire company in a tailspin. We're desperately trying to keep up with the constant onslaught of death and violence.

"Same MO, it's definitely him," Theo confirms. "All five victims were sex workers and off the radar. The bodies are being dated at roughly seven years old."

"He had me in the cage then," I finish for him.

"Yeah. The timeline checks out."

"So what? Maybe he just didn't think to bring these victims down there to kill them. That formality came later."

Theo cocks his head. "Perhaps these were practice kills. The ritual wasn't right, so he didn't display them for the police to find."

"And he stuffed them under the floorboards instead." I rub my temples, feeling sick to my stomach. "They were there all along. Buried and forgotten."

"I'm sorry, Harlow. I know this is hard."

When his phone vibrates with an incoming phone call, Theo offers me an apologetic look and accepts. He mutters a strained *okay* before hanging up.

"You're wanted in Hunter's office."

"Something wrong? Is it Hunter?"

Theo avoids my eyes. "To do with the case. Enzo and the Cobra team are waiting. I'll finish up here."

Seized by anxiety, I quickly press a kiss to his lips. "Will you meet us at the hospital?"

"I'll be there later on."

"Okay. Be safe."

He catches me in another kiss. "You too."

Leaving the underground morgue, it's a long elevator ride up to the office levels back amongst the living. I've spent a lot of time here this past week, more than ever before.

None of us are able to face being at home with Hunter's discarded ties, the growing pile of unread newspapers and boxes of English tea. Without him, it's a house. Not a home.

I was more than happy to throw myself into the case and help the others wherever possible. It's given us reason to keep going rather than drowning in the uncertainty that's currently wrecking our lives.

Reaching Hunter's carpet-lined office, I take a breath for courage before letting myself inside. Expecting everyone to be waiting for me, I'm surprised to find Enzo alone, his burly shoulders hunched over.

He's staring at the collection of framed photographs behind the desk. The precious memories of his family are one of Hunter's most prized possessions. Several more frames have been added in recent months, and I've only just noticed.

"Enz? You wanted to see me?"

He waves me forward. "Yeah."

I click the door shut and approach. Enzo's tanned, sinewy form slumps when my arms wrap around his waist from behind. I can barely get my arms around his muscular body.

Burying my nose in his back, I breathe in deeply. The scents of moss, pine trees and bonfire embers still cling to his usual black t-shirt, despite the days camped out in this office.

"What is it?" I ask fearfully.

"Michaels has made contact."

His voice is hard, clipped.

"Is Candace... alive?" I gulp hard.

"Fuck, Harlow. I want to protect you so badly, but I can't keep you safe from this. We're fighting a losing battle."

"I know. You don't have to."

"Looking after you is the only thing that matters to me, but we're taking fire on all sides. I don't know what else to do."

Slipping around his mountainous torso, I slide into his arms and force him to hug me back. Enzo has to bend in half to cuddle me close, and his chin rests on my head.

"Feel me," I say into his abdomen.

He shudders with an unsteady breath.

"I'm here, Enz. Safe. Protected. We're good. You're going to make yourself sick with worry at this rate."

"I almost watched my best friend die last week," he answers gruffly. "I have no idea if he will ever come back to us. I'm allowed to worry."

"Not when I'm in your arms. That's when you hold me close and tell me everything's going to be okay. That's when you believe it yourself too."

His chuckle smooths over me, soft and broken. "Jesus, little one. I have no clue how you're still standing after everything that's happened these past few months."

"You're holding me up, dummy."

He kisses the top of my head. "I'll always be here to do that. No matter what happens. Nothing will tear this family apart while I'm still alive and kicking."

We cuddle for several silent minutes, our breathing aligned and heartbeats hammering together. When Enzo sighs and pushes me away, I know reality has come knocking.

"He contacted Channel Ten News," Enzo reveals.

"Pastor Michaels did?"

"Yeah. Our old friend, Sally Moore, broke the news an hour ago."

Great. I bet she loved that.

"How bad is it?" I wince.

"He sent a grainy photograph of Candace and a warning. She looked to be badly beaten and shackled in some kind of abandoned property. No cage this time."

My meagre breakfast of dry toast and tea threatens to resurface. Enzo's hands gripping my shoulders are the only thing preventing me from crumpling to my knees.

"What was the warning?"

He shakes his head. "You don't need to read it."

"Yeah, Enz. I do. Show me."

"No."

"You asked me to trust you again," I remind him. "Don't break that trust now. I need to know what we're dealing with."

Cursing, he stares deep into my eyes for a moment, seeing my resolve. We're past him wrapping me in cotton wool now. I steel myself as he reaches for the iPad on the desk and pulls up a breaking news report.

The bright-red letters blur on the screen as I fight to remain calm. It's the longest message he's sent us in several months. My monster is still alive and kicking in the darkness.

Harlow,

I know you've found my playthings in their shallow grave. I've saved them for all these years. It's brought me happiness to know they rotted alone in the dark. The devil's spawn deserves no less.

Say hello to Candace.

She's running out of time.

Have you found out our little secret yet? I'm sure you'll want to talk when you do. I'll be waiting with answers. My offer still stands.

A life for a life.
With love,
Your father.

"He sent this to the national press. Why?"

Enzo studies the note with narrowed eyes. "Showmanship. The more pressure he applies, the quicker he thinks we'll break and surrender you back to him."

I read the warning again, more confused than ever. There's something here, whispered between the written lines. He's luring me closer with his lies and I can feel the inevitable pull, but I'm powerless to stop myself from being hooked like bait.

"Do you think he's telling the truth?" I bite my lip.

"About what? The man's a fucking lunatic."

"I mean... does he know something I don't? About my past? I feel like I'm missing something huge. I just can't remember what. It's driving me crazy."

Taking the iPad away from me, Enzo switches it off. "No. I think he's unhinged and desperate to get you back. This is another tactic, nothing more."

Enzo believes what he wants to. I know that now. He can't bear the thought of another twist in the road, not while we're on the back foot and battling to remain afloat.

"Are my parents still trying to contact me?"

"Daily," he answers. "Giana's called five times since the article dropped alone. Your father keeps calling too."

"I was going to go and see him when the news hit about the bodies, but then we had the memorial, then... Hunter."

He bumps my shoulder. "Don't beat yourself up. Our lives are a fucking disaster zone right now. He can wait his turn."

Staring at the photographs that first occupied his attention, I try to hold the swell of burning hot tears back. Hunter selected these new memories to add to his collection.

Various crappy selfies taken over the span of the last year, our tongues flopping out and lips stretched wide. Decorating the Christmas tree. Family dinners. Walks with Lucky.

It's our life. Together.

He treasured every moment.

To the world, he's brash, unemotional, cruel even. Hunter has spent the last eight months battling his urges to both control and cherish me. He's threatened the very foundation of his life, determined to have me to himself.

But in private?

This right here is the truth about Hunter Rodriguez. He is absolutely nothing without the people he cares about. That survival instinct I recognise so clearly within him is a fearsome drive to protect the one thing he loves most in the world. His fucking family.

"We need to go back to the hospital to see Hunter's consultant this afternoon." Enzo's heat meets my back as we face the photos together. "They're easing the sedation."

"You think he'll wake up?"

"The doctors seem to think so. His scans are looking better, and the swelling has gone down. We have to give it a go."

He doesn't need to say what we're all thinking. We all want Hunter back in fighting form, but today could change his entire life. Forever. All of our lives.

None of us know how much of his hearing has survived the accident. He'll be recovering from his injuries for months to come as it is, but once he's awake, they can perform the relevant tests to answer that terrifying question.

"I don't know if I can be there when he wakes up," I make myself admit. "He should be with his family, not… me."

Enzo turns me around. "You are his family."

"He's lying in that hospital bed because of my stupidity." I feel the tears spill over. "That bullet was meant for me."

"You should know by now that Hunter will always throw himself in harm's way if it keeps the people he loves safe."

"Maybe he shouldn't," I murmur back. "I wish that bullet had hit me. Enz… I wanted it to. I actually wanted it to."

Stroking a roughened thumb over my wet cheek, the pain in Enzo's expression makes me regret my confession. It's no secret that I'm lurching from one breakdown to another.

The accident has tipped me over the edge into a very dark place. Not even the case has kept the whisper of ghosts from my mind, their daily taunts increasing. More than once, I've considered leaving and returning to Pastor Michaels.

When Hunter does wake up, he should have his family and loved ones around him. Not the baggage he got lumped with from the case that's ruined his life and career. That's all I am now. A threat. A burden. The girl who almost got him killed.

"Whatever you're thinking, stop," Enzo scolds. "This wasn't your fault. Hunter would say the same thing."

"Because none of you will admit the truth."

Teeth gritted, his defeat dissipates into red-hot anger. The emotion swirls in his golden eyes, spreading agony and indignation with each furious breath he sucks in.

"You want the truth?" Enzo entreats.

I try to back away from him and end up colliding with Hunter's nearby desk. The solid press of wood meets my tailbone, and Enzo steps into the space between us.

I'm caught between two obstacles, pinned and out of escape

routes. His hands stroke down my arms to encircle my wrists like handcuffs. He's grinding my bones together.

"The truth is that our family would've fallen apart long ago if you weren't here," he says fiercely. "You are the only thing holding us all together."

I try to wriggle free and fail.

"Enz, I'm the one tearing you apart."

"No," he disagrees. "You're wrong, and I'm so fucking glad that you are. You will never know just how much you've changed our lives for the better."

Bending to press his plump lips to my cheek, he plants a soft kiss, his stubble scratching against my skin. I pull again at my wrists, but it's no use. I can't run from him.

"Enzo..."

"Shut up and let me kiss you."

When his mouth crashes onto mine, I'm too tired to fight it. The inevitable road to disaster is careening towards us, right on target. Enzo has always wanted to own me—inside out, from the moment we met. He stamped me with his seal of possession the day we bonded over unlaced Chucks.

I saw then what I see now.

Possession. Hunger.

But more than that, the security and certainty that comes with imprisoning those you love most. For months, I've thought that he wanted to entrap me. Control me. Force me to live in the shadows while they risk their lives.

No. I was wrong.

He wants me to be his equal.

Releasing one wrist, he grabs my jean-covered hip and lifts me up. I fall backwards onto the desk, scattering pencil pots and stacks of paperwork across the carpet.

"We can't do this here," I gasp loudly.

"I need to feel you, little one."

"Enz—"

"Please. I need to know that we're okay."

My legs part without being told, letting him pin me against the polished wood. His mouth is hot on mine, demanding, seeking, torturing the answers from me that he needs to hear.

I'm on fire. Pins and needles spread everywhere as his hand pushes my shoulder, forcing me to lie down on the wide desk. Every carved muscle pressed against me adds to the sense of spiralling. I'm falling in a rapid, dizzying corkscrew.

Maybe he'll catch me.

Maybe he'll follow me to hell.

Lifting the hem of my blue sweater, his calloused hand leaves a searing path against my stomach. Everywhere he touches erupts into flames. This is wrong. We can't be doing this right now, but I do not give a fuck.

We're in Hunter's office while our entire world crumbles around us with each passing day. I shouldn't be wet and writhing in my desperation to taste him, but I am. I can't live with this tension suffocating me for a second longer.

Enzo growls under his breath as he tugs my sweater over my head. His hands are everywhere, unbuttoning my jeans, pushing my bra cups aside, rolling my nipples between his roughened fingers.

"You're so beautiful," he grunts into my lips. "Fuck, Harlow. I've wanted to touch you so bad these past few months."

"Why didn't you?"

"Because I'm an idiot. I'll make up for that now."

"Enzo, we can't do this here," I repeat.

"Nobody can get in without the code."

I want to protest more, but his hand shoves inside my jeans and finds the delicate lace of my panties. Unlike the gentle exploration of our previous collisions, he's almost delirious with need this time. There's no slow build up.

We're both on the verge of ruin.

I need him to make everything better.

"Do you want me to stop?"

His fingers are a short walk from heaven. I'm desperate to feel his touch between my thighs, relieving the burning ache that nothing else will fix. My pussy is his to own.

"No," I moan. "Don't stop."

When his thick finger parts my folds, swirling moisture and desire, I see stars. My moans grow louder as he drives a digit deep inside me.

"So tight, little one."

Each thrust of his finger threatens to unhinge my grip on the world. This is so inappropriate, and it's turning me on even more. I'm soaking wet, more than ever before.

"Can you take another finger?"

"Yes," I plead.

"That's right. I heard you've been fooling around with our Leigh. Why did that asshole get to fuck you first?"

When I don't answer him, Enzo pumps the two fingers in and out of my slit with a smirk lighting his face. He's packed inside me, moving fast and hard to force me into submission.

"Answer the damn question."

"It... just happened," I mewl.

Enzo snickers with a dark grin. "I'm going to fuck you so hard, you'll forget all about the other men battling for a taste of you. My name is the only one allowed on your tongue now."

His other hand moves to clasp my throat. It's a loose necklace at first, but his grip gradually tightens until I can't breathe properly. The promise of danger only adds to my anticipation. He literally owns the air in my lungs.

"I'm your God now, Harlow."

I release a strangled gasp.

"You want to breathe, baby?"

My head bobs.

"Just a quick one. That's all you're allowed."

Loosening his grip long enough for me to suck a breath deep into my lungs, his fingers tighten again.

"Do you understand how this works now?" Enzo asks with inky darkness in his eyes.

I blink, silent and complacent.

"You belong to me, angel. That means you breathe when I say so. Spread your legs when I order. Show me your gorgeous fucking tits if I want them in my face."

If he keeps going like this, I'm going to come from his words alone. Old Harlow would've been terrified by this demanding beast. I'm glad we waited, because I'm ready for him now.

Ready to surrender.

I'll worship at his feet.

When his hand releases, allowing me to suck in a glorious mouthful of air, his fingertips move to let his teeth pierce my skin. He sucks so hard, I can feel the bruise forming for the entire world to see.

"I'm going to leave my marks all over your perfect skin," Enzo announces. "When the others want to fuck you, they'll have to plead on their knees for my permission."

"P-Permission?" I rasp.

"I'm willing to share you with my brothers, but not without conditions. They'll have to beg me for a taste of your cunt."

His path of destruction sweeps over my skin. Everything feels overly sensitive and swollen beneath his lips. I'm putty in his hands, my nipples reacting with the coldness of the room outside of my bra cups.

Touching the harsh zigzag of scars cutting deep into my pale skin, Enzo's eyes search my body. I hate how inadequate I feel beneath his gaze. He could do so much better.

"Stop," he warns as I squirm to escape. "You are forbidden from hiding or being ashamed. Fucking *forbidden*."

Sucking my breast into his mouth, Enzo tortures my tingling skin, leaving another dark bruise to form. I feel like I'm covered in his scent and marks of possession.

"All mine," he declares. "Say it, Harlow."

When I don't immediately respond, his hand crashes against my bare breast in a painful slap.

"Argh," I cry out.

"I said say it."

"I'm yours. I always have been."

"Good little angel," he praises.

Hand pressed against my lower belly, he traps me on my back. The desk is hard beneath my spine, but the delicious pressure of his cock brushing my panties is all I can think about. It's so close to being inside me.

Enzo tugs off my jeans, one leg at a time, and tosses them over his shoulder. If someone were to walk in right now, they'd see every scrap of my scarred skin on display outside my remaining bra and panties.

The sound of tearing fabric is the final straw. He does not give a fuck right now. Enzo holds my ruined panties in his hand like a trophy, an eyebrow cocked in amusement.

"You won't be needing these."

A shiver rolls down my spine.

"I want to see every inch of you," he adds.

The human facade that conceals Enzo's monster from the world has fallen away. I'm staring at a crouched tiger, preparing to pounce on its prey. He's going to consume me.

Left hand returning to clasp my throat, he smashes our lips back together. His tongue steals any remaining doubt from my mind, battling with mine to claim ultimate ownership.

I allow myself to be dominated by him. His touch. His tongue. Hips grinding against mine. Hands roaming my goosebump-covered skin. Chest rumbling with a contented purr.

"Turn over," he orders into my lips.

"Now?"

Amber eyes burning, Enzo grabs my hip and tugs until I'm forced to flip over. My arms stretch across Hunter's desk as my breasts and body meet the cool surface of the wood.

My feet barely touch Hunter's office carpet. Enzo pulls me into a position that leaves nothing to the imagination. My butt is raised high, laying bare the wet heat of my slit for him to see from behind.

"Look at this perfect ass just begging for my handprint," he comments hoarsely.

"Enz," I whine.

"Yes, little one?"

The ache inside me is so intense, it steals my breath. I feel like one stroke of his hand will make me explode. Months of anticipation and tension are swirling inside me.

"Please. I just... want to forget, for a moment. Help me."

The buckle on his black jeans clicks open and causes my pulse to spike. I recognise the rustle of foil being ripped as his body heat shifts behind me. My exposed pussy lips feel every small movement.

"We can forget together," he replies as his palm stokes my ass cheek. "The world can wait."

When his hand draws back and collides with my skin in a hard spank, the sizzle of pain causes my self-control to snap. I cry out, unable to swallow the sound in case anyone can hear us. I don't care who knows what we're doing in here.

Huge hands engulfing my hips, Enzo pulls my behind even higher, at the perfect angle for the tip of his length to tease my soaked opening. He's so close to crossing that final line.

"Last chance," Enzo advises.

I'm so sick of them treading carefully around me. Hands gripping the edge of Hunter's desk, I use the position to push myself backwards so that Enzo's cock slips inside.

"Fuck, Harlow!"

The sheer size of him causes a satisfying burn. Shifting my hips, he pulls out and pushes back inside me at a deeper angle, making me swallow more of his huge length.

"We're gonna start slow. I don't want to hurt you."

I can't answer beyond tiny, frenzied pants. Every time he surges back into me, I feel myself stretching around him. This feels easier than my first time, and the tingle of pain soon melts into pleasure.

Every inch of me is screaming with satisfaction. I want more. All of it. With him filling me, the overwhelming darkness in my head falls silent for the first time in days. He leaves no space for the devil or his machinations.

"Take my cock, baby. Take it all."

"More," I groan.

"Such a greedy little slut, aren't you?"

His hand cracks against my ass again, harder this time. It sends spikes of sizzling electricity through my body. My legs are trembling with each thrust, his speed slowly increasing.

Pots of fountain pens and stray paperclips rattle. More papers fall, and the desk lamp crashes loudly on the floor. We're causing mayhem as the desk threatens to collapse beneath his weight slamming into me.

Enzo doesn't hesitate for a second. It's the surest he's ever been around me. His grip on my hips turns bruising, but I don't care. Let him break me. I want the punishment. I deserve to be disciplined for what I've done to them all.

He's finally letting himself go with me. His control is fraying, falling apart, leaving us adrift in no man's land. I gasp and moan with each pump of his hips.

Enzo slips free from my pussy and quickly flips me back over. I squeak in surprise, sitting on the very edge of the desk. He roughly shoves my legs open and steps between them.

"I want your beautiful eyes on me. Do you understand?"

My legs sneak around his waist. "I understand."

"Say *I understand, sir.*"

Thighs clenched, I fight back a groan. I never expected the formal title that the company uses to refer to him to be so hot.

"I understand... sir."

"Good, angel."

I place my hands on the wide, threatening set of his shoulders. At some point, he discarded his t-shirt. The corded muscles and exquisitely carved V of his hips are hard to look away from. He's a deliciously toned boulder of masculinity.

When he pushes back inside me from this angle, I cry out again. The pressure is reaching a boiling point. He's almost completely buried inside me now; it's too much for my control to take.

Digging my nails deep into his bronzed skin, I feel the warmth of his blood against my fingertips. Each second of sweet torture is setting off fireworks beneath my skin.

"That's it," he purrs. "Let me see my pretty girl come. Are you gonna scream my name, angel?"

"Yes," I submit.

"Then let's see it."

His hips move like steel engines. Faster. Harder. Coaxing my obedience with each pump. I scream out his name just as the desk groans ominously, on the verge of collapsing.

Enzo gasps and picks me up right before one of the legs breaks. The slabs of solid wood crumple with a loud bang, semi-destroying Hunter's office in the process.

I'm holding on to Enzo's huge body, a tiny limpet clinging to his chest in comparison. He buries his face in my neck as he walks across the office and slams me against the wall instead.

"Again," he demands, his teeth cutting into my neck. "I want to hear that gorgeous scream of yours again."

It's a good thing he's holding me against the wall, else I'd be tangled in a boneless puddle at his feet. My limbs have turned to jelly with my first mind-melting orgasm.

"Come." Enzo slams into me with a loud thump. "For." His mouth is hot on mine. "Me." He licks my pulse point. "Again."

That's all it takes.

"Arghh!" I cry out.

The room fades into blackness as the most intense release I've ever had shatters my consciousness. I'm all light and sensation, floating untethered in space.

Enzo's face hides in the rapid rise and fall of my breasts as he bellows through his own intense climax. We're both gasping dramatically for air and struggling to remain upright.

"Jesus," he curses. "Are you okay? Did I hurt you?"

I struggle to form a sentence.

"Harlow! Answer me."

"No… I'm okay. That was crazy."

When he has the willpower to move, Enzo lets me slide down his frame. His eyes are ducked low as he pulls the condom from himself and tosses it into Hunter's bin.

That's when he gets a good look at the war zone we've created. The office is a complete wreck. It looks like a bomb exploded in here.

"Well, shit."

"Uh-huh," I echo.

"If he saw this, he'd kill us both."

That sobers me up.

The carefree haze draped over me slinks away without warning, leaving me cold and ashamed. Hunter's lying in intensive care while I'm hooking up with his best friend.

"Hey." Enzo clasps my jaw firmly. "Let's get dressed and we'll go straight to the hospital to see Hunter."

"How did you know I was thinking about him?"

"I can tell." He shrugs. "You love him."

"You got all that from a look?"

"I can read you easily enough. Please don't feel guilty about this. You've done nothing wrong, alright?"

I blow out a breath. "Then why does being with all of you feel so wrong and yet so right at the same time?"

His smile softens. "Because the world wants us to stay in our tidy little boxes. We're just choosing not to."

"So, what are we choosing instead?"

"Love," he answers without missing a beat.

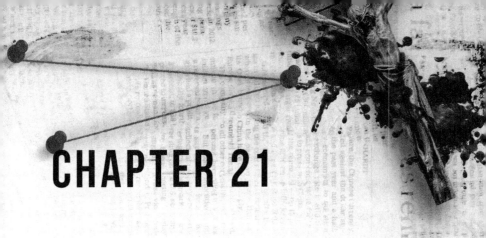

CHAPTER 21

Harlow

DRIFTING - NF

The intensive care unit's dreary waiting area is packed. Hunter's whole family is here—us, his parents, the Cobra team and several steely-eyed agents glowering at anyone not with us.

We've been here for a few hours, tense and silent, awaiting any news as they attempt to ease Hunter off sedation. Leighton has stepped outside to smoke with Hudson and Brooklyn, needing an escape.

We're all on edge.

You could hear a pin drop.

When the click of Hunter's hospital room door opening draws all our heads up, my heart leaps into my throat. Doctor Lane, accompanied by two nurses and an anaesthetist, steps outside.

Ben is the first one on his feet, even faster than his wife. The doctor gestures for Hunter's parents to follow them into the quiet family room down the corridor to talk in private.

"This is bad," I mutter to myself. "Why are they speaking to them alone?"

Next to me, Richards is half-heartedly reading an article in a psychiatry magazine he pulled from his briefcase. He spares me a small, tense smile.

"Standard procedure. They have to update Hunter's next of kin first."

Pulling the hair tie wrapped around my wrist, I snap the band against my skin several times. It's one of the techniques Richards advised upon seeing the mess I'd made of myself. It sears, but the pain is nowhere near enough.

Anxiety is eating me alive.

I can't pull and rave like I want to with everyone's eyes primed for any movement. I'm sure that's why they arranged for Richards to be here. That decision has Enzo written all over it.

"Shall we take a walk?" Richards suggests. "Some fresh air might be good."

"I don't want to miss anything."

"I'm sure they'll call if you do."

"No. I'm staying," I insist.

Avoiding looking up at his perceptive eyes, I can feel him studying me behind polished spectacles and bushy grey eyebrows. My trust in Richards is hanging on by a shoestring.

He hasn't mentioned the inpatient idea since our last session, but I can still see it in his eyes. I'm not so sure he isn't a threat. Inching my chair further away, I fold my hands in my lap.

At least I can fool the others and hide the guilt shredding me apart until it's physically painful to breathe. Richards isn't so easily fooled. He sees too much after months of exploring the deepest depths of my brain.

Someone nudges my shoulder, and a steaming styrofoam cup appears in front of me. I look up at Eli's pursed lips and bright-green eyes, softened with concern.

"Uh, thanks, Eli." I take the cup of tea and place it at my feet to cool down.

"You got it. Want something to eat?"

He's always so sweet and thoughtful.

"No, I'm okay," I decline. "But thanks."

He looks uncertain for a moment before clasping my shoulders and dragging me into a quick hug. I'm stunned for a second before cuddling him back.

He's comfortable around me now, but physical contact is usually a no-go. His narrow frame and bird-like bones feel delicate in my arms as we embrace tightly.

"I won't bother saying that everything is going to be okay," Eli whispers in my ear. "I know that means fuck all right now. But we're all here with you. Remember that."

A lump gathers in my throat.

"Thank you for being here."

"Of course," he murmurs. "If you change your mind about food, let me know. I'll locate ice cream."

"Okay." I laugh through tears. "Thanks."

"Don't mention it."

Returning to the nearby drinks machine, Eli works his way around the rest of the room, ensuring everyone has a hot drink clasped in their hands.

Phoenix takes his black coffee and pulls Eli into his lap after he's finished his rounds. The pair cling to each other, neither saying a word yet somehow conversing through little glances and smiles. It's rare to see them apart.

They're a package deal outside of their relationship with Brooklyn. But in a different way to how I've caught Hudson and Jude locking lips. They love to hate each other.

Leighton, Brooklyn and Hudson return, retaking their seats with the rest of the Cobra team. Enzo paces up and down the linoleum. Richards pretends to read his magazine.

Tick, tock.

Tick, tock.

I want to smash that clock.

Tick, tock.

Tick, tock.

I'm losing my mind here.

Tick, tock.

Tick, tock.

When the sound of crying emanates from the family room after a while, I lose patience. I'm about to storm into Hunter's hospital room when the doctors finally reappear.

Enzo halts, wound tighter than a coiled spring. "Well? Can we see him now?"

Doctor Lane dismisses her colleagues. "Hunter regained consciousness a little while ago. His parents are going in to spend some time with him."

"And?" he urges. "What's the verdict?"

"I'm sorry, Mr Montpellier. I can't disclose anything without Hunter's consent. You'll have to wait."

"Enough waiting! We're his family!"

Stopping beside him, Leighton clasps his bicep. "Enz, calm down. Mum and Dad will fill us in soon."

"I want to see him right now."

"That isn't how this works." Doctor Lane offers a placating smile. "Excuse me."

She disappears to guide Della and Ben into their son's hospital room. Hunter's mum is leaning on her husband for support, and she doesn't look up at us as she dabs her red eyes. I have a very bad feeling about this.

We all sit back down, even more on edge than before. Enzo cracks his knuckles with menace, glowering down the corridor, while Leighton taps out a text message.

I send a silent prayer up to the heavens.

Please, God.

Don't punish him for my mistakes.

"Where the fuck is Theo?" Enzo growls under his breath. "He was supposed to be here an hour ago."

Leighton shrugs, his eyes glued to his phone. "The post-mortems are done. I don't know why he's held up."

"Fuck." Enzo rakes a hand over his unshaven face. "I'll go and call him. We shouldn't be separated right now; it isn't safe. The damn press is camped outside the hospital."

"It's their fault that Hunter's here," Leighton agrees angrily. "This is a clusterfuck. Nowhere is safe."

Enzo stands to stride from the intensive care ward, but a newcomer stops him by entering the waiting area. She's short and round, her jet-black hair brushing her jaw in dense curls.

The duo of agents immediately crowd her, demanding identification and answers. She disappears behind their towering physiques and visible weaponry.

"Stop," Enzo shouts, heading for the foray. "Stand down. She's not a threat."

Grumbling to themselves, the two agents dip their heads in respect and backtrack. The woman is left to dust herself off, her olive complexion flushed a light shade of pink.

"What are you doing here?"

She opens her arms for Enzo to step into. "I heard today was the day, so I'm here. There are a lot of reporters and angry people outside."

"I know. Did they recognise you?"

"Not a chance. I snuck around the back."

The pair embrace tightly, exchanging hugs and kisses. She barely reaches Enzo's shoulder, not much taller than me. The moment I see them entangled, I spot the resemblance.

Studying the beautiful, middle-aged woman hanging off him, it's clear to see the relation between them. She shares the same strong Spanish heritage as her sister, Enzo's mum.

"That's Hayley," Leighton whispers in my ear. "Enzo's aunt. My mum's kept her posted on Hunter's condition."

Smoothing my rumpled blue jeans and sweater tucked in at the waist, I blow out a nervous breath. Enzo hugs his aunt close and directs her over to us.

"Leigh," she gasps with tear-filled eyes. "You've grown up so much. It's been years since I last saw you."

"Hey, Hayley." He doesn't move, keeping a reassuring arm around my waist. "Thanks for coming."

"Of course. I wanted to be here."

I stammer a timid hello before I'm yanked from Leighton's arms and bundled into a tight hug. Hayley's hair tickles my face, thick and glossy, as she whispers my name.

She smells like rose-scented perfume and freshly baked bread, wafting off her plain blouse and flared black jeans. I can't help but panic a little when she doesn't let go.

"Oh, Harlow." Her lips press against my head. "I'm so sorry it took this long for us to finally meet. Are you okay?"

"Um." I try to peel her off, but she clings on even tighter. "I'm f-fine. You're... uh, Hayley?"

"Hay," Enzo says. "Let her bloody breathe."

"Gosh, I'm sorry," she apologises again. "I've just heard a lot about you from my nephew. All good, I swear."

Swiping a painted fingernail under her sparkling gold eyes, Hayley smiles sweetly. I plaster what feels like a grimace on my mouth and attempt to smile back.

"Hayley is my aunt," Enzo grumbles. "And absolutely terrible at respecting boundaries."

"Excuse me," Hayley complains with a playful scowl. "I'm a hugger. That is not a bad thing."

After pinching her nephew's cheeks, Hayley works her way around the room for hugs. She seems to know everyone and gasps when she spots the black-diamond engagement ring on Brooklyn's finger.

"Those bastards finally decided to make it official, eh?" She winks at Hudson and Kade, both grinning themselves.

Brooklyn kisses her cheek. "Well, you threatened all five of them with a beating enough times if they didn't."

"She's scarier than you are, Brooke," Hudson agrees with a wince. "Nice to see you again."

Hayley messes up his hair. "Good job on the ring, hot shot. Nice touch with the black diamond."

"I had some help." Hudson chuckles. "The colour choice was all Eli's and Phoenix's doing."

Still snuggled on Phoenix's lap, next to where Jude is answering emails on his work phone, Eli shrugs off the compliment.

"When's the wedding?" Hayley enquires.

Brooklyn smiles. "September."

"Not long to go now!"

"We still have a shitload to do, but we'll get there."

All settling back in our seats, we wait together and converse in low whispers. The tension has eased with Hayley's arrival. She's a light, easy presence, doling out physical affection without blinking an eye. I like her already.

"What's the latest?" Hayley asks.

Enzo resumes cracking his knuckles. "Della and Ben are in there now. He's awake."

She touches his hands to make him stop. "Patience, *querido*. It's going to be okay."

"Did you close the bakery to come over here?"

Hayley waves him off. "Gordon is closing up shop for me this evening."

"I hate that douchebag," Enzo complains. "Why are you still dating him? Is he still driving that shitty car?"

"Because he's a nice man and you aren't in charge of my dating life, as I've said a million times before." She clips him around the ear. "His car choice is none of your business."

"We'll see about that," Enzo mutters.

"Is he this much of a pain in the ass to you too, Harlow?"

I choke on a mouthful of lukewarm tea. "Uh."

"That's a yes," she concludes.

Enzo narrows his eyes at me. "Traitor."

Leighton is trying his best not to laugh as he hides behind his phone. Glowering at his aunt, Enzo makes a point of laying a possessive hand on my thigh.

"I am not a pain in the ass," he defends.

My skin tingles where he touches me. I had to deal with Brooklyn's smug, knowing grin when I semi-limped into the waiting area earlier. I'm sore after our earlier activities.

"Yeah, right," Hayley continues with a snort. "Enz, we've discussed this. You'll scare poor Harlow off if you keep acting like a caveman for all your life."

"I am not a caveman," Enzo protests.

"That's debatable." Hudson coughs to conceal his words. "No one has ever defined the word caveman more than you do, Enz."

When Enzo shoots him a death glare, he grins wide. I think Hudson's the only one who isn't afraid of our less-than-cuddly resident enforcer. Enzo trained him too well to feel such fear. I wouldn't want to watch them fight.

The tentative banter ceases when Hunter's father emerges from the hospital room. Ben doesn't even cast us a look, striding out of the ward without a second glance.

Leighton watches him go with unease. "I should go after him. He looked upset."

I gently nudge him. "Go."

"You'll be okay?"

"I'm fine, Leigh. Your family needs you."

Nodding, he grabs me by the chin to plant a heavy kiss against my lips. I linger for a second before his mouth is torn from mine and he chases after his father's hurried footsteps.

The pressure of Hayley's eyes burning a hole in my head causes me to blush. I get the impression that nothing escapes her attention. While I have no idea what Enzo's told her, she doesn't seem surprised by them all touching me.

Della's splotchy, tear-stained face appears around the hospital door next, and we all stand up at the same time. Her smile is appreciative, but strained.

"Harlow," she rasps.

I clutch Enzo's arm tight. "Yeah?"

"Can you come here, please?"

When the ever-present shadow at my side steps forward, Della shakes her head, causing Enzo to freeze.

"Just Harlow for now."

He looks crestfallen, but nods as he sits back down. Releasing his arm, I catch sight of Hayley's reassuring smile. I must look as terrified as I feel right now.

Passing Richards and his discarded magazine, I leave the waiting room and meet Della in the corridor. She's been sobbing. Her face and greying hair are a stressed-out mess.

I freeze outside the door. "Yes?"

"You can come in," she encourages, offering me a withered hand. "Come and say hello."

Reluctantly accepting her offer, I'm ushered into the shadows of the hospital room. The plain-white blinds are drawn against the dreary, cloud-covered day.

The moment I set eyes on the bandaged, wire-wrapped figure in the bed, I know this is going to hurt. Buried amongst the medical paraphernalia, Hunter is hardly recognisable.

"He's awake?"

Della squeezes my hand. "He woke up a few hours ago from the coma. They've just been running some tests."

"Is he okay?"

She pushes me forwards. "He needs you right now. I'll give you two some privacy."

I wait for the door to click shut behind me before taking another breath. I'm petrified of the contents of that bed. The person I'm staring at isn't Hunter, but the consequences of my cowardice.

I practically begged that bullet to pierce my chest and end it all. With the cruel, malicious irony of a God that has forsaken me, it almost took Hunter's life instead.

He should've died.

His survival is a miracle.

Trembling all over, I stop an inch from his bedside. Hunter's head is partially swathed in bandages. His scruff-covered face and two open eyes peek out through the cotton, the only sign that he isn't a mummified corpse.

The endless, intelligent brown depths are locked on me for a brief second before he returns to staring up at the pocked hospital ceiling. Not a single word of greeting.

"Hunt," I whimper. "It's me."

Hunter blinks but still doesn't acknowledge me. Throat seizing, I dodge several tangled IV lines and stroke my fingertips over his forearm. No response.

He could be dead.

There's no light left in him.

"I know you don't want to talk to me right now, and that's okay. But I need you to know that I love you."

Nothing.

Watching his pale, gaunt face for any glimmer of recognition, I choke up when a solitary tear escapes down his cheek. It's soaked up by the rough scruff of his beard.

"Please don't cry," I say through my own tears. "You're going to get back on your feet. We're all here to help you."

He still isn't looking at me or saying anything. My worst fears are confirmed. Hunter hates me. I'm the reason he's confined to this bed, unable to walk or feed himself.

Driven by wild desperation, I duck down to brush my lips against his cheek. There isn't much skin on display amongst the bandages protecting his butchered ear and fractured skull. They performed surgery to staple everything back together. He resembles the infamous monster created by Frankenstein that I've read so much about.

When I begin to retreat, his eyes finally slide over to me. I'm caught in a storm of horrific pain staring back at me. My breath catches. I feel like I'm drowning in his palpable misery. It's crawling up my nose and throat.

"It's g-g-gone," he stammers.

"What's gone? What is it?"

It takes great exertion for his pinkie finger to lift and capture mine. Linked together, he squeezes ever so softly before releasing. The brief moment of contact doesn't comfort me. This feels like a goodbye.

"I can't..."

His voice is garbled and sounds off.

I lean closer. "Can't what? Tell me what you need. Please, Hunt. I'll do anything to make this right."

More tears soak into his sunken cheeks, highlighting his weight loss while trapped in this hospital. My own cheeks are dripping wet. I reach out to brush the moisture aside.

"Hunt," I croak. "Please talk to me."

Our eyes collide again. He's always been my strength. My certainty. My protector. The irrevocable storm that sweeps all into its tide, powered by the promise of justice beyond the horizon.

That strength is gone.

I'm staring back at myself. The familiar prison of terror is reflected in his irises now too. His pinkie squeezes mine again. A silent apology. A plea. I can't give him what he wants.

I already know what pain-stricken words are struggling to leave his tongue. Even if I don't want to hear them.

"Can't h-hear you," he finishes with a silent sob. "Can't hear a-a-anything."

"Your hearing aid? Where is it?"

Hunter blinks twice and I recognise the message. He's saying no.

There's a couple of hearing aids on the bedside table, but they've been dismissed. Deemed useless.

His next stuttered word slams the final nail in the coffin of my guilt. My head falls and his pinkie releases mine.

"D-Deaf."

CHAPTER 22

Theo

Kijo – Memorist

"**A**fter the tragic accident earlier this month, we understand that Sabre's director, Hunter Rodriguez, remains under medical supervision."

Propped against the cold brick wall of the basement gym, I tug my hood up to cover my blonde curls while listening to the news report through my headphones.

Enzo asked me to flick the heating on before he comes down to train, but it's still fucking freezing sitting on the floor in the corner of the well-equipped gym.

April has arrived with the first sprigs of fresh grass, constant random rainfall and chirp of birds, but we're too busy being held prisoner in our own home to enjoy it.

"What about their appeal for information?"

Sally Moore rolls her eyes as she gestures towards the familiar, Victorian-style mansion behind her, the curtains drawn to conceal the inside occupants. It's a livestream.

"Clinging at straws, Clive. Since uncovering the mass grave, we've been given a vague timeframe for the killings and Sabre has asked for any witnesses to come forward."

"So, no connection to our killer?"

"Not yet," she responds with a smile. "We'll keep our viewers informed of any developments as this story continues. Now, let's go back to the studio for the weather."

Exiting the trashy news channel's website, I crash the heel of my palm against my forehead. These gossiping sell-outs are filling the airwaves with the stupidest of speculations.

The case is complex and difficult enough to manage without them adding fuel to the fire of furious public opinion. With cases like this, it's guaranteed that the world will turn on you somewhere down the line.

We've become the bad guys.

The scapegoats.

Even the enemies.

I just never thought that it would lead to abject violence. Some, perhaps. But nothing on this scale. We're confined to the house while reporters and protestors crowd the front gate.

It was only a matter of time until our home address was leaked online. The added security threat comes at the worst possible time, with Hunter still in the hospital, out of action.

We have a full team of agents posted outside, armed and very much prepared to use force if needed. Nobody leaves the house alone and without the protection of an armed convoy.

"I am not going down there."

Harlow's stubborn complaint echoes down the concrete staircase from the floor above me.

"You agreed to learn some self-defence after what happened,"

Enzo reminds her. "Move it."

"Yeah, but not in the basement!"

"Would you prefer to train outside under the glare of the media's helicopters? Be my guest. I couldn't care less."

"You're an asshole."

"*Your* asshole," he snips back.

"Stop trying to butter me up."

The sound of annoyed footsteps stomps down the staircase. I quickly minimise the pages of countryside house listings I was trawling through while watching the news.

It's official.

We're moving.

Enzo made the decision that we need to leave London behind, in light of recent events. I don't blame him. If the world knows where we live, then so does Pastor Michaels. It isn't safe here anymore.

"Theo?" Harlow exclaims.

Pausing on the threshold of the cold room, she anxiously peeks around the well-lit space. Her shoulders are drawn tightly together with anxiety.

I offer her a wave. "Hey."

"What are you doing down here?"

"Leighton was singing in the shower again. I couldn't concentrate in the office upstairs. His voice carries."

"He's auditioning for a new career, apparently." Harlow places a tentative foot inside. "Something about running away to Hollywood and leaving this madness behind."

"Somehow, I doubt Hollywood is holding its breath for Leighton and his terrible rendition of *Mamma Mia*."

Sneaking up behind her, which is a seriously impressive feat at his size, Enzo swoops Harlow off her feet. She screams in shock before beginning to yell her head off.

"It's a gym," he scolds, his palm cracking across her behind. "It won't bite. Stop being a wimp."

"You know why I haven't been down here," she shouts while hammering his back. "Let me down, now."

All of the screaming attracts Lucky's attention as she comes bounding down the staircase next. After declaring the room safe with a loud sniff, she curls up next to me, her nose buried in my faded-blue jeans. Bloody hypervigilant dog.

"Good girl." I pet her ears.

Enzo deposits Harlow in the middle of the spongy workout mat surrounded by state-of-the-art machines, weights and equipment. Don't ask me what any of this stuff does.

I keep in decent enough shape by running around like a lunatic after Hunter and his constant list of demands, not working out. Physical exercise is really not my thing.

Shaking my head to clear the automatic stab of worry, I refocus on my laptop screen. Enzo's keeping Harlow busy as he orders her around, watching with interested eyes when she stretches in front of him in a pastel workout set.

"I'm going to take you through some basic self-defence." He rolls his broad shoulders. "We'll train for two hours a day until I'm satisfied you can defend yourself."

"Two hours?" Harlow groans.

Folding his arms, Enzo huffs. "Hunter's been working in the field for over a decade, and he got shot in the fucking head. Don't argue with me on this. You need to learn fast."

Gulping hard, Harlow ducks her eyes to the workout mat. I shoot Enzo an exasperated glare. He doesn't need to guilt trip her into doing this. She's beating herself up enough.

"Let's start with your form. You're gonna have to come closer, little one."

Sneaking forward with her chin tucked down, Harlow stands opposite him, her arms loose at her sides. I watch over my laptop screen as Enzo holds her by the hips to correct her posture.

"Eyes up and alert," he scolds her. "Shoulders back, feet planted, hands raised to block an attack. You never know when one might come."

With her body correctly positioned, Enzo scans over Harlow with an expertly trained eye. I sure as hell hope he's not going to teach her in the same way he taught his other recruits. That won't go down well with anyone.

Hudson spent months walking around with black eyes and split lips throughout his induction to Sabre. I'm convinced Enzo beat the shit out of him on a daily basis, purely for his own entertainment. He's a sadistic fuck at times.

"You're small and light." He pushes her shoulder in demonstration, almost causing her to fall.

"I feel like I should be offended by that."

"Quite the opposite," Enzo compliments. "Use it to your advantage. Speed is your best friend in a combat situation. How did you escape Diablo before?"

Harlow's face drains of colour. She clears her throat, looking uncomfortable.

"I bit him," she admits quietly. "Then I ran for my life."

Enzo actually looks impressed. "That's so hot."

"Enz! Christ."

"Thinking outside of the box. I like it. Ideally, you don't want your attacker close enough to bite. Basic evasive manoeuvres can help you there."

Without warning, he flashes across the mat and wrenches her up into the air. Harlow squeals in shock, her body restrained by the vice-like suffocation of Enzo's arms trapping her in place.

"Your first instinct is to panic," he breathes in her ear. "You want to beg and plead for me to let you go, right?"

She attempts to stomp on his foot and snarls when he doesn't react by bellowing in pain.

"The trick is to detach yourself." His hands roam down her arms, crossing a multitude of professional boundaries. "Allow your breathing to slow, and your movements to halt."

I feel kinda weird watching this private moment. He sure as fuck didn't semi-molest Hudson like this while kicking his ass. Harlow's eyes flutter shut as she takes a measured breath.

"There you go," Enzo purrs. "Let them think you're compliant. Play into their judgement. They aren't worried about a little slip like you."

"I am not a little slip," she seethes.

He tilts his head to brush his lips against her temple from behind. "When their guard is down, that's your chance to show them exactly that. No one expects you to fight back."

Harlow's eyes meet mine with half-lidded curiosity. I hastily look back down at my laptop again, caught red-handed. I need to pretend to be immersed in something until it's safe for me to resume watching them.

"Twist your wrists outwards, like this." Enzo pulls her arms into the correct form. "You're going to feint to the left and tug hard. Slip beneath my arm when the hold breaks."

Teeth gritted together, Harlow relaxes against his towering height. Enzo's enjoying this far too much. Leighton will kill him when he finds out what he missed by working out first, then showering.

With his guard down, Harlow decides to strike out. She twists her arms and moves fast, lurching forward to slip through his heavily muscled prison. Enzo lets her escape without much of a fight.

"I did it!" she says excitedly.

His smile is broad. "See? Simple but effective."

Dancing backwards on the mat, she pumps the air in a very un-Harlow like manner. Hell, she's too darn cute. I'd happily pin her to the ground and kiss the life out of her right now.

My cock twitches just watching her small, inviting curves straining against the tight material of her Lycra leggings and t-shirt. These workout clothes should be illegal for her to tease me with.

"Again," Enzo commands with a grin. "We're going to practise until you can do this with your eyes shut. No hesitation. Understood?"

More enthused now that she's had her first win, Harlow nods and jumps back into his arms. He tightens his grip and they run through the manoeuvre again.

Refocusing on my laptop to distract myself from the blood rushing to my dick, I flick back through the houses I've narrowed down. Enzo's criteria is obsessively detailed.

There are several viable options outside of London, but still close enough to commute. The city is too risky for us to consider, even though we have a range of different safe houses scattered throughout. Too many prying eyes.

When my laptop dings with an email on our secure server, I check again to make sure Harlow's absorbed in her training. She's ducking from fake punches now as Enzo chases her around the room, laughing his head off.

Logging in with a scan of my thumbprint in the top corner of my keyboard, I open the password-protected report from the team. My eyes race over the complicated jargon.

Forensics would've been my second career choice if I didn't fall into tech and programming. It offers similar insight into a world that most are content to let pass them by.

For me, I want to understand the complex systems and invisible rules that dictate our reality. The more we know, the easier it is to control. Techies can do more damage within half an hour at a terminal than the president in his Oval Office.

"Enz," I summon.

He glances over at me, pulling his blow short at the last minute before he would've struck Harlow in the gut. She's already ducked sideways to avoid the collision.

"Yeah?" he snaps.

I wave him over. "You need to see this."

Sighing, he plants a kiss on Harlow's braided hair. "Keep practising for a minute."

She swats him away. "Like hell. What's happening?"

Scanning back over the results, I feel giddy. It's unnerving. These conversations usually begin with disappointment, but this time, I'm staring at the biggest breakthrough we've had in months. About fucking time.

"Forensics found hair fibres on one of the bodies," I quickly recite. "We have a positive DNA match with the samples taken from Northumberland. It's him."

"Pastor Michaels?" Harlow squeaks.

"We have evidence tying the two crime scenes. One perp. This proves that Lee Heston and Pastor Michaels are the same person."

"Fuck." Enzo crouches to look over my shoulder. "Fuck! This is enough to go public. We can issue an arrest warrant and flush this son of a bitch out."

"How?" Harlow frowns at him. "We still have no idea where he's hiding. What difference will this make?"

"The photograph from Frederick Houghton," I remind her. "We can release it to the press. Someone's seen him in the last six months. We spread this far and wide."

Enzo rises to his feet. "What about the landlord?"

"In Newcastle?" I clarify.

"Yeah. I want him arrested and brought in for questioning. He rented that damn place to Michaels five years ago and allowed another family to live above a crime scene."

"You think he knew?"

"Doubtful, but I don't want any loose ends. We need to send someone to monitor Frederick Houghton's residence too. Michaels knows we've linked his two identities. He may decide to retaliate."

"Seems risky."

"I wouldn't put it past him though," Enzo argues.

His phone rings, and Enzo sighs as he notes the caller ID. Hunter's mum. She's at the hospital with the Cobra team, keeping an eye on things while we're trapped by the madness going on outside.

"Take it." I shrug without looking up from my email reiterating his instructions. "I'll tell Becket and the Anaconda team to hit the road. They can track down the landlord."

Enzo nods and heads upstairs for some privacy. Lucky bounds after him, yipping for attention, leaving Harlow to sink down next to me on the floor. Her expression is conflicted.

"What's up?" I ask while typing furiously. "This is good news. We're getting closer to Michaels. All it takes is one tip-off to expose his current location."

She worries her bottom lip. "It's nothing."

Setting my laptop aside once finished, I tentatively reach out and stroke my fingers against her clenched hand. She's staring at her folded legs, doing her best to ignore my touch.

"Beautiful," I murmur.

"I just… it's selfish of me, but I know that when we catch him, it will all be over. Everything will change."

"What do you mean? Us?"

"Yeah. I'll have to leave, and you'll all go back to your lives without me."

Is she being serious right now? I will never understand how her brilliant mind can be so fucking naïve at times.

"Don't look at me like that."

"Um, hard not to." I tug her hand into mine. "Do you actually think that Michaels is the only reason we're all here? Nothing else?"

Harlow shrugs. "I don't know."

The anger comes rushing back.

We've sacrificed everything to get to this point—a DNA match and solid lead that could bring the entire house of cards crashing down. We're getting close.

"Like I said, it's stupid and selfish." She winces at her own words. "I sound like a spoiled brat, complaining about this while Hunter's lying in a hospital bed."

"I understand how you're feeling," I admit.

Her iridescent blue eyes lock onto me. "You do?"

"Yeah. Ever since you came into our lives… I feel like I've started to get my family back." I pick at a loose thread in my jeans. "I'm scared of losing them all over again when this is over. In a fucked-up way, the case has brought us together."

"You know that won't happen though."

"Won't it?" I point out.

"The only reason they're getting hurt is because of me. Look at Hunter. Look what I did to him. You'd all be better off with me far away."

"You still don't get it, do you? None of this matters without you. Literally none of it."

She tries to shy away from me, and my patience fizzles out. I pull her hand and hook an arm underneath her slim legs. Harlow lands in my lap, sprawled out with her head tipped up towards me.

Our mouths gravitate together. I'm not in control of it, and neither is she. Something greater ties us together now. Something that can't be undone, no matter how much she worries it will all fall apart the minute Michaels is caught.

Harlow tastes like everything bright and good in the world. Her lips are velvety, moving against mine in a nervous waltz. We're too alike for our own good, but I feel stronger around her.

More capable.

Confident.

Whole.

It's a feeling I only ever experienced around one other person. I know that Harlow matters to me, on a level that cannot be described, because I no longer dream about Alyssa. She's been absent for a while now.

My nights are haunted by another face. Sweetheart-shaped and innocent, framed by inquisitive blue eyes that excite the people pleaser within me. I want to please her. Protect her. Love her. All of it.

Harlow has snuck into my system and planted her exploit. Now, my code is failing, and I cannot safely reboot as the malware corrupts my hard drive. She has become my new master. Everything I am, I want to give to her.

"With or without that son of a bitch in custody, we all belong to you," I whisper into her mouth. "None of us have the power to walk away. In our world, family is forever."

"Forever," she echoes. "You don't mean that."

Her fingers knot in my t-shirt and tug, betraying her uncertainty. She still doesn't believe me. It's infuriating.

"I fell in love with you before we even met, beautiful. For months, you existed in the printed ink of case files and witness statements. I didn't need to see you to know that you were something special."

"I'm nobody," she hushes out.

"Respectfully, Harlow, shut the fuck up."

Bursting into anguished laughter, her eyes flutter shut. "I don't want to wake up from this dream. When we find Pastor Michaels… everything will shatter. I feel like the worst person on the planet for admitting that out loud."

Nudging her nose with mine, I force her eyes to reopen. There she is. The kind-hearted, curious angel that stole my attention from the pages of police reports and crime scene photographs. She's far better than any book I've ever loved.

"That's when our lives will really begin," I reply. "We'll be free to live without fear. I cannot bloody wait to see what you do with that freedom."

A tentative smile blooms on her pink lips, and it's the most breathtaking sight I've ever seen. I know she still feels guilty as hell, but that tiny hint of positivity is enough for me.

"What *we* will do with it," Harlow corrects.

"What *we* will do with it," I repeat. "Together."

"I don't want to do this alone."

"And you'll never have to. That I can promise."

We kiss again, and the gym melts away around us. Enzo's and Leighton's voices talking upstairs become background noise. All that exists is the pressure of Harlow's sweet body cradled in my lap.

Clasping her chin, I deepen the kiss, needing more than her lips can give me. I want an eternal vow, signed in blood across the tender flesh of her soul, that she'll never abandon us.

Alyssa's death demanded its own solemn oath from me—the promise that I'd never let myself love again. Not for the toll it eventually extracts when that love is stolen away. Yet here I am, head over heels. I have no idea how it happened.

Her hand slips beneath my plain t-shirt and strokes over my ribcage. Every touch sends my heart into palpitations. I've wanted to taste every damned inch of her since that night we spent in the underground station.

"We need to go upstairs and deal with this fiasco," I gasp.

"No." Harlow yanks my lips back to hers when I pull away. "I need... I need something else from you first."

She shifts on my lap and moves to straddle me instead. My throat seizes with the weight of her rocking against my hard dick. Fuck. She has no idea how much she turns me on.

"And what's that, beautiful?"

Harlow's lips brush my clavicle. "Your trust."

"You already have it."

"Prove it then. No more hiding."

She shimmies backwards and lets her mouth travel down my body. When her hands move to the waistband of my jeans, I flinch with surprise. The guys are mere metres above us. They could return at any moment.

"Harlow—"

The button pops as she eases a hand inside the denim folds, cutting my complaint off. I hardly recognise the sexy confidence of the angel cupping my cock. Eyes rolling back, I let the protests die on my tongue.

"You'll need to be quiet," she instructs, easing my length out of my boxers. "I don't want them to interrupt us."

Wrapping a hand around the base of my shaft, Harlow sneaks a look up at me through her thick lashes. I stroke my hand over her hair, feeling like my heart is ready to burst.

"Is this okay?" she checks.

"As long as you're okay with it."

Grinning to herself, I watch her mouth descend on my erection. The minute it enters the warm, welcome prison, I have to swallow a grunt of pleasure. Her lips feel incredible tightening around me.

"Fuck, beautiful."

The light graze of her teeth against my shaft is a silent warning. Neither of us wants an audience for this, no matter the times I've shared with Hunter and Enzo in the past. I want her to myself for now. The sharing will come later.

Carefully holding her two thick braids to avoid triggering her, I lean back against the brick wall. Her mouth is tentative at first before she begins to take me deeper into her throat.

Her head rotates with each suck, determined to squeeze every last drop of pleasure from me. After the longest period of celibacy, I won't last long, riding her mouth like this.

Enzo's voice sneaks into my awareness as his footsteps begin to descend the stairs. Harlow doesn't seem to notice, too absorbed by her task. I try to pull her head back, but she holds firm.

A hot wave of awkwardness washes over me as Enzo's headful of sweaty black hair pokes around the corner. He freezes in the doorway the moment he spots me, pinned and gasping, while Harlow lets me fuck her mouth.

Enzo grins ear-to-ear and shoots me a pleased thumbs up. *Oh Lord, kill me now.* Flipping him the bird, I wave him away while trying not to burst into humiliated flames.

Biting down on his lip to suppress a laugh, he spreads his hands in surrender and ducks back upstairs. Perfect timing, as I'm about to finish in Harlow's mouth if she doesn't stop.

"Beautiful," I warn her.

She takes my warning as encouragement and sneaks a hand downwards to take a handful of my balls. *Jesus H Christ.* Someone taught her this shit. My money is on Leighton, the sneaky little asshole.

With a gentle squeeze of my balls, I'm driven to the edge. My hand fists in her braids as my release explodes out of me. Her lips tighten, milking my cock with a final suck.

I don't know why I'm stunned to silence that she swallows, glancing up at me with glistening lips. This dirty, gorgeous angel is a different creature entirely to the Harlow I know and love.

I'm not complaining.

That was incredible.

"Who taught you that?" I ask suspiciously.

Her lips contort in a rueful grin. "I had some help. Was it good?"

"You're asking me if I enjoyed you giving me a blow job?"

"Well... yeah."

Now I know exactly what Enzo means when he talks about loving her innocence. I didn't quite get it until now. It's so goddamn hot.

I stroke the pad of my thumb along her lips, stealing the droplets of come that have slipped out. Her luminescent eyes widen when I lick the remnants of my own release up.

She has no idea of the things I could show her. I've only held back for so long because I was confused about my feelings, and frankly, a little nervous about the kind of relationship I would need with her.

Alyssa understood me perfectly. She respected my need to be dominated and controlled in the bedroom. It was her domain. That's why I was more than happy for Harlow to take control of this moment. I need her to lead.

"Is it safe to come down?" Leighton bellows from upstairs.

Sitting back on her heels, Harlow watches me straighten my clothing back into place. There's a healthy dose of intrigue in her hot and heavy gaze. I'll happily be her guinea pig again for anything else she learns.

"It's safe," I call back.

"Could've lied," she mumbles. "Now he's gonna come and sing *Mamma Mia* down here too."

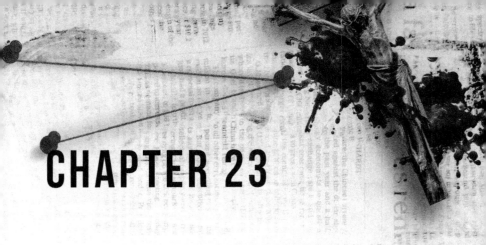

CHAPTER 23

Harlow

Sad Money — Call Me Karizma

ulling Leighton's baseball cap lower to cover my face, I tug the collar of my coat upwards for extra protection. With my long hair down, I'm hoping to blend into the buzz of people exploring Hyde Park in the sunshine.

Families hum around me, pushing prams or carrying picnic baskets. Kids squeal and race through the ancient bodies of oak trees. This undisturbed green space is a bizarre contrast to the city, a slice of nature in the heart of London.

"There's a bench up ahead opposite the lake," Enzo's voice whispers into my ear. "Sit down there. We have a perfect line of sight."

I adjust my headphones. "I don't need a team of agents watching my every move. He isn't going to hurt me."

"The last we saw of your father, he broke into our house with a weapon. I'm not taking any chances. If I had my way, you wouldn't be meeting that wanker at all."

"He's out of rehab," I justify under my breath. "That's something.

I have to give him a chance to explain himself."

"Doesn't make him any less of a security risk," he cuts back. "Stay alert and keep it short. If you need anything, you know the signal. Our agents will come running."

"Got it."

"Good luck, little one. I'll give you some privacy."

He ends the call, and I tuck my headphones away in my pocket. The peeling varnish on the bench is cool beneath my butt as I take a seat. In front of me, a glimmering lake wraps around the intimidating presence of trees far older than London's industrialisation.

The request came in a few days ago as we were leaving the hospital. It was another painfully silent visit, with Hunter staring into space, unresponsive. He refuses to interact with anyone, and I can't look at him without sobbing my eyes out.

I broke him.

And I'm scared that it's permanent.

When Enzo showed me the email from my father, I finally cracked and agreed to meet him. I can't fix Hunter's agony right now, but I can offer my father the chance to explain himself. That's still within my control, if nothing else.

Leg jiggling with nerves, I watch the ducks bob across the lake water. It feels good to be out in the fresh spring air after being cooped up inside all week, only leaving the house for therapy or to visit the hospital.

"Harlow?"

I recognise his voice without looking up. Shuffling up to me in jeans, a dark zip-up jumper and an oversized raincoat, my father halts a few feet away. He looks like a completely different person to the gaunt, inebriated ghost who first re-entered my life.

"You know my name."

His narrow lips hook upwards in a smile. "I wish I could take the credit, but your security team threatened some pretty horrific stuff if I called you Letty again."

Huh. Sounds about right.

Swiping a hand over his clean, dark-blonde hair, freshly trimmed and hanging over sharp blue eyes that match my own, he gestures towards the space next to me.

"Mind if I sit?"

I shuffle over to make room. "Sure."

Sinking down next to me, Dad spares me a fast, searching glance. I try not to squirm as he studies my features. Even if it's subconscious, I trust him for reasons I can't fathom. My racing heart recognises him even if my brain doesn't.

"You're so grown up," he croaks. "I wasn't sure if I'd recognise you when we met again. I spent so many years picturing what you'd look like now."

"When?" I repeat in surprise. "Not if?"

He wrings his hands together. "I never stopped believing that you were still alive. Did you... read my letters?"

My chest constricts with grief. "A couple with my therapist. You wrote to me a lot. I've kept them safe."

"Not much else to do in prison. I needed to find a way to keep you alive in my head. It helped me."

Staring ahead as a couple strolls past us, their limbs entwined while flirting, I clear my throat. The stark difference from Giana and her actions is indisputable. Dad never gave up on me. She did. That's something.

"How did you find me?" I ask tightly. "You tracked me down months ago."

"The answer to that question is a little complicated."

"Then uncomplicate it." I look up and meet his uncertain eyes. "I've taken a huge risk to meet you. I need to know what happened thirteen years ago."

Sighing heavily, he nods and looks ahead at the lake. I watch him from the corner of my eye. Everything about him is familiar—from the smile lines etched around his mouth, to the sparkle of his eyes and the wide set of his shoulders.

I know him.

We had a life together.

Distant fragments of a memory crash over me. Those same shoulders held my child-sized weight as we bounded across a quiet beach. He splashed into the water and threatened to throw me in before swooping me upwards and planting a kiss on my cheek.

More often than that, I dream about that beach. It featured in so much of my childhood. The pieces of it that I can remember, at least. Grandma Sylvie took me there. It was a place of happiness, before that was ripped away forever.

His voice drags me back to the present.

"Whatever Giana's told you… it isn't the truth. She's been playing an elaborate game for all these years."

My skin breaks out in gooseflesh.

"What kind of game?"

"Two truths and a lie," he answers flatly. "I'm no saint. I've always owned up to that. But she choreographed the whole thing, and even I couldn't stop her plan from working."

I pull the elastic band wrapped around my wrist and repeatedly snap it against my skin. If I didn't know that Enzo and his army spooks are watching our meeting, I'd be tearing whole chunks of hair out.

"You know about the drugs." He crosses his arms. "I'm not proud of it. She was so temperamental to live with, especially after you were born. Her mood swings were unpredictable."

My thoughts go back to the day she grabbed me during our meeting at HQ. I can still feel her nails cutting into my wrist.

"I'm not sure when things got out of control," Dad admits. "I owed people money, a lot of it. Work was fine, but it didn't cover the cash I was snorting on a daily basis."

"What did you do?"

He looks uncomfortable. "I worked for the Home Office at the time. Anti-fraud division, if you can believe it. That's where I got the idea to start forging identities."

Another family settles on the bench next to us. They're sitting close enough to overhear our conversation. Rising to my feet, I gesture for him to come with me.

"Come on. Let's walk."

"I don't want to piss off your protection any more than I already have," he frets.

Glancing around, I can feel the weight of invisible eyes. "Don't worry. They will follow us, I'm sure."

Nodding, Dad falls into step next to me as we set off down the winding path through the park. He's a lot steadier on his feet than the unstable wreck who recklessly broke in before.

"I swore to myself that once my debts were paid, I'd stop," he says in a low voice. "But Giana was getting worse. It wasn't her violence towards me that I cared about; I was used to it."

I startle as his hand brushes my arm before releasing. The brief touch causes my heart to stutter.

"When I came home from work one night, you were doing your homework with a black eye." His voice chills. "She scared you into silence, but we both knew who did it."

"I don't remember that," I admit.

"It wasn't the first time it happened either."

Tiny sparks are firing in the back of my mind. The memories are there, swelling and growing in size. His words resonate, even if I don't want them to.

"She started to behave strangely," he continues. "I was convinced that she was having an affair, but when I caught her with a Bible one night, I knew it was something else."

"Wait, a Bible?"

Dad rolls his shoulders back. "She was carving scripture into her arm with a kitchen knife. I tried to get her to stop, but she came for me instead."

Pulling the collar of his zip-up hoodie to the side, he flashes a stretch of skin. The deep, uneven scar twists beneath his collarbone. I've got enough knife marks of my own to recognise one.

"She was never religious." He pulls his clothes back into place. "Things got worse. She was obsessive, borderline manic. Convinced the rapture was coming and we all needed to repent."

Dread slips down my spine. I should be disturbed by his story, but it all sounds sickeningly familiar. I've had the same fanatical nonsense crammed down my throat before, accompanied by the beat of fists on flesh.

"That's when I decided to keep forging identities. I was saving the money from every single job, ready for us to start a new life. We were ready to go. Passports, flights, the lot."

Halting on the pavement, I frown up at him. "You were going to run away with me?"

"I had no other choice," he pleads with widened eyes. "You weren't safe with her. She was getting out of control."

"Like how?"

"She'd plastered the house in printed-out hymns and scripture about Hell. I caught her yelling at people in the street, getting violent when I challenged her. It scared me to death."

I blink back tears. It's hard not to wonder how my life might have turned out if we did run away together.

"And then, you were gone."

He suddenly stops, looking up at the heavens while taking a breath. I fidget on the spot. I'm torn between wrapping him into a hug and running in the opposite direction. I don't know who to believe.

"She played it so well," Dad chokes out. "Her alibi was solid. Giana convinced the world that she was a hysterical, heartbroken mother trapped in an abusive marriage."

"They said I decided to walk home from school that day," I add through my own rising nausea. "Giana was running late from work, apparently."

"You didn't decide to walk." Dad gives me a grief-laden look. "I usually took you, but I was too out of it that day. She'd broken my rib, and I was in agony. Regardless, I made you swear long before then that you'd never walk alone."

"Then why would she say that?" I ask in confusion.

"Because it was all planned, Harlow. She told you exactly where to go. The kidnapping was a setup."

"W-What?" I stammer.

He tries to reach for me, grimacing when I take a protective step backwards.

"I could never prove it, no matter how hard I tried." Tears leak down his face. "I kept pushing for months, searching for any clues. Giana knew I was on to her and got me arrested."

"This can't be right."

"She testified that I was an abusive addict, and she was the victim.

It all fit together like a lock and key."

"No…" I moan.

"The perfect lie. I was quickly convicted, and your case was left to rot. Giana skipped off into the sunset."

I want to scream and run for my life. This is another flight of fantasy, a horror-filled fiction being sold to gain my loyalty. He wants to destroy my mother. I know that. I'm being used.

"You're lying," I say as my courage fails. "She isn't perfect, but Giana isn't a monster. She would never do that to me."

"Harlow, please. I'm telling the truth. You've been lied to… she isn't the person you think she is."

"Neither are you."

"I'm still your dad, petal."

"No. You're not. I haven't had a father for thirteen years… and I don't need one now."

I turn to leave, and he grabs my arm. Immediately, I spot movement from the treeline ahead of us. Two black-clothed agents are already racing towards us to contain the threat.

"Let go of me."

"You aren't safe here," Dad urges. "That's how I tracked you down. I still have connections in the Home Office. Say the word, and I'll have us on a flight to Mexico with brand-new identities by tomorrow."

"You seriously think I'd run away with you?"

"Giana knows her days are numbered." His voice raises as panic takes over. "She's been threatening me for months. I don't know what she'll do to keep her secret intact."

"I'll take my chances."

"No! You're in danger here."

"The only danger to me right now is you," I reply sternly. "I heard you out. Now, we're done. I'd like you to leave me alone."

His grip on my coat tightens. "Please, Harlow. You have to listen to me. I won't lose you a second time."

Security is almost upon us. They'll batter him senseless if he doesn't let go, and no matter how messed up this whole charade is, I don't want to see that happen to him.

"I'd like both of you to leave me alone and settle your fight without involving me. I have enough going on as it is."

Peeling his fingertips from my coat, I shove his hand back towards him. The hurt written across Dad's face is a punch in the gut, but I clamp down on my emotions. He and Giana are cut from the same cloth.

"I'm so sorry," he hushes, tears glittering in his blue eyes. "I should've protected you from her. It was my job, and I failed. I understand why you hate me."

"That's the thing." I step backwards, needing space to breathe. "I don't hate you... or Giana, for that matter. Even though I should."

Dad nods with an unhappy smile. "I won't make the same mistakes again. You know where to find me when you're ready. Don't forget my offer."

Before he can be beaten to within an inch of life at Enzo's command, Dad turns on his heel and walks away. The two agents are about to blur past me to chase after him when I shout for them to stop.

Hyland halts at my side, searching for any injuries. "Are you okay? Did he hurt you?"

"I'm fine. Let him go."

"But—"

"Forget it. I want to go home now."

Looking conflicted, Hyland nods. I'm sandwiched between the two agents and ushered towards the park's exit where Enzo is waiting in a blacked-out SUV, hidden from the world and cameras constantly tailing us.

At the last second, I look over my shoulder. Dad has stopped at the edge of the clustered oak trees, watching us leave. Anguish is written across his entire shivering frame.

He lifts a single hand and waves.

I don't wave back.

CHAPTER 24

Hunter

Taurus – Machine Gun Kelly & Naomi Wild

Propped upright in the raised hospital bed, I half-heartedly read the closed captions on the TV screen. I'm like the rest of the world now. Deafened by silence and desperate for unreachable answers.

The statement from Sabre has been signed off with Lucas's name, on behalf of management. Not Hunter Rodriguez. He doesn't exist anymore. My authority has vanished along with my hearing.

Officials are appealing for any information relating to Mr Lee Heston, also known by the alias Pastor Michaels. DNA evidence has tied this individual to the discovery of a mass grave in Newcastle.

It feels poetic that it's Sally Moore delivering the news on my screen. We finally have our killer pinned down by real, tangible evidence. It's the single biggest breakthrough in the whole case, and I'm not there to see it.

Her bright-red lips move with each sentence, but her words are lost in translation. I can't hear her sharp, irritating voice. Nor the dramatic channel's music associated with a breaking news story. The busy hospital ward around me is lifeless too.

There's nothing.

Endless, empty nothingness.

This man is the prime suspect in Sabre's ongoing serial killer investigation. The public is being urged to contact law enforcement and not approach this extremely dangerous individual if seen.

Pastor Michaels stares back at me from the screen. The single photograph that Frederick Houghton provided has been joined by many others from over the years. People are discovering that this bastard has been living right under their noses and coming forward to testify.

Years of aliases and bolt holes.

He's been hidden in plain sight.

The screen fades to black as the remote is deposited on the table over my bed. Her usual forced smile in place, Mum begins chatting like everything is normal as she arrives for her daily visit. I can see her lips moving, but nothing comes out.

She's been doing this for the past couple of weeks. I treat her the same as the others who've rotated through this room, bringing with them pitiful smiles and tears that turn my stomach. I tune them out.

After the explosion six years ago, I had a glimpse of the hellish reality waiting for me down the road. Partially losing my hearing back then was the scariest experience of my life.

Far more terrifying than assassinations, car chases, espionage and landing in war zones. Nothing compared. Nor did I think it ever would.

I was wrong.

That terror pales into insignificance compared to the moment my consultant explained the situation with a whiteboard and pen. The damage to my left eardrum is so severe, the limited hearing I had left has been permanently obliterated.

I've lost my last lifeline.

It's gone, forever.

Mum's hand touches mine, and I flinch in surprise. She appeared next to me without warning. Lips moving in an apology for catching me off guard, she automatically moves to brush my hair aside, but it's gone.

My head was shaved before the surgery performed to pin my broken skull. I haven't looked at myself yet. I don't need to see how closely I resemble a monster. Feeling the lumps and bumps of my bald head was horrifying enough.

"Doctor's buying a farm," she mouths.

I squint at her lips. "Wait, what?"

Mum speaks more slowly. "Doctor… thawing… pram."

"I have no clue what you're saying to me!"

Eyes softening, she sits on the edge of the bed and spells out a word at a time until it finally clicks into place in my head.

"Doctor… drawing up… discharge plan."

"Oh."

"Home soon… tough weeks… on the mend."

"No," I quickly blurt.

She frowns at me. "No?"

It's disconcerting to speak without hearing my own voice echoing inside my head. Another grim reminder. I've barely spoken to avoid the pain it causes to lance through my chest.

"I don't want them caring for me."

Mum shakes her head, appearing dumbfounded at me. She speaks so fast, I can only distinguish bits and pieces of her words. She's pissed at me now. Great.

"Your family!" Her lips carve out the words. "Love you."

"No, they don't," I repeat. "I'm a burden."

Eyes narrowed, she grabs me by the chin like I'm an insolent child. Leighton was regularly on the receiving end of her lectures. I was more obedient than him as a kid. Apparently, we've reversed. I fucking hate irony.

"Harlow." The word filters through as I follow her lips. "Guilty... enough... home."

The rest of her response is shattered into confusing fragments. I can only ever pick up odd words here and there.

"This isn't Harlow's fault," I insist.

"Tell... yourself," Mum mouths angrily. "*Home.*"

She slaps something hard into my hand. I look down at the slim metal of my phone. The soft vibrating is almost thrilling now in a world of black and white, silence and numbness.

Harlow's name is on the screen. She texted me dozens of times this morning alone. Throat burning, I scroll through the increasingly upset messages. I never respond to them.

> **Harlow:** I'll come after my therapy session to see you. Do you need anything?
>
> **Harlow:** Please stop ignoring me, Hunt.
>
> **Harlow:** If you don't want me there... just say.
>
> **Harlow:** I dropped by. You were asleep. Coming back later.

Now, it's my turn to feel guilty. I was only pretending to be asleep earlier. She stayed for almost an hour, staring at the wall while clasping my limp hand in hers. All she did was cry, and it killed me inside to see.

I couldn't bring myself to butcher a conversation in mouthed words and scraps of paper. The quicker they realise the person they know is gone and never coming back, the easier this drawn-out goodbye will be.

The other texts vary in tone.

I'm sent regular updates from the team as Sabre continues to tick over in my absence. Leighton makes the most effort to keep me in the loop, weirdly enough. He's been helping out more and supporting Enzo at a senior management level.

> **Enzo:** The press release went well. Tips are pouring in. We're close.
>
> **Leigh:** Turn on the news. We're gonna catch this motherfucker.
>
> **Enzo:** Harlow called me crying. Text her back.
>
> **Theo:** I've found an auditory specialist in the States. Emailing you the details now.

Mum gently shakes my arm again to guide my eyes back up to her mouth. The fucking tears are back. When she cries and looks at me like that, I wish the bullet actually had killed me.

"They love you," she repeats. "We all do."

And that's the problem.

Their love. It will drag them to the pits of this miserable existence with me. I've had a lot of time to think while holed up in here, and I won't do that to them. It's no life.

I don't need an audience for the slow death that lies ahead. Will I ever be able to work again? Live a normal life? I got used to the idea of living with partial hearing.

That was hard enough.

But I was grateful for that glimmer of hope, and I treasured it for years. Now, I'll never hear Harlow's laugh again. High-pitched and laced with such zest for life, it's impossible not to smile in her incandescent presence.

It's gone forever. I'll never hear that bright spark of hope ever again. Nor my parents' voices. Leighton's shitty attitude. Enzo's gruff complaints. Theo's sarcastic quips. Hell, my kids' first cries. Endless unrealised possibilities.

Gone. Gone. Gone.

It's all been stolen.

I squeeze my eyes shut and ignore the pressure of Mum's hand attempting to regain my attention. Eventually, she gives up. When I dare to peek an eye open again, she's left me in peace. Probably gone to cry in private this time.

The nurses helped me to stand and walk around last week. I've been moving more with each day. Without them here, it's difficult to wrench my legs into position, but I manage to stand up alone.

Disconnecting my IV port from the line attached to a bag of painkillers, I grab the nearest piece of clothing—a discarded hoodie. Leighton must've left it here. It covers my sweats and loose, black t-shirt.

I need out of this room. This hospital. This world. Nobody can look at me. Not even the doctors and specialists. I know what they're all thinking. *Oh, the tragedy.* It makes me fucking sick that I've become the gossip of tea breaks.

I'm not a charity case dependent on their pity to figure out what the fuck I'm going to do now. The last month has proven that I'm not needed. Sabre is safe. My family is fine without me. The case is being wrapped up.

I'm dead weight.

It's time for me to go.

Leaning against the wall, I pull on a pair of shoes and stumble over to the door to peek out at the male ward I was moved to not long after I woke up. The usual afternoon nurse is dozing, her chin propped on her hand.

Pulling the hood up to cover my bald, stapled head, I slip out and hope I'm moving as silently as the world is to me now. The ward passes in a soundless blur. It's easy to limp through the barely organised chaos of the hospital without being seen.

With no direction, I begin walking. My steps are slow and awkward, with regular pauses to regain my balance. London continues to thrive around me. I'm the silent ghost, locked out from its sensual whispers.

Afternoon fades into night. Office blocks become billboards for advertising, while coffee shops transition into packed bars for after-work drinks. To the world, I could be another jogger, taking a stroll.

They don't need to know the truth—that I'm a failed case study, the millionaire businessman brought to his knees by a single motherfucking bullet. In that instant, years of hard-won success vanished. My legacy died an early death.

Without my phone on me, I have no idea what time it is. The darkness is a cold prison that I walk into willingly. I don't want to be found this time.

I cross the Millennium Bridge, and wind whips around me. The twisted metal structure offers me a wordless welcome as cold air lashes against my face. From here, I can see the bright lights of St Paul's Cathedral, all lit up at night.

God is my witness here.

I won't take another step.

Stopping halfway, my elbows propped on the handrail, I study the domed structure of the cathedral. Warm strobe lights break the suffocation of shadows. Perhaps they're singing inside. What I wouldn't give to hear it.

Leaning forward on the railings, I look down at the black water of the River Thames beneath me. It's choppy, lashing against the bank. I can imagine the sound of crashing waves.

This entire city used to mean something to me. It represented a land of opportunity, the tempting luxury that success and fame afforded my family for our hard work. London is my home.

Like everything else, it's lost.

Just like me.

I'm not sure how long I stand there for, shivering in the frigid night. A storm is approaching. I can taste the electricity in the air. I'm left undisturbed as pedestrians rush to take cover before the heavens open.

I don't want to live anymore. This is no life. Don't get me wrong, I know that deaf people can function. Scrape by. Make do. Relearn their whole existence. I don't want to do any of that. I refuse, and that's my fucking choice.

I'll jump.

Quick and painless.

Hooking one leg on the railing, I take a step up. It's a big drop down to the river. Glancing around me, there's no one in sight. Not a single soul to stop me from doing this. I'm thankful.

This wasn't the plan. My life isn't supposed to end this way. I'd rather die doing what I do best than take the coward's way out, but I'm backed into a corner.

I don't want this life.

I should be back at Sabre, fighting for justice and battling corruption in the most sinister corners of the world. Protecting those who can't do it themselves. That's who I am.

Who I was.

Who I'll never be again.

Taking another step up, I teeter in the air. Fear takes hold, no matter how hard I try to crush it down. Don't blink. Don't hesitate. Don't even think about it.

If I do, I'll stop.

On the verge of taking the final step, the tension in the air breaks. Clouds release the first specks of rain. Sweet droplets kiss my skin in the most excruciating way, entrapping me on the verge of oblivion.

It's raining. Heavier and heavier. Water soaks into my skin and brings sharp sensations. The pleasure is so intense, like each individual feeling has been dialled to ten without my hearing.

Gasping for a breath, I tilt my head upwards. Fuck. It feels so good. Like I'm breathing for the first time in weeks. Air bursts in my lungs as I swallow the lash of rain on my tongue.

It's sweet.

Almost metallic.

I could cry in relief. Part of me thought I'd never feel again. Numbness had become my new normal in the hospital, but that smothering tomb is breaking wide open.

Swinging my other leg over the railing, I sit down on the edge of a dangerous drop. The metal beneath my backside is the only thing holding me in this world.

I'm soaked to the bone. The heavens are pouring down on me. Near hypothermic, I almost don't notice when someone taps my shoulder. It startles me back to the real world, where normal people don't sob in the middle of a violent rainstorm.

Phone pressed to his ear, Leighton sweeps his viridescent eyes over me, checking for injury. I watch his lips move in the angry vortex of the storm encapsulating us.

"Found him," he recites.

His hand snags on my stolen hoodie. Unpeeling his fingers, I push him backwards. "Leave me alone."

Shaking his head, he tries to reply, but I turn my head to silence his words. London has vanished in the blur of falling water, obscured from sight. The temptation of darkness still lashes below me, but the whisper in my head has quietened for a second.

Clarity comes, and I panic.

I can't do this with him here.

Slapping his hands on the railing, Leighton boosts himself up and hooks his stocky legs over the metal poles. He sits down next to me, holding on for dear life.

Waving his hand to get my attention, he sticks his phone beneath my nose. I look down at the text message he's typed out for me to read.

What the hell are you doing up here? Why did you leave the hospital without telling anyone?

"I want to be alone, Leigh. You can go."

His thumbs batter his phone screen as he types a response.

That's not going to happen. Please come down. Whatever this is... you don't need to do it.

"Just go. We're not discussing this."

Come home with me then. No talking required.

"Home?" I scoff back. "So you can all sit around, staring at me? Feeling fucking sorry for me? I'll pass."

He wavers in the air for a second when there's a powerful gust of wind. I move on instinct, grabbing hold of his sleeve so he doesn't fall. Leighton rights himself and types a reply.

Give me a chance to help you, Hunt. Just like you did for me. I know you're hurting, but this isn't the answer.

"I don't need anyone's help."

But we need yours. I need you. Harlow needs you.

I shove his phone away. "Nobody needs the help of a deaf man. You're better off without me dragging you down."

He sticks it back under my nose.

Deaf or not, you're our leader. We don't give a shit about your hearing. You're still you. So get the fuck up and lead.

Leighton tucks his phone back into his pocket, abandoning our stunted conversation when I scowl in defiance. He slings his legs back over the other side of the railing and lands on his feet.

When I think he's going to leave me in peace, he grabs my arm and tugs hard. I teeter for a breathless second, a millimetre from falling to my death, before gravity takes hold.

I fall backwards and hit the hard floor of the bridge with a gasp. The impact is absorbed by my shoulder as pain burns through the smacked limb. Leighton hovers over me, poised to block my path back up onto the railing.

"What the fuck?" I yell at him.

His lips move, but I can't make out what he's shouting back at me. The rain is falling thick and fast as I attempt to stand up. The burst of energy that led me here is gone. I'm cold and exhausted, in every way possible.

He won't move.

Leighton stands between me and the promise of death. I bat his phone aside when he shoves it back in my face, but he grips my hoodie tight and makes me read the message.

If you jump, then I will too.

"No!" I shout in a rush.

Leighton cocks an eyebrow. The challenge is clear. We're facing off on opposite sides of an impasse, neither one of us willing to back down or compromise.

"Please." I break down. "I can't do this anymore."

Kneeling down next to me, Leighton holds my shoulder tight as I decipher his words. "You can."

J ROSE

I'm bundled into his arms before I can fight him off. Leighton hugs me so tight against his chest, we could melt into each other. It's the first time my brother has hugged me in years.

I try to push him backwards to escape. His grip only strengthens, no matter how hard I shove him away. He clings on tighter and tighter, swallowing every punch I throw at him. Blow after blow. Insult after insult. He takes it all.

It's no use.

He won't fight back.

My body turns against me. I can't battle the fatigue anymore. I slump into his embrace and my head falls. Shoulders slump. Throat tightens. Eyes burn. Gripping my shoulders, he forces me to try to read his lips.

"Brother... will not leave... bridge. Staying... so am I. In... together."

Angry wind freezes the stray tears on my cheeks that have dared to escape my control. His cheeks look wet too, beyond the lash of rain. We're a pair of sobbing idiots, both trying to keep the other alive.

"I'm fucking scared," I admit.

Leighton's forehead wrinkles as he stares into my eyes.

"Me too," he mouths back. "Why... don't do... alone."

His hand claps my forearm and squeezes.

"I can't go back to that hospital, Leigh."

"Home."

The word clings to his lips in a tempting poison. More than anything, I want to be with my family. This isn't my choice. This pain. This dark, desperate walk, looking for an easy escape. Leighton's offering a different way out.

"I can't face them," I stumble. "None of you can bear to look at me. Especially not Harlow. She's disgusted."

414

He punches me in the shoulder so hard, it reignites the forming bruise from where I was pulled off the bridge's edge.

"Harlow... guilty," he spells out.

"She feels guilty?"

Leighton nods. "Really... bad."

Nausea curls in the pit of my stomach. I let her sit there today, sobbing her goddamn eyes out. Maybe she wasn't crying for me, but for herself. The sins she feels guilty for. I'm such an idiot for not spotting it sooner.

This wasn't her fault. I chose to jump in front of that bullet. That was my decision and, given another chance, I'd do exactly the same thing. It was worth it to save her life.

I can't leave her like this.

Not while she's blaming herself.

Reaching out a hand, I let Leighton drag me back onto my feet. His arm encircles my shoulders. Both of us are violently trembling from the freezing cold rain.

"Home," I whisper back.

We walk back down the Millennium Bridge, fighting to stay upright in the worsening weather. Leighton nudges his phone back into my hand with another message.

Can you have a mental breakdown somewhere warm and dry next time? I think I have hypothermia now.

He's fucking grinning at me, even though this is a complete shitshow. I came out here to throw myself off the damn bridge, and yet, I break into semi-neurotic laughter.

"I'll consider it."

Leighton claps my shoulder. "You pepper."

"Pepper?"

He rolls his eyes. "Better."

It takes all of my remaining brain power to decipher his next words, even when he talks deliberately slowly.

"Want... take home... compromised."

"Compromised? What?" I demand.

"Moving... safer location."

"Why? What happened?"

His lips move fast as I fight to keep up.

"Whole world... address... no choice."

Shitting hell. I've spent too long staring at hospital walls while they've been firefighting a growing disaster. I can feel his eyes on the flash of my bald head.

Tugging the hood further up to cover the gnarly staples pinning my skin back together, I pretend not to notice the concern on his face, even as it kills me inside.

Inside the warmth of my parked convertible down a side street, I discover my hospital bag already packed and thrown in the back seat. Leighton slides behind the wheel and passes my phone over.

I raise an eyebrow.

He shrugs. "Coming... bust out... anyway."

Shaking my head, I quickly bring up my text messages. The dark, depressive fog that's clouded my mind is still there, but I can think clearly enough to see the pain I've caused. I need to make this right before it's too late.

Hunter: I'm sorry. Still owe you that date.

It doesn't take long for her reply to come. She must've been clutching her phone, waiting for an update from Leighton's trek across London to fetch me.

Harlow: I'll hold you to it. Come home.

CHAPTER 25

Harlow

Room To Breathe – You Me At Six

Curled up in the back of Hudson's throaty Mustang GT, the tap of Theo's fingers abusing his laptop blurs with the latest pop song blaring from the radio.

Lucky is crammed between us, snoring her head off. She's been clingy all day. I think she's missed us despite staying with Enzo's aunt while we've been caught up at HQ and the hospital.

Our empty home disappears into the distance. I can't help but feel a twinge of grief. When Enzo revealed that we were moving, I understood the decision. This was my first real home in a very long time, though, and I'm sad to see it go.

Behind the steering wheel, Hudson is fighting off a yawn, his pierced face tired after a late night of packing bags. Only the Cobra team is being trusted with our new location.

I'm exhausted too, but for a different reason. Since speaking to my father, sleep has become an elusive luxury. My nightmares have gotten worse, and with the guys working all hours at Sabre, I've been sleeping alone most nights.

I scrub my sore eyes. "How far away is the house?"

"About an hour." Theo scans over another anonymous tip with pinched eyebrows. "I swear, people have nothing better to do than email us fake information. It's pathetic."

I glance over his shoulder to read the email sent to Sabre's tip line. This moron actually thinks their teacher is Pastor Michaels. Their *female* teacher. Another childish prank and, unfortunately, one of many received. Time wasters.

"You hear from Enzo?"

Theo nods while opening the next batch of emails to be checked over. "He's loading the last boxes up. It was a good call moving the big furniture last night. The press saw nothing and haven't caught on yet."

"Leighton and Hunter?" I worry. "They're safe?"

"Waiting for us at the new house."

Fear wraps around my spinal cord. "How is he?"

Theo glances at me over the black-framed glasses balanced on his nose. "He's... Hunter."

"And you're very Theodore. What's your point?"

He snorts in derision. "I don't know what else to say, beautiful. Leighton talked some sense into him for now. He's in a dark place. We need to help him get through it."

"Did you tell him about the auditory specialist you found in the States? That might help him."

Theo's lips purse. "He didn't respond."

"Crap. We can talk to him tonight."

"Worth a shot, I guess."

I stroke a hand over Lucky's head in my lap beside the red-leather journal I was jotting in. I don't own much, but the pages of dreams and secrets matter to me as much as the gold ring tucked into my bra for safekeeping.

Writing has kept me sane. There are months of entries here, documenting the fascinating world around me. Jude told me to take back control, and I've filled these pages in an attempt to piece my past back together.

As Sabre swims through a barrage of information, inching ever closer to the end of this chaotic case, I'm far behind, drowning in a sea of secrets.

I now know this is a battle that I have to fight alone. The priority is catching Pastor Michaels, and we're closer than ever. I can't distract the guys now with my mental anguish, especially not with Hunter still in a fragile mental state. We're both balancing on a knife's edge. He's the priority.

Over an hour later, we arrive at the red-bricked streets of a quiet Midlands town. It's close enough to the motorway for the guys to commute into London, but removed from the risk of cameras tracking us down again.

"How did you find this place so quickly?" I stare out of the window at billowing cherry trees, bright-pink blossoms and middle-class families walking their pampered pets.

"We're cash buyers," Theo replies. "Made the owners an offer they couldn't refuse, and here we are. There's still paperwork to do, but they were happy for us to move in."

At the end of a winding cul-de-sac, Hudson parks up on the curb and shuts off the purring engine. He flicks the remains of his half-smoked cigarette out of the open window.

"Time to pay up," he declares. "This taxi ain't free."

Theo shuts his laptop. "Do you accept takeout as payment?"

"I could be persuaded," Hudson submits. "The moving vans should already be here."

Sliding out of the car, Theo stretches his arms high above his head. My mouth turns into the Sahara Desert as his t-shirt rides up, exposing his firm stomach, narrow waist and the flash of blonde hair trailing into his jeans.

He flashes me a smile. "Let's take a look inside."

"Okay."

With a bone-tired sigh, I stuff the journal back into my bag. Lucky hops over me to escape the car, already yipping and wagging her tail as she drinks in the fresh, blossom-scented air. She hates travelling in cars.

"You like it here, girl?"

She barks loudly, and I follow her up the steep, brick-lined driveway surrounded by flowering trees that cast shade against the warmth of sparkling sunshine.

Two moving vans are parked up next to Hunter's cherry-red convertible that Leighton has been using to get around. Two heads poke out of the vans, bickering between wrapped furniture and boxes.

"I'm just here to supervise," Phoenix protests, tucking lime-green hair behind his ear. "You're the one with the brains, Eli."

"You don't need brains to lift boxes." Eli grimaces as he hefts a box over his shoulder. "Stop being a lazy son of a bitch."

"It's my day off work!"

"You think I give a shit?"

I watch Lucky launch herself into the back of the first van. She rugby-tackles Phoenix, and he ends up on his ass beneath her huge limbs and overexcited tongue.

"Fucking dog!" he bellows. "Argh."

Eli shoots me a thumbs up as he hops down, a box in hand. He offers Theo a nod of greeting before heading for the two-story house tucked amongst billowing greenery.

It's beautiful, adorned with white hatched windows, a wraparound porch and cute balcony swing. It's smaller and cosier than our old home, perfectly matching the quiet farmer's fields surrounding the small town.

An arm winds around my waist and squeezes.

"You like it?" Theo asks.

"It's beautiful. I love it."

"Good." He beams at me. "I know this situation is less than ideal, but I wanted to find somewhere that would make you happy. Silver linings and all that."

I'm distracted as Phoenix saunters past us, carrying two boxes labelled with Theo's name in permanent marker.

"Are you moving back in?" I ask hopefully.

Theo releases my waist with a shrug. "Figured it's about time. We need to pull together now more than ever."

My stomach flips. I can't help but ask.

"Is that the only reason?"

His lips stroke against my cheek in a breathless kiss. "You might have something to do with it. I don't want to live in my office anymore. I want to be with you every day."

Burying my fingers in the perfect blonde curls hanging over pale-blue eyes, I pull his lips to mine. He kisses me back with the biggest smile I've ever seen on his usually shy face.

"Does this mean we can make our own shared library in the house?"

Theo rests his nose against mine. "That sounds like the best idea I've heard all day. Go and take a look around, I'll help these two."

"I'll see you inside."

Shifting my bag higher on my shoulder, I run after Phoenix. Inside the house, multicoloured tiles meet polished, light-brown bannisters on the staircase leading upstairs. To the left, an archway leads into a decent-sized living room with an open-plan kitchen attached.

Complete with an original fireplace and stripped flooring, I spot the gleam of cupboards and checked tiles around the corner. The kitchen is a decent size, with a space at the back for a family-sized table.

Compared to the sleek modernity of Hunter's London mansion, this place is a welcome departure. I love the traditionalism and quirky sense of character.

"Leigh?" I call out.

Shooting upright from his perch inspecting TV brackets, Leighton curses as he smacks his head on the solid oak beam built above the fireplace's chimney.

"Shit!" he curses.

I wince as he rubs the sore spot on his head.

"Did you knock your brains out?"

"According to my idiot brother, I haven't got any for agreeing to buy this place," he complains. "Was the journey okay?"

"Bit cramped in Hudson's car with Lucky as well, but it was fine. Does Hunter hate it that badly?"

"You know he hates anything that isn't made of stainless steel."

He strides across the room with determination. Hands landing on my shoulders, Leighton backs me up against the papered wall and peppers kisses along my jawline.

"Fancy christening the place? The others can unload the boxes."

"Leigh," I gasp as his hips grind into mine. "Get off me, you lunatic. We have a houseful of people."

"I feel like I haven't seen you in days," he purrs throatily. "Don't take this the wrong way, but you look like shit. Are you not sleeping again?"

"Thanks for the insult. I'm fine."

"I'm sorry. How can I redeem myself, princess?"

"Stop being a fucking sleazeball and come help," Hudson's loud voice heckles from the hall. "Want me to punch him for you, Harlow?"

Utilising one of the new techniques Enzo taught me, I bend my knees and push my elbow out. It connects with Leighton's stomach, and he stumbles backwards from the sharp blow.

"She can punch him herself if needed," I retort.

Leighton groans as he rubs his stomach. "I'm never leaving you with Enzo again. He'll have you jumping out of helicopters in no time."

"I'm not sure secret-agent school is my kinda thing."

"I'm not sure co-running the company is my calling either," he admits. "Honestly, I've been making it up as I go along and pretending like I know what I'm talking about."

I nuzzle his bristled cheek. "You're doing a great job. I'm sure Hunter appreciates you stepping up to cover for him."

His eyes cloud over. "He's out back. You should go say hi."

"Has he spoken?"

"Not much since I dragged him off that bridge."

Patting his shoulder, I sneak past him and head for the glass door leading to the back garden. Eli is in the spacious, slightly dated kitchen, unloading utensils and plates. He waves at me with a spoon as I pass.

"Good luck with that chatterbox."

Coming from someone like Eli, that's more than a little worrying. He's hardly the biggest talker around. Hunter must be stealing all his introverted awards from him now.

"Thanks," I mumble back.

Outside, the first hints of impending summer are beginning to reveal themselves as May approaches. The garden is bathed in shades of lush green ivy and sprouting wildflowers. It's overgrown and chaotic with weeds, but I love the untamed feeling of the shrubbery.

Far down the lawn, a long tangle of limbs and wiry muscles is sitting cross-legged amongst blooming daisies. Hunter is staring up at the cloudless sky, tearing out handfuls of grass while lost in thought.

My lungs seize up.

I have no idea what to say to him.

The baseball cap on his head almost hides the devastation underneath. The edges of a white bandage peek out the back, but I won't tell him that. This veneer of normality is the only thing keeping him semi-sane.

Sinking down on the soft pad of grass, Hunter's eyes follow me. He's dressed in his grey sweatpants and a loose, black t-shirt that conceals the weight that's dropped from his frame in the past month or so.

"You okay?"

He shrugs, his lips pursed.

I gesture to the house behind us. "Good?"

"Can we not do this?"

His defeated words strike me across the face, and I try to conceal my hurt.

"Do what?"

Hunter's eyes flit back to his bare feet. "You don't have to sit out here and babysit me. I didn't come home from the hospital for that."

If he wasn't recovering from a near-death experience, I'd throttle him myself. Instead, I snatch his hand and lace our fingers together. Hunter relents and glances back up at me.

"Do you have any idea how much I missed you?"

His eyes narrow. "Huh?"

"I missed you," I emphasise.

"You want... fruit tea?"

I bury my face in his broad shoulder. This is impossible. When I look back up, Hunter's eyes are drenched in sadness, and I feel awful for letting my frustration win out.

"I'm sorry. Still working on my lip reading."

"No, no. I'm so sorry," I try to enunciate. "We should learn sign language."

Hunter shrugs. "I know a little bit. Enzo learned some when I first lost my hearing."

Leaning close, I rest my hand over his cheek and stroke the softness of his beard. "Missed you."

A brief smile touches his lips. "Gotcha. Yeah, me too."

"Hungry? Theo's going to order takeout."

Hunter frowns in confusion. "Cake?"

I blink back the rising tears that want to spill over. I'm too tired to control my emotions, but he really doesn't need my pity right now. We'll get used to communicating like this soon. I need to be strong for him. We all do.

Hand dipping into his sweats pocket, Hunter pulls out his phone and drops it in my hands. I look down at the notes app open on the screen.

"Type," he explains.

With a nod, I tap out my previous question.

"Oh," he echoes. "Yeah, I could eat."

Standing up, I offer him a hand. Our fingers interlink as we walk back up the lawn together. In the kitchen, Eli has finished unboxing and now sits on the counter with a beer in hand.

He's watching Phoenix heft the dining table into place with Hudson, the pair sweating and cursing repeatedly. Leighton's in the living room, shoving our sectional sofa into place before wiping off his gleaming forehead.

"We're never moving again," he huffs. "Too much work. Where the fuck are the other three?"

"Jude's working late," Phoenix answers.

Theo appears in the doorway. "Brooklyn and Kade are keeping the press occupied while Enzo moves the last of the stuff. She already soaked Sally Moore while driving past on live TV."

"Please tell me that's gonna make the six o'clock news," Leighton hoots gleefully. "I will pay to see that shit."

"I'm sure the other channels will show it."

"Score." He celebrates with a fist pump.

Right on time, the front door slams shut. Everyone stiffens until the shadow of Enzo's intimidating frame enters our new kitchen. He's carrying several plastic bags of groceries and wearing a tired grimace.

"We are never, ever moving again," he grunts.

"That's exactly what I just said!" Leighton grins and helps himself to the multipack of beers in one of the bags. "Fuck the rest of the boxes. Let's drink and order food."

"Amen," Enzo praises. "I am shattered."

Everyone gravitates towards the living room, helping themselves to beers and seats. Tucking himself into the corner where no one can engage him in conversation, Hunter sits on the floor and begins to drink alone.

It causes intense pain to flare through my heart again. He looks as broken as I feel inside. This move hasn't patched over the wounds that are still threatening to break us for good.

"Angel?"

Enzo wraps his arms around me from behind and rests his chin on the top of my head. I relax into his embrace, letting my forced brave face fall off. We're alone in the kitchen.

"This place is really nice. Looks like you might get that quiet, countryside life after all."

"I'm glad you like it," he rumbles. "I'd go back to the city in a heartbeat if we could, but it isn't safe anymore."

"Why? You hate London."

"Because Hunter hates hiding," Enzo replies. "I'd suck it up for him. He said anything?"

"Not much. Communicating is a bit tricky. I didn't know that you could speak sign language."

He cuddles me tighter. "Only the basics. We started learning years ago, but when the hearing in Hunter's left ear stabilised, we stopped."

"Can you teach me?" I request.

My heart rate triples when his hand smacks my ass. He's fully obsessed with spanking me at this point.

"You want a lesson, little one?"

Gripping the countertop, I push backwards against his crotch. Enzo grunts under his breath, a meaty palm moving to clasp my hip.

"Depends on how good of a teacher you are," I return.

"Why don't I bend you over this counter and eat your cunt to prove myself? Feel free to rate my performance then."

My core quivers at his filthy words. The mental image alone is enough to make me wet. He's become an insatiable animal since we slept together for the first time.

"Somehow, I think the others might have a problem with you doing that in front of Hudson, Phoenix and Eli."

"I've seen their pasty asses sprawled out after fucking enough times. Brooklyn loves an audience."

"Thanks for that mental image."

Enzo snorts. "You're so welcome."

"Hey, guys," Theo calls from the living room. "Come and choose what you want. We found a decent Mexican restaurant a few miles away."

Leaning over my shoulder to graze my ear with his teeth, Enzo mutters a curse word that makes me blush. I disentangle myself from his arms and head for the living room, leaving him to adjust his snug jeans.

"I'll have anything." I snag Leighton's beer from his hand. "The spicier, the better."

Theo wrinkles his nose. "I can't believe they corrupted you into liking spicy food."

"Don't be a pussy, Theodore." Phoenix snickers, his head pooled in Eli's lap on the sofa. "We'll win you over to the dark side one of these days."

"Not gonna happen."

With my stolen beer in hand, I plonk down next to Hunter. He's frowning at the spider-like cracks in the bricks around the fireplace. Amidst the bickering and insults, his silence has already been forgotten.

He's becoming a ghost.

No. I won't allow that.

I won't let him fade away. Even if he wants us to let him do exactly that. We vowed to face this as a family, and that's what we're going to do. Leighton dragged him home for a reason.

Tapping his leg, I point towards Leighton's phone. "Food?"

Hunter shrugs. "Sure."

Ditching my beer, I curl up on the hardwood floor and use his shoulder as a pillow. My eyes are so heavy, even the hard floorboards don't bother me. Hunter hesitates before his arm wraps around my torso to pull me closer.

His heart is pounding fast, panicked even. Something isn't right. Sliding the phone from his pocket, I manoeuvre his thumb to unlock the screen and bring the notes app back up.

What's wrong?

He hesitates before whispering back. "Nothing."

I can feel your heart going crazy.

"I'm fine."

I subtly point a finger around the room, indicating to the others still arguing over food choices. No one is listening to our conversation. I feel Hunter's chest vibrate with a sigh.

"I hate this," he murmurs, barely audible. "I can't hear a word of what anyone's saying, and it's freaking me out. I feel like I don't exist."

My breath catches as I tap out a response.

I know how that feels. It's terrifying, but you didn't let me go through it alone.

"That was different. I need to get a fucking grip."

You're allowed to struggle. That doesn't make you weak.

"Doesn't it?" he sighs back.

Before I can jab him in the ribs, Leighton's loud voice interrupts our conversation. He's managed to turn on the TV, though it's still resting haphazardly against the fireplace. The six o'clock news is playing a report from outside our old house in London.

"Brooklyn West, former resident of the infamous Blackwood Institute, has never been one to play well with media requests."

Phoenix laughs at the reporter's sarcastic tone. "That's one word for it."

"She'll love that," Eli concurs.

A clip is shown of Brooklyn reversing out of the driveway in a company car, the window rolled down as she lights a cigarette caught between her teeth. Reporters are screaming questions about us and the case at her.

It's raining heavily in London. She takes full advantage of the torrential downpour, yelling while hitting a huge puddle next to the nearest news crew. It sprays outwards with the impact.

"Fuck you, goddamn vampires!"

Sally Moore emerges from the dirty tidal wave of water, soaking wet with mascara trailing down her cheeks. She walks up to the camera and forcibly shoves it away to stop filming her embarrassment.

"Oh my God." Leighton clutches his belly as he falls into hysterics. "That's the best thing I've ever seen. I'm gonna print her face off and frame it."

Even Hunter is smirking as he drinks his beer, watching Phoenix replay the clip several times. I bet the rival news station thanked their lucky stars they captured this footage. It plays very badly for Sally's channel and her reputation.

"Serves her right," Enzo remarks.

Theo nods in agreement. "I hope she gets sacked."

"Or goes viral looking like a soaking wet clown."

Flicking over to a movie, Leighton bounces from the room to retrieve more beers. I gesture for Enzo to pass me the remote and quickly flick the subtitles on so Hunter can read them.

He drops a kiss on my forehead. "Thanks."

"Welcome," I mouth back.

Snuggling closer to him, I let my aching eyes glide shut. Hunter's head slumps as he nestles his face in my hair. With his arms around me, I try to lock the plague of bad thoughts into a little box. Numbness is approaching.

I'm so tired.

Five minutes won't hurt.

CHAPTER 26

Harlow

Hotel - Montell Fish

The vibrating engine of a car hums beneath me. Details come in flashes—the swinging dice hanging from the mirror, a radio playing, morning mist leaking across the road.

I'm... scared.

"Get your dirty feet off the dashboard, Letty," a cold voice lashes.

With fear straightening my spine, I watch the mud-caked leather of my school shoes lower from the dashboard. Someone's clicking their tongue in the seat next to me.

"Why are you taking me to school?"

"Your father is passed out drunk." Mummy's voice is thick with disgust. "After school, you will walk home by yourself. Understood?"

I'm frozen by confusion.

"Why, Mummy?"

"Because," she snaps. "Walk through the field with the blackberry bushes. You'll be fine."

"I'm not supposed to walk home alone. Daddy said so."

"I'm telling you, Letty. Not him. Do as you're told."

"What if I get scared?"

"I don't give a shit! You will walk home."

Grabbing my wrist, she twists until tears burn in my eyes. The ink splotches of dark bruises beneath her grip peek out from underneath my uniform. It still throbs from the other night.

I tried to ease the Bible from her hands—she was asleep with it on the sofa again. Mummy attacked me instead, smashing the worn leather into my body over and over as she wrenched me around the room.

"You never do as you're told. The devil's in your blood, Letty. I'm trying to save you from him."

"The d-devil?"

Her bloodshot eyes meet mine, lit with a manic gleam. "This will be our redemption. We have to atone before the rapture comes."

"I d-don't understand."

The scream of brakes accompanies my body being thrown forwards against the seatbelt. Mummy slams her hands on the wheel and her cheeks soak with tears as she screams abuse at me.

Her palm slaps my cheek so hard, I bite down on my tongue. Blood floods into my mouth, hot and coppery. Holding my aching cheek, I look through my tears up at her.

"Please, Lord," she mumbles to herself. "Show me the righteous path away from my sins. Forgive me for what I must do."

I tug on her shirt sleeve, bracing myself for another slap.

"Mummy? Are you okay?"

Wiping her tears aside, she spares me a frenzied look. "This is for your own good. You're a sinner, just like me."

"But, Mummy—"

"Enough! He's going to save us both, Letty. Everything will be okay now. The Lord is going to forgive us. I just have to pay the price first."

"P-Price?" I stammer.

She strokes my tears aside with a sick grin.

"That's you."

†

Someone roughly shaking me awake cuts through the hazy dream. I shoot upright in a state of panic. The darkness of the room is cut by moonlight soaking through the window.

I'm lying on tangled, sweaty sheets. Gasping for air, my lungs feel like they're on fire. I can still feel the car vibrating beneath my butt and the rush of blood to my sore, swollen cheek as my mother struck me over and over again. Her anger knew no bounds, even then.

The real world settles around me, but the widened torment of my mother's eyes is superimposed over the room. Her voice clings. Echoing. Sinking deep into the depths of my brain and dissolving into bloodied shimmers.

"Harlow! Snap out of it."

I scoot backwards to get away from the giant in front of me. He's kneeling upright in the bed, sandwiching me in with another lump of muscle on the other side. Their faces settle into focus.

Hunter. Enzo.

Both look wide-eyed with terror.

"Where am I?" I whimper.

"Your new bedroom," Enzo explains in a rush.

"But we were... the dinner, then... I can't remember..."

"That was earlier on. We came upstairs hours ago," he explains calmly. "You've been thrashing and crying out for a while, but we couldn't wake you up."

His explanation redoubles my anxiety. It happened again. I've lost time. It's been a while since I last fell into one of dissociation's bottomless pits. I can't remember a thing after falling asleep on Hunter's shoulder. It's a complete blur.

"She knew," I pant, fisting the sheets. "She knew!"

"Harlow, breathe. You're not making any sense."

"Giana knew!"

"Knew what?" Enzo demands.

"She did it… it was all her…"

His fear-laden eyes widen further. "What do you mean?"

Unable to answer him, I fall back into hyperventilating. Another pair of arms bands around me, and I'm pulled against Hunter's bare, tattooed chest. His lips meet my ear as he squeezes tight, and the burst of pain is welcome.

"Take a breath," he advises. "In for four, out for four."

"No… no… she knew. I don't understand."

"Calm down," Enzo urges. "What did Giana know?"

"No! Please, don't let him take me!"

Throwing out a fist, it catches Enzo right in the jaw. He barely flinches, grabbing my wrist instead to prevent another blow. In an instant, he vanishes. My mother is bruising my skin all over again, slashing into my veins with her hatred.

"Get away from me! No!"

He lets go like I've burned him.

"Please, Harlow. It's me."

Shoving Hunter away next, I fall from the bed and cower in the furthest corner from them both. I can't do this. It was staring me in the face all along. The harrowing truth.

Right there, reality was taunting me with the future that was stolen through blood and violence. She took it. Her. The one person in the world whose job it was to keep me safe.

I didn't believe it.

Dad tried to warn me.

I threw it all back in his face and refused to believe the truth. That scenario was too disturbing to contemplate. I should've known by now that nothing is ever too evil. Humans hold the depraved ability to exceed all expectations.

"Please," Hunter begs from the bed.

"Say something," Enzo implores.

Shaking my head, I grab handfuls of my hair instead. Enzo lunges for me too late. I tear at the fragile strands, ignoring the sharp sting and light trickle of blood on my scalp.

"Harlow! Stop!"

"Leave me alone!" I shout back.

Waving at Enzo to back off, Hunter kneels on the bare floor of my new bedroom and knee-walks towards me. I watch him approach through the hot blur of tears.

Without his baseball cap on as armour, he looks worse than me now. We're both sporting balding heads and visible anguish. How the tables have turned.

"Sweetheart." He raises his hands. "It's just me."

"Too much… too much…"

"Can I hold you? Is that okay?"

Rubbing my face with trembling hands, I manage a timid nod. Hunter nods back and his hands curl around my forearms. I'm gently eased into his lap, and the moment his arms pull me close, I let myself implode.

"Shhh, I've got you," he hushes. "You're not alone, remember? That's what you said to me. The same goes for you."

Burying my face in the warmth of his neck, he smells the same as he did a few months short of a whole year ago, holding me in the darkness of the hospital as we hid from the media's first show of depravity.

We've always kept each other safe, but he can't protect me from the past. Not this time. It's rushing up to meet me.

A calloused hand strokes down my spine, and I feel the brush of Enzo's head against mine. He boxes me in from behind until I'm enveloped in both of them.

I'm safe.

My guys are here.

The monster isn't waiting for me amongst the blackberry bushes. They hold me in silence until I can draw a ragged breath. We're sitting on the floor in darkness, shivering from the cool air while the rest of the house sleeps.

"Alright, let's move to the bed," Enzo implores. "It's cold on the floor. I don't want you to get sick."

Too tired to lift my head, I let him pull me from Hunter's lap. My legs band around his midsection as I cuddle closer to his warmth. I'm so cold and tired. More than physically. Every single part of me is done with this world.

I want this all to be over, but it won't end when Pastor Michaels is rotting behind bars. It won't even end when I figure out why the memories of my mother haunt my nightly dreams.

The damage is done.

It'll always be there—festering, digging deeper, nesting into the pits of my brain. I need to dig it out. Tear it fibre by fibre if necessary. I can't keep living like this.

"No, stop that." Enzo traps my hand as I begin to pull again. "Please, baby. We're here."

"I can't escape what he did to me, no matter where I go," I choke out. "It's always going to be there, isn't it?"

"Maybe," he admits uncertainly.

A sob tears from my chest.

"But you're so much more than what he did to you. Don't let him win now. We've come too far for that."

The bed dips as Hunter slides back in, his anxious eyes darting over us. Blinking through my tears, I catch Enzo's hands moving fast. Hunter replies with several waves. I think they're speaking sign language.

"What are you saying?"

Enzo halts, kissing my temple. "Hunter's suggesting that we jump on a plane and leave the country tomorrow."

"For real?"

Hunter bobs his head. "I'm done. You are too."

Sucking in a breath, my cheeks sting with tears. "It's my fault, isn't it? I've done this to you all."

"Harlow, no."

"The media rampage, Sabre falling apart, Hunter's accident, the move... everything. I've ruined your lives."

"Don't you dare," Enzo scolds again.

The cruel lash of his voice causes me to flinch. Engulfing my face in his huge hands, he forces me to meet his fiery amber eyes. Determination still burns bright.

"You are the best thing that's ever happened to us, Harlow Michaels. I won't hear you talk about yourself like that. We've been dealt a shitty hand, but that is not your fault."

Hunter's hand snakes out and takes mine. It's the first contact he's initiated for a long time. I meet his widened cocoa eyes, the irises spiked with defeat.

"I love you," he says simply.

Enzo's thumbs stroke across my cheeks. "I love you."

My eyes flutter shut in pain. The truth tears itself free. I'm being selfish, but I can't let them go. Not now. They're the only thing keeping me alive and fighting.

"I love you," I reply to them both. "Too much."

"No such thing as too much," Enzo murmurs.

Leaning close to press a kiss on my nose, he hesitates, battling with himself. Despite Hunter's gaze trained on us both, I break his indecision and slant my mouth against his.

Enzo's hesitant at first, then his mouth melts into mine and we collapse into each other. The tip of his tongue brushes mine, asking a silent question. I reply by letting my lips part, inviting him to deepen the kiss.

A hand lands on my thigh, teasing bare skin as the oversized t-shirt I'm wearing rides up to my waist. But Enzo's hands are still on my face. It's Hunter drawing slow circles against the sensitive flesh of my upper thigh.

With both of them touching me, a spark is lit deep inside my core. The suffocation of pain and fear gives way to a low burn of desire. I can't hold back the darkness in my head alone. I'm going to drown if they don't offer me a lifeline.

"We need to stop," Enzo says against my mouth. "I don't wanna take advantage."

Feeling emboldened by the intimacy of midnight darkness, I nudge him aside and drag Hunter closer instead. Unlike Enzo, his lips greedily meet mine. I can see the same gaping chasm in his eyes. We both need this right now.

Dragging a hand down the sharp blades of his clavicles, I trace the dark swirls of tattoos that paint the violent thunderstorm on Hunter's skin. Muscles tightening, I stroke down his firm abdominals next.

Every inch of him is a canvas to be explored, from the curling smoke of his tattoos to the healing stitches that traverse the entire length of his skull. Hunter is a patchwork quilt of his stubborn will to survive, no matter what.

"You're giving him all the attention now?" Enzo growls out. "I don't mind sharing, but I'm gonna need to see more of your gorgeous body first."

"Thought you didn't want to take advantage?"

"Fuck it," he decides.

"Such a gentleman," I quip back.

"I'll show you a fucking gentleman."

He lifts the hem of my t-shirt, and I'm forced to break the kiss with Hunter so it can be tugged over my head. Beneath it, I'm wearing a pair of bright-pink girl boxers and nothing else. Goosebumps race over my skin.

"On your back, brother," Enzo orders.

Hunter must've read that on his lips. He eases backwards on the bed, stretching his long legs out. I'm left dangling over him as Enzo holds me by the hips, raising my behind into the air like I'm his puppet.

"Remember what I said in the kitchen?" Enzo's lips tease the edge of my panties. "I'm gonna eat your cunt while Hunter watches now. Would you like that, angel?"

I gasp as he tugs my panties down, exposing the wet heat between my thighs. The cool air kisses my pussy lips in the most excruciating way. I'm left completely naked and at his mercy from behind.

"Answer me," Enzo demands.

"Yes, please."

He smacks my ass, sending spikes of electricity up my spine. "What did I tell you to call me?"

"Sorry... sir."

"Good girl. I want to see you looking after my brother too."

Pressing my lips against Hunter's pectorals, I drag my lips

downwards. "What should I do, sir?"

Pain spikes through me as Enzo's palm cracks against my ass cheek again. "Suck his cock. If you do a good job, I'll let him fuck you next. He's waited for a very long time."

Breath held, I meet Hunter's gaze before dipping a hand inside his sweatpants. *Ah, hell.* He hasn't bothered to put any boxers on. The generous sheath of steel trapped inside is hard and eager to see me.

"Fuck," he moans.

I wrap a hand around the base of his dick. Feeling emboldened by their gazes fixed solely on me, the whispers in my head die down to a low murmuring. All of my attention is on the task at hand as I drop a kiss against Hunter's length.

His hips raise, silently seeking more. Trailing my lips to the head of his dick, I spare him a quick glance beneath my eyelashes before taking it deep into my mouth. His eyes roll back in his head with another moan.

My confidence has grown so much when it comes to being physically intimate. I'm no longer terrified of someone else's touch, and seeing the power I hold over them is so empowering.

They make me feel beautiful and wanted. With my mouth driving them to the edge of falling apart, I become their deity. They worship me and fall victim to whatever I desire.

It's heady. I'm more than the timid shell of a person they rescued from the hospital, broken and alone in the world. I can bring these men to their knees.

"So perfect," Enzo praises, stroking my tingling skin. "Don't stop."

Keeping a gentle grip on Hunter's length as I bob my head up and down, my focus is derailed by the warmth of Enzo's breath on my entrance. His lips are planting open-mouthed kisses against my quivering pussy.

"Focus," I hear him whisper as I pause to moan.

Taking Hunter's cock back into my mouth, it hits against the back of my throat. I want to gag but swallow it down, loving the intensity of taking him deeper. He's huge, as I expected.

Enzo's tongue slides between my folds as he dives into his meal. It's a challenge to maintain my focus. When Hunter's hand reaches down to clench around my neck, I feel the first flickers of a release building.

I'm overstimulated, set to fall apart fast with both of them demanding my attention. The pressure of a finger easing inside my entrance is another shove towards that inevitable explosion. Enzo thrusts it inside me, curling his digit at the perfect angle to brush the tender spot I can't find myself.

"You're soaked, angel." Enzo's stubble scratches against my clit in a painful taunt. "I'm dying to fuck this perfect pussy, but I think Hunter's waited long enough. Don't you?"

I gasp as his lips are torn away. Enzo smacks my ass again with a chuckle. He seriously loves marking up my skin. The sharp burst of pain blurs with the desire swelling in my veins. It feels so good when he punishes me with a firm spank.

Releasing Hunter's cock, glistening with moisture and the first beads of pre-come, I sit up. The hand that was wrapped around my throat moves to my arm as Hunter tugs me closer so that I fall on top of him.

"Hunt," I gasp in shock.

I'm terrified of hurting him.

"I'm okay," he assures me.

This isn't quite what I imagined for our first time, but we almost lost him, and I hated myself in that moment for never showing him how much he means to me. Time is precious.

Raising a hand, Hunter catches the foil packet that's thrown over my shoulder. I hear the shuffle of Enzo dropping his sweats back on the floor before he settles behind me again.

Hunter's eyes don't leave mine as he rolls the condom on to his long, thick length. When he crooks a finger, inviting me closer, I move to straddle his waist. It feels weirdly good to be on top for once.

"I don't want to hurt you," I mouth.

"Go slow," he whispers back, running a finger over my skipping pulse. "You look like a fucking queen on top."

Positioning myself, I push the remaining flickers of insecurity aside and slowly sink down on his cock. Hunter's head slumps against the pillows as he groans loudly. He breaches me, and the pressure is exquisite.

I love watching his reactions. The others were more controlling in the bedroom, but this is on my terms. Hunter is trapped beneath me. Circling my hips, I adjust to his length before taking it all inside.

"Fuck, sweetheart," he cusses.

Hunter is big, but not as intimidating as Enzo's monstrous sheath. That was a bruising, blissful experience. Holding Hunter's biceps for balance, I begin to grind on him, being careful not to disturb his injuries.

His hips rise to meet me, but without the frantic urgency of the others. He's surprisingly loving and tender. His fingertips stroke every inch of my skin as he stares up at me with adoration.

One hand gripping my hip, his thumb finds my clit and begins torturously circling. I roll my hips and take him deeper, chasing my own explosions of painful pleasure. I've imagined this moment so many times.

The giant running a teasing fingertip up and down my spine never featured in these daydreams, but I love knowing that Enzo's watching every thrust. He's giving me permission, just like he said.

"Good job, angel," he encourages.

We're being choreographed while he watches us both from his throne, never once taking his eyes off our tangle of limbs. Every gasping pump of our hips is under his control. We're his puppets, performing on demand.

"You're not allowed to come until he does," Enzo says darkly. "Disobey my command and you'll be getting punished. I want you to hold it in."

Hunter chooses that moment to surge up into me, his hands now holding my hips to deepen his thrusts. Every slam of his cock into me sets my nervous system alight.

"Please," I whimper. "I can't hold it."

"I won't lay a finger on you if you finish now," Enzo warns. "Make my brother come first. That's an order."

He is turning out to be a strict master in the bedroom. I love how rough and unfiltered he is with his temperament. It's a glimpse of the man that the rest of the world sees. Around me, he melts. In the bedroom, he becomes a monster again, long enough to choke submission from my lungs.

Biting back a moan, I splay my hands across Hunter's chest and ride him as fast as my protesting legs will allow. He tweaks my nipple, sending sparks flying across my chest. His palm kneads my breast as he worships me with his eyes.

"You're so damn beautiful," he rumbles.

I'm so close. All it would take is a little nudge over the edge of the cliff, and I'll be falling into bliss. It takes all of my control to walk the tightrope until Hunter's nails are digging into my skin.

The biting lash of pain threatens to unseal the box of demons seething in my head, but I focus on Hunter's eyes trained on me. He's got me. Nothing can hurt me while I'm in his arms. Not even the invisible monsters that like to play in my head.

He grunts and smashes his eyes shut, still gripping me tightly as his release peaks. Being able to watch him come feels intimate. No one else sees this side of him, defenceless and vulnerable. I'm one of a privileged few.

Watching his implosion finishes me off. I did that. With a mewl, I feel my core clench tight. It hits me in an overwhelming influx of tingles, racing over my skin and driving me to cry out his name.

When his eyes flutter open, they're dark, almost black with the rapid expansion of his pupils. Slumping on his chest, I press a fervid kiss to his lips. His breath tangles with mine as we rest for a moment.

"Christ," Hunter gasps.

I tap his forehead. "You okay?"

He nods, his throat bobbing. "Yeah."

"Was it weird, not being able to hear me?"

His eyebrows knit for a moment. I repeat myself and he eventually catches on.

"It was different. Intense. I could almost feel more in the silence."

When I've caught my breath, Enzo's voice pops our bubble.

"Time's up, Rodriguez. Hand her back."

My cheeks flame. "I'm not some toy to be passed back and forth."

Enzo's hand snakes around my torso and takes a handful of my breast, squeezing tight. My nipples are hard as studs.

"Aren't you?" he snickers in my ear. "How disappointing. I thought my beautiful little slut didn't mind a bit of sharing."

Flushed, I kiss Hunter's lips in full view of Enzo and his snide attitude. Only I dictate when I'm done. Not him.

"And if I want to fuck Hunter again just to make you mad?" I challenge him without fear. "You'll have to play nice and wait your turn."

"Play nice?" Enzo repeats, teeth bared. "I'm not sure I know how."

"Better learn, Enz."

Pecking Hunter's mouth again, I stretch to my full height and twist to face Enzo's frown. He's perched behind me, a thick eyebrow raised beneath his shock of raven hair.

"Careful," I warn.

"How so, angel?"

"You're dangerously close to getting everything you wanted. Don't mess it up now by getting cocky."

"I'm just enjoying my victory. Don't pretend like you aren't too. You're fucking loving being shared. Admit it."

"I'll admit no such thing."

I attempt to climb off the bed to aggravate him further, but he darts up and blocks my exit. Stark naked, I put my hands on my hips and raise an eyebrow right back at him.

"Problem?" I sigh.

"You think you're done here?"

"You told me to look after your brother. Last I checked, he's more than satisfied."

Skulking towards me with palpable menace, Enzo backs me up until my legs hit the bed. His fingers wrap around my nipple and tug so hard, it causes my breath to catch.

"What about you?" Enzo smirks down at me. "Are you satisfied, little one? You only came once."

My knees knock together as he ducks down, taking a hardened nipple into his mouth. I was right. He really is the devil in disguise.

"Poor little angel," he breathes against my flushed chest. "Bend over for me. Hell, Hunter can even watch."

My pulse skitters at the thought. I offer him an innocent smile and rotate. With my hands fisting the bed sheets, facing Hunter and his interested eyes, I bend over the end of the bed.

"Damn." Enzo's voice is accompanied by the tearing of a condom wrapper. "Now that's a fine sight. All that dripping wet pussy laid out for me to see."

His mouth is going to be the death of me. I groan as his hardness brushes against me, one tiny move from surging inside my entrance. I'm still soaked from being with Hunter.

If this is what sharing will be like, then I could get used to it very quickly. I feel like a completely different person splayed out between them, begging to be touched and owned.

"You can't look away from him," Enzo grumbles in my ear. "I want him to see every single moan that leaves your lips. I want him to know that you're mine, first and foremost."

"You're cruel."

"Nope. This is me being fucking fair, my love."

Taking a handful of my long hair, Enzo pulls until my head rises up. I meet Hunter's gaze again. There's still heat there, even as he ties off the condom, full of his release. He looks ready to fuck me all over again.

"That's it," Enzo encourages. "Show him who owns every inch of your gorgeous body. Let him see it all."

The bed shakes as he shifts behind me. I gasp out in surprise when he thrusts inside my slit, quickly burying himself to the hilt since I'm already warmed up. I moan so loud, it's certain to wake up even the snoring Leighton from his dead sleep.

Enzo pulls back before surging into me again, taking long, punishing strides. He fucks like he rules—without mercy or restraint. We're all pawns to be manoeuvred in his eyes.

"My girl's still so tight," he grunts.

Eyes locked on Hunter's while Enzo fucks me from behind, he refuses to look away from the show we're putting on. This should be humiliating, but I find myself even more turned on.

This whole thing is a performance drenched in desire. If I wasn't a sinner before, I'm dancing with the devil now.

Slamming into me with each pump, Enzo batters his ownership over every inch of my mind. I can't think straight. My senses are overwhelmed by the sheer intensity of being trapped between two greedy men, both determined to devour me.

"You can come now, angel," Enzo obliges through ragged breaths. "Let him see you scream my name."

Twisting the sheets in my hands, I release a strangled pant for air. It's too much. My consciousness is splintering apart. I'm overwhelmed by sensations and the lick of flames burning through me.

Taking a scrap of control back, Hunter sits forward and claps my chin between two fingers. His mouth crashes against mine, and his tongue plunges between my lips. It tangles with mine in a sensual tango that causes my release to peak.

Crying out through the dizzying rush of my orgasm, Hunter swallows every last syllable. It's Enzo's victory, but his best friend won't let him have it. He still wants the final say.

I feel Enzo's movements grow stilted. He pounds into me with a final grunt and his grip on my hair slackens. The roar of him coming apart will probably wake up our neighbours.

"Harlow," he breathes unsteadily.

When he pulls out of me, I slump on the bed. Enzo collapses next to me in a heap, fighting for air. I don't think I can move a muscle. My limbs have turned into spaghetti.

I poke Enzo's side. "You alive?"

He groans under his breath. "Just about."

Shifting with a wince, I wriggle to ease the burn between my legs. Having them both inside me was an experience. My mind can't help but wonder if anyone else would be up for it.

"If we're sharing her, this better be a regular occurrence," Hunter supplies.

"I've never had a problem with him watching me have sex," Enzo whispers to me. "Want to know a secret?"

"Always."

"Hunter loves it too. He's a total voyeur."

I smother a laugh. "You can't tell me his secrets just because he can't hear us. That's mean."

Enzo smirks. "It seemed to me like you quite enjoyed an audience too, based on that little performance."

I bury my face in the sheets to shield my embarrassment, even though the growing bonfire of curiosity inside me wholeheartedly agrees. I did secretly love it, and I want more.

I can imagine Leighton and Theo being a good team.

Now that's one hell of a thought.

CHAPTER 27

Theo

Dead – 228k

"Jesus, Enz. I really don't wanna die in this car."

"Quit whining."

Careening down the motorway at breakneck speed, Enzo pisses off a right-lane hogger driving a dated estate car. At this rate, we'll arrive at HQ in road-splattered pieces.

"Ben said to come quickly," he justifies while undercutting another driver. "This guy's refused to go on record for months. He could back out if we leave him waiting."

Glancing down at my laptop, I look over the case file again. Rosetta Stone is an important piece of the puzzle, but she's fallen to the wayside as we've assigned the full might of Sabre to narrowing down Michaels' current location.

That was before Ben's police contact finally broke and agreed to meet late last night. We had been sitting tight since he rejected our interview request. It was another dead end. Now, we have a second chance to nail this lead down.

All we need is an eyewitness to confirm our children's home theory and we have a solid connection between Michaels and Rosetta Stone. Our case against the sick bastard is getting stronger by the day.

The end is coming.

I can fucking feel it.

I look over my shoulder into the backseat. Harlow's curled up against the door, headphones tucked in her ears as she furiously scribbles in her leather journal. Something's been eating at her all weekend.

She hasn't been herself while slowly unpacking and settling in. Everyone has noticed it. Harlow refuses to discuss her violent nightmares any further, retreating into herself instead.

"She said anything else about Giana?" I ask quietly.

Enzo checks the mirror before answering. "Not a word after the other night. She says it was a bad dream, that's all."

"You believe that?"

"Not a chance in hell, but I can't force her to talk to us."

"Maybe she'll talk to Richards in her session today. He'll fill us in if we should be worried about something."

"I warned Hunter about this happening the minute he gave Giana Kensington the attention she wanted. Harlow's parents are screwing with her head for their own benefit."

"Isn't that what parents do best?"

He gives me a side look. "I wouldn't know. Mine are dead, remember?"

"Better dead than heartless assholes," I snip back. "At least you had parents."

Enzo winces, running a hand over his messy hair. "Didn't think. I'm knackered."

"Forget it. We're all wrecked at the moment."

"Ain't that the truth."

Looking out of the tinted-black window, I study the blur of greenery morphing into cinder-block buildings and drooping train wires. The team knows better than to broach the subject of parents with me. Usually, it's an off-limits topic.

Enzo may have lost everyone apart from his aunt, but he had something to lose in the first place. They will always be with him. My parents abandoned me before I could walk, and England's fucked-up foster care system became my family instead.

The team has always blamed me for walking away first after Alyssa's death tore our lives apart. There's a reason why. Truthfully, I abandoned them, just like I'd been taught to do before I could speak for myself.

That was my default reaction, regardless of the pain it caused them. It's one of many regrets I have about the last six years. I'm trying to fix that now.

"You get an update from Kade on that potential sighting?" Enzo asks.

Bringing up the file, I squint over the lines of information. "The tip came in from a bus driver in Exeter. Reckons he spotted Michaels leaving a church last week."

"Is it legit?"

"Hard to say. The whole country thinks Michaels is their next-door neighbour based on the bullshit sightings we've had coming through. Hudson's driving to Exeter to scout it out with Brooklyn."

Enzo nods as London's outskirts come into view. "We have to be thorough. If this bastard slips through our fingers now, I'll never forgive myself. We're too close."

I know his tormented thoughts are on our silent passenger in the back seat. I pack my laptop away and clear my throat.

"We'll get him, Enz. It's just a matter of time."

"Time." Enzo scoffs. "We've wasted enough of that."

"Nothing's wasted if it guarantees Harlow's future," I correct him. "This is her life we're talking about. Her justice. We promised to get that for her."

He scrubs his face and sighs. "Fuck off, Theodore. I'm all too aware of that fact."

"Then bloody remember it."

We fall silent as London's outskirts melt into busy city streets and mid-morning traffic. The blacked-out windows of his car hide us from any onlookers as we approach HQ's glittering height on the horizon.

After we've parked in the relative safety of the garage, we hop out and prepare to head inside the building. Harlow's tucked her journal into the bag hooked under her arm, but she leaves her headphones in, discouraging any conversation.

Her eyes are sagging with painfully obvious exhaustion. She's woken the whole house up with blood-curdling screaming for the past few nights. Even Hunter wakes up, deaf as a damn bat. It's like he can sense her distress.

I approach her and ease an arm around her shoulders. She offers me a weak smile as I tug a headphone out and peck my lips against her cheek before dropping my voice low.

"Come and find me after your session with Richards. Enzo's interviewing the witness. I'll be in my office watching the livestream."

"Sure," she replies. "You'll fill me in?"

"Of course, beautiful."

"Thanks, Theo. I appreciate you."

My chest warms. "Anytime."

ID badges scanned and stray employees greeted, we bundle into the elevators together. Enzo smashes his lips against Harlow's when the doors slide open on the tenth floor.

She's without an escort today—Leighton is taking Hunter to the hospital for a checkup with the audiologist. The whole team seems to be scattered across the country.

"You'll be okay on your own?" Enzo worries.

Harlow steps out into the foyer. "Richards is just down the hall. I'll see you guys later."

Her tentative smile is plastered on as we mutter our goodbyes before the doors slam shut. Enzo shifts impatiently on his feet, eyeing the floor numbers ticking upwards.

"Stop fidgeting. Whatever's going on, Richards will get it out of her. We need to worry about this perp first."

"Yeah," he grunts.

Enzo storms out of the elevator without another word as he reaches the interrogation floor. *Chatty son of a bitch.* I continue upwards until my office is in sight.

Despite settling into the blank walls and bare carpets of my new bedroom, this place still feels like home. I've missed its book-lined corners and warm light dappled across old case files.

The live feed from the room holding our tight-lipped ex-police officer fills my screens as I make a coffee to perk myself up. By the time I sit down, Enzo's slid into his seat opposite the silver-haired, elderly man in his cheap blue suit.

"Mr Prescott," Enzo greets. "Thanks for coming in."

Ben didn't go into great detail about how he tracked this dinosaur down using his old law enforcement contacts. We know this constable was on the lead investigating team that dismantled Genesis Home and three of its sister branches.

Like many others back then, Mr Prescott was silenced with a healthy pension and a promise that the government would punish the powers that be behind our string of children's homes.

Complete crap, of course.

We now know that the wealthy Catholic churches running our less-than-legal homes escaped punishment, buying off their victims instead. History was erased with crumpled cash and pursed lips, as it often is.

"No problem," he answers stiffly.

"May I begin by asking why you changed your mind? Last we spoke, you were very reluctant to engage with our investigation."

Mr Prescott straightens his striped tie. "We all signed non-disclosure agreements when we exited the force. I'm putting my neck on the line by being here today."

Enzo cocks his head. "Interesting. Is this standard procedure for a retiring officer of your rank?"

"Depending on their division. I worked for the major crimes unit up in Sunderland. Certain aspects of my career have been made classified."

This guy has clearly been around the block. It's rare that police investigations are hidden from public record, but it's not unheard of. Some information is deemed too sensitive.

"I understand you spent many years investigating a string of child abuse cases involving private children's homes in the area."

"That's correct."

Enzo leans forward on the table. "I'm interested in Genesis Home, in particular."

Mr Prescott swallows hard. "My partner and I spent many years building a case on that particular location. We visited on numerous occasions between the late seventies and mid-eighties."

"It has since been demolished."

"I'm aware," he confirms.

"We have reason to believe a person of interest to our current case resided at the property within this time period."

Nodding again, he twists the wedding band strangling his wrinkled finger. "We developed a relationship with the owners. Both devout Catholics and church members."

I sit back in my chair. In our line of work, we call out red flags like winning numbers on a bingo card. This entire timeline has been screaming of suspicion since we uncovered Rosetta's real identity. There's far more to the story.

"Did you find any instances of abuse?" Enzo asks brusquely.

"Numerous cases. We kept tabs on a number of minors as we built a case for prosecution. Excuse my bluntness, but I've seen a lot of battered children. The kids in this case were next-level messed up."

Enzo doesn't waste time taking notes. My fingers are blurring across my keyboard instead, and I know the rest of the intelligence department is watching in their own offices.

"I've seen the photographs you released on the news," Mr Prescott interjects. "That's why I changed my mind."

"The photographs of our suspect?" Enzo clarifies.

"He's been using a false name. Sickos like this always do. My partner and I knew him by another alias back then."

I lean closer, locked on the movement of his lips. Our hair-brained theory from months ago is on the verge of validation or destruction.

"You recognised him from recent photographs?"

Mr Prescott nods. "He was sixteen at the time, but the resemblance is there. I followed the cases of two children before they absconded from custody together."

"Rosetta Stone," Enzo guesses.

He does a double take. "You know her?"

Enzo waves for him to continue. "We do."

"Well, Rosetta was a person of interest in our investigation. She was in a relationship with a fellow resident that came to our attention for his… frankly, worrying behaviour."

"Worrying?"

"Another resident reported him, several months into the case." Mr Prescott's expression hardens. "He was accused of sexually assaulting a female. Rosetta, in fact."

My blood chills.

What the fuck?

"Rosetta? I thought you said they were romantically involved?" Enzo asks, confused. "Why would he rape her?"

"Rosetta maintained that story, but the witness was certain of what she saw occur between them. We performed a follow-up interview and the story changed."

"Changed how?"

"Our witness was sitting there with two black eyes and a crucifix-shaped bruise on her damn cheek. She refused to say another word."

Holy. Shit.

Pastor Michaels didn't just know his bloody accomplice from childhood. They attended the same abusive hellhole, and he already had a proclivity for rape as a sixteen-year-old child. She was his first fucking victim… that we know of.

Gotcha.

We were right.

"You're suggesting that management, *ahem*, intervened?" Enzo narrows his eyes. "I assume Rosetta refused to press charges?"

He shrugs it off. "She never spoke to us again. We returned to Genesis Home several more times. A matter of months later, she'd run off in cahoots with her supposed abuser."

Fists clenched on the table, Enzo shakes his head. "And none of this was deemed valuable for the public record? These sickos got off without prosecution. Not even a slap on the wrists."

"You think I wanted that?" Mr Prescott argues back. "Watch your tone, son. We tried our best to close that place down. I was just one man against a whole corrupt system."

Taking a moment to restrain himself, Enzo pushes his hair back and refocuses. We know better than most that money talks in this world, and it takes a whole army to dismantle something this insidious.

"I kept tabs in the years before I retired. Neither of them ever showed up again. They disappeared into thin air and left us with nothing but questions and no answers."

"I want a name," Enzo presses.

The suspense shatters into spectacular pieces as our entire case changes with two words.

"Michael Abaddon."

My hands are flying before Enzo's even caught a breath. I'm across all the systems that we're granted access to and some I've hacked myself—prison records, bank accounts, prosecution files—and there isn't a single shred of evidence after 1978.

Another ghost.

But our killer finally has a name.

"Michael Abaddon," I repeat to myself. "Pastor... Michaels. Fucker."

From the evidence I pulled when I hacked the High Court's sealed case files, I have a list of the children allocated to Genesis Home. Three rows down, there the bastard is.

Michael Abaddon.

It seems so innocuous, the typed letters of a child's name, lost to the gradual erosion of history and its sins. No one knew this kid would become a vicious killing machine decades down the line.

"Strange boy." Mr Prescott frowns to himself. "It was clear that Rosetta was being abused by him. Even at sixteen, Abaddon was a master manipulator. He scared the crap out of my partner."

Part of me wonders what Harlow would think of this. To her account, Mrs Michaels was a perpetrator herself. Not a victim of the same monster that imprisoned our girl.

"Are you aware of the suspect having any family?" Enzo questions.

"Not that I ever saw. Genesis Home didn't attract many kids with families. I was glad to see it demolished in the nineties."

Turning away from the interview, I trawl back through the scanned documents on my screen but find no more information on Michael Abaddon. By the time the case went to trial in 1994, he'd been gone for over two decades.

A perfect monster, born from the hottest depths of Hell. No prizes for guessing where Pastor Michaels got his extreme religious beliefs and love of violence from. This place practically birthed him.

The creator of evil incarnate.

My concentration is shattered by the scream of our emergency alarm erupting. The lighting shifts to a deep red as I startle, fumbling to reach for my laptop and open the secure server.

With a few clicks, I've narrowed the triggered alarm down to the third floor. Relief comes fast before dissipating again. It's not Harlow's floor, but she could still be in danger.

Tripping over myself, I tear from the room, swiping my gun from my under-desk safe along the way. My hands shake as I quickly fire off a text message to Enzo, telling him to meet me downstairs.

With my gun cocked and ready, the elevator feels like it's moving at a snail's pace. My ears are aching from the deafening alarm still screaming for attention.

The doors *ding* open on a floor now unrecognisable, doused in shadows and the neon tinge of emergency lighting. When the door to the adjacent staircase slams open, admitting a red-faced Enzo and several armed agents, I wave him forward.

This area is dedicated to staff—an expansive break room, showers and a cafeteria serving freshly cooked meals twenty-four hours a day. All are in chaos as people flood out, disgruntled and covering their ears.

"Fan out!" Enzo barks loudly. "If we have an intruder, I want them found."

"I'm gonna go check on Harlow," I shout above the noise. "She's probably freaking out."

He shoves two of his men towards me. "Take backup and make sure she's secure. This might be Michaels."

Flanked by the two agents, we return to the elevator and climb out on Harlow's floor. It's empty compared to the madness downstairs. Not many people come here as it's reserved for more informal meetings or appointments.

With an invisible hand strangling my windpipe, we clear the whole floor, heading for the final therapy room on the right. The door is slightly ajar, and my terror triples.

Stepping in front of me with a wordless conversation in hand signals, the two agents storm into the room. It's a matter of seconds before they shout back for me to enter.

Every step seals my dread. The room is empty apart from two still-warm, half-drank cups of tea on the low table and Richards' discarded binder of notes. They were here.

As I'm ordering the agents to sweep the whole floor again, I check my phone and notice an incoming message from fifteen minutes ago.

> **Harlow:** I'm sorry. I have to find the truth on my own. It's the only way to save me from myself.

"Fuck!" I scream at the screen.

This can't be happening.

She wouldn't be that stupid.

Logging in to our tracking software, I search for the small dot that represents Harlow's live location. It's in the same fucking building as me.

When I call, a soft vibrating fills the therapy room. Tucked down the side of the high-backed armchair, I find Harlow's phone stashed inside the pages of her leather journal.

Her stuff is here, but she isn't. The pages of her journal blur with a hot, heady wave of sheer panic. Her phone was tucked in at the most recent entry, leaving it open for me to find.

Control is an illusion.

Control is an illusion.

Control is an illusion.

Ice spikes through my veins. The frenzied scrawl continues across three pages. The same four words, over and over again. This is bad; she's spiralling worse than we thought.

Enzo's contact flashes up on my phone and I stick him on loudspeaker while flicking back through her journal, searching for any clues.

"Yeah?"

"Tenth floor is secure," he growls down the line. "I've got Richards down here. He was locked outside in the staff garden and set off the alarm. His security pass is gone."

"Where the fuck is Harlow?"

"He brought her down here for some fresh air when she was triggered. She lost her shit and attacked him. Sounds like he was out cold for a while."

"Goddammit!" I slam a hand on the table, rattling a vase. "She

466

must've set off the alarm herself as a distraction to escape. This was planned."

"What is she thinking?"

The journal is a crushing weight in my hands.

Control is an illusion.

"I think she's going for Michaels," I suggest.

We were so busy worrying about the threat that Michaels poses to Harlow, we forgot about the more destructive enemy lapping at her heels.

Herself.

"Motherfuck! She can't have gotten far." Enzo's gravelly voice is spiked with fear. "Not unless she had help."

We are in so much shit if she did. This wasn't a mere accident. It was choreographed and planned to take full advantage of the opening in her security.

"I'll mobilise all units and alert the local police departments to set up traffic blocks. We don't have much time."

"What is her plan here?" he asks, mostly to himself. "We're supposed to be in this together. I don't understand."

Pain practically spills from the journal's pages. I know what Harlow wants. The biggest thing that's been taken from her.

"She's looking for something."

"What?" Enzo snarls at me.

"Control."

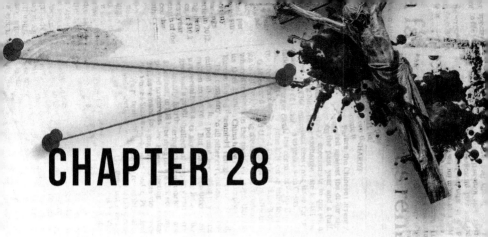

CHAPTER 28

Harlow

Make This Go On Forever - Hahlweg

Silvery bullets of rain slam into the ground like machine-gun fire. God's violent wrath is punishing the earth for daring to challenge his almighty rule.

I watch with fascination from my resting place against the school's painted railings. The swollen storm clouds in the sky scream with the same rage keeping me upright.

It was impossible to sleep on the road while knowing what chaos and heartbreak I've left behind. I batter the life out of that thought before it takes over and I change my mind.

I don't have time to feel.

Not until this is done.

Beneath the brim of a baseball cap and oversized hoodie concealing my face, I wear a pair of sunglasses to hide from the world. Parents are running in all directions, dropping off children in their hurry to get to work.

It isn't long before a familiar headful of brown hair joins the crowd of disgruntled parents running from the morning rain. Her green eyes are downturned, hidden by a navy-blue raincoat.

Clutching his mother's hand tight, my half-brother, Ulrich, squeals in excitement as he splashes into a muddy rain puddle. Giana shouts at him to stop and drags him along, her annoyance clear.

Ulrich doesn't look much like her, aside from his hair. We all have the same mousy shade of brown on our heads. They disappear inside the bustling school, and that's when I move.

My feet splash through excess rainwater in a rhythmic thump. Each footstep mirrors my calm heartbeat. A cloud of determination has slipped beneath my skin and silenced my fear.

I've waited long enough.

The truth won't find itself.

When Giana emerges from dropping her kid off, I fall into step behind her. She's cowering beneath an umbrella to protect her from the stormy weather for the walk home.

The small coastal village of Croyde passes us by as we leave the school behind. I never thought I'd be back here again, but this time, I'm not running away from my demons.

This is a head-on collision.

My face is still tucked low, and I maintain a safe distance, ensuring she can't hear my footsteps. Giana walks all the way home in the rain from her son's local school.

The irony isn't lost on me. We've found ourselves back at the beginning, walking home from school together on a day that will change the course of our lives. I'm rewriting my own history.

When the bright-red door of her home appears, I falter. There's no telling what she's capable of. I've sacrificed my safety in the name of sanity, but this is a risk I had to take.

"Why did you do it?" I call out.

She freezes halfway through the picket-fence gate. Turning to find me standing a few short metres away, Giana's mouth falls open in shock.

"Letty? What are you doing here?"

I inch closer. "Did he pay you? Was that it?"

"What are you talking about? Where is your security team?"

"Or perhaps it wasn't for the money," I continue, removing my sunglasses to reveal my bloodshot eyes.

"Money?" she repeats. "What is this? Are you... having another episode? Do you know where you are?"

"I know where I am, Giana. Nobody else will be joining us. This is between me and you."

She hesitates, clutching her phone tight. I make a point of pulling out my coat pockets, showing that I'm unarmed with no secret phone or weapon stashed.

"It's just us," I assure her.

Giana bites her lip. "Why did you come here alone?"

"I thought you wanted to see me."

"I... I do," she stumbles, glancing behind her at the house. "Foster is at work. You should come inside."

With a quick look up and down the street, I nod and approach her. Giana's hands shake as she fights to unlock the front door, her eyes darting from side to side.

I take the house keys from her hands and unlock the door myself, gesturing for her to head inside. Her bag-lined eyes are locked on me. It's there again.

That look.

Fear-fuelled mania.

With a gulp, she enters her home and removes layers of clothing. I take a deep breath and follow suit. The last time I was in this house, it ended in disaster.

"Take a seat," she invites, opting for the cramped, carpeted living room on the left. "You want tea?"

"I don't have a lot of time."

Giana nods and perches on the sofa opposite. "I heard about the accident. How is Hunter?"

"He's alive."

"I'm sorry, Letty. You must've been terrified."

Even her apologies are tainted with lies. I can see it now. Everything became crystal clear as soon as I made the decision to retake control. Arms folded, I stare straight into her eyes.

"I remember," I deadpan.

She flinches. "Excuse me?"

"Let's cut the small talk. We've done enough of that. I'd like to have an honest conversation for once."

"I should call someone," Giana worries as she eyes me. "You're not well, darling. Let me call for some help."

"I'm finally thinking clearly for the first time ever. Put the phone down. You owe me the truth... for Ulrich's sake."

The blood drains from Giana's face. "What?"

"Nice school. Good to see you walking your kid to class now. Learned your lesson, did you?"

Her hands clench in her lap. I can see the blueish lightning strike of veins popping against her pale skin.

"You followed me?" Giana accuses. "What is this? Some kind of game? I won't have you threatening my son."

"I'm not you," I fight back. "I'd never threaten a child. But frankly, I think the safest place for him is far away from you. That can be arranged."

Her pink-painted nails are digging into her palms. She's slowly turning bright red, accompanying the rising hysteria gathering in her gaze.

The wolf has been backed into a corner, its sheep's clothing stripped off. We don't need to pretend to be strangers anymore. This charade has gone on for long enough.

"Walk through the field with the blackberry bushes." I brace my elbows on my knees. "You sent me to him, wrapped like a Christmas present."

"I d-don't know what you m-mean," Giana splutters.

"He was supposed to save us from the rapture, right? I remember that much. Why did you believe his lies?"

"Letty, please..."

"I won't say it again. My name is Harlow. You should know, it's the name *he* gave to me. Was that planned too?"

She looks ready to bolt from the room and call the police herself. The obnoxiously loud tick of her grandfather clock is the only sound above the downpour of angry rain outside.

I never considered Giana to be my mother, not in the real sense. Still, it's a painful stab in the heart to see the slow realisation spread across her face as she realises I'm not kidding around.

"I know everything," I repeat again. "So, drop the pretence and tell me the truth."

Her mouth snaps open and shut as the tears pool in her eyes. Panic and hysteria reign chaos across her face.

"Your father is lying. He's tricked you! I warned you to stay away from him for this reason."

"He is the only person that has never lied to me. I was just too stupid to believe what was right in front of me."

"Please," Giana begs. "You don't understand. He was always so controlling. You're being used by him."

There's that word again. Control. The invisible thread that undercuts our lives, whether we acknowledge it or not. I've been grasping in the dark for that elusive power long enough.

"I have never been in control of my own life," I admit, looking around her comfy family home. "All these months, I've been pretending. Acting like I'm the one in control."

Giana's poised on the edge of her seat, ready to run. "I don't know what he's told you…"

"Enough! Shut up and listen."

Fury jolts through me as I stand up, on the verge of wrapping my hands around her throat. The anger I've been suppressing for months on end is making it hard to see straight.

"You hurt me," I force out. "Not him. That morning, you were the one who told me where to go. For my own good, right? That's what you said to me."

She gulps hard. "This isn't what you think it is."

"I was scared. It was getting dark, but I had no choice. You warned me what would happen if I disobeyed you again. I was already limping and covered in bruises."

"Please—"

"Pastor Michaels was there, waiting for me." I let the tears splash across my cheeks. "He seemed… so nice. All I wanted was for someone to take care of me for once."

"I can't… I don't…"

"Don't what, huh? You don't remember agreeing to sell me to a mass murderer? You can't believe how unlucky you are that it didn't work, and I escaped? What?"

"I did not sell you!" she snaps, rising to her feet. "He… he told me that it was the only way. I had to repent, Letty. He was going to save us all from damnation."

"No!" I jab an accusing finger in her face. "He didn't save me, Giana. That monster stole everything from me, and the women he murdered in God's name. That isn't salvation."

She breaks down, crumpling until her knees hit the carpet. "I d-didn't know what h-he'd become... I thought I was doing the right thing by tracking him down."

I freeze mid-rant. "Tracking him down?"

Her hands cover her face. "Sylvie told me not to look for him when my mother passed away, but I had to know. I wanted so badly to have a real family."

"Grandma S-Sylvie wasn't your real mum?"

"I was adopted," Giana hiccups. "My real mother was a s-sex worker. She abandoned me. Just l-like she did to him."

The sound of rainfall is drowned out by the ringing in my head. I stumble into the sofa and almost fall over, struck by a wave of fearsome dizziness.

"Pastor Michaels... he's..."

"My half-brother," she finishes with a sob. "Your uncle."

I feel like the whole house is shaking as my world falls apart. We're trapped in the same earthquake, neither able to save ourselves from the inevitable destruction in the road ahead.

"When we reunited, I was so happy," she continues, her head lowered. "I finally h-had a real family. But Michael... he was so angry with our mother."

"M-Michael?"

"His real first name. Our mother abandoned him too, but he wasn't adopted like me. S-Something was broken in him. He got in my head and... and... twisted everything."

The puzzle pieces click into place with Dad's words and scraps of memories. Her frantic, terrified praying. Pouring over Bibles late at night. The obsession, the fear. Lashing out in waves of uncontrolled violence.

That wasn't Giana.

It was all him.

Planting a poisonous seedling and fanning the flames until it grew into a semi-psychotic, unhinged obsession. The same obsession he distilled into Mrs Michaels and those fanatics.

"I did everything he told me to." Giana weeps into her hands. "But the d-demons, they still whispered to me. I was losing my m-mind, and he told me that he could make it all stop... if I let him take you."

With vomit burning my throat, I kneel down in front of her. Giana's head lifts when I slide a finger under her chin.

"You gave me to him," I whisper in horror.

Her mouth contorts into a pleading smile. "The things I was seeing, Letty... the voices, everything. He convinced me the rapture was coming, and I had to repent."

"You just... sacrificed me?"

"I tried to forget." Her tears flood faster. "Afterwards, I realised what I'd done. I wanted to fix it, but it was too late. Michael was gone. You were gone."

"You got Dad arrested instead when he began to figure it out," I fill in the gaps. "And you found yourself a perfect new family to cover up the mistakes of the past."

"I'm sorry, Letty. I never meant for any of this to happen! It all spiralled out of control so quickly."

"Out of control? You fed me to the wolves!"

She screams as I launch myself at her, our bodies colliding and rolling across the carpet. I latch my hands around her throat and begin to choke with all my God-given strength.

"You ruined my life!"

Giana's nails scratch against my hands. Pinned beneath me, her limbs writhe and buck. All I can see is red—anger, hatred, the stain of Laura's blood on my hands, Kiera's body being sliced into easily disposable pieces.

Spit bubbles slip from Giana's lips as she gasps for air, the tear of her nails slowly losing steam. I want her to lose everything. She needs to know how it feels to be unmade.

With her eyes on the verge of falling shut forever, Brooklyn's voice cuts through the haze that's fallen over me. She could be in the room, I hear it so clearly.

Trust me when I tell you, there isn't a bad bone in your body.

My hands fall from Giana's neck as I scream out my rage. She splutters, grappling at her throat. I hang over her, my own chest on fire as an ugly sob escapes my mouth. I can't do it. She hurts people—not me. I'm not like them.

"You're going to admit to everything," I choke through tears. "You will never see Ulrich again. He deserves to be loved, and you're not capable of it."

Staring up at me with every heaving breath she sucks in, Giana's eyes widen at something over my shoulder. The sound of creeping footsteps registers too late for me to react.

"You shouldn't have come back," she whispers.

Something heavy smashes against my head, followed by the sound of ceramic shattering. Pain. It overcomes me.

I slump over her body, feeling the gush of hot, sticky blood spreading across my scalp, littered with shards of a broken vase. With the room swaying, a dark shadow approaches.

"I knew you'd find your way home." Pastor Michaels grins down at me, his silver crucifix glinting. "All lost lambs do in the end."

His laced boot hovers over my face, obscuring the insidious grin stretching his mouth wide open. It slams down with an audible crunch that blackens my vision.

Darkness swallows me whole.

I'm welcomed back into its arms.

CHAPTER 29

Harlow

Hold Your Breath – Astyria

T he rugged coastline stretches out in front of me. Waves lap at the shore, and the tang of salt rests on my tongue. The summer sunshine casts a brilliant glow that I welcome with open arms.

Digging my toes into the wet sand, I let my eyes slide shut.

I'm home. Safe.

This is paradise.

I can't remember a time I ever felt content. Even my happiest moments have been tinged with darkness. But here, in this beautiful, windswept place, all I feel is peace at last.

"Hey, Harlow!"

Running down the beach, Laura's platinum-blonde hair streams over her shoulders in a glistening curtain. With a huge smile on her face, she races towards me, the floral fabric of her dress trailing behind her.

We meet in the middle, and she tackles me to the golden sand. Falling over in peals of laughter, we scream when the tide rolls back in. Water soaks into our clothes and I shove Laura off me with a squeal.

"I'm soaked!"

"What kind of idiot stands next to the sea if they don't wanna get wet?" she teases, wringing out her dress.

Clambering to my feet, I offer her a helping hand up. She curls her arm around my waist, and we walk along the shore, both barefoot and laughing in the glow of sunshine.

"What are you doing here?"

"I'm here to see you," she answers like it's obvious. *"Figured you could use a friend right about now."*

I glance around the empty beach. "But... where are we?"

She offers me a knowing grin and taps her temple.

My smile falters. "You're not real."

"Hey, I'm no more real than you are. Why should that matter? Imaginary friends are still friends."

We walk in companionable silence, our steps swallowed by the swill of water and chirping seagulls flying above us. There isn't another soul in sight. We're alone in our own personal utopia.

"I wish you were still alive," I blurt.

"You've been blaming yourself for my death for too long." Laura squeezes my waist. *"I know you're hurting right now. That's why I'm here."*

We stop and wait for the sea water to return. It races back up the sand in a twinkling wave, hitting us with a rush of warmth that laps at our ankles. Laura turns to face me, her smile understanding.

"Only you can forgive yourself for what happened."

I shake my head. "I think it's too late for that. I'm dead."

"Dead? Oh, no. Not yet. You are in danger, though, and I need you to wake up. You can't let him win again. Not when he's taken so much from us both."

The wind picks up as storm clouds roll in. Our pocket of happiness is swept away with the rising winds, leaving us both shivering and doused in shadows.

"What do I do?"

Laura presses a kiss to my cheek. "You fight, Harlow Michaels. Fight like hell for all of us. We'll be here watching."

Her eyes flick over to the sandbank high above us, wrapped in swaying patches of grass. Their faces stare back at me—too many to count now. The girls that filled my childhood, intermixed with the new victims.

Some don't have faces, their mottled skin smoothed over in an eyeless, mouthless blur. Five souls extinguished without anyone knowing, butchered and buried out of sight. I'll never know their names.

At the forefront, two faces stand out. One dead. One alive. Candace's fiery auburn hair stirs in the wind. She's small, petite, her body covered by a dress that hides the assortment of vicious bruises from sight. I recognise her from my dreams.

She nods once.

Breath held, I nod back.

Next to her, Kiera has found her final resting place. Her purpose has been fulfilled now. She blows me a kiss, slinking backwards to join the other girls. They all turn and begin to walk away, hand in hand.

With a loud crack of thunder, the shadows stretch outwards, swallowing the whole beach. Laura's hand brushes against my cheek, tracing the path of her kiss.

"Forgive yourself," she repeats.

It's the last words to leave her lips. She vanishes into the blackness that takes over, wrapping around me in ice-cold tendrils. The beach disappears from sight and the real world rushes up to meet me.

†

All-consuming pain is the first sensation that reality brings. Fierce, pounding pain, like someone peeled the skin from my skull and started smashing it to death with a hammer.

I groan while battling to open my heavy eyes. It's hard to breathe. Everything feels stuffy, and the sharp, coppery taste of blood is clogging up my throat.

"Hey," someone hisses.

Blinking to settle my vision, I lift a shaking hand to my face and search my blood-crusted nose. It's bent out of shape and pulsating.

"Hey!"

Darkness surrounds me on all sides. The scent of unwashed filth, sweat and urine welcomes me home. This is more familiar than the luxury I've spent so long living in.

"Are you awake? Say something!"

"I'm awake," I garble.

Trapped in a litter-strewn room, the bare walls are coated in damp and rotting cream wallpaper that sags from the exposed bricks. Ancient, bare floorboards dig into my spine.

When I attempt to roll over, something metal clanks, and I gasp in pain. A pair of handcuffs are cutting deep into my left wrist, securing me to the wall.

"Are you Harlow?"

Across the room, her skin is painted in nasty shades of black, blue and green. Blood streaks cover her face and naked body, blending with weeks of layered dirt.

Her auburn hair tips me off. This isn't a dream. I haven't wound back the clock and returned to my imprisonment in Pastor Michaels' basement. This is a new iteration of hell.

"Candace," I gasp. "You're alive."

Her laugh is choked. "I'm not sure I'd call it that. You've been out for hours. I thought you were dead."

The numbness shatters. This is it. He's got me again. As terror sets in, I scream out, tugging sharply on the handcuff pinning me in place. Candace watches with a tired look.

"No use. You don't think I tried that?"

"Where is he? Pastor Michaels?"

She recoils, staring down at her bare legs. She has one hand free, the other cuffed high above her at a painful angle. She won't look at me now that I've named the elephant in the room.

"Candace," I say more gently. "I know you're afraid, but I won't let him hurt you again. You aren't alone."

"He's been waiting for you. At first, I believed him when he said you'd come, and I could go home."

"He... said that?"

Candace winces as she pulls her legs up to her chest, exposing raw, oozing ulcers eating into her skin. Jesus. They look infected. It's a miracle she's still here.

"That woman carried you in here earlier and just left me here. They'll never let me go home, will they?"

My stomach lurches, and I strain against the handcuff, a hot burst of vomit surging up my throat. Tears sear the backs of my eyes with each heave.

She was helping him all along.

"Woman?" I cough out. "Giana?"

"Never told me her name. Some miserable-looking, brown-haired bitch. Loves to throw a punch or two. She feeds me whenever she remembers to."

Throwing up again, I splutter and sob until there's nothing left inside me but resentment. The pit of darkness keeps burrowing deeper. I won't make it out alive this time.

"*He* comes for prayers every night."

I know what that means. If there was anything left in me, I'd be sick again. All these weeks, I've slept in a warm bed, had a bellyful of food and the love of an incredible family.

All while Candace was being beaten, starved and raped on a daily basis. My freedom has cost her an unfathomable price. One she will never be able to take back.

"Does he sleep here?"

Candace shudders. "No. It's just me."

Searching around the room, I look for any clues as to our location. There's nothing beyond piles of energy bar wrappers, squashed water bottles and an array of mice droppings.

This wasn't part of the plan. I had it all laid out. Exposing Giana's lies was all I wanted. I didn't know her deceit would lead to a rabbit hole of evil, landing me straight back in Pastor Michaels' grasp.

"What do you remember?" I urge her. "Where are we?"

"There's nothing here," she mumbles back. "I screamed and screamed, but no one has ever heard me. Only him."

Shit, this is bad. We know from the taunting image he sent that Candace has been held captive in some kind of abandoned building. We could be anywhere in England.

But if Giana's involved, that narrows down the search radius. We must be reasonably close to Croyde for her to be feeding Candace on a semi-regular basis.

"Don't worry," I whisper into the dark. "They'll come for us soon. I'm going to get you out of here."

"Don't make promises you can't keep, Harlow."

Her words lash against me in a painful whip. I did the same thing for Laura—promised her salvation as our pinkies linked between rusted cage bars. I failed her.

It won't happen again.

This is my chance to fix the past.

We lapse into silence as the sound of heavy rain continues to patter in the dark night, lashing against the grimy window high above us.

Hours pass, and the sun rises, illuminating the dank room. In the cold light of day, Candace's condition is further revealed. If we have to fight our way out of here, she will be in trouble.

Her entire body is beaten and slashed while her face is misshapen from too many blows. She's in bad shape, nursing infected wounds and probably severe dehydration.

"Are you in pain?"

She shrugs, cursing when it jolts her handcuffed arm. "I don't really feel it anymore. How's the nose?"

"I'm okay. It's not the first time."

"Jesus. How long did he... you know, have you?"

"Thirteen years."

Candace gapes at me. "All that time? How did you survive? I feel like I'm going insane in here on my own."

"I don't remember a lot of it," I admit. "After a while, you learn to switch off. It was years before he brought the first girl to torture and kill."

"So, you were alone for all that time." She shakes her head as tears streak down her dirty face. "I'd rather die. I don't know how much more of this I can take."

"That's not happening. We're getting out of here together or not at all."

She stares back down at her toes. "How long have I been here? Did anyone even look for me?"

"I think it's been eight weeks or so. The whole country has been looking for you. There's been huge protests about the case. Your brother was looking, too."

"My brother?" She laughs weakly. "That can't be right. I haven't spoken to him in years. Why would he care?"

Biting my tongue, I hold back that he's staring down the barrel of a lengthy prison sentence for attempted murder. She needs hope right now, not more heartbreak.

"He was devastated," I say vaguely.

"Huh. I wasn't expecting that."

"I guess people can surprise you. Stuff like this either brings out the best or worst in them."

We lapse back into silence until she breaks it.

"I don't get it," she mumbles. "How has he gotten away with this for so long? Why did no one care before?"

"Pastor Michaels has spent years picking off the invisibles." I wince, attempting to get comfortable. "That's what allowed him to remain hidden."

Candace sniffles as she cries even harder.

"But that's changing now," I add.

"Nothing's changed, Harlow."

"No, it has. People are finally waking up. Violence against women isn't okay, no matter who they are or what they do."

She manages a thin smile. "Things have always been different for people like me. To the world, we're whores up for a cheap fuck. Not people."

"You're a person," I assure her. "You matter. The people out there who love you have fought for you since day one."

"Who? My waste-of-space brother who disowned me the day he found out how I was paying the bills?"

"Well, it was your friends who alerted the police."

"They did?" She perks up.

"You were reported missing by the next morning."

"Holy shit."

"They came all the way to London to be interviewed by Sabre and help with the investigation. Do you believe me now?"

Candace's tears are still flowing, but her smile widens. She nods, wiping her face off with her free hand.

"What about you? Who's looking for you?"

My heart aches behind my ribcage, broken into jagged pieces that slice against the fragile remains of my hope. I wouldn't blame the guys if they didn't look for me.

I did this to myself. One day, they will get sick of constantly worrying about me, and that'll be it. The end of the road. This could very well be it this time.

Before I can choke out an answer, the creak of footsteps sounds out from the floor below us. A door slams, followed by the murmurings of two voices.

"Is that help?" Candace asks, but her hope dies quickly. "Shit. It's him. I recognise his voice."

Wrestling myself as upright as possible, I stretch my limbs and attempt to move into a prepared position. I need every defence I can get if we're going to survive this.

"Be quiet and let me handle him," I order her. "Don't get involved. He'll leave you alone as long as you do that."

"Wait," she rushes out. "I won't sit here and watch him... hurt..."

"Don't worry." I plaster on a smile, even if it feels alien on my lips. "I'm the one he wants. You're safe."

"No! Harlow, please."

"Be quiet!"

Heavy, aggressive steps preclude the devil's arrival, cutting off her frantic pleas. My heart is pounding so fast, I can feel it throbbing throughout my body.

Fear is my automatic response, bred into me after years of violence and death. It quickly fades into newfound determination. Pastor Michaels won't lay another finger on her.

Even if I have to take every cut and punch he needs to inflict, I'll keep her safe. I have to keep him occupied long enough for backup to track us down.

At the last second, I fall back on old habits and send a silent, desperate plea up to the heavens.

Please, Lord.

Give me the strength to survive.

I don't want to die here.

The door slams open and cracks against the wall. Broad shoulders are cloaked in thick, perfectly pressed robes. The twinkle of a crucifix resting on his chest sets my pulse alight.

No more running.

Pastor Michaels looks as I remember him, albeit wearier, his grey-streaked hair a little overgrown and his beard scraggly. Sunken cheeks sit below piercing green eyes that steal my breath.

Oh my God.

I never realised it before now, but his eyes are identical to Giana's bright shade of green, down to the tiny flecks of brown blurring with emerald irises.

Pastor Michaels steps into the room and sweeps his gaze over us both, a slimy grin slashed across his face. When his eyes land on me, trapped and bloodied, that grin triples.

"Let us be thankful, and so worship God with reverence and awe, for our God is a consuming fire."

I lift my chin and, for the first time ever, meet his gaze head on. I'm no longer afraid to stare into the depths of pure, unadulterated evil. Cowering never protected me.

"Hebrews, 12:28."

"You remember your scripture," he praises as he touches his crucifix. "I'm impressed."

"You made me recite it enough."

Scanning over my dirty, ripped clothing, matted hair and blood-slick face, he chuckles darkly.

"You look different. It's been a long time, Harlow. But you're home now, with me. Exactly where you belong."

I swallow the lump in my throat. "I was never yours, Uncle. That was just one of your lies."

His bushy eyebrows raise. "I see you've stumbled across our family secret. Took you long enough. Let's dispense with the formalities then, shall we?"

"Please do."

Kicking aside a crushed water bottle, Pastor Michaels crouches down in front of me, his wrinkled hands braced on his robe-covered knees.

He still smells the same. Blood, sweat and fresh tears. I wonder how much of it is my imagination, blurring with countless excruciating memories from the past.

"Your mother is downstairs," he reveals gleefully. "Say the word, and I'll slit her throat for you. Call it a welcome home present."

I flinch. "You would kill your own sister?"

"You think she matters to me?" He cracks his knuckles. "That whore is no better than the poisonous slut who birthed us. Giana's the reason we ran away together."

"You kidnapped me," I snarl back.

"No, I wanted to save you from her."

"Save me? Really?"

"You had the chance to repent. The women in this family are cursed with the devil's blood."

He is genuinely insane. More than I remember.

"I saved you from her corrupted ways and raised you in the Lord's light. That was your repentance, Harlow."

His delusions stare back at me in the insidious depths of his eyes. He truly believes every twisted word. Seized by fury, I gather saliva in my mouth and spit right in his face.

"You took everything from me," I shout at him. "I hope you both rot for what you've done to us all."

His hand strikes out, and my head snaps to the side, fire racing across my cheek. Punching me again, his ring slices into my top lip. I savour the warm splash of blood.

As long as it hurts, I'm still alive. He hasn't won. I'll swallow whatever self-obsessed, psychotic bullshit he wants to throw at me as long as it keeps him distracted.

"Filthy sinner," he screams in my face. "I see you've forgotten all the lessons I taught you. I'm disappointed, but not surprised. This world is full of temptations."

"The only thing you taught me was hatred! You aren't the Lord's saviour. God is disgusted by you."

His meagre patience expires.

"Silence, demon!"

Hitting me harder, I feel the blood begin to pour from my broken nose again. The pain barely registers. This is child's play compared to what he's done to me before.

"I know who you really are." I cough up blood-flecked saliva at his feet. "Why did you kill Rosetta? Another failed experiment?"

He flinches, his knuckles stained red. "Mrs Michaels outlived her usefulness."

"Is that why you left her body for me to find?"

"I killed her for you!" he bellows. "Now, you can take her place at my side. We will face the rapture together."

My near-hysterical laughter echoes around us, over and over. With each wheezing chuckle, his rage metastasises, leaching into every limb. I watch the cloud of sickness descend over his face.

"I would rather hang like her than help you kill more innocent women. You'd be better off killing me now."

The tip of his steel-capped boot slams into my stomach. I double over, heaving and sobbing in pain.

"You dare to defy me? After all I've done for you?" Pastor Michaels howls. "You will take your rightful place at my side."

"Fuck you! I'll die instead."

Another sharp kick. The air is torn from my lungs with each strike. I try to curl inwards and protect my ribs.

"Those men have deceived you," he screeches. "Look what they've made you into! A sinful whore, just like the rest of them."

With another laugh, I drop the killer blow.

"I'd rather be their whore than your prisoner."

Pastor Michaels freezes. "You dare speak such words."

"They love me more than you ever could."

His glare is enraged. "I can still save you. It isn't too late. Only I can lead you back to the path of the righteous."

"No," I wheeze out. "You will always be alone, unloved and unwanted. I won't join you. Not now, not ever."

"Disobedient bitch! You will surrender to me!"

My eyes squeeze shut as I take another furious blow, retching up the blood that runs down my throat. He's sweating now, his eyes wild with untamed madness.

"Rosetta was a puppet under your control. You victimised her too. How does it feel, knowing you killed the only person who was ever loyal to you?"

Pastor Michaels snarls as he looms over me, hand raised for another punch. "Enough of this. We're leaving."

"You indoctrinated Giana next, twisted her mind and convinced her to surrender me to you," I stall further.

"Giana needed saving! I gave her the second chance she wanted. You were the price for her redemption."

"She was just another woman for you to control. That way, we can't abandon you like your mother did, can we?"

That stops him dead in his tracks.

"No," he falters. "That whore has nothing to do with this. Stop these lies before I cut your filthy tongue out."

"You told me to call you Daddy," I continue defiantly. "And tortured me until I spouted the same ugly lie. It didn't work, though, did it? You had to keep on killing."

"I saved you from a sinner's life," he spits out. "I am your God, Harlow. Your salvation. You're nothing without me."

"No, that's where you're wrong. My God doesn't hate the world and everyone in it. My God doesn't preach violence and evil."

"Enough!"

"My God isn't you," I finish. "You're an animal, and you'll get what you deserve for killing those women. I'll see to it."

When he boots me in the side of my tender rib cage, I slump against the rotten floorboards. Blinding pain is tearing through every inch of me.

Candace's eyes connect with mine across the room. She looks utterly terrified of Pastor Michaels, frozen in horror while watching our power struggle.

I try to shake my head, warning her off speaking. I can take it. He's losing control and unravelling fast. The sooner his madness consumes him, the quicker this will end.

"You could've had it all, my child. A seat in the kingdom of paradise while the rapture razes this world to ash."

My eyes flutter shut for a brief, exhausted moment of reprieve. I'm so tired. Adrenaline and pain have sapped my strength to its last reserves.

"Instead, you have forsaken me. Your own flesh and blood! Lucifer was thrown from Heaven for less."

He slams my head against the wall with each hateful word, reigniting the sore, swollen egg on the top of my skull. I scream myself hoarse, unable to hold it in.

"We'll have to start again," he decides with a nod. "From the beginning. Let God decide your fate now that you've been tainted by temptation and sin."

Opening the flap of his ceremonial robes, the glint of the ornate ritual knife catches my eye. Pastor Michaels slides it free, inspecting the sharp blade with an excited smile.

"You survived the ritual once before. Let's see if the Lord will forgive your sins twice. I will abide by his will."

"No!" Candace wails. "Stop! Leave her alone!"

Reaching above me, Pastor Michaels ignores her shouts and unlocks my handcuff. My arm screams in protest as it falls down into my lap, limp and completely numb.

He hovers over me. "Beg the Lord for forgiveness. Pray for his divine mercy. You have much to atone for."

I blink through my tears. "Never."

"I said fucking pray!"

With the sharp blade poised to slice through my clothing, the sound of voices causes him to halt. Giana's shouting at someone downstairs, her voice high with fright.

I sag in relief. "Time's up."

Pastor Michaels' lip curls. "What did you do?"

"Did you think I wouldn't bring backup?"

Footsteps thud up the staircase before two shadows cross into the room. A blood-slick knife pressed against her exposed throat, Giana's escorted inside by her captor.

It's a family reunion.

Dad looks around the room as he holds his ex-wife's life in his hands. He's wearing the same rumpled clothing as yesterday when we travelled to Croyde together.

I knew that I couldn't escape Sabre's protection alone. Knocking Richards out and stealing his security pass was merely the first step. We came to find the truth.

Father and daughter.

Retaking our stolen lives, together.

It took his masterminding and experience to evade capture long enough for me to confront Giana myself. This was a road that needed to be travelled alone.

But I knew it was a risk to leave the security of Sabre's protective custody and the four men determined to keep me there, even as I died more inside with each passing day.

That's why I left my father with strict instructions—if anything went wrong, his job was to raise the alert. If he's here, that means the guys can't be far behind him.

"Step away from my daughter," he shouts. "Or the bitch dies. You're done, Michaels. The game is over."

Poised over me, Pastor Michaels' eyes shut for a second. The ceremonial blade is primed and ready to sink deep into my flesh. My life is hanging on a literal knife's edge.

"Oliver," he greets with an air of exasperation. "How nice of you to join us. This truly is a family affair now."

"Knife down!" Dad barks at him.

"Do what you please with Giana."

"Don't test me! I'll do it."

"In fact, if you plan to slit her throat, I would be quite happy to watch the show myself. Go right ahead."

Giana sobs even harder, a thick stream of blood staining her neck and soaking into the collar of her blouse. She blinks at me, pleading as the knife slices ever closer.

"She's your sister, isn't she? You both kept that secret very quiet. My own wife… related to a fucking serial killer."

Pastor Michaels shrugs. "She's from the demon seed of my mother. That's all that binds us. Kill her and end her pitiful existence, once and for all."

My father's face twists, and I can see the indecision in his agitated blue eyes. The temptation. One slip of the hand and the woman who ruined his life will be dead.

"Dad," I wheeze. "Don't do it."

He looks over to me, his eyes shining with unshed tears. We found our truth, and it's an ugly sight to behold. I wipe blood from the corner of my mouth and try to sit up.

"Please. Killing her won't bring anyone justice. She needs to be punished for what she's done. If you do this, you're no better than she is."

"Goddammit," he curses. "She did this to us, Harlow! It was all part of her plan. She gave you to this bastard."

"And I want to see her punished for it. Death would be too kind for the pain she's inflicted."

The tears spill from his eyes and begin to pour in thick, defeated trails of sadness. His determination broken, Dad lowers the knife from her throat.

Giana moves before I can scream his name, taking advantage of the opening rather than collapsing in relief as I thought she would.

Reaching inside her coat pocket, her hand reappears clutching a gun. She's fumbling with inexperience, but Dad's movements are too slow to escape even her terrible aim.

"No!" I shriek.

It's too little, too late.

Blood sprays across the floor as the bullet pierces Dad's left thigh. He flops backwards with a bellow of agony, leaving Giana to crumple, staring at the gun in her hands.

Her lips move on a remorseful whisper. "I'm sorry. I have no other choice."

"Well," Pastor Michaels singsongs. "I didn't think you'd have it in you. Well done, sister. Perhaps you aren't so useless after all."

Dad's hand is pressed over his bleeding thigh as he writhes in pain on the dirty floor. He lashes out when Giana attempts to approach, her face overcome with regret.

"Should've shot me in the head if you wanted to stop me," he threatens. "You're going to pay for what you did to our family."

"Shut up, Oliver," she blusters. "Take some damn responsibility. Harlow had two parents who failed her."

Pastor Michaels locates my handcuffs and kicks them across the room to her. "Secure him while I finish this."

When Giana pauses, his voice raises.

"Remember our deal. I have no problem taking another child from you if you start disobeying me now."

Her face turning ash white, Giana bows her head, following his orders without further question. That's when it all clicks into place. She's being blackmailed with Ulrich's life.

Dad is handcuffed across the room, his wrist secured to a rusted pipe. With the task done, Giana breaks down. She collapses and curls into a tight, sobbing ball.

"Now, where were we?" Pastor Michaels crouches over me, pressing the knife to my sternum. "Let's make this quick. I don't have time for any more delays."

Cutting my sweater, he exposes the twisted, silvery scars crisscrossing my torso from the last time we played this game. I look away from Dad's tear-filled eyes as he shouts his head off with each knife flick.

"This is for your own good," Pastor Michaels whispers as he works. "You've been led astray. We must pray to God for mercy. If you live, we will escape together."

"Do whatever you want to me," I fire back. "You will never own me ever again. I'm free now. I'm alive."

"Feeling brave? Perhaps this will change your tune." The knife slices through my bra strap. "Time to pray, sinner. You know the words."

As my bra slumps, the sound of something metallic bouncing against the floor halts his movements. Mrs Michaels' shining gold wedding ring has fallen from its hiding place.

Pastor Michaels wavers. I know he recognises it. The strangest of looks crosses his face. A glimmer of... regret.

"She's dead because of you," I accuse.

"Rosetta had to die," he justifies with a bobbing throat. "Her sins were too great. I couldn't help her anymore."

"Help her? That's what you were doing? She helped you butcher my friends! She was a fucking monster!"

Infuriated, he disregards the wedding ring and slashes the knife with an enraged roar. When the first cut parts the skin of my rapidly bruising rib cage, Candace's sobs ricochet throughout the room. She's curled into herself to hide from the inevitable.

Dad's panicked yelling mingles with her cries, echoing into a maelstrom that does little to distract Pastor Michaels from his task. The feeding frenzy has set in.

"Why do none of you obey me?" he screeches.

I hold back a sob as the knife digs into my stomach and begins circling, cutting over old scars to lay new, oozing wounds. He digs deeper, mixing fresh blood with slashed flesh, parting skin and cutting muscle fibres.

"I said fucking *pray!*" His spittle hits my face. "Beg the Lord for his divine retribution, heathen child."

Teeth locked together, it takes all my mental strength to hold back the screams. I won't give him what he wants. Not now, not ever. His complacent songbird is long gone.

When the knife moves up to slice the first line of the Holy Trinity, his concentration breaks. Pastor Michaels' head cocks to the side, listening intently.

Wind.

Beating rotors.

Someone's coming. The sound of an approaching helicopter rattles the bricks of the abandoned house. I almost choke on a sob of relief.

"No," he mutters to himself. "I'm not done!"

"They're coming for you."

Face hardening, he glances over my sliced, blood-slick frame, cuts and scars melding into a grotesque portrait. The ritual isn't complete. With a low curse, he straightens to his full height.

"It's too late to run," I warn him.

His feet are already retreating. The rotors of the helicopter still sound a way off. Pressing a hand to the deep slashes in my stomach to stem the bleeding, I grab the edge of his robes.

"Scared now? How does it feel?"

"Let go, whore!"

Pastor Michaels kicks me in the face, his dark eyes flitting around the room. I'm slammed backwards, agony ripping through my mouth. A tooth is pulled loose, and I spit it out.

"No," I garble. "Never."

He tries to retreat again, intent on running. It takes all of my energy to stumble after him, woozy and weak. I'll follow him for as long as it takes. Pain be damned.

The throaty growl of an approaching car engine causes his movements to halt again. The brief flicker of hope in my chest is extinguished by his pleased smile.

"You think I didn't bring backup too?" He leers at me. "There are plenty of people who believe in my mission."

I grapple with his robes, trying to hold on to something. "No! I won't let you get away. Not this time."

"Don't worry, child. I'll be seeing you again. We won't stop until every sinner has been exposed to God's wrath."

The car's horn blares. I stumble while gripping his robes, driven by desperation. Pastor Michaels wrestles with me as I attempt to scratch my nails down his face in a last-ditch effort.

I'm smashed so hard into the wall, the air is knocked from my lungs. Blackness is eating at my vision as I fight to remain conscious, even though my body wants to shut down.

I sway on my feet, verging on collapse. "Is that all you've got? God's mightiest servant is running like a scared child."

Pastor Michaels holds the knife high above him, prepared to inflict one final stab that will silence my taunts forever. His eyes narrow into slits as he contemplates me.

"I gave everything to you. I'm the one that saved you from

damnation. You've thrown it all away, and for what?"

I bare my blood-stained teeth. "Freedom."

"That is pathetic."

"How would you know? I love, and I am loved. That's something you'll never understand."

He lowers the knife with a cackle. "You're right. But what fun I'm going to have, ripping those you love away from you, one by one. I want you to live to heed my words."

Pivoting on his heel, he launches towards the door. I throw myself across the room and wrap a hand around his ankle with my absolute last glimmer of strength.

Pastor Michaels kicks me in the stomach again, throwing me onto my back. With the knife in his hand, he catches me off guard by going for Candace instead.

"Aha," he taunts.

"Leave her alone!"

"Let's play one last game. Keep following me and let her die if that's what you want more. Your choice."

Candace screams at the top of her lungs as Pastor Michaels lifts her up by the throat. In one brutal slash, he cuts deep into both of her wrists, unleashing the arterial spray of veins.

A crimson waterfall splashes across the sagging wall, and she hits the floor with a thud, her eyes blown wide and breathing laboured. Blood is pouring out of her in a petrifying river.

"Your choice," he repeats.

I watch Pastor Michaels bounce from the room with a final, deranged laugh. Doubt holds me prisoner. The helicopter is close. If I delay him, they'll be able to track the escaping car.

"Go, Harlow," Candace murmurs, turning a ghostly shade of translucent white. "Stop h-him. I'm f-fine."

Every fibre inside me is screaming so loud, I can't think straight. I have to chase after him. It's the only way to end this, once and for all. He's going to escape again.

Candace's head smacks against the floorboards as the last of her consciousness dissipates. Blood is pooling in a copper-tinged puddle, framing her auburn hair in a halo.

No.

I can't do it.

Not again.

Revenge isn't worth more than her life. I couldn't give Laura the freedom she wanted, but I can give Candace a fighting chance at survival. Only if I stay.

Hauling myself past Dad's slumped, bleeding form, I swim through warm blood and gather Candace into my arms. She's too weak to protest, her eyes fighting to remain open.

Clasping her slashed wrists, I apply as much pressure as my weakened state will allow. She's losing too much blood. Flashes overtake my vision with awful déjà vu.

Bright-red spit bubbles sliding from Laura's parted lips. Her pained gasps as I squeezed her throat, choking the final wisps of life from her veins. The echoing rattle of my sobs around the basement.

"You're not allowed to die," I say fiercely.

Her head is limp, lifeless.

"Please. I have a promise to keep. We're getting out of here together, remember?"

The inherited strength of countless stolen lives keeps my eyes open, even as unconsciousness threatens to overwhelm me. Candace will live. The ghosts in my head demand it so.

"Harlow."

A shaking hand touches my shoulder. Dad protests weakly, but

Giana ignores him as she shuffles closer to me.

"Here, use this."

Her swollen, bloodshot eyes lock on mine. She pulls off her cardigan and presses the fabric against Candace's gaping wounds.

"I'm sorry," she offers with finality. "All I wanted was to protect my child. Everything I've done has been for him."

Blood quickly soaks through the cardigan. Giana cuddles up to me, shaking as hard as I am and silently crying into my hair.

I let myself sag against her. "You kept him safe. It's done now. I can't control what happens next. You hurt people."

"I know, darling. For what it's worth, I'm sorry for all of it. I'll take my punishment. Just promise me one thing."

My eyes fall shut as the helicopter roars directly above us. The rotors are slowing down. It's preparing to land.

"What is it?" I mumble.

"Please tell Ulrich that I love him."

Unconsciousness is pulling me into her warm, newly protective embrace. Barked orders and frantic voices echo from outside the building. Our saviours have arrived.

"Please, Harlow," she begs. "Promise me."

My name leaving her lips seals my defeat.

"I promise, Mum."

EPILOGUE

Enzo

We Are Not Okay — NIKKITA

Staring into the depths of my empty suitcase, I glower at the lack of clothing. Leighton had one fucking job while we cleaned out our desks at Sabre—pack the damn suitcases in time for our early morning flight.

My mind is too weary to fight with him about it. Turns out, Hunter was right about one thing. We're done. All of us. This case has broken our family; left, right and centre.

My phone vibrates with another phone call. It must be Lucas calling with more shitty news. Press coverage of Pastor Michaels' daring escape has been absolutely brutal.

I accept the call with an exhausted sigh. "If this is another depressing update, you can thoroughly fuck off."

"Mr Montpellier."

Shitting fuck!

"Superintendent." I clear my throat. "My apologies. It's been a trying few days, to say the least."

She sniffs in derision. "I've been notified that your team is leaving the country. Care to explain yourself?"

Tucking the phone under my chin, I start tossing clothes at random into the case. No idea where the fuck we're headed. Out of England and hopefully, far away.

"Our staff will continue the investigation while we take a short break," I reply tiredly. "I'm taking my family somewhere safe. Not even you can begrudge me that."

Her own sigh rattles down the line. "I understand that you've all been through a great ordeal, but we still have a serial killer to catch, and his new accomplices."

"We have reason to believe that the suspect is being aided by his... *ahem*, fan group. Sabre is following up with our current leads. He won't get far."

"I need results, Mr Montpellier. You are not the only one with superiors to answer to. The Prime Minister is very concerned about recent events."

Abandoning my haphazard packing, I glance outside at the wild, overgrown garden stretching behind our new home. The sun is setting in a blazing, fiery riot.

In her usual place, Harlow sits on the lawn, a hand buried in Lucky's fur as they watch the sinking horizon together. The hospital discharged her this morning, to our collective relief.

She's silent and still, her battered face hidden from sight. Finding her unconscious and bathing in a pool of blood almost stopped my heart for the last time.

Our family is broken.

Exhausted.

Beaten and bruised.

We have to leave and heal these wounds, or I fear we'll never recover from the chaos of the past few months.

"Mr Montpellier," the superintendent repeats. "Are you listening to me? I'm not paying you to skip off on bloody holiday when the country is in crisis!"

"With all due respect, I will hand back your money and leave with my family regardless. We have sacrificed everything for this case. Enough is enough."

She hesitates, muttering to someone in the background to wait their turn to speak. I slam my bedroom door shut and head downstairs, almost too tired to walk.

"Candace Bernard's rescue will sate the Prime Minster for the time being," she submits. "When you return, we will be having a full and frank conversation about your actions."

"Can't wait. Please contact Hudson or Kade Knight if you have any further concerns during our absence. They will be acting as interim directors."

"Is that appropriate, given their history?" she scoffs.

Annoyance prickles across my scalp. Too weary to act like I give a fuck about her fancy title, I prepare to end the call.

"They are fine agents, and if you wish to receive our continued support with this investigation, you'll treat them with some fucking respect."

My thumb jabs against the red button. Head colliding with the wall, I allow myself a sliver of satisfaction. I've been wanting to stick her stupid cheques and bad attitude up her ass for well over a year now.

"Enz?" Theo calls from the kitchen.

Tucking my phone away, I sidle into the room. He's cleaning out the fridge, throwing away anything perishable that will turn to sludge while we're abroad.

"Yeah?"

He spares me a glance. "Um, did you just hang up on the superintendent? You know she pays our wages, right?"

"Fuck her and the damn money. She won't pull our contract. We all know the police can't handle this case."

"Can we handle it?" Leighton interrupts.

He's sitting at the family table, crouched over a laptop. Next to him, the printed plane tickets sit with five passports.

"Right now?" I reply flatly. "No, we can't handle it. That's precisely why I'm calling time. We need this break."

"Not arguing with you, bro." Leighton takes a slurp from his beer. "The case can survive a few weeks without us."

Slapping his shoulder, I peer out through the glass door leading to the garden. Harlow hasn't moved an inch in hours. The sun has almost vanished entirely now.

"She spoken to any of you?"

"A little," Theo answers as he pours milk down the drain. "The doctor signed her off for air travel."

"Candace Bernard is still in the ICU," Leighton chimes in. "Two transfusions and sixteen stitches later, she's alive. Bloody miracle."

"That's great news."

"Hudson's gonna do the debrief and take her full statement once she's stabilised. I've arranged a security team for her protection until Michaels is apprehended."

I nod. "Good work, Leigh."

"Um, thanks," he stumbles.

The doorbell rings, and Theo darts out of the room to answer it. In the living room, sprawled out on the sectional sofa, Hunter's glaring at the newspaper while slurping his millionth cup of tea.

The exact details of what happened have been kept under wraps. As far as the public is concerned, Candace is alive, and Pastor Michaels escaped with an unnamed accomplice.

We were lucky to find them, following Oliver Kensington's emergency call from the middle of fucking nowhere, several miles into the Devonshire countryside.

I'm not sure if any of us are ready to forgive Harlow for skipping out and deliberately putting herself in harm's way. She knows that. It's exactly why she's hiding from us.

But I get it.

Very begrudgingly.

This clusterfuck is enough to scramble anyone's mind, and she's done a hell of a good job keeping it together for this long. Now, at least, she has her truth. She can finally begin to heal from the past.

Theo returns with company in tow. Limping and favouring his right leg, Oliver's dressed in casual jeans and a loose t-shirt. He offers us all cool nods of greeting.

"What are you doing here?"

"Came to say goodbye," he says gruffly. "Heard you're leaving for a while. I wanted to check on Harlow."

"She'd be fine if it wasn't for you," Leighton grumbles darkly. "Dickhead."

Ignoring him, I shake Oliver's outstretched hand. Leighton is right. He's lucky we didn't murder him. Just about. If he wasn't her last decent relative, he'd be dead and buried.

"How's the leg?"

"No permanent damage." He runs a hand over his dirty-blonde hair. "Doctor says I'm gonna be just fine."

Theo wipes off his hands on a tea towel. "I heard Giana's been transferred to Bronzefield Prison while awaiting trial."

Oliver nods. "She's facing a minimum of fifteen years and they're still adding charges. The trial's been set for December."

"Does Harlow know?" I ask with a frown.

"I called to let her know last night," he answers. "She was relieved, I think. Hard to tell. She didn't say much else."

We all exchange worried glances. None of us can truly understand what happened between Harlow and her mother, but we know it's left her gutted. Even if she hated the bitch.

"Where are you guys going?" Oliver takes a seat at the table. "Harlow mentioned something about a trip."

We all turn to Leighton.

"Costa Rica," he declares proudly.

"You're serious?" Theo gapes at him.

"You guys told me to go wild, so I did. Blue waters, sandy beaches, floating cocktail bars. I know, I'm the best."

"Costa Rica? It's the other side of the world," I complain. "What if we need to come home? It's so far away."

"Wasn't that the whole point?" Theo pipes up. "We need total removal from reality for a bit. I think it's a great idea."

Leighton punches the air in triumph. "Knew it. Fuck me, I'm too good. Maybe I should work as a travel agent."

"The further away from me, the better." I level him with a glare. "You almost broke the company managing it for one bloody month. You know, I saw the credit card statement."

He winces, caught red-handed. "Wasn't that supposed to be used for, uh, business expenses?"

"How is a year-long pizza subscription and a Christian Bale cardboard cut-out a business expense?"

Theo doubles over, laughing hard. "For fuck's sake."

"Don't start on the Batman bullshit with me again," Leighton defends. "I have experience now. I'm basically an assassin. I can kick your ass for insulting my man, Christian."

"Assassin." Theo snorts. "The country would implode if you were its replacement for James Bond."

"Watch it, four eyes. I can soon lose your plane ticket to Costa Rica. No more topless waitresses for you."

"You hired a topless waitress?!"

Leighton smirks over his beer. "Kidding."

Gaze bouncing between all three of us, Oliver's smiling to himself. We may have threatened to break his neck if he steals our girl again, but I think we got the old man's approval.

Leaving the sofa, Hunter walks straight up to the bin and tosses the newspaper in it. He spins around, catching us all staring at him, and flicks us the bird instead.

"You know it pisses him off when you stare." Leighton slides the paperwork to his brother. "He punched me the other day for touching his stitches."

"Why the hell did you touch them?" I exclaim.

He shrugs. "Curious. Wanted to see if the doctors managed to staple his brain back in there or if I'm the smart brother now."

Theo buries his face in his hands. "I don't think that I can survive an international trip with you."

"Zip it, Theodore. You're gonna love it."

Picking up the collection of papers, Hunter leans against the wall and runs his eyes over them. He checks the plane tickets and I nearly fall over when he... smiles? Weird.

"We have a private beach?" he asks.

Leighton nods. "And a villa."

"Huh? What filler?"

"*VILLA*," he shouts loudly.

"Great plan." I facepalm. "Shout louder so the deaf man can hear you. Clearly, you're not the smart brother."

Hunter's hand collides with the back of my head. His eyes are narrowed as he smacks me hard enough to rattle my teeth.

"I can read your lips," he warns. "I've been out of action, but I'm still your damn boss, Montpellier. Tread carefully."

Unable to suppress a grin, I bundle Hunter into a tight hug. He squeezes back with that weird, smiley thing still twisting his lips. It's starting to freak me out a bit.

"Well, I should go." Oliver moves to stand up. "Got a meeting at the rehab centre tonight. Jude's a stickler for punctuality."

"We're shocked," Leighton says under his breath.

"Mind if I say hey to Harlow before I go?"

I gesture for him to go ahead. "Be my guest. Try to run away with her again, though, and I'll shoot you in the head."

"Yeah, I got the message the last two hundred times you threatened to do that. Loud and clear, sarge."

With a mock salute, Oliver slips outside into the garden. I watch him go, keeping a watchful eye. It's not that I don't trust Harlow… but I don't fucking trust her. Not right now.

This shit is still a red-hot mess and she's got a lot to come to terms with. We need some time to figure out how to move past what happened, and how she chose to go about it.

"I like him," Theo announces.

Leighton laughs him off. "He's the douchebag who put Harlow in danger. You're not allowed to like him."

"He's got some skills." I shrug casually. "Sabre could use a new forger. We can keep an eye on him that way."

"You want to offer him a job?" Leighton looks gobsmacked. "He's an ex-junkie criminal who broke into our house. Don't get me started on the last forty-eight hours, too."

"We've hired worse. Look at the Cobra team and their rapsheet.

Besides, that's a good resume in my mind."

We bicker amongst ourselves until Oliver returns, his smile strained. He offers us a short goodbye before leaving, requesting we keep in contact.

Harlow is still sat outside, even as night descends. I send Theo and Leighton out to pick up some takeout, giving us some privacy. The pair arm wrestle for who gets to drive Hunter's convertible.

"I win!" Leighton declares.

Theo curses in displeasure. "How are you so strong?"

"Come on, Clark Kent. We can discuss my admittedly fantastic biceps on the way out."

"Fucking kill me now," he complains.

With the arguing idiots gone, Hunter follows me into the garden. It's warm enough now to sit outside even without the sun. Lucky barks loudly as we approach, her tail wagging. She chases the ball that Harlow throws half-heartedly.

We take a seat on either side of her. She's staring down at the flower-laced grass, her technicolour face shielded by a curtain of uneven hair. I reach out to tuck the thinning strands aside.

"Talk to us, little one."

Harlow doesn't stir.

Meeting my eyes over her lowered head, Hunter's fingers spell out a simple command. *You yelled at her. Fix this.*

"Hey," I try again, kissing her temple. "I was rough on you at the hospital. We need to talk about this."

"You were right," she replies in a small voice. "I know that I betrayed your trust."

"I was so afraid when we realised that you were gone," I admit. "That fear turned into anger when we got you back. I shouldn't have taken it out on you."

"You were right to. I scared you all."

Sliding a finger underneath her chin, I raise her bottomless blue eyes to mine. Her broken nose is strapped into place over the bloom of devastating, pitch-black bruises.

I've seen her in worse states, but this shit never gets easier. The thought of that asshole daring to hurt what's mine makes my vision dim with rage. When I find him, he's fucking dead.

I channelled my anger in the wrong direction. I've grown enough to see the tendency I have to do that. Harlow knows she fucked up. She had her reasons for taking that risk, and harrowing injuries and near-death experiences aside, she got what she was looking for.

The truth.

Now, she has to live with it.

We all do.

"I'm so sorry, Enz," she whispers tearfully. "I couldn't take the not knowing any longer. I did what I had to."

I stroke her tears aside with my thumbs. "I know, angel. Sometimes, we're backed into a corner and forced to make a shitty decision. You played your last move."

She nods timidly. "Yeah."

"Just wish you'd talked to us."

"Would you have let me go alone?"

"Not a chance in hell."

Harlow lifts an eyebrow. "Case in point."

"Alright, don't get sassy. I'll still spank your ass raw even if you look like you've gone three rounds with Mike Tyson."

"Who on earth is that?"

Chuckling, I lean in and lock our lips together. We can figure out an appropriate punishment for her as soon as we're in the air, leaving England and its chaos behind.

I doubt Hunter will mind if I tie Harlow to the bed and fuck her senseless while he rides her smart mouth. Then she can lecture us about being overprotective.

"What's the plan?" She leans against Hunter's shoulder, looking between us both. "We're really going?"

Hunter kisses her temple after deciphering her words. "I told you that I'd show you the world one day."

She looks up so that he can clearly read her lips.

"Pastor Michaels is still out there. The work isn't done."

"The work can wait," he replies sternly. "We were attacked. I lost my hearing. You got tortured by a serial killer. We're taking a motherfucking holiday."

"Amen to that," I chime in.

Snuggling between us, Harlow accepts the slobber-covered ball caught between Lucky's fangs. She strokes over her ears with a low coo of appreciation.

"I'm gonna miss you, girl."

"Brooklyn's on babysitting duty while we're gone," I say, watching Lucky skip after the ball. "She's very excited to be a dog mum again after losing their pup last year."

"How long will we be gone for?"

Hunter meets my eyes with a frown. I quickly reiterate her question in sign language. We're picking it up fast, thanks to some helpful YouTube tutorials.

He brushes his lips against Harlow's ear, his teeth briefly sinking into her lobe. A shudder runs over her body.

"As long as it takes," he whispers.

Harlow lets out a long-held breath. "What if Pastor Michaels hurts someone else? We have to find him."

"We have our best agents on it," I remind her. "But none of us can pour from an empty cup. We're going, no arguments."

Lips pursed, Harlow's head falls on Hunter's shoulder as her eyes slide shut. We sit on the grass, wrapped around each other and playing fetch with Lucky, until the other two return.

"I come bearing pizza!" Leighton calls from inside. "Courtesy of my brand-spanking-new subscription. Thank you, Sabre Security."

"Little asshole," I mutter.

Harlow snorts. "Heard that."

"You don't pay the credit card bill. Have a word with your boyfriend about his Batman obsession too. It's unhealthy."

She stills, her aquamarine eyes coasting up to meet mine. "Boyfriend, huh?"

I brush our noses together. "That's what we are to you, aren't we?"

"All of you?" she clarifies.

"Well, why not?"

"I didn't realise we were finally doing labels. You guys were still sizing each other up last time we discussed this."

With an eye roll, I yell for Theo and Leighton to join us outside. A blush overtakes Harlow's cheeks, but it's too late. She's admitted it's bothering her. I'm gonna settle this, once and for all.

All seated in a circle, several pizza boxes laid across the grass between us, I clear my throat. Leighton freezes, a huge slice of pepperoni pizza halfway down his throat.

"Harlow has a very serious question for us."

She covers her face with her hands. "I really don't."

"What is it?" Theo asks anxiously.

"Nope, nothing."

He's glancing between all of us in a panic. I stifle a laugh while relaying the situation to Hunter in sign language. He grins evilly, elbowing Harlow in the waist.

"Come on," I goad her. "Put Anxious Nelly over here out of his misery before he explodes."

"Screw you, Enz," Theo cusses. "Harlow, what is it?"

She's flaming a bright tomato red. Even the tips of her ears are pink. It's so damn cute, my dick is actually hard.

"Please," Leighton pleads around a mouthful. "Pinkie swear, we won't laugh if it's embarrassing."

"Why would it be embarrassing?" Theo frowns to himself. "It's not... about periods, is it? Because Leighton's next on the rotation to buy tampons. I did my duty."

"No!" Harlow squeals. "You guys are such idiots."

I ruffle her hair. "Your idiots?"

Still blushing hard, she glances between all four of us. Her face is turned towards Hunter for his benefit, but her words are for everyone.

"Well... I was just asking if... you know, erm. If we're... or you're... well. *Ahem*. The thing is, ah—"

"Fuck me gently," I interrupt her rambling. "Harlow wants to know if we're *all* her boyfriends."

Leighton chokes on his pizza and Theo has to hammer him so hard on the back, a chunk of pineapple shoots out of his nose. Hunter curses up a storm as it lands in his lap.

"Leigh! Jesus!"

"Sorry!" Leighton splutters, his eyes streaming. "That was fucking cool. Reckon I can do it again?"

When he's done coughing a lung up, Leighton offers Harlow a bright smile.

"I've been yours since day one, Goldilocks. If they don't want you, I'll happily steal you away."

"Watch it, fucker," I warn in a low voice. "That's the kind of talk that gets you buried at the bottom of a lake."

"Forget we ever had this conversation," Harlow begs.

I tuck her into my side and inhale her fresh, sweet scent. If I died with her in my arms, blushing like a maniac and being cute as hell, I think I'd be okay with that.

"I'm all in too," I whisper to her.

She smiles to herself, glancing up at Hunter next. He's been tracking the whole conversation and takes her hand into his. Harlow shivers as his lips graze her knuckles.

"I miss the sound of your voice," he murmurs. "But I can live without it as long as I have you by my side for the rest of my life. Hearing or not."

"You're... okay with sharing?"

He nods, deadly serious. "We've all lost enough. I'm ready to risk it all to feel a bit of happiness again."

They kiss passionately, his fingers sliding through her hair. I catch Leighton watching as intently as I am, and we exchange knowing smirks. Looks like the younger Rodriguez doesn't mind a bit of voyeurism either.

Theo's the last one to answer. He's been flagging behind the group since the first time Harlow blew into our lives, and the descent of chaos began. His grief never quite left him.

Straightening his crooked glasses, he bites his bottom lip and looks up at Harlow. She's holding her breath.

"I am in love with you," he finally answers. "I don't give a fuck if I have to share, as long as you're in my life."

With a grin blossoming, Harlow launches herself over the pizza boxes and ends up tackling Theo back onto the grass. She grunts in pain, yet it doesn't seem to slow her down.

After kissing Theo until he's sporting a similarly red face, Harlow comes up for air. We're all hanging on for her reaction. She takes the time to look between us all.

"Let's get the first plane out of here."

THE END

To be concluded in

Hollow Veins (Sabre Security #3)

PLAYLIST

Black Water – The People's Thieves
Empty – Letdown
All I Have – NF
The Kid I Used To Know – Arrested Youth
Put It On Me – Matt Maeson
No More Hiding – Gina Brooklyn
Fool & The Thief – THE HARA
Me and My Brain – Airways
2008 – cleopatrick
Do It For Me – Rosenfeld
My Hand/Lawless Dream – Matt Maeson
Pray – Ready the Prince
Fantastic – Blame My Youth
Hard To Be Alone – Barns Courtney
Villain – MISSIO
Into It – Chase Atlantic
Via – Voices From The Fuselage
Too Far Gone – The Plot In You
The Way That You Were – Sleep Token
Two Weeks – FKA Twigs

DRIFTING — NF
Kijo — Memorist
Sad Money — Call Me Karizma
Taurus — Machine Gun Kelly & Naomi Wild
Room To Breathe — You Me At Six
Hotel — Montell Fish
Dead — 228k
Make This Go On Forever — Hahlweg
Hold Your Breath — Astyria
We Are Not Okay — NIKKITA

Want more from this shared universe?

If you loved Brooklyn and her merry band of psychopaths, check out their completed stories in the Blackwood Institute trilogy—a dark, why choose romance set in an experimental psychiatric institute where monsters walk among us and nothing is quite what it seems.

https://mybook.to/TwistedHeathens
https://mybook.to/SacrificialSinners
https://mybook.to/DesecratedSaints

ACKNOWLEDGEMENTS

Here we are again, friends.

Book baby number thirteen is done and dusted.

This is the part of the book where I usually have something meaningful to say, but honestly, this was a tough write. Not because of the subject matter—I've never been one to shy away from darkness—but because it was painful to sit down and confront the harsh reality of guilt on a daily basis while writing.

Every single character deals with their own baptism of fire in this book. Character development is one of my absolute favourite parts of writing, but it's also the most taxing. If nothing else, I hope that you take this message away from Harlow's story:

We're all imperfect humans, making imperfect decisions while navigating an imperfect world. The trick is to find someone (or someones, no judgement) whose flaws complement your own and never fucking let them go.

Let's dive in.

As always, I have to thank my two biggest supporters. To Eddie, my fiancé. You're my rock and even when we drive each other crazy, you inspire me to keep going. Thank you for saving my life every single day.

Kristen, I never have the right words to express just how much you mean to me. I'll settle for this; I fucking love you, wife, and every book I publish is for you.

Of course, I need to thank my incredible team for keeping my chaos in line. My PA, Julia, and my two amazing editors, Kenzie and Lauren, who all work tirelessly behind the scenes with me. You're rock stars and I couldn't do it without your love and guidance.

Thank you to everyone on my dedicated street and ARC teams for being there to support me. I appreciate every single one of you. And thank you to Savannah at Peachy Keen Author Services for being fabulous in supporting me with this release.

I'm so lucky to have met the most amazing friends—Lilith, Lola, Dani, Rosa, Emma, Nat, Mallory—and so many others who inspire me with their creativity and passion for writing. That's what the book community is all about.

Finally, I want to thank every single reader who has bought my work, supported every book I've released and enabled me to live out this crazy, chaotic dream. I feel truly blessed.

Stay wild.

With love,

J Rose x

ABOUT THE AUTHOR

J Rose is an independent dark romance author from the United Kingdom. She writes challenging, plot-driven stories packed full of angst, heartbreak and broken characters fighting for their happily ever afters.

She's an introverted bookworm at heart, with a caffeine addiction, penchant for cursing and an unhealthy attachment to fictional characters.

Feel free to reach out on social media, J Rose loves talking to her readers!

For exclusive insights, updates and general mayhem, join J Rose's Bleeding Thorns on Facebook.

Business enquiries: j_roseauthor@yahoo.com

Come join the chaos. Stalk J Rose here...
www.jroseauthor.com/socials

NEWSLETTER

Want more madness? Sign up to J Rose's newsletter for monthly announcements, exclusive content, sneak peeks, giveaways and more!

www.jroseauthor.com/newsletter

ALSO BY J ROSE

www.jroseauthor.com/books

Blackwood Institute
Twisted Heathens
Sacrificial Sinners
Desecrated Saints

Standalones
Forever Ago
Drown in You

Sabre Security
Corpse Roads
Skeletal Hearts
Hollow Veins

Writing as Jessalyn Thorn
Departed Whispers

Printed in Great Britain
by Amazon

38364294R00297